Patricia Cornwell— ̶A̶ ̶n̶u̶m̶b̶e̶r̶-̶o̶n̶e̶ ̶b̶e̶s̶t̶s̶e̶l̶l̶i̶n̶g̶ *crime writer—brings us this extraordinary new Kay Scarpetta novel, full of twists and turns and the kind of cutting-edge technology that only she can deliver . . .*

Leaving behind her private forensic pathology practice in Charleston, South Carolina, Kay Scarpetta takes an assignment in New York City, where an injured patient in Bellevue Hospital's psychiatric prison ward has specifically asked for her. While Scarpetta examines him, she listens to one of the most bizarre stories she has ever heard.

Oscar Bane says his injuries were sustained in the course of a murder . . . that he did not commit. Is Bane a criminally insane stalker who has fixated on Scarpetta? Or is his paranoid tale true, and it is he who is being spied on, followed, and stalked by the actual killer? The one thing Scarpetta knows for certain is that a woman has been tortured and murdered—and more violent deaths will occur . . .

In the days that follow, Scarpetta, her forensic psychologist husband, Benton Wesley, and her niece, Lucy, who has recently formed her own forensic computer investigation firm in New York, will undertake a harrowing chase through cyberspace and the all-too-real streets of the city. It is an odyssey that will take them at once to places they never knew but also much, much too close to home.

Praise for the novels of Patricia Cornwell

The Front

"[A] classically written crime novel."   *—USA Today*

At Risk

"Highly entertaining."   *—St. Louis Post-Dispatch*

continued . . .

"A thriller that is neither predictable nor mundane."

—The Canadian Press

"Scary."

—*The Boston Globe*

Book of the Dead

"Compelling."

—*Richmond Times-Dispatch*

"What a walloping, riveting mix of . . . adventure and psychology. Author Cornwell certainly is skilled at dissecting the not always attractive innards of human nature." —*Forbes*

Predator

"Cornwell continu[es] to stretch her muscles . . . a fine psychological thriller."

—*The Denver Post*

"Sensationally plotted, with a twist at the end that will leave you gasping for breath." —*Daily Express* (U.K.)

"[Scarpetta] comes out swinging, and pity the fool who gets in her way."

—*The Clarion-Ledger*

Trace

"Dr. Kay Scarpetta . . . is back with a vengeance."

—*The New York Times Book Review*

"Cornwell gets her Hitchcock on . . . [She] can generate willies with subtle poetic turns." —*People*

"Fun [and] flamboyant."

—*Entertainment Weekly*

Blow Fly

"[A] grisly fast-paced thriller . . . utterly chilling."

—*Entertainment Weekly*

"Patricia Cornwell is on target—and spectacularly so—with her latest Kay Scarpetta thriller, a story so compelling that even longtime readers will be stunned by its twists and turns." —*Chicago Tribune*

"Gruesome and suspenseful." —*New York Daily News*

The Last Precinct

"Ignites on the first page . . . Cornwell has created a character so real, so compelling, so driven that this reader has to remind herself regularly that Scarpetta is just a product of an author's imagination." —*USA Today*

"Plots within plots, fraught atmosphere and unrelenting suspense keep readers on tenterhooks while one trap after another springs under unwary feet. Cunningly designed, ingeniously laid out, composed with Cornwellian skill, this far-from-the-*Last Precinct* is a model of the art." —*Los Angeles Times*

"The most unexpected of the Kay Scarpetta novels so far . . . Compelling . . . Terrific." —*The Miami Herald*

Black Notice

"Brainteasing . . . one of the most savage killers of her career . . . [a] hair-raising tale with a French twist." —*People*

"The author's darkest and perhaps best . . . a fast-paced, first-rate thriller." —*The San Francisco Examiner*

Point of Origin

"Cornwell lights a fire under familiar characters—and sparks her hottest adventure in years." —*People*

"Packed with action and suspense." —*Rocky Mountain News*

Patricia Cornwell

Scarpetta

BERKLEY BOOKS
NEW YORK

THE BERKLEY PUBLISHING GROUP
Published by the Penguin Group
Penguin Group (USA) Inc.
375 Hudson Street, New York, New York 10014, USA
Penguin Group (Canada), 90 Eglinton Avenue East, Suite 700, Toronto, Ontario M4P 2Y3, Canada
(a division of Pearson Penguin Canada Inc.)
Penguin Books Ltd., 80 Strand, London WC2R 0RL, England
Penguin Group Ireland, 25 St. Stephen's Green, Dublin 2, Ireland (a division of Penguin Books Ltd.)
Penguin Group (Australia), 250 Camberwell Road, Camberwell, Victoria 3124, Australia
(a division of Pearson Australia Group Pty. Ltd.)
Penguin Books India Pvt. Ltd., 11 Community Centre, Panchsheel Park, New Delhi—110 017, India
Penguin Group (NZ), 67 Apollo Drive, Rosedale, North Shore 0632, New Zealand
(a division of Pearson New Zealand Ltd.)
Penguin Books (South Africa) (Pty.) Ltd., 24 Sturdee Avenue, Rosebank, Johannesburg 2196,
South Africa

Penguin Books Ltd., Registered Offices: 80 Strand, London WC2R 0RL, England

This is a work of fiction. Names, characters, places, and incidents either are the product of the author's imagination or are used fictitiously, and any resemblance to actual persons, living or dead, business establishments, events, or locales is entirely coincidental. The publisher does not have any control over and does not assume any responsibility for author or third-party websites or their content.

SCARPETTA

A Berkley Book / published by arrangement with CEI Enterprises, Inc.

PRINTING HISTORY
G. P. Putnam's Sons hardcover edition / December 2008
Berkley premium edition / September 2009

Copyright © 2008 by CEI Enterprises, Inc.
Interior cover photograph by Jacob Silberberg/Polaris.
Cover design by Richard Hasselberger.

ISBN: 978-0-425-23016-9

BERKLEY®
Berkley Books are published by The Berkley Publishing Group,
a division of Penguin Group (USA) Inc.,
375 Hudson Street, New York, New York 10014.
BERKLEY® is a registered trademark of Penguin Group (USA) Inc.
The "B" design is a trademark of Penguin Group (USA) Inc.

PRINTED IN THE UNITED STATES OF AMERICA

10   9   8   7   6   5   4   3   2   1

To Ruth
(1920–2007)

And as always, with gratitude—
to Staci

The mental state of the madman, indeed, may be described as a walking and disordered dream.

MONTAGU LOMAX,
The Experiences of an Asylum Doctor, 1921

1

Brain tissue clung like wet, gray lint to the sleeves of Dr. Kay Scarpetta's surgical gown, and the front of it was splashed with blood. Stryker saws whined, running water drummed, and bone dust sifted through the air like flour. Three tables were full. More bodies were on the way. It was Tuesday, January 1, New Year's Day.

She didn't need to rush toxicology to know her patient had been drinking before he pulled the shotgun's trigger with his toe. The instant she'd opened him up, she detected the putrid, pungent smell of booze as it breaks down in the body. When she was a forensic pathology resident long years ago, she used to wonder if giving substance abusers a tour of the morgue might shock them into sobriety. If she showed them a head opened up like an egg cup, let them catch the stench of postmortem champagne, maybe they'd switch to Perrier. If only it worked that way.

She watched her deputy chief, Jack Fielding, lift the shimmering block of organs from the chest cavity of a university student robbed and shot at an ATM, and waited for his outburst. During this morning's staff conference, he'd made the incensed comment that the victim was the same age as his daughter, both of them track stars and pre-med. Nothing good happened when Fielding personalized a case.

"We not sharpening knives anymore?" he yelled.

The oscillating blade of a Stryker saw screamed, the morgue assistant opening a skull and yelling back, "Do I look busy?"

Fielding tossed the surgical knife back on his cart with a loud clatter. "How am I supposed to get anything fucking done around here?"

"Good God, somebody get him a Xanax or something." The morgue assistant pried off the skull cap with a chisel.

Scarpetta placed a lung on a scale, using a smartpen to jot down the weight on a smart notepad. There wasn't a ballpoint pen, clipboard, or paper form in sight. When she got upstairs, all she'd have to do is download what she wrote or sketched into her computer, but technology had no remedy for her fluent thoughts, and she still dictated them after she was done and her gloves were off. Hers was a modern medical examiner's office, upgraded with what she considered essential in a world she no longer recognized, where the public believed everything "forensic" it saw on TV, and violence wasn't a societal problem but a war.

She began sectioning the lung, making a mental note that it was typically formed with smooth, glistening visceral pleurae, and an atelectatic dusky red parenchyma. Minimal quantity of pink froth. Otherwise lacked discrete gross lesion, and the pulmonary vasculature was without note. She paused when her administrative assistant, Bryce, walked in, a look of disdain and avoidance on his youthful face. He wasn't squeamish about what went on in here, just offended for every reason one might be, and he snatched several paper towels from a dispenser. Covering his hand, he picked up the receiver of the black wall phone, where line one was lit up.

"Benton, you still with me?" he said into the phone. "She's right here holding a very big knife. I'm sure she told you today's specials? The Tufts student is the worst, her life worth two hundred bucks. The Bloods or the Crips, some gang piece of shit, you should see him on video surveillance. All over the news. Jack shouldn't be doing that case. Does anybody ask me? About to blow an aneurysm. And the suicide, yup. Comes home from Iraq without a scratch. He's fine. Have a happy holiday and a nice life."

Scarpetta pushed back her face shield. She pulled off her bloody gloves and dropped them in a bright red biohazard can. She scrubbed her hands in a deep steel sink.

"Bad weather inside and out," Bryce chatted to Benton, who wasn't fond of chatting. "A full house and Jack's irritable depression, did I mention that? Maybe we should do an intervention. Maybe a weekend getaway at that Harvard hospital of yours? We probably could qualify for a family plan . . . ?"

Scarpetta took the receiver from him, removed the paper towels, and dropped them into the trash.

"Stop picking on Jack," she said to Bryce.

"I think he's on steroids again, and that's why he's so cranky."

She turned her back to him and everything else.

"What's happened?" she said to Benton.

They had talked at dawn. For him to call again several hours later while she was in the autopsy suite didn't bode anything good.

"I'm afraid we've got a situation," he said.

It was the same way he'd phrased it last night when she'd just gotten home from the ATM homicide scene and found him putting on his coat, headed to Logan to catch the shuttle. NYPD had a situation and needed him immediately.

"Jaime Berger's asking if you can get here," he added.

Hearing her name always unnerved Scarpetta, gave her a tightness in her chest that had nothing to do with the New York prosecutor personally. Berger would always be linked to a past that Scarpetta preferred to forget.

Benton said, "The sooner the better. Maybe the one-o'clock shuttle?"

The wall clock said it was almost ten. She'd have to finish her case, shower, change, and she'd want to stop by the house first. *Food,* she thought. Homemade mozzarella, chickpea soup, meatballs, bread. What else? The ricotta with fresh basil that Benton loved on homemade pizza. She'd prepared all that and more yesterday, having no idea she was about to spend New Year's Eve alone. There would be nothing to eat in their New York apartment. When Benton was by himself, he usually got take-out.

"Come straight to Bellevue," he said. "You can leave your bags in my office. I have your crime scene case ready and waiting."

She could barely hear over the rhythmic rasping of a knife being sharpened in long, aggressive sweeps. The buzzer from the bay blared, and on the closed-circuit video screen on the countertop, a dark-sleeved arm emerged from the driver's window of a white van as attendants from a delivery service buzzed.

"Can someone please get that?" Scarpetta said at the top of her voice.

On the prison-ward floor of the modern Bellevue Hospital Center, the thin wire of Benton's headset connected him to his wife some hundred and fifty miles away.

He explained that late last night a man was admitted to the forensic psychiatric unit, making the point, "Berger wants you to examine his injuries."

"What's he been charged with?" Scarpetta asked.

In the background, he could hear the indistinguishable voices, the noise of the morgue—or what he wryly called her "deconstruction site."

"Nothing yet," he said. "There was a murder last night. An unusual one."

He tapped the down arrow on his keyboard, scrolling through what was on his computer screen.

"You mean there's no court order for the examination?" Scarpetta's voice moved at the speed of sound.

"Not yet. But he needs to be looked at now."

"He should have been looked at already. The minute he was admitted. If there was any trace evidence, by now it's likely been contaminated or lost."

Benton kept tapping the down arrow, re-reading what was on the screen, wondering how he was going to approach her about it. He could tell by her tone she didn't know, and he hoped like hell she didn't hear it from someone else first. Lucy Farinelli, her niece, had damn well better abide by his wish to let him handle it. Not that he was doing a good job so far.

Jaime Berger had seemed all business when she'd called him a few minutes earlier, and from that he'd inferred she wasn't aware of the trashy gossip on the Internet. Why he didn't say something to her while he'd had the chance, he wasn't sure. But he hadn't, and he should have. He should have been honest with Berger long before now. He should have explained everything to her almost half a year ago.

"His injuries are superficial," Benton said to Scarpetta. "He's in isolation, won't talk, won't cooperate unless you come. Berger doesn't want anyone coercing him into anything and decided the exam could wait until you got here. Since that's what he wants . . ."

"Since when is it about what the inmate wants?"

"PR, political reasons, and he's not an inmate, not

that anybody on the ward's considered an inmate once they've been admitted. They're patients." His nervous ramblings didn't sound like him as he heard himself talk. "As I've said, he's not been charged with any crime. There's no warrant. There's nothing. He's basically a civil admission. We can't make him stay the minimum seventy-two hours because he didn't sign a consent form, and as I said, he's not been charged with a crime, at least not yet. Maybe that will change after you've seen him. But at this moment, he can leave whenever he wants."

"You're expecting me to find something that will give the police probable cause to charge him with murder? And what do you mean he didn't sign . . . ? Back up. This patient signed himself into a prison ward with the proviso he can walk out the door whenever he pleases?"

"I'll explain more when I see you. I'm not expecting you to find anything. No expectations, Kay. I'm just asking you to come because it's a very complicated situation. And Berger really wants you here."

"Even though he might be gone by the time I get there."

He detected the question she wasn't going to ask. He wasn't acting like the cool, unflappable forensic psychologist she had known for twenty years, but she wasn't going to point that out. She was in the morgue and she wasn't alone. She wasn't going to ask him what the hell was wrong with him.

Benton said, "He definitely won't leave before you get here."

"I don't understand why he's there." She wasn't going to let that go.

"We're not entirely sure. But in a nutshell? When the cops arrived at the scene, he insisted on being transported to Bellevue. . . ."

"His name?"

"Oscar Bane. He said the only person he'd allow to conduct the psychological evaluation was me. So I was called, and as you know, I left immediately for New York. He's afraid of doctors. Gets panic attacks."

"How did he know who you are?"

"Because he knows who you are."

"He knows who I am?"

"The cops have his clothes, but he says if they want any evidence collected from him physically—and there's no warrant, as I keep emphasizing—it will have to be you who does it. We hoped he'd calm down, agree to let a local ME take care of him. Never going to happen. He's more adamant than ever. Says he's terrified of doctors. Has odynephobia, dishabiliophobia."

"He's afraid of pain and taking his clothes off?"

"And caligynephobia. Fear of beautiful women."

"I see. So that's why he'd feel safe with me."

"That part was supposed to be funny. He thinks you're beautiful, and he's definitely not afraid of you. I'm the one who should be afraid."

That was the truth of the matter. Benton didn't want her here. He didn't even want her in New York right now.

"Let me make sure I understand. Jaime Berger wants

me to fly there in a snowstorm, examine a patient on a prison ward who hasn't been charged with a crime—"

"If you can get out of Boston, the weather's fine here. Just cold." Benton looked out his window and saw nothing but gray.

"Let me finish up with my Army Reservist sergeant who was a casualty in Iraq but didn't know it until he got home. And I'll see you mid-afternoon," she said.

"Fly safe. I love you."

Benton hung up, started tapping the down arrow again, then the up arrow, reading and re-reading, as though if he read the anonymous gossip column often enough, it wouldn't seem so offensive, so ugly, so hateful. "Sticks and stones," Scarpetta always said. Maybe that was true in grammar school, but not in their adult lives. Words could hurt. They could hurt badly. What kind of monster would write something like this? How did the monster find out?

He reached for the phone.

Scarpetta paid scant attention to Bryce as he drove her to Logan International Airport. He'd been talking nonstop about one thing or another ever since picking her up at her house.

Mainly, he'd been complaining about Dr. Jack Fielding, reminding her yet again that returning to the past was like a dog returning to its own vomit. Or Lot's wife looking back and turning into a pillar of salt. Bryce's biblical analogies were endless and irritating and had nothing to do with his religious beliefs, assuming he had any, but were leftover pearls from a college term paper he'd done on the Bible as literature.

Her administrative assistant's point was you don't hire people from your past. Fielding was from Scarpetta's past. He'd had his problems, but then who hadn't? When she had accepted the position up here and had started looking for a deputy chief, she wondered what Fielding was doing, tracked him down, and found out he wasn't doing much.

Benton's input had been unusually toothless, maybe even patronizing, which made more sense to her now. He'd said she was looking for stability, and often people move backward instead of forward when they are overwhelmed by change. Feeling the desire to hire someone she'd known since the early days of her career was understandable, Benton had said. But the danger in looking back was that we saw only what we wanted to see, he'd added. We saw what made us feel safe.

What Benton had chosen to avoid is why she didn't feel safe to begin with. He hadn't wanted to get within range of how she really felt about her domestic life with him, which was as chaotic and dissonant as it had ever been. Since their relationship began with an adulterous affair more than fifteen years ago, they'd never lived in the same place, didn't know the meaning of day-to-day togetherness, until last summer. Theirs had been a very simple ceremony in the garden behind her carriage house in Charleston, South Carolina, where she'd just set up a private practice that she then was forced to close.

Afterward, they'd moved to Belmont, Massachusetts, to be near his psychiatric hospital, McLean, and her new headquarters in Watertown, where she'd accepted the position of chief medical examiner of the Commonwealth's Northeastern District. Because of their proximity to New York, she thought it a fine idea for them to accept John Jay College of Criminal Justice's invitation to serve as visiting lecturers there, which included offering pro bono consultation for the NYPD, the New York Medical Examiner's office, and forensic psychiatric units such as the one at Bellevue.

". . . I know it's not the sort of thing you'd look at or maybe even be a big deal to you, but at the risk of pissing you off, I'm going to point it out." Bryce's voice penetrated her preoccupations.

She said, "What big deal?"

"Well, hello? Don't mind me. I was just talking to myself."

"I'm sorry. Rewind the tape."

"I didn't say anything after staff meeting because I didn't want to distract you from all the shit going on this morning. Thought I'd wait until you were done and we could have a little heart-to-heart behind your closed door. And since nobody's said anything to me, I don't think they saw it. Which is good, right? As if Jack isn't pissy enough this morning. Of course, he's always pissy, which is why he has eczema and alopecia. And by the way, did you see the crusty lesion behind his right ear? Home for the holidays. Does wonders for the nerves."

"How much coffee have you had today?"

"Why is it always me? Kill the messenger. You zone out until what I'm trying to convey reaches critical mass, and then kaboom, and I'm the bad guy, and bye-bye messenger. If you're going to be in New York more than a night, please let me know a-sap so I can get coverage. Should I set up some sessions with that trainer you like so much? What's his name?"

Bryce thought, touching a finger to his lips.

"Kit," he answered himself. "Maybe one of these days when you need me as your boy Friday in New York, he can have a go at me. Love handles."

He pinched his waist.

"Although I hear liposuction's the only thing that works once you turn thirty," he said. "Truth serum time?"

He glanced over at her, his hands gesturing as if they were something alive and not part of him.

"I did look him up on the Internet," he confessed. "I'm surprised Benton lets him anywhere near you. Reminds me of, of what's-his-name on *Queer as Folk*? The football star? Drove a Hummer and quite the homophobe until he hooked up with Emmett, who everyone says looks just like me, or the other way around, since he's the one who's famous. Well, you probably don't watch it."

Scarpetta said, "Kill the messenger because of what? And please keep at least one hand on the wheel since we're driving in a blizzard. How many shots did you get in your Starbucks this morning? I saw two Venti cups on your desk. Hopefully not both of them from this morning.

Remember our talk about caffeine? That it's a drug, and therefore addictive?"

"You're the whole damn thing," Bryce went on. "Which I've never seen before. It's really weird. Usually it's not just one famous person, you know? Because whoever the columnist is, he roams around the city like some undercover asshole, and shits on a lot of celebs at once. The other week, it was Bloomberg, and, oh, what's her name? That model always getting arrested for throwing things at people? Well, this time she was what got *thrown*—out of Elaine's for saying something lewd to Charlie Rose. No, wait a minute. Barbara Walters? No. I'm crossing over into something I saw on *The View*. Maybe what's-her-name the model went after that singer from *American Idol*. No, he was on *Ellen*, not in Elaine's. And not Clay Aiken or Kelly Clarkson. Who's the other one? TiVo's simply killing me. It's like the remote surfs through channels when you're not touching anything. You ever have that happen?"

Snow was like a swarm of white gnats hitting the windshield, the wipers hypnotically useless. Traffic was slow but steady, Logan just a few minutes out.

"Bryce?" Scarpetta said in the tone she used when she was warning him to shut up and answer her question. "What big deal?"

"That disgusting online gossip column. *Gotham Gotcha*."

She'd seen ads for it on New York City buses and taxicab tops, the anonymous columnist notoriously vicious. The guessing game of who was behind it ranged from a nobody to a Pulitzer Prize–winning journalist who was having great fun making mean-spirited mischief and money.

"Nas-ty," Bryce said. "Now, I know it's supposed to be nasty, but this is nasty below the belt. Not that I read such tripe. But for obvious reasons, I have you as a Google alert. There's a photograph, which is the worst part. It's not flattering."

2

Benton leaned back in his desk chair, looking out at his view of ugly red brick in the flat wintry light.

"Sounds like you got a cold," he said into the phone.

"I'm slightly under the weather today. Which is why I didn't get back to you sooner. Don't ask me what we did last night to deserve it. Gerald won't get out of bed. And I don't mean it in a good way," Dr. Thomas said.

She was a colleague at McLean. She was also Benton's psychiatrist. There was nothing unusual about it. As Dr. Thomas, who was born in the coal-mining hinterlands of western Virginia, liked to say, "Hospitals are more incestuous than hillbillies." Practitioners treated one another and their families and friends. They prescribed drugs for one another and their families and friends. They fucked one another, but hopefully not their families and friends. Occasionally, they got married. Dr. Thomas had married a McLean radiologist who scanned Scarpetta's niece, Lucy, in the neuroimaging lab where Benton had his office. Dr. Thomas knew Benton's business, pretty much all of it. She was the first person he'd thought of some months back when he'd realized he had to talk to someone.

"Did you open the link I e-mailed to you?" Benton asked her.

"Yes, and the real question is who are you more worried about? I think the answer might be you. What do you think?"

"I think that would make me incredibly selfish," Benton said.

"It would be normal to feel cuckolded, humiliated," she said.

"I forgot you were a Shakespearean actor in an earlier life," he said. "Can't remember the last time I heard someone refer to anyone as cuckolded, and it doesn't apply. Kay didn't wander out of the nest and into the arms of another man. She was grabbed. Were I to feel cuckolded, it should have been when it happened. But I didn't. I was too worried about her. Don't say 'the lady doth protest too much.' "

"What I'll say is when it happened, there wasn't an audience," Dr. Thomas said. "Perhaps it makes it more real when everybody knows? Did you tell her what's on the Internet? Or had she already seen it?"

"I didn't tell her, and I'm sure she hasn't seen it. She would have called to warn me. Funny how she's like that."

"Yes. Kay and her fragile heroes with their feet of clay. Why didn't you tell her?"

"Timing," Benton said.

"Yours or hers?"

"She was in the morgue," he said. "I wanted to wait and do it in person."

"Let's retrace our steps, Benton. You talked to her at the crack of dawn, let me guess. Isn't that what you always do when you're away from each other?"

"We talked early this morning."

"So when you talked to her early this morning, you already knew what was on the Internet, because Lucy called you when?" Dr. Thomas said. "At one a.m. to tell you, since your hypomanic niece by marriage has audible alarms programmed into her computer to wake her up like a fireman if one of her search engines finds something important in cyberspace?"

Dr. Thomas wasn't joking. Lucy did have alarms that signaled her when one of her search engines found something she needed to know about.

He said, "Actually, she called me at midnight. When the damn thing was posted."

"But she didn't call Kay."

"To her credit, she didn't, and she let it go when I said I would handle it."

"Which you didn't do," Dr. Thomas said. "So we're back to that. You talked to Kay early this morning, by which time you'd known for many hours what's on the Internet? Yet you said nothing. You've still said nothing. I don't believe it's about telling her in person. Unfortunately, there's a good chance she might find out from someone other than you—if she hasn't already."

Benton took a deep, quiet breath. He pressed his lips together and wondered when it was, exactly, that he'd begun to lose faith in himself and his ability to read his environment and react accordingly. For as far back as he could remember, he had possessed the uncanny ability to size up people at a glance or a quick listen. Scarpetta called it his party trick. He'd meet someone or overhear a snippet of a conversation, and that was it. Rarely was he wrong.

But he'd completely missed the danger at the door this time, and still didn't fully comprehend how he could have been so devastatingly obtuse. He'd watched Pete Marino's anger and frustration build over the years. He knew damn well it was a matter of time before Marino's self-loathing and rage reached flashover. But Benton didn't fear it. He didn't give Marino enough credit to be feared like that. He wasn't sure he'd ever imagined Marino having a dick prior to its becoming a weapon.

It made no sense, in retrospect. For virtually everybody else, it was impossible to get past Marino's rough-hewn machismo and volatility, and that particular recipe was Benton's bread and butter. Sexual violence, no matter its catalyst, was what kept forensic psychologists in business.

"I'm having homicidal thoughts about him," Benton said to Dr. Thomas. "Of course, I wouldn't do it. Just thoughts. I'm having a lot of thoughts. I believed I'd forgiven him and felt proud of myself, really proud of myself, because of the way I handled it. Where would he be without me? All I've done for him, and now I want to kill him. Lucy wants to kill him. The reminder this morning didn't help, and now everyone knows. It's made it happen all over again."

"Or maybe happen for the first time. It feels real to you now."

"Oh, it feels real. It always felt real," Benton said.

"But it's different when you read it on the Internet and know a million other people are, too. That's a different level of real. You're finally having an emotional response. Before, it was intellectual. Out of self-defense, you processed it in your head. I think this is a break-through, Benton. A very unpleasant one. I'm sorry for that."

"He doesn't know Lucy's in New York, and if she sees him—" Benton intercepted his thought. "Well, not true. She wouldn't really think about killing him, because she's been through that. She's long past that. She wouldn't kill him, just so you know."

Benton watched the gray sky subtly change the red-ness of the old bricks beyond his window, and when he shifted in his chair and rubbed his chin, he caught his own male scent and felt stubble that Scarpetta always said looked exactly like sand. He'd been up all night, had never left the hospital. He needed a shower. He needed a shave. He needed food and sleep.

"Sometimes I catch myself by surprise," he said. "When I say things like that about Lucy? It's literally a consideration and a reminder of what a warped life I live. The only person who never wanted to kill him is Kay. She still thinks she's somehow to blame, and it makes me angry. Just incredibly angry. I avoid the subject completely with her, and that's probably why I didn't say anything. The whole goddamn world is reading about it on the goddamn Internet. I'm tired. I was up all night with someone I can't tell you about who is going to be a major problem."

He stopped looking out the window. He didn't look at anything.

"Now we're getting somewhere," Dr. Thomas said. "I've wondered when you'd cut the crap about what a saint you are. You're angry as hell, and you're no saint. There are no saints, by the way."

"Angry as hell. Yes, I'm angry as hell."

"Angry at her."

"Yes, I really am," Benton said, and admitting it frightened him. "I know it's not fair. Good God, she's the one who was hurt. Of course she didn't ask for it. She'd worked with him for half her life, so why wouldn't she let him into her house when he was drunk and half out of his mind? That's what friends do. Even knowing what he felt about her doesn't make it her fault."

"He's wanted her sexually since they first met," Dr. Thomas said. "Rather much the way you felt. He fell in love with her. As did you. I wonder who fell in love with her first? Both of you met her around the same time, didn't you? Nineteen-ninety."

"His wanting her. Well, that had been going on for a long time, true. His feeling that way and her stepping around it and trying so hard not to hurt his feelings. I can sit here and analyze it all I want, but honestly?"

Benton was looking out his window again, talking to the bricks.

"There isn't anything different she could have done," he said. "What he did to her absolutely wasn't her fault. In many ways, it wasn't his fault. He would never do that sober. Not even close."

"You certainly sound convinced," Dr. Thomas said.

Benton turned away from the window and stared at what was on his computer screen. Then he looked out his window again as if the steely cold sky was a message for him, a metaphor. He removed a paper clip from a journal article he was revising and stapled the pages together, suddenly furious. The American Psychological Society probably wasn't going to accept yet another damn research article on emotional responses to members of social outgroups. Someone from Princeton just published basically the same damn thing Benton was about to submit. He straightened the paper clip. The challenge was to straighten it without a trace of a kink. In the end, they always snapped.

"Of all people, to be so irrational," he said. "So out of touch. And I have been. From day one. Irrational about everything, and now I'm about to pay for it."

"You're about to pay for it because other people know what your friend Pete Marino did to her?"

"He's not my friend."

"I thought he was. I thought you thought he was," Dr. Thomas said.

"We never socialized. We have nothing in common. Bowling, fishing, motorcycles, watching football, and drinking beer. Well, not beer. Not now. That's Marino. That's not me. Now that I think about it, I don't recall ever even going out to dinner with him, just the two of us. Not in twenty years. We have nothing in common. We'll never have anything in common."

"He's not from an elitist New England family? He didn't go to graduate school, was never an FBI profiler? He's not on the faculty of Harvard Medical School? Is that what you mean?"

"I'm not trying to be a snob," Benton said.

"Seems as if the two of you have Kay in common."

"Not that way. It never went that far," Benton said.

"How far did it need to go?"

"She told me it never went that far. He did other things. When she finally got undressed in front of me, I could see what he did. She made excuses for a day or two. Lied. I knew damn well she hadn't shut the hatch-back on her wrists."

Benton remembered bruises as dark as thunderclouds and shaped exactly the way they would be had someone pinned her hands behind her and held her against the wall. She'd offered no explanation at all when Benton finally saw her breasts. No one had ever done anything like that to her before, and he had never seen anything like that before except in cases he worked. When he'd sat on the bed looking at her, he'd felt as if a monstrous cretin had mangled the wings of a dove or mauled a child's tender flesh. He'd imagined Marino trying to eat her.

"Have you ever felt competitive with him?" Dr. Thomas's voice was distant as Benton envisioned stigmatas he didn't want to remember.

He heard himself say, "What's bad, I guess, is I never felt much of anything about him."

"He's spent a lot more time with Kay than you have," Dr. Thomas said. "That might make some people feel competitive. Feel threatened."

"Kay's never been attracted to him. If he were the last person on the planet, she wouldn't be."

"I guess we won't know the answer to that unless there's just the two of them left on the planet. In which case, you and I still won't know."

"I should have protected her better than I did," Benton said. "That's one thing I know how to do. Protect people. Those I love, and myself, or people I don't know. Doesn't matter. I'm an expert at it or I would have been dead a long time ago. A lot of people would be."

"Yes, Mr. Bond, but you weren't home that night. You were up here."

Dr. Thomas may as well have thrown a punch. Benton silently took it, could barely breathe. He worked the paper clip back and forth, bending and unbending, until it broke.

"Do you blame yourself, Benton?"

"We've been through this. And I've had no sleep," he answered.

"Yes, we've been through all sorts of facts and possibilities. Such as you've never allowed yourself a chance to feel the personal insult of what Marino did to Kay, who you quickly married afterwards. Maybe too quickly? Because you felt you had to hold everything together, especially since you didn't protect her, didn't prevent it? No different than what you do when you handle a criminal case, really. You take over the investigation, handle it, micromanage it, keep it a safe distance from your psyche. But the same rules don't apply in our personal lives. You're telling me you have homicidal feelings toward Marino, and in our last several conversations, we've delved into what you call your sexual acting out with Kay, although she isn't necessarily aware of it, is that still correct? Nor is she aware that you're aware of other women in a way that's unsettling to you? Still true?"

"It's normal for men to feel attractions they don't do anything about."

"Only men do that?" Dr. Thomas asked.

"You know what I mean."

"What's Kay aware of?"

"I'm trying to be a good husband," Benton said. "I love her. I'm in love with her."

"Are you worried you'll have an affair? Cheat?"

"No. Absolutely not. I would never do that," he said.

"No. Not. Never. You cheated on Connie. Left her for Kay. But that was a long time ago, wasn't it."

"I've never loved anybody as much as I love Kay," Benton said. "I would never forgive myself."

"My question is whether you completely trust yourself."

"I don't know."

"Do you completely trust her? She's very attractive, and now she must have a lot of fans because of CNN. A powerful, good-looking woman can have her pick. What about her trainer? You said you can't stand the thought that he puts his hands on her."

"I'm glad she's taking care of herself, and a trainer's a good thing. Prevents people from injuring themselves, especially if they've never worked with weights and aren't twenty years old."

"I believe his name is Kit."

Benton didn't like Kit. He always found excuses not to use the gym in their apartment building if Scarpetta was working out with Kit.

"Truth of the matter," Dr. Thomas said. "Whether you trust Kay or not, it won't change her behavior. That's her power, not yours. I'm more interested in whether you trust yourself."

"I don't know why you continue to push me on this," Benton said.

"Since you got married, your sexual patterns have changed. At least that's what you told me the first time we talked. You find excuses not to have sex when the opportunity is there, and then want it when you, quote, shouldn't. Again, what you told me. Still true?"

"Probably," Benton said.

"That's one way to pay her back."

"I'm not paying her back for Marino. Jesus Christ. She didn't do anything wrong." Benton tried not to sound angry.

"No," Dr. Thomas said. "I think it's more likely you're paying her back for being your wife. You don't want a wife. You never have, and that's not what you fell

in love with. You fell in love with a powerful woman, not
a wife. You're sexually attracted to Kay Scarpetta, not to
a wife."

"She's Kay Scarpetta and my wife. In fact, in many ways,
she's more powerful than she's ever been in her life."

"It's not the rest of us who need convincing, Benton."

Dr. Thomas always gave him special treatment, meaning
she was more aggressive and confrontational than she was
with her other patients. She and Benton shared a com-
monality that went beyond their therapeutic bond. Each
understood how the other processed information, and
Dr. Thomas could see right through linguistic camou-
flage. Denial, evasion, and passive communication simply weren't options. Long sessions of silent staring as the
shrink waited for an uptight patient to launch into what
was bothering him weren't going to happen. One minute into the void, and she was going to prompt Benton
as she did last time: *Did you come here for me to admire
your Hermès tie? Or do you have something on your mind?
Maybe we should pick up where we left off last time. How's
your libido?*

Dr. Thomas said, "And Marino? Will you talk to him?"

"Probably not," Benton said.

"Well, it seems you have a lot of people not to talk
to, and I'll leave you with my quirky little theory that at
some level we intend everything we do. That's why it's
extremely important to root out our intentions before
they uproot us. Gerald's waiting for me. Errands. We're
having a dinner party tonight, which we need like a hole
in the head."

It was her way of saying "Enough." Benton needed to process.

He got up from his desk and stood before his office window, gazing out at the leaden winter afternoon. Nineteen floors below, the hospital's small garden was barren, its concrete fountain dry.

3

GOTHAM GOTCHA!

Happy New Year, everyone!

My resolution is all about you—what will really grab you, and as I was mulling it over . . . ? Well, you know how they roll back the year? Remind us of every awful thing that happened so we can get depressed all over again? Guess who filled my to-die-for fifty-eight-inch HD Samsung plasma TV?

The to-die-for queen herself: Dr. Kay Scarpetta.

Walking up courthouse steps to testify in another sensational murder trial. Her sidekick investigator Pete Marino in tow—meaning the trial was at least six, seven months ago, right? I think we all know the poor fat maggot's not her sidekick anymore. Has anybody seen him? Is he in a cosmic jail somewhere? (Imagine working for a forensic diva like Scarpetta. Were it me, I might just commit suicide and hope she's not the one who does the autopsy.)

Anyway, back to her walking up the court-house steps. Cameras, the media, wannabes, spectators everywhere. Because she's the expert, right? Gets called in from here to Italy because who better? So I poured another glass of Maker's Mark, cranked up Coldplay, and watched her for a while, testifying in that pathological language of hers so few of us understand beyond getting the drift that some little girl was raped from stem to stern, even found seminal fluid in her ear (thought you could get that only from phone sex), and her head was bashed against the tile floor and *blunt force trauma* was what killed her. It dawned on me:

Who the hell is Scarpetta, anyway?

If you took away the hype, would there be anything behind it?

I began doing a little research. Start with this. She's a politico. Don't fall for bullshit about her being a champion for justice, a voice for those who can no longer speak, the lady physi-cian who believes in "First Do No Harm." (Are we absolutely sure Hippocrates isn't where the

word *hypocrite* comes from?) Fact is, Scarpetta's a
megalomaniac who manipulates us on CNN into
believing she's serving an altruistic social service
when the only thing she's serving is herself. . . .

Scarpetta had seen enough and dropped her BlackBerry
into her handbag, disgusted that Bryce had suggested she
look at such rot. She was as annoyed with him as she would
be if he had written it, and she could have done without his
critique of the photograph that accompanied the column.
Although the display on her BlackBerry was small, she saw
enough to get a good impression of what he'd meant when
he'd said the photograph was unflattering.

She looked like a she-devil in bloody scrubs, a face
shield, a disposable hair cover reminiscent of a shower
cap. Her mouth was open mid-sentence, her bloody
gloved hand pointing a scalpel, as if she was threatening
someone. The black rubber chronograph watch she was
wearing was a birthday gift from Lucy in 2005, meaning
the photograph had been taken at some point in the last
three and a half years.

Taken where?

Scarpetta didn't know. The background had been
whited out.

"Thirty-four dollar, twenty cent," her driver said
loudly as the taxi abruptly halted.

She looked through her side window at the closed
black iron front gates of Bellevue's former psychiatric
hospital, a foreboding red-rock building some two
centuries old that hadn't seen a patient in decades. No

lights, no cars, nobody home, the guard booth behind the fence empty.

"Not here," she said loudly through the opening in the Plexiglas partition. "Wrong Bellevue."

She repeated the address she'd given him when he'd picked her up at La Guardia, but the more she explained, the more insistent he got, jabbing his finger at the entrance, where *Psychiatric Hospital* was carved in granite. She leaned closer to him, directing his attention several blocks ahead where tall buildings were etched in gray, but he was bullish in his bad English. He wasn't taking her anywhere else, and she must get out of the cab right now. It entered her mind that he truly didn't know that the Bellevue Hospital Center wasn't this creepy old horror that looked like something out of *One Flew Over the Cuckoo's Nest*. He probably thought his passenger was a psychiatric patient, a criminally insane one suffering a relapse. Why else would she have luggage?

Scarpetta decided she'd rather walk the rest of the way in arctic blasts of wind than deal with him. Paying the fare, she got out of the cab, shouldered two bags, and began rolling her suitcase full of home cooking along the sidewalk. She pressed a button on her wireless earpiece.

"I'm almost here—" she started to tell Benton. "Dammit!" Her suitcase flopped over as if someone shot it.

"Kay? Where are you?"

"I just got thrown out of a taxi—"

"What? Thrown out of what? You're breaking up . . ." he said, right before the battery went dead.

She felt like a homeless person as she struggled with

her luggage, the suitcase falling over every other minute, and when she'd bend down to set it upright, her other bags would slide off her shoulders. Cold and irritable, she made her way to the modern Bellevue at First Avenue and East 27th, a full-service hospital center with a glass atrium entrance, a garden, a renowned trauma unit and ICU, and a forensic psychiatric floor for male patients whose alleged crimes ranged from jumping a turnstile to murdering John Lennon.

The phone on Benton's desk rang just minutes after he and Scarpetta were disconnected. He was sure it was her, trying him back.

"What happened?" he said.

"I was about to ask you that." Jaime Berger's voice.

"I'm sorry. I thought you were Kay. She's having some problem—"

"I'd say. Nice of you to mention it when we spoke earlier. Let's see. That would have been six, seven hours ago? Why didn't you say something?"

Berger must have read *Gotham Gotcha*.

"It's complicated," Benton said.

"I'm sure it is. We have a number of complications to deal with. I'm two minutes from the hospital. Meet me in the cafeteria."

Pete Marino's one-bedroom walk-up in Harlem was close enough to Manna's Soul Food that he lived and breathed fried chicken and short ribs. It was unfair to a man whose deprivation of food and drink had created an insatiable appetite for everything he couldn't have.

His makeshift dining area was a TV tray and straight-back chair overlooking the constant traffic on Fifth Avenue. He stacked deli turkey on a slice of whole-wheat bread, which he folded in half and dipped into a puddle of Nathan's Coney Island mustard on a paper plate. He drank a Sharp's nonalcoholic beer, about a third of the bottle in two swallows. Since he'd fled from Charleston, he'd lost fifty pounds and certain parts of his personality. Boxes of biker clothes, including an impressive collection of Harley-Davidson leather, went to a bazaar on 116th Street, where in exchange he got three suits, one blazer, two pairs of dress shoes, and a variety of shirts and ties, all knockoffs made in China.

He no longer wore his diamond stud, leaving a tiny hole badly located in his right earlobe, which somehow seemed a symbol of his have-not, off-center life. He'd quit shaving his scalp as smooth as a bowling ball, and what gray hair hadn't abandoned him circled his large head like part of a tarnished silver halo held up by his ears. He'd made a pact to give up women until he was ready, and his motorcycle and pickup truck were pointless when there was no place to park, so he'd given them up, too. His therapist at the treatment center, Nancy, had helped him comprehend the importance of self-control in his day-to-day interactions with other people, no matter what was wrong with them or what they had coming to them.

She said in her descriptive way that alcohol was the lighted match that ignited the bonfire of his anger, and had gone on to explain that his drinking was a fatal disease he'd acquired honestly from his blue-collar, uneducated, and inadequate father who got drunk and violent every payday. In short, Marino had inherited this fatal disease, and based on the brisk business at every bar and liquor store he quickly walked past, it was an epidemic. He decided it had been around since the Garden of Eden, where it wasn't an apple but a bottle of bourbon that the snake had given to Eve, which she in turn had shared with Adam, and that had led to sex and being thrown out of paradise with nothing but the fig leaves on their backs.

Nancy warned Marino if he didn't religiously attend AA meetings, he would become a dry drunk, which was an individual who got angry, nasty, compulsive, and out of control without the benefit of a six-pack or two. The nearest gathering place of the AAs, as Marino called them, was a church not far from the Professional African Hair Braiding Center, and therefore quite convenient for him. But he hadn't become a regular or even an irregular. When he'd first moved here, he'd attended three times in three days, uncomfortable as hell when the participants, suspiciously kind and friendly, had gone around the room, introducing themselves, giving him no choice but to solemnly swear himself in, as if he were on trial.

My name's Pete and I'm an alcoholic.

Hi, Pete.

He sent Nancy e-mails explaining that it went against

the nature and training of a cop to confess to anything, especially in a room packed with strangers, any one of whom might turn out to be a potential dry-drunk shit-can Marino might have to lock up someday. Besides, it had taken only three meetings for him to complete all twelve steps, although he'd decided against making a list of persons he'd harmed and making amends. His reason was step nine, which clearly stated that one shouldn't make amends if it would only further injure whoever had been harmed, and he decided that was everyone.

Step ten was easier, and he had filled an entire note-book with the names of those who had wronged him throughout his life.

He hadn't included Scarpetta on either list until a strange coincidence occurred. He found the apartment where he now lived, made a deal with the landlord to lease it at an affordable price in exchange for services, such as handling evictions, only to discover the location was so close to former President Bill Clinton's office that Marino often walked past the fourteen-story building on his way to the subway station at 125th and Lenox. Thinking of Bill Clinton caused Marino to think of Hil-lary Clinton, and that caused him to think about women who were powerful enough to be the president or some other world leader. That led to thoughts of Scarpetta.

It had gotten to where he almost confused the two in his fantasies. He would see Hillary on CNN, then see Scarpetta on CNN, and by the time he changed chan-nels in a desperate attempt to divert his attention with ESPN or maybe a pay-per-view movie, he was depressed.

His heart would ache like an abscessed tooth. He would obsess about Scarpetta and the lists she wasn't on. He would jot her name on one list, then scratch through it and jot it on the other. He fantasized about what it would be like if she were president. He would suddenly find himself on the Secret Service's security threat list and have to escape to Canada.

Maybe Mexico. He'd spent several years in South Florida and could handle Spanish-speaking people better than he could those who spoke French. He'd never understood the French, and didn't like their food. What did it say about a country that didn't have a national beer, like Budweiser, Corona, Dos Equis, Heineken, or Red Stripe?

He finished a second turkey roll-up, took another slug of Sharp's, and watched people whose only ambitions were West Indian take-out, boutiques, juice bars, tailor shops, or maybe the nearby Apollo theater, the noise of cars, trucks, and pedestrians a jarring orchestra that Marino didn't mind in the least. In warm weather he kept his windows open until he couldn't stand the dust. What he avoided was silence. He'd had plenty enough of that in rehab, where he wasn't allowed to listen to music or watch TV, couldn't fill his head with anything but the confessions of drunks and drug addicts, and his own haunted thoughts and memories of embarrassingly naked talks with Nancy.

He got up from his chair and collected his soggy paper plate, his napkin, his empty Sharp's bottle. The kitchen was no more than six steps away, with a small window above the sink that afforded him a view of artificial turf–covered concrete and aluminum tables and chairs surrounded by a chain-link fence—what was advertised as the apartment building's backyard.

On the counter was his computer, and he read the gossip column from this morning that he'd saved on the desktop, determined to discover who was behind it, then find the scumbag and do something that would rearrange his or her body parts permanently.

No investigative tool he knew of worked. He could Google *Gotham Gotcha* until the cows came home, and nothing that popped up told him a damn thing he didn't already know. It was useless trying to trace the columnist through the advertising companies that paid to push foods, liquor, books, electronics, movies, and TV shows. There was no pattern, only the validation that millions of fans were addicted to a fucking gossip column that this morning had made the worst episode of Marino's life its centerpiece.

His phone rang.

It was Detective Mike Morales.

"What's up," Marino said.

"Data mining, bro," Morales said in his slow, lazy way.

"I'm not your bro. Don't waste your rapper-talk shit on me."

Morales's MO was to come across as half asleep and bored, and doped up on sedatives or painkillers, which Marino doubted, but then again, he didn't know. Behind Morales's haze was a snobby bastard who had gone to Dartmouth, then Johns Hopkins, where he'd completed medical school and decided he'd rather be one of New York's finest, a cop, which Marino didn't take at face value. Nobody who could be a doctor would end up a cop.

Besides, he was a bullshit artist who circulated all sorts of wild stories about himself and laughed his ass off when other cops believed him. Supposedly, his cousin was the president of Bolivia, and his father had moved the family to America because he believed in capitalism and was tired of herding llamas. Supposedly, Morales had grown up in the projects of Chicago and had been a pal of Barack Obama until politics interfered, which seemed reasonable to those who didn't know better. No presidential candidate would want to be friends with someone who used words like *bro* and looked like a member of a street gang, right down to his half-mast baggy jeans, big gold chains and rings, and cornrow hair.

"Been running queries all day—not to be confused with homos, bro," Morales said.

"Got no idea what the hell you're talking about."

"Queer-ies? I forgot you got no sense of humor and barely finished high school. Looking for the usual patterns, trends, modus operandi, complaints, from here to Dollywood, and I think I hit on something."

"What besides Berger?" Marino said.

"What is it about women like her and Kay Scarpetta? It might be worth dying to have her hands all over me. Goddamn. Can you imagine doing her and Berger at the same time? Well, who am I talking to? Of course you can imagine it."

Marino's dislike of Morales instantly turned to hate. He was always screwing with Marino, putting him down, and the only reason Marino didn't screw him back, only harder, was Marino's self-imposed probation. Benton had asked Berger for a favor. If she hadn't granted it, God knows where Marino would be. Probably a dispatcher in some shitbox small-town police department somewhere. Or a drunk in a homeless shelter. Or dead.

"It's possible our killer's struck before," Morales said. "I've found two other homicides that are somewhat similar. Not New York, but remember Oscar's self-employed and doesn't, quote, go to the office. He's got a car. He's got disposable income because he gets a tax-free check from his family every birthday, and right now the limit's up to twelve grand—their way of not feeling guilty about their freako only son. He's got no one to support but himself. So we got no idea how much he travels or what he does, now, do we? I might just get a couple of oldie goldies cleared while I'm at it."

Marino opened the refrigerator, found another Sharp's, twisted off the cap, and hurled it into the sink, where it clattered like shotgun pellets smacking a pop-up metal target.

"What two other homicides?" he asked.

"Got hits on two possibles in our database. Like I said, not New York cases, which is why they didn't come to mind. Both in the summer of 2003, two months apart. A fourteen-year-old kid hooked on oxys. Found nude, hands and ankles bound, strangled with a ligature that was missing from the scene. From a good family in

Greenwich, Connecticut. Body dumped near the Bugatti dealership. Unsolved, no suspects."

Marino said, "Where was Oscar the summer of 2003?"

"Same place he is now. Same job, living his whacked life in his same apartment. Meaning he could have been anywhere."

"I'm not seeing the connection. The kid's what? Doing blows for drugs and got picked up by the wrong customer? That's what it sounds like to me. And you got reason to think Oscar Bane's into teenage boys?"

"You ever notice we don't know what the hell people are into until after they start raping and murdering and it comes out in the wash? It could have been Oscar. Like I said, he drives. He can afford to get around and has plenty of time on his hands. He's strong as hell. We should keep an open mind."

"What about the other case? Another teenage boy?"

"A woman."

"So tell me who and why Oscar might have done her," Marino said.

"Oops." Morales yawned loudly. "I'm reshuffling my paperwork. Out of order, me, oh, my. She was first, then the kid. Beautiful, twenty-one, just moved to Baltimore from a rural town in North Carolina, got a nothing job with a radio station, was hoping to get into television, and instead got involved in some extracurricular activities to keep herself in oxys. So she was vulnerable to being picked up. Nude, hands bound, strangled with a ligature that wasn't found at the scene. Body found in a Dumpster near the harbor."

Marino said, "DNA in either case?"

"Nothing useful, and there was no sign of sexual assault. Negative for seminal fluid."

"I'm still waiting for the connection," Marino said. "Homicides where people are probably doing tricks for drugs and end up bound and strangled and dumped are a dime a dozen."

"You aware Terri Bridges had a thin gold chain around her left ankle? Nobody knows where it came from. Kind of weird she had no other jewelry on, and when I pushed Oscar about the ankle bracelet, he said he'd never seen it before."

"And?"

"And these other two cases, same thing. No jewelry except a thin gold bracelet around the left ankle. Same side as the heart, right? Like a leg iron? Like, you're my love slave? Could be the killer's signature. Could be Oscar's signature. I'm getting the case files together, still data-searching and digging for other info. Will put out alerts to the usual suspects—including the posse from your past."

"What posse from my past?" Marino's thoughts went from dark to black.

He couldn't see through the storm clouds rolling in his head.

"Benton Wesley. And that hot young former agent-cop-whatever who's unfortunately untouchable to yours truly here, if rumors are to be believed. Of course, your little discovery of the laptops when you dropped by the scene earlier today without my permission just threw her a bone."

"I don't need your permission. You're not my den mother."

"Nope. The den mother would be Berger. Maybe you should ask her who's in charge."

"If I need to, I will. Right now, I'm doing my job. Investigating this homicide, exactly like she expects me to do."

He drained the last of the Sharp's and glass clanked inside the refrigerator as he went for another one. By his calculations, if each bottle was point three percent alcohol, he could achieve the first hint of a buzz if he drank at least twelve in quick succession, which he had tried before, and had felt nothing but an urgency to pee.

Morales said, "She's got this forensic computer company Berger's eager to use. Lucy, as in Kay Scarpetta's niece."

"I know who she is."

Marino also knew about Lucy's company in the Village, and that Scarpetta and Benton were involved with John Jay. He knew a lot of things he chose not to discuss with Morales or anyone else. What he didn't know was that Lucy, Benton, and Scarpetta were involved in the Terri Bridges case, or that Scarpetta and Benton were in the city right this minute.

Morales's cocky voice: "It may relieve you to know that I don't believe Kay will be around long enough for you to have any awkward encounters."

There could be no doubt. Morales had read that fucking gossip column.

"She's here to examine Oscar," Morales said.

"What the hell for?"

"Looks like she's the blue plate special on Oscar's menu. He demanded her, and Berger's giving the little guy whatever his little heart wants."

Marino couldn't stand the thought of Scarpetta being alone with Oscar Bane. It unnerved him that Oscar had requested her specifically, because that could mean only one thing: He was far more aware of her than he ought to be.

Marino said, "You're suggesting he might be a serial killer, so what's he doing with the Doc? I can't believe Berger or anybody set her up for something like this. Especially since he could get out any minute. Jesus."

He was pacing. In a dozen steps, he could cover his apartment's entire square footage.

"Once she's done, maybe she'll buzz back to Massachusetts and you got nothing to worry about," Morales said. "Which is good, right? Since you got plenty to worry about already."

"That right? Why don't you tell me."

"I'm reminding you this is a sensitive case, and you didn't handle it all too well when Oscar Bane poured his heart out to you last month."

"I did it by the book."

"Funny thing about that. Nobody gives a shit once there's a problem. As far as your former boss Kay goes, I advise avoidance. Not that you have any reason to be in her company or show up unexpected at Bellevue. For example."

It inflamed Marino to hear Morales call her Kay. Marino had never called her Kay, and he'd worked side by side with her, had probably spent ten thousand hours with her in the morgue, in her office, in the car, at crime scenes, in her home, including on holidays, and even having a drink or two in her hotel room when they worked cases out of town. So if he didn't call her Kay, who the hell did Morales think he was?

"My advice to you is to make yourself scarce until Kay's back in Massachusetts," Morales said. "She doesn't need any more stress, you hearing me, bro? And what I don't want is next time we call her in for assistance, she says no because of you. We don't need her quitting her position at John Jay, quitting as a consultant because of you. Then Benton would quit next, if he wants to keep the wife happy. So we lose both of them because of you. I plan on spending a lot of years working with both of them. Being the Three Musketeers."

"You don't know them." Marino was so angry, his heart was pounding in his neck.

"They quit and it will hit the news," Morales said. "And you know how things get passed down the line. A scandal because it will be the front page of the *Post,* a headline ten feet tall that Jaime Berger, the ace prosecutor of sex crimes, hired a sex offender and maybe she gets fired. Unbelievable how you can bring down the house of cards, man. Anyway, I gotta get off the phone. About what's on the Internet, what happened between you and Kay. Not to pry—"

"Then fucking don't," Marino snapped.

4

Oscar Bane's hairless, shackled legs dangled over the edge of the examination table inside one of the several infirmaries in the psychiatric prison ward. His eyes, one blue, the other green, gave Scarpetta the unsettling sensation that two people were staring at her.

A Department of Corrections officer had the solid, silent presence of the Rockies as he stood near the wall, allowing her space to work, but close enough to intervene should Oscar become violent, which seemed unlikely. He was frightened. He'd been crying. She sensed nothing aggressive about him as he sat on the table, self-conscious in a thin cotton gown that was long on him but periodically sneaked open below the tie at his waist. Chains quietly clanked whenever he shifted his shackled legs or cuffed hands to cover himself.

Oscar was a little person, a dwarf. While his extremities and fingers were disproportionately short, his flimsy gown revealed that he was well endowed elsewhere. One might go so far as to say that God had overcompensated him for what Scarpetta suspected was achondroplasia, caused by a spontaneous mutation of the gene responsible for the formation of bone, primarily targeting the long bones of the arms and legs. His torso and head were disproportionately large for his extremities, and his short, thick fingers diverged between the middle and ring fingers, giving his hands a somewhat trident appearance. Beyond that, he appeared normal anatomically except for what he had done to himself at considerable misery and expense.

His startling white teeth had been bonded or bleached, possibly crowned, and his short hair was dyed bright yellow-gold. His nails were buffed and perfectly squared, and although Scarpetta couldn't swear to it, she credited his tranquil brow to injections of Botox. Most remarkable was his body, which looked as if it were sculpted of beige Carrara marble with bluish-gray veining. Perfectly balanced in its musculature, it was almost completely devoid of hair. The overall effect of his appearance, with his intensely different eyes and Apollo-like radiance, was rather surreal and bizarre, and she found Benton's comment about Oscar's phobias quite strange. He could not look the way he did without worshipping at the feet of pain and the practitioners who inflicted it.

She felt the probe of his blue-green gaze as she opened the crime scene case Benton kept in his office for her. Unlike those whose professions didn't demand forceps, evidence envelopes and bags and containers, or camera equipment, forensic light sources, sharp blades, and all the rest, Scarpetta was forced to live a life of redundancy. If bottled water couldn't make it through airport security, a crime scene case certainly wouldn't, and flaunting her medical examiner's shield only drew more unwanted attention.

She'd tried it once at Logan and had ended up in a room where she was interrogated, searched, and subjected to other invasions to make sure she wasn't a terrorist who, the TSA officers had to admit, just happened to be the spitting image of that lady medical examiner on CNN. In the end, she wasn't allowed to carry the crime scene case on the plane anyway, and refusing to check it in baggage, she ended up driving. Now she kept duplicates of all security threats in Manhattan.

She asked Oscar, "Do you understand the purpose of these samples and why you're under no obligation to give them?"

He watched her arrange envelopes, forceps, a tape measure, and various other forensic items on the white paper–covered examination table. He turned away from her and stared at the wall.

The corrections officer said, "Look at the doctor when she talks to you, Oscar."

Oscar continued to stare at the wall.

In a tense, tenor voice, he said, "Dr. Scarpetta, could you repeat what you said, please?"

"You signed a release, agreeing it was all right for me to take certain biological samples," she replied. "I'm confirming you understand the scientific information these samples can provide, and that no one has asked for them."

Oscar still hadn't been charged with a crime. She wondered if Benton, Berger, and the police interpreted his malingering to mean he was going to confess any minute to a murder Scarpetta knew nothing about. This forced her into an untenable and unprecedented position. Since he wasn't under arrest, she couldn't divulge anything he revealed to her unless he waived the doctor-patient privilege, and the only waiver he had signed so far was one that allowed her to take biological samples.

Oscar looked at her and said, "I know what they're for. DNA. I know why you need my hair."

"The samples will be analyzed and the labs will have your DNA profile. Hair can tell us if you're a chronic substance abuser. There are other things the police, the scientists look for. Trace evidence . . ."

"I know what it is."

"I'm making sure you understand."

"I don't do drugs, and I'm certainly not a chronic substance abuser of any description," he said in a shaky voice, facing the wall again. "And my DNA and fingerprints are all over her apartment. My blood's in there. I cut my thumb."

He showed her his right thumb, a Band-Aid around the second knuckle.

"I let them fingerprint me when they brought me in," he said. "I'm not in any database. They'll see I've never committed a crime. I don't get parking tickets. I stay out of trouble."

He stared at the forceps she picked up, and fear shadowed his mismatched eyes.

"I don't need those," he said. "I'll do it myself."

"Have you showered since you got here?" she asked, putting down the forceps.

"No. I said I wouldn't until you looked at me."

"Have you washed your hands?"

"No. I've touched as little as possible, mainly the pencil your husband had me use during certain psychological tests. Projective figure drawings. I've refused to eat. I didn't want to do anything to my body until you looked. I'm afraid of doctors. I don't like pain."

She tore open paper packets of swabs and applicators while he watched, as if at any moment he expected her to do something that might hurt.

"I'd like to scrape under your nails," she said. "Only if it's all right. We can recover trace evidence, DNA, from under fingernails, toenails."

"I know what it's for. You won't find anything that shows I did anything to her. Finding her DNA means nothing. My DNA's all over her apartment," he repeated himself.

He sat very still while she used a plastic scraper to scrape under his nails, and she could feel his stare. She sensed his blue-green eyes like warm light as they touched her head and other parts of her, as if he was examining her while she was examining him. When she was done with the scraping and looked up at him, he was looking at the wall. He asked her not to watch while he plucked his own head hair, which she helped him place inside an envelope, and then his pubic hair, which went into another envelope. For someone so averse to pain, he didn't flinch, but his face was tense and his forehead was beaded with sweat.

She peeled open a buccal brush, and he swabbed the inside of his cheek, and his hands trembled.

"Now please make him leave." He meant the corrections officer. "You don't need him here. I'm not talking with him here."

"Doesn't work that way," the officer said. "It's not your choice."

Oscar was silent. He stared at the wall. The officer looked at Scarpetta, waiting to see what she was going to do.

"You know," she decided, "I think we'll be fine."

"I'd rather not do that, Doc. He's pretty keyed up."

He didn't seem keyed up, but she didn't comment. What he seemed was dazed and upset, and on the verge of hysteria.

"What you mean is chained up like Houdini," Oscar said. "It's one thing to be in lockup. But I don't need to be shackled like some serial killer. I'm surprised you didn't roll me out in a Hannibal Lecter cage. The staff here obviously doesn't know that mechanical restraints in psychiatric hospitals were abolished in the mid–nineteenth century. What have I done to deserve this?"

He raised his cuffed hands and was sputtering, he was so incensed.

"It's because ignorant people like you think I'm a circus freak," he said.

"Hey, Oscar," the guard replied. "Here's a news flash. You're not in a normal psychiatric hospital. This is the prison ward you checked yourself into." He said to Scarpetta, "I'd prefer to stay, Doc."

"A freak. That's what ignorant people like you think."

"We're fine," she repeated to the officer, and she could understand why Berger was exercising caution.

Oscar was quick to point out anything he perceived as unfair. He was quick to remind everyone he was a little person, when in fact that wasn't the first thing people probably noticed about him, unless he was standing. Certainly, it wasn't what had caught her attention the instant she'd walked into the infirmary. His different-colored eyes had flashed at her, and seemed a more startling green and blue in contrast to the brightness of his teeth and hair, and although his features weren't flawless, the way they fit together had invited her to stare, to study. She continued to wonder just what it was that Oscar Bane reminded her of. Perhaps a bust on an ancient gold coin.

"I'll be right out here," the officer said.

He left, shutting the door, which like every door on the ward had no handles. Only the corrections officers had keys, so it was important to keep the double-cylinder deadbolt in the locked position. If the bolt was out, the door wasn't going to shut all the way and accidentally trap a member of the staff or visiting consultant such as herself inside a small room with a two-hundred-pound man who'd just dismembered some woman he'd met in a bar, for example.

Scarpetta picked up the tape measure and said to Oscar, "I'd like to measure your arms and legs. Get your exact height and weight."

"I'm four foot and a quarter," he said. "I weigh one hundred and nine pounds. I wear a size-five shoe. Sometimes a four. Or a six and a half if it's a woman's. Sometimes a five and a half. It depends on the shoe. I have a wide foot."

"Left arm from the glenohumeral joint to the tip of your third finger. If you don't mind holding your arms as straight as you can. That's perfect. Sixteen and one-eighth inches for the left. Sixteen and two-eighths for the right. Not unusual. Most people's arms aren't precisely the same length. Now your legs, if you can hold them straight out. I'm going to measure from your acetabulum, your hip joint."

She felt it through the thin cotton of his gown, and measured the length of his legs to the tip of his toes, and the shackles clacked quietly and his muscles bulged as he moved. His legs were only about two inches longer than his arms, and slightly bowed. She wrote down the measurements and retrieved other paperwork from the countertop.

"Let me confirm what they gave me when I got here," she said. "You're thirty-four, your middle name is Lawrence. You're right-handed, according to this," and she got as far as his date of birth and address in the city before he interrupted her.

"Aren't you going to ask why I want you here? Why I demanded it? Why I made sure Jaime Berger was informed I wouldn't cooperate unless you came? Screw her." His eyes were watering and his voice wavered. "Terri would still be here if it wasn't for her."

He turned his head to the right and looked at the wall.

"Are you having trouble hearing me, Oscar?" Scarpetta asked.

"My right ear," he said in a voice that intermittently shook and changed octaves.

"But you can hear with your left ear?"

"Chronic ear infections when I was a boy. I'm deaf in my right ear."

"Do you know Jaime Berger?"

"She's cold-blooded, doesn't give a shit about anybody. You're nothing like her. You care about victims. I'm a victim. I need you to care about me. You're all I've got."

"In what way are you a victim?" Scarpetta labeled envelopes.

"My life's been ruined. The person who means most to me is gone. I'll never see her again. She's gone. I have nothing left. I don't care if I die. I know who you are and what you do. I would even if you weren't famous. Famous or not, I would know who and what you are. I had to think fast, very fast. After finding . . . after finding Terri . . ." His voice cracked, and he blinked back tears. "I told the police to bring me here. Where I'd be safe." .

"Safe from what?"

"I said I might be a danger to myself. And they asked, 'What about to others?' And I said no, only to myself. I requested solitary confinement on the prison ward because I can't be in general population. They're calling me the Midget Murderer up here. Laughing at me. The police have no probable cause to arrest me, but they think I'm deranged and don't want me disappearing, and I do have money and a passport, because I come from a good family in Connecticut, although my parents aren't very kind. I don't care if I die. In the minds of the police and Jaime Berger, I'm guilty."

"They're doing what they can to accommodate you. You're here. You met with Dr. Wesley. Now I'm here," Scarpetta reminded him.

"They're just using you. They don't care about me."

"I promise not to let anybody use me."

"They already are. To cover their asses. They've already convicted me, aren't looking for anybody else. The real killer's out there somewhere. He knows who I am. Someone will be next. Whoever did this will do it again. They have a motive, a cause, and I was warned but I didn't think they meant Terri. It never occurred to me they intended to hurt Terri."

"Warned?"

"They communicate with me. I have these communications."

"Did you tell the police this?"

"If you don't know who they are, you have to be careful who you tell. I tried to warn Jaime Berger a month ago about how unsafe it was for me to come forward with what I know. But I never imagined I was putting Terri at risk. They never communicated with me about Terri. So I didn't know about that, about the danger to her."

He wiped tears with the backs of his hands, and his chains clanked.

"How did you warn Jaime Berger? Or try to warn her?"

"I called her office. She'll tell you. Get her to tell you what a cold-blooded human being she is. Get her to tell you how much she cares. She doesn't." Tears rolled down his face. "And now Terri's gone. I knew something bad was going to happen, but I didn't know it would be to her. And you're wondering why. Well, I don't know. Maybe they hate little people, want to wipe us off the planet. Like the Nazis did to the Jews, the homosexuals and gypsies, the handicapped, the mentally ill. Whoever threatened Hitler's Master Race ended up in the ovens. Somehow they've stolen my identity and my thoughts, and they know everything about me. I reported it but Berger didn't care. I demanded to have mind justice, but she wouldn't even get on the phone with me."

"Tell me about mind justice."

"When your mind is stolen. Justice is getting it back. It's her fault. She could have stopped it. I don't have my mind back. I don't have Terri. All I have is you. Please help me."

Scarpetta slipped her gloved hands into the pockets of her lab coat and felt herself slipping deeper into trouble. She didn't want to be Oscar Bane's physician. She should tell him right now she wanted no further relationship with him. She should open that beige-painted steel door and never look back.

"They killed her. I know they did it," Oscar said.

"Who do you think *they* are?"

"I don't know who they are. They've been following me, some specialized group supporting some cause. I'm their target. It's been going on for months, at least. How can she be gone? Maybe I am a danger to myself. Maybe I do want to die."

He began to cry.

"I loved her more than anyone . . . ever in my life. I keep thinking I'll wake up. It isn't true. It can't be true. I'm not really here. I hate Jaime Berger. Maybe they'll kill someone she loves. See how that feels. Let her live that hell. I hope it happens. I hope someone murders whoever she loves most in her life."

"Do you wish you could kill someone she loves?" Scarpetta asked.

She tucked several tissues into his cuffed hands. Tears fell, and his nose ran.

He said, "I don't know who they are. If I'm out there, they'll follow me again. They know where I am right this minute. They try to control me through fear. Through harassment."

"How are they doing this? Do you have reason to believe someone is stalking you?"

"Advanced electronics. There are countless unclassified devices you can order off the Internet. Microwave-transmitted voice to skull. Silent sound. Through-the-wall radar. I have every reason to believe I've been selected as a mind-control target, and if you don't think things like this happen, think back to the human radiation experiments conducted by the government after World War

Two. Those people were secretly fed radioactive materials, injected with plutonium for purposes of nuclear warfare research. I'm not making this up."

"I'm aware of the radiation experiments," Scarpetta said. "There's no denying that happened."

"I don't know what they want from me," he said. "It's Berger's fault. All of it's her fault."

"Explain that to me."

"The DA's office investigates identity theft, stalking, harassment, and I called and asked to talk to her, and they wouldn't let me. I told you. They put me on the phone with this asshole cop. He thought I was a lunatic, of course, and nobody did anything. There was no investigation. No one cares. I trust you. I know you care about people. I've seen it with my own eyes. Please help me. Please. I'm completely unprotected. I have no shields here. No protections."

She checked shallow abrasions on the left side of his neck, noting that the stage of scab formation looked relatively fresh.

"Why would you trust me?" she asked.

"I can't believe you'd say that. What manipulation are you trying?"

"I don't manipulate people. I have no intention of manipulating you."

He studied her face as she studied more abrasions.

"Okay," he said. "I understand you have to be careful what you say. It doesn't matter. I respected you before all that. You don't know who they are, either. You have to be careful."

"Before all what?"

"You were brave to discuss Bhutto's assassination. Terri and I watched you on CNN. You had a long day and night on CNN, talking about it, were so compassionate and respectful about that terrible tragedy. And brave and matter-of-fact, but I could tell what you felt in your heart. I could tell you were as devastated as we were. You were devastated, and it wasn't for show. You worked hard to hide it. I knew I could trust you. I understood. Terri did, too, of course. But it was disappointing. I told her she had to think of it from your perspective. Because I knew I could trust you."

"I'm not sure why seeing me on TV would make you think you could trust me."

She retrieved a camera from her crime scene case.

When he didn't answer her, she said, "Tell me why Terri was disappointed."

"You know why, and it was completely understandable. You respect people," Oscar said. "You care about them. You help them. I stay away from doctors unless I have no choice. I can't stand pain. I tell them to put me under, give me an injection of Demerol, do anything if it's going to hurt. I admit it. I'm afraid of doctors. I'm afraid of pain. I can't look at a needle if I'm injected. I can't see it or I'll faint. I'll tell them to cover my eyes or inject me where I can't see it. You aren't going to hurt me, are you? Or give me a shot?"

"No. Nothing I do should be painful," she said as she checked abrasions under his left ear.

They were shallow, with no sign of epithelial regeneration at the edges. Again, the scabbing was fresh. Oscar seemed reassured by what she said, and soothed by her touch.

"Whoever's following me, spying on me," he started on that again. "Maybe the government, but whose government? Maybe some hate cell or some cult. I know you're not afraid of anyone or any government or any cult or group or you wouldn't talk about the things you do on TV. Terri said the same thing. You're her hero. If only she knew I was sitting in this room with you, talking about her. Maybe she knows. Do you believe in the afterlife? That the loved one's spirit doesn't leave you?"

His bloodshot eyes looked up, as if looking for Terri.

"I don't know what I'm going to do," he said.

"Let me make sure you understand something," Scarpetta said.

She pulled up a plastic chair and sat close to the table.

"I know nothing about this case," she said. "I don't know what you supposedly did or didn't do. I don't know who Terri is."

Shock registered on his face. "What are you saying?"

"I'm saying I was called in to examine your injuries, and agreed to do so. And I'm probably not the person you should be speaking to. Your well-being is of my utmost concern, so I'm obliged to tell you that the more you talk to me about Terri, about what happened, the bigger the risk."

"You're the only one I should be speaking to."

He wiped his nose and eyes, and stared at her as if he were trying to figure out something very important.

He said, "You have your reasons. Maybe you know something."

"You should have a lawyer. Then every word you say is privileged, unconditionally."

"You're a physician. Whatever we discuss is privileged. You can't allow the police to interfere with my medical care, and they have no right to any information unless I give permission or there's a court order. You must protect my dignity. That's the law."

"It's also the law that if you're charged with a crime, my records can be subpoenaed by the prosecution or the defense. You need to think about that before you continue to talk to me about Terri, about what happened last night. Anything I say could be subpoenaed," she emphasized.

"Jaime Berger had her chance to talk to me. She's nothing like you. She deserves to be fired. She deserves to suffer the way I am and to lose what I've lost. It's her fault."

"Do you want to cause Jaime Berger harm?" Scarpetta asked.

"I'd never harm anybody. But she's harmed herself. It's her fault. The universe repays in kind. If she loses someone she loves, it will be her fault."

"I'll try to impress it upon you again. If you're charged with a crime, I can be subpoenaed and will have no choice but to disclose anything I've observed. Yes. I absolutely can be subpoenaed by Jaime Berger. Do you understand that?"

His different-colored eyes stared at her, his body rigid

with anger. Scarpetta was aware of the heavy steel door, wondering if she should open it.

"They won't find any justifiable cause to pin this on me," he said. "I didn't stop them from taking my clothes, my car. I've given consent to go inside my apartment because I've got nothing to hide, and you can see for yourself the way I'm forced to live. I want you to see it. I insist you see it. I said you have to see it or they can't go in. There's no evidence I've ever hurt Terri unless they make it up. And maybe they will. But you'll protect me because you're my witness. You'll watch after me no matter where I am, and if anything happens to me, you'll know it's part of a plan. And you can't tell anyone anything I don't want them to know. Right now, legally, you can't reveal anything that goes on between us. Not even to your husband. I allowed him to do my psychological eval, and he'll tell you from my mental-health assessment that I'm not crazy. I trust his expertise. More important, I knew he could get to you."

"Did you tell him what you're telling me?"

"I let him do the eval, and that's all. I said he could check my mind and you could check the rest of me. Otherwise, I wouldn't cooperate. You can't tell him what I say. Not even him. If that changes and I get falsely accused and you get subpoenaed? By then you'll believe in me and fight for me anyway. You should believe in me. It's not like you've never heard of me."

"Why would you think I've heard of you?"

"I see." His stare was fierce. "You've been instructed not to talk. Fine. I don't like this game. But okay. Fine.

All I ask is you listen to me and not betray me or violate your sworn oath."

Scarpetta should stop now. But she was thinking about Berger. Oscar hadn't threatened Berger. Not yet. Unless he did, Scarpetta couldn't reveal a word he said, but that didn't stop her from worrying about Berger, about anybody close to Berger. She wished he would come right out with it and say in no uncertain terms that he was a danger to Berger or to someone. Then no more confidentiality, and at the very least, he would be arrested for communicating a threat.

"I'm going to take notes, which I'll keep in a file as a consultation," Scarpetta said.

"Yes, notes. I want a record of the truth in your hands. In case something happens."

She slipped a pad of paper and pen out of a pocket of her lab coat.

"In case I die," he said. "There's probably no way out. They'll probably get me. This will probably be my last New Year's Day. Probably I don't care."

"What makes you say that?"

"Whatever I do, wherever I go, they know."

"What about right now?"

"Maybe. But you know?" He looked at the door. "There's a lot of steel to get through. I'm not sure they can get through it, but I'm going to be careful what I say and what I think. You need to listen carefully. You need to read my mind while you can. Eventually, they'll completely control what's left of my free will, my thoughts. Maybe what they're doing is practice. They have to practice on someone. We know the CIA's had covert behavior-modification neuro-electromagnetic programs for half a century, and who do you think they practice on? And what do you think happens if you go to the police? Mysteriously, no report is filed. Same thing that happened when I reported it to Ms. Berger. I was ignored. And now Terri's dead. I'm not paranoid. I'm not suffering some schizoid, psychotic episode. I don't have a personality disorder. I'm not delusional. I don't believe the Air Loom Gang is after me with their infernal machine, although one has to wonder about the politicians and if that's why we're at war in the Middle East. Of course, I'm being facetious, although not much would surprise me anymore."

"You seem very well versed in psychology and psychiatric history."

"I have a Ph.D. I teach the history of psychiatry at Gotham College."

She'd never heard of it and asked him where it was.

"It's nowhere," he said.

5

Her username was Shrew because her husband used to call her that. He didn't always mean it as an insult. Sometimes it was a term of endearment.

"Don't be such a goddamn shrew," he would say, verbatim, after her complaints about his cigars or not picking up after himself. "Let's have a drink, my darling little shrew" usually meant it was five p.m. and he was in a decent mood and wanted to watch the news.

She'd carry in their drinks and a bowl of cashews, and he'd pat the cushion next to him on the tawny corduroy couch. After a half-hour of the news, which, needless to say, was never good, he would get quiet and not call her a shrew or talk to her, and dinner would be the sounds of eating, after which he would retreat to the bedroom and read. One day he went out on an errand and never came back.

She had no illusions about what he'd have to say were he still here. He wouldn't approve of her being the anonymous system administrator for the *Gotham Gotcha* website. He would call what she did disgusting detritus that was intended to ruthlessly exploit and inflict disease upon people, and would say it was insane for her to work a job where she'd never met any of those involved or for that matter didn't know their names. He would say it was outrageously suspicious that Shrew did not know who the anonymous columnist was.

Most of all, he would be aghast that she had been hired over the phone by an "agent" who wasn't an American. He said he lived in the UK, but he sounded about as English as Tony Soprano, and had forced Shrew to sign numerous legal documents without her own counsel reviewing them first. When she'd done everything asked of her, she was given a trial run of one month. Without pay. At the end of that period, no one had called to tell her what a marvelous job she'd done or how thrilled the Boss (as Shrew thought of the anonymous columnist) was to have her onboard. She'd never heard a word.

And so she continued, and every two weeks, money was wired into her bank account. No taxes were withheld, and she received no benefits, nor was she reimbursed for any expenses she might incur, such as when she'd needed a new computer some months back and a range extender for the wireless network. She wasn't given sick leave or vacation days or paid overtime, but as the agent had explained, it was part of the job description to be "on the call twenty-forty-seven."

In an earlier life, Shrew had held real jobs with real companies, her last one a database marketing manager for a consulting firm. She was no tabula rasa, was all too aware that her current employment demands were unreasonable and she had grounds to sue the company if she knew whom she worked for. But she wouldn't think of complaining. She was paid reasonably well, and it was an honor to work for an anonymous celebrity whose column was the most talked-about one in New York, if not the entire country.

The holidays were an especially busy time for Shrew. Not for personal reasons, because she really wasn't allowed to have personal reasons for anything. But website traffic inevitably surged, and the banner on the home page was a tremendous challenge. Shrew was clever, but admittedly had never been an especially gifted graphic artist.

This time of year the publishing schedule was escalated as well. Instead of three columns per week, the Boss picked up the pace to please the fans and sponsors, and rewarded them for a year of being a faithful, enthusiastic, lucrative audience. Beginning Christmas Eve, Shrew was to post a column daily. On occasion, she was fortunate and got several at once and made adjustments, and they waited in a queue for auto release, and she was allowed a respite, could run a frivolous errand or two, or get her hair done, or go for a walk, instead of waiting for the Boss to get on with things. The Boss never thought twice about Shrew's inconveniences, and the truth was, it might be more dismal than that.

Shrew suspected the Boss deliberately orchestrated it, no doubt through programming, so that columns were shipped one at a time although several days of them had been done in advance and were already in the can. What this implied was two important bits of intelligence.

First, unlike Shrew, the Boss had a life and stockpiled work so he or she could do other things, maybe take a trip or be with friends or family, or simply rest. Second, the Boss did think about Shrew, was invested enough in their relationship to remind her regularly that she was small and unimportant, and was owned and controlled by whoever the anonymous celebrity might be. Shrew's was a nonexistence, and it was not her right to be granted a day or two when the work was done and she didn't need to think about it. She was to wait on the Boss and serve at the Boss's pleasure. The Boss answered Shrew's prayers or didn't, rather much with a finger on the mouse, the cursor on send.

It was fortunate, really, that Shrew would dread the holidays were she given the opportunity to enjoy them, because they were nothing more than an empty ship that took her from one year into the next, reminding her of what she didn't have and what wasn't ahead, and that biology was unkind and played mischievous tricks on the mind. She didn't recall the process being a gradual one, as logic had always told her it would be—a little gray hair here, a wrinkle or stiff joint there.

It seemed that one day she looked in the mirror and didn't find the thirty-year-old she was inside or recognize the ruin looking back at her. Whenever she'd put on her glasses these days, she discovered she was surrounded by loose, crinkled skin. She'd find that pigmented spots, like squatters, had taken up residence all over her body, and hair, like neglected landscaping, had moved from where it belonged to areas well outside the garden. She had no idea why she needed so many veins unless it was to rush extra blood to cells bent on dying for the hell of it.

It suited her that during this joyless journey between Christmas Eve and New Year's Day she'd not had a moment to herself, and was on hold, waiting for the next column, no matter how many of them might already be done, the momentum building in a crescendo to New Year's Day, when the Boss posted twice. These, naturally, were always the most sensational.

Shrew had received the second one a little while ago and was surprised and puzzled by it. The Boss never headlined with the same public figure twice in a row, especially for today's Daily Double, and this second column, like the first one, was solely devoted to Dr. Kay Scarpetta. No doubt it would be quite the hit because it covered all the bases: sex, violence, and the Catholic Church.

Shrew expected a swarm of comments from the fans, and possibly yet another coveted Poisoned Pen Prize, which would leave everybody guessing, just like last time, when no one showed up to collect it. But she couldn't help puzzling rather nervously. What was it about the well-respected lady medical examiner that had set off the Boss like this?

Shrew carefully re-read the new column, making sure there were no typos or misspellings she might have missed. She fine-tuned the format as she wondered where on earth the Boss had gotten all this highly personal information she had flagged with the familiar NBS in red. Never-before-seen information was the most coveted. With rare exception, it and all gossip came from anecdotes, sightings, rumors, and fabrications sent in by fans, which were sifted through by Shrew and moved to an electronic research file accessed by the Boss. But none of the NBS information about Dr. Scarpetta was anything Shrew had sorted through or selected.

So where had the Boss gotten it?

Apparently, assuming this was true, Dr. Kay Scarpetta had grown up in a poor, uneducated Italian family: a sister who was screwing boys before puberty, a dumb cow of a mother, and a blue-collar father just off the boat, whom little Kay helped in the small family grocery store. She played the role of doctor for many years while he died of cancer in his bedroom, thus explaining her eventual addiction to death. Her priest felt sorry for her and arranged for a scholarship at a Miami parochial school, where she was the resident nerd, a whiner, and a tattletale. For good reason, the other girls hated her.

At this point in the column, the Boss switched to story mode, which was always when the writing was strongest.

> . . . On this particular afternoon, little Florida cracker Kay was alone in the chemistry lab, working on a project for extra credit, when Sister Polly suddenly appeared. She flowed across the empty room in her black scapular, her wimple

and veil, and nailed her severe little pious eyes
onto little Kay.

"What does our Father instruct us about
forgiveness, Kay?" Sister Polly demanded, her
hands on her virgin hips.

"That we should forgive others as He for-
gives us."

"And did you obey His word? What do you
say?"

"I didn't obey."

"Because you tattled."

"I was working on a math problem and had
my pencils on my desk, Sister Polly, and Sarah
broke them in half. I had to buy more, and she
knows my family is poor . . ."

"And now you've just tattled again." Sister
Polly reached into a pocket and said, "God
believes in restitution." She pressed a quarter
into the palm of little Kay's hand before slapping
her across the face.

Sister Polly told her to pray for her enemies
and to forgive them. She severely reprimanded
little Kay for being a sinner with a wagging
tongue, and said she clearly needed reminding
that God didn't look kindly upon tattlers.

In the bathroom across the hall, Sister Polly
locked the door and took off her black leather cinc-
ture as she ordered little Kay to remove her plaid
tunic and Peter Pan collar blouse and everything
under it, and bend over and hold her knees. . . .

Satisfied that the column was ready to go live, Shrew typed her system administrator password to get into the website programming. She posted the column, but not without misgiving.

Had Dr. Scarpetta done something of late that might have incited hatred in the Boss, whoever the Boss was?

Shrew gazed out the window behind her computer, momentarily reminded that throughout the entire day, a police car had been parked in front of the brownstone apartment building directly across the street. Perhaps a policeman had moved in, although she couldn't imagine that the average policeman could afford the rents in Murray Hill. It occurred to her that the policeman might be on a stakeout. Perhaps there was a burglar or lunatic on the loose. Her thoughts returned to the Boss's obvious intention of ruining the New Year for the lady medical examiner whom Shrew had always admired.

The last time she had seen Dr. Scarpetta on TV was a few days after Christmas, after Benazir Bhutto was assassinated, and Dr. Scarpetta was explaining, diplomatically and tastefully, the damage shrapnel or a bullet or blunt-force trauma could cause, depending on what part of the brain or spinal cord was injured. Might that have something to do with the Boss's first column this morning, and now the bonus column? Perhaps Dr. Scarpetta had touched a nerve of extreme prejudice. If so, what sort of person did Shrew work for? Was it someone who hated the Pakistanis or Islam or democracy or human rights or women in charge? Perhaps the timing was simply coincidental and completely unrelated.

But somehow Shrew didn't think so, and her intuition gave rise to an awful speculation she'd never before considered. How did she know she didn't work for a terrorist organization that used the infamous, highly profitable Internet gossip column to subliminally communicate with extremist sympathizers and spread propaganda and, most important, fund terrorist plots?

Shrew didn't know. But if she was right, it was simply a matter of time before someone came looking for her, either Homeland Security or a member of the very terrorist sect behind Shrew's highly secretive and, frankly, suspicious job—one she had never uttered a word about to anyone.

To her knowledge, the only people who knew she worked for *Gotham Gotcha* were the Italian agent who had hired her over the phone (a man she'd never met and whose name she didn't know), and the anonymous celebrity who actually wrote the columns and e-mailed them to Shrew for a light copyedit and format. Then she'd post them, and the programming would do the rest, and the columns would go live at one minute past midnight. If terrorists were involved, then Dr. Scarpetta was a target. They were trying to destroy her professionally and personally, and her life could be in danger.

Shrew needed to warn her.

How could she do that without admitting she was the anonymous system administrator for the anonymous website?

She couldn't.

She pondered this as she sat in front of her computer,

staring out her window at the police car, wondering if there might be a way to get an anonymous message to her.

At the very moment she was having these paranoid and decidedly unpleasant thoughts, someone pounded on her door, startling her. Maybe it was that strange young man in the apartment across from hers. Like most people who had caring families, he had gone away for the holidays. Maybe he was back and wanted to borrow something or ask a question.

She looked through the peephole and was shocked to see a big rugged face, a balding head, and out-of-style wire-rimmed glasses.

Oh God in heaven.

She snatched up the phone and called 911.

Inside Bellevue's cafeteria, Benton Wesley and Jaime Berger sat in a pink booth against the back wall, where they could have privacy. People who didn't recognize Berger often noticed her anyway.

She had compelling good looks, was of medium height and slim, with deep blue eyes and lustrous dark hair. Always smartly dressed, today she wore a charcoal cashmere blazer, a button-up black sweater, a black skirt with a slit in back, and black pumps with small silver buckles on the sides. Berger wasn't provocative, but she wasn't afraid to look like a woman. It was well known that if the attention of lawyers, cops, or violent offenders began wandering over her physical landscape, she'd lean close, point at her eyes, and say, "Look here. Look right here when I'm talking to you."

She reminded him of Scarpetta. Her voice had the same low timbre that commanded attention because it didn't ask for it, her features similar in their keenness, and her physical architectural style completely to his liking, simple lines that led to generous curves. He had his fetishes. He admitted it. But as he had emphasized to Dr. Thomas a short while ago over the phone, he was faithful to Scarpetta and always would be. Even in his imagination, he was faithful to her, would instantly change channels when his fantasies strayed to erotic dramas that didn't feature her. He would never cheat on her. Never.

His behavior hadn't always been so virtuous. What Dr. Thomas had said was true. He'd cheated on his first wife, Connie, and if he was honest about it, the betrayal had begun early on when he'd decided it was perfectly admissible and, in fact, healthy to enjoy the same magazines and movies other males did, especially during his four monk-like months at the FBI Academy when there was little to do at night except have a few beers in the Boardroom, then return to his dorm where he could briefly relieve his stress and escape his uptight life.

He had maintained this clandestine but healthy sexual routine throughout his sensible marriage until he and Scarpetta had worked one too many cases together and ended up in the Travel-Eze Motel. He'd lost his wife and half of a considerable inheritance, and their three daughters continued to have nothing to do with him. To this day, some of his former colleagues from his FBI past still had no respect for him, or at least they blamed it on his morals. He didn't care.

Worse than not caring and a vacuum where there should be a spark of remorse was the truth that he would do it all again, if he could. And he did do it all again, often, in his mind. He would replay that scene in the motel room, where he was bleeding from cuts that required stitches, and Scarpetta had tended to him. She'd barely dressed his wounds before he was undressing her. It was beyond fantasy.

What always struck him when he looked back on it was how he'd managed to work around her for the better part of five years and not succumb sooner. The more he'd flipped back through the pages of his life during his talks with Dr. Thomas, the more amazed he was by a number of things, not the least of which was Scarpetta's imperviousness. She honestly hadn't known how he felt, was far more aware of how she felt. Or at least that's what she told him when he'd admitted that with rare exception, whenever she'd seen him with his briefcase in his lap, it meant he was hiding an erection.

Including the first time we met?

Probably.

In the morgue?

Yes.

Reviewing cases in that awful conference room of yours at Quantico, going through reports, photographs, having those relentless, endless, serious conversations?

Especially then. Afterward, when I'd walk you back to your car, it was all I could do not to get in it and . . .

If I'd known, Scarpetta had told him one night, when they were drinking a lot of wine, *I would have seduced you immediately instead of wasting five goddamn years singing solo.*

Singing solo? Do you mean . . . ?

Just because I work around dead people doesn't mean I am one.

"This is the main reason I'm not going to," Jaime Berger was saying to Benton. "Political correctness. Political sensitivity. Are you paying any attention to me at all?"

"Yes. If I seem glazed, I'm slightly sleep-deprived."

"The last thing I want is a perception of prejudice. Especially now, when there's much more public awareness about dwarfism and the misconceptions and stereotypes historically associated with it. This morning's *Post,* for example. The headline about this big." She held her hands about two inches apart. "*Midget Murder.* Horrible. Exactly what we don't want, and I expect a backlash, especially if other news sources pick it up and it's all the hell over the place." Her eyes were on his, and she paused. "Unfortunately, I can't control the press any more than you can."

She said it as if she meant something else.

It was the something else that Benton was anticipating. He knew damn well the Terri Bridges case wasn't Berger's only agenda. He'd made a tactical error. He should have brought up the *Gotham Gotcha* column while he'd had the chance.

"The joys of contemporary journalism," she said. "We're never sure what's true."

She would accuse Benton of lying to her by omission. But technically he hadn't, because technically Pete Marino had committed no crime. What Dr. Thomas had said was correct. Benton wasn't in Scarpetta's house when it happened and would never know the nuances of what Marino had done to her that warm, humid Charleston night last May. Marino's drunken, grossly inappropriate behavior had gone unreported and largely undiscussed. For Benton to have made even the slightest allusion to it would have been a betrayal of Scarpetta—and of Marino, for that matter—and in fact would constitute hearsay that Berger would never tolerate under other circumstances.

"Unfortunately," Benton said, "the same sort of thing is being passed around on the ward. The other patients are calling Oscar names."

"Vaudeville, carnivals, the Wizard of Oz," Berger said.

She reached for her coffee, and every time she moved her hands, Benton noticed the absence of her large-carat diamond ring and matching wedding band. He had almost asked her about it last summer, after not seeing her for a number of years, but refrained when it became apparent that she never mentioned her multimillionaire husband or her stepchildren. She never made any reference to any aspect of her private life. Not even the cops were talking.

Maybe there was nothing to talk about. Maybe her marriage was intact. Maybe she'd developed an allergy to metals or worried about being robbed. But if it were the latter, she should think twice about the Blancpain she had on. Benton estimated it was a numbered timepiece that cost in the neighborhood of a hundred thousand dollars.

"Negative portrayals in the media, in the entertainment industry," Berger went on. "Fools, dimwits. The movie *Don't Look Now*. Folktale dwarfs, imperial court dwarfs. And rather apropos, the omnipresent dwarf who witnesses everything, from the triumph of Julius Caesar to the discovery of Moses in the bulrushes. Oscar Bane was witness to something, and at the same time accuses others of being witness to everything. His claims of being stalked, spied on, subjected to some sort of electronic harassment, and that the CIA might be involved and is torturing him with electronic and antipersonnel weapons as some sort of experiment or persecution."

"He didn't go into that kind of detail with me," Benton replied.

"It's what he reported when he called my office a month ago, and I'll get back to that momentarily. What's your assessment of his mental state?"

"His evaluation is perplexing in its contradictions. MMPI-Two indicates traits of social introversion. During the Rorschach, he had perceptions of buildings, flowers, lakes, mountains, but no people. Similar pattern with the TAT. A forest with eyes and faces in the leaves, indicative of someone disconnected from people, someone profoundly anxious, paranoid. Aloneness, frustration, fear. Projective figure drawings were mature, but no human figures, just faces with empty eyes. Again, paranoia. A feeling of being watched. Yet nothing indicative that his paranoia is long-standing. That's the contradiction. That's what's disconcerting. He's paranoid, but I don't believe his paranoia is long-standing," he repeated.

"He's afraid of something right now that to him is real."

"In my opinion, yes. He's afraid and depressed."

"His paranoia," Berger said. "Based on your experience and the time you spent with him, you don't believe it's his inherent disposition? It doesn't go back to his childhood? As in, he's always been paranoid because he's a little person? Perhaps was made fun of, mistreated, discriminated against?"

"For the most part, it doesn't appear he had those early experiences. Except with the police. He repeatedly told me he hates the police. And he hates you."

"Yet he's cooperated with the police. Excessively. Let me guess. His excessive cooperation won't prove helpful." As if she hadn't heard the part about Oscar hating her.

"I hope you'll get your chance with him," Benton said.

The saying was, if a broken window were the victim, Berger could get a confession from the rock.

"I'm fascinated by his cooperation with a group of people he certainly doesn't trust," she said. "Yet he's rather much given us free rein. Biological samples and his statement, as long as Kay's the one he gives them to. His clothing, his car, apartment, as long as Kay is right there. Why?"

"Based on his fears?" Benton said. "I would venture

to say that he wants to prove there's no evidence linking him to Terri Bridges's murder. Most of all, prove this to Kay."

"He should be more worried about proving it to me."

"He doesn't trust you. He does trust Kay. Trusts her irrationally, and that worries me a lot. But back to his mind-set. He wants to prove to her he's a good guy. He didn't do anything wrong. As long as she believes in him, he's safe. Physically, and in how he views himself. At this point, he needs her validation. Without her, he almost doesn't know who he is anymore."

"Guess what. We do know who he is and what he probably did."

Benton said, "You need to understand this fear of mind control is very real to thousands of people who believe they are victims of mind weapons. That the government is spying on them, reprogramming them, controlling their thoughts, their entire lives, through movies, computer games, chemicals, microwaves, implants. And the fears have gotten exponentially worse in the past eight years. I was walking through Central Park not so long ago, and here's this guy talking to the squirrels. I watched him for a while, and he turns around and tells me he's a victim of the very thing we're discussing. One of the ways he copes is to visit the squirrels, and if he can get them to eat peanuts out of his hands, then he knows he's still grounded. He's not letting the bastards get him."

"That's New York, all right. And the pigeons wear homing devices."

"And Tesla gravity radar waves are being used to brainwash the woodpeckers," Benton said.

Berger frowned. "Do we have woodpeckers here?"

"Ask Lucy about advances in technology, about experiments that sound like a schizophrenic's bad dreams," he said. "Only this stuff is real. I don't doubt Oscar thinks it's real."

"I don't think anybody doubts that. They just think he's crazy. And they worry his craziness led him to murder his girlfriend. I alluded to his rather unusual protection devices. A plastic shield glued to the back of his cell phone. Another plastic shield in the back pocket of his jeans. A magnet-mounted external antenna on his SUV that seems to have no purpose. Investigator Morales—you haven't met him yet—says this is anti-radiation stuff. That—and let me see if I can remember this right. A TriField meter?"

"To detect frequency-weighted electric fields in the ELF and VLF range. A detector, in other words. An electromagnetic measurement tool," Benton said. "You hold it up in the middle of a room to see if you get readings that might indicate you're being electronically monitored."

"Does it work?"

"It's popular in ghost hunting," Benton said.

6

For the third time, Investigator P. R. Marino refused tea, coffee, soda, or a glass of water. She tried harder.

"It's five o'clock somewhere," she parroted her husband's old quip. "How about a little spot of bourbon?"

"I'm all set," Investigator Marino said.

"You sure? It's no trouble. I might have a taste of it myself."

She returned to the living room.

"No, thanks."

She sat back down and there was no might about it. She'd poured herself a generous one. Ice rattled as she set down the glass on a coaster.

"I'm not usually like this," she said from the corduroy couch. "I'm not a drunk."

"I don't go around judging people," Investigator

Marino said, his eyes lingering on her drink as if it were a pretty woman.

"Sometimes a person needs something for the nerves," she said. "I'd be dishonest if I pretended you didn't scare me a little."

She was still shaky after a good ten minutes of back and forth about whether he really was the police. Holding up a badge to the peephole was a trick she'd seen numerous times in violent movies, and had the 911 operator not stayed on the line, assuring her that the man at her door was legitimate, and continued to stay on the line while she let him in, he wouldn't be sitting in her living room right now.

Investigator Marino was a big man, with weathered skin and a red hue to his complexion that caused her concern about his blood pressure. Mostly bald with unfortunate wisps of gray hair in a crescent moon around his pate, he had the look and demeanor of one who did everything the hard way, listened to no one, and certainly wasn't to be trifled with. She was quite sure he could pick up two thugs by the scruff of the neck, one in each hand, and simultaneously toss them across the room as if they were made of hay. She suspected he'd cut quite a figure when he was young. She also suspected he was single at this time, or would be better off if he were, because if he had a sweetheart and she let him out the door looking the way he did, either she didn't care about him or she was of questionable breeding.

Oh, how Shrew would love to give him a tip or two about the way he dressed. If a man was large-boned, then the rule was that cheap, skimpily cut suits, especially black ones, and white cotton shirts without a tie, and rubber-bottomed black leather lace-up shoes tended to make him look a bit like Herman Munster. But she wasn't about to offer him advice, for fear he would react the same way her husband had, and she was careful not to study the investigator too closely.

Instead, she continued to make nervous comments and to reach for her drink, and to ask him if he wanted something as she sipped and set her drink back down. The more she talked and reached for her drink, the less he said as he occupied her husband's favorite leather recliner.

Investigator Marino had yet to tell her the purpose of his visit.

Finally she said, "Well, enough about me. I'm sure you're very busy. What kind of investigator did you say you are? Burglary, I imagine. This is the time of year for it, and if I had my way about it, I'd certainly live in a full-service building with a doorman. What happened across the street. I suppose that's why you're here."

"I'd appreciate whatever you can tell me about it," Investigator Marino said, and his huge presence in the recliner seemed to shrink the image she had of her husband sitting there. "You find out from the *Post*, or did a neighbor say something?"

"Neither one."

"I'm curious because nothing much about it's made the news yet. We're not releasing details, for good reason. The less known at this time, the better. You can see the logic in that, right? So you and me having this private little conversation's between the two of us. Nothing said to the neighbors or anyone. I'm a special investigator for the DA's office. That translates into court. I know you wouldn't want to do anything that might mess up a case in court. You ever heard of Jaime Berger?"

"Yes, I certainly have," Shrew replied, regretting she'd implied she knew something, and worrying what trouble she'd just caused herself. "I appreciate her advocacy of animal rights."

He looked silently at her. She looked silently at him until she couldn't stand it anymore.

"Did I say something wrong?" she asked, reaching for her drink.

His glasses glinted as his attention poked around her apartment like a flashlight searching for something hidden or lost. He seemed especially interested in her extensive collection of porcelain and crystal dogs, and photographs of her with her husband and the various dogs they had owned throughout their lives together. She loved dogs. She loved them far more than her children.

Then the investigator stared down at the tan-and-blue braided rug under the old cherry coffee table.

"You got a dog?" he asked.

Obviously he'd noticed the tiny white-and-black dog hairs embedded in the rug, which weren't really her fault. She'd had no success vacuuming them up, and didn't feel like getting on her hands and knees, plucking them out, one at a time, as she continued to mourn the untimely death of Ivy.

"I'm not a bad housekeeper," she said. "Dog hairs tend to work their way into things, and it's difficult getting them out. Sort of like they do to your heart. Work their way in. I don't know what it is about dogs, but God had a hand in it, and anybody who says they're just animals has no soul. Dogs are fallen angels, while cats don't live in this world. They just visit. Dog hairs can actually stick into your skin like splinters if you walk around barefoot. I've always had dogs. Just right now I don't. Are you involved in Ms. Berger's crusade against cruelty to animals? I'm feeling the bourbon, I'm afraid."

"What do you mean by animals?" he asked, and maybe he was trying to ease the tension, but she couldn't be sure. "You talking four-legged or two-legged?"

She decided it was best to take him seriously and said, "I'm sure you deal with your share of two-legged animals, but in my book, that's a terrible misnomer. Animals don't have cold hearts and cruel imaginations. They just want to be loved, unless they're rabid or have something else wrong with them or it's about the food chain. Even then, they don't rob and murder innocent people. They don't break into apartments while people are gone for the holidays. I can only imagine what it was like to come home to find something as awful as that. Most of these apartment buildings around here are easy pickings, if you ask me. No doormen, no security, very few burglar-alarm systems. I don't have one, I'm sure that hasn't escaped your attention. Being attentive is your training, your job, and by the looks of you, you've been at it for a while. I meant the four-legged kind."

"What four-legged kind?" Investigator Marino seemed on the verge of smiling, as if he found her entertaining.

It was probably her imagination. And the bourbon.

"Pardon my non sequitur," she said. "I've read articles about Jaime Berger. What a fine woman. Anybody who's a champion of animals is a decent person in my book. She's cleaned up a number of these dreadful pet stores that sell sick and genetically compromised creatures, and maybe you've helped. If so, I thank you very much. I had a puppy from one."

He listened with no discernible reaction. The more he listened, the more she talked and tentatively reached for her bourbon, usually three times before picking up the glass and taking a sip. She'd gone from thinking he found her interesting to believing he suspected her of something. All in a minute or two.

"A Boston terrier named Ivy," she said as she clutched a tissue in her lap.

"I asked about a dog," he said, "because I was wondering if you went out much. As in walking a dog. I'm wondering if maybe you're observant about what goes on in your neighborhood. People who walk dogs notice what goes on around them. Even more than people with babies in strollers. That's a little-known fact." His glasses on her. "You ever observe how many people cross the street, pushing the stroller in front of them? What gets hit first? Dog owners are more careful."

"Absolutely," she said, elated that she wasn't the only one who had noticed the same imbecilic thing about people letting strollers lead the way when they crossed busy New York streets. "But no. I don't have one at the moment."

Another long silence, and this time he broke it.

"What happened to Ivy?" he asked.

"Well, it wasn't me who bought her in that pet shop around the corner. Puppingham Palace. 'Where pets get the royal treatment.' What it ought to say is 'Where vets get the royal treatment,' because vets around here must get most of their business from that unspeakable place. The woman across the street got Ivy as a gift, and couldn't keep her and gave her to me in a panic. Not a week later, Ivy died of parvovirus. This wasn't that long ago. Around Thanksgiving."

"What lady across the street?"

It occurred to Shrew with a jolt of disbelief. "Please don't tell me Terri's the one who was burglarized. I wouldn't have thought it since she's the only one home over there, and her lights are on, so it wouldn't dawn on me that someone would break into an apartment where the resident was home."

She reached for her glass and held on to it.

"I suppose she might have been out last night like most people on New Year's Eve," she said.

She drank more than a sip.

"I wouldn't know." She kept talking. "I always stay in and retreat to my bedroom. I don't wait to see the ball drop. I really have no interest. One day is the same as another."

"What time did you turn in last night?" Investigator Marino asked.

She was certain he asked it as if he thought she was

implying she hadn't seen a thing, and he didn't believe it for one minute.

"Of course, I understand what you're leading up to," she said. "It's not exactly a matter of when I went to sleep. What I'm telling you is I wasn't sitting at my computer."

It was directly in front of the window that afforded a perfect view of Terri's first-floor apartment. He looked right at it.

"Not that I'm staring out my window, down at the street, every other minute, either," she said. "I ate in the kitchen at my usual time of six o'clock. Leftover tuna casserole. After that, I read for a while back in my bedroom, where the drapes are always drawn."

"What are you reading?"

"I see, you're testing me, as if I'm making this up. Ian McEwan's *Chesil Beach*. It's the third time I've read it. I keep hoping they'll find each other again in the end. Have you ever done that? Read a book or watched a movie again, thinking it will end the way you wish?"

"Unless it's reality TV, they end the way they end. A lot like crime and tragedy. You can keep talking about it for a hundred years, and people are still mugged, killed in a terrible accident, or, worst of all, murdered."

Shrew got up from the sofa.

"I'm topping it off. You sure?" As she headed to her tiny kitchen that hadn't been updated in forty years.

"Just so you're aware," his voice followed her, "no one else was home last night, not in your building or the one across the street. All the residents, except you, are gone for the holiday and have been since before Christmas."

He'd run background checks. He knew all about everyone, including her, she thought, splashing more Maker's Mark into her glass, the hell with ice. Well, so what? Her husband was a well-respected accountant, and neither of them had ever gotten into any kind of trouble or associated with unsavory people. Other than her secret professional life, which not even a police investigator could possibly know about, Shrew had nothing to hide.

"It's very important you think hard," he said as she returned to the couch. "Was there anything at all you saw or heard at any point yesterday that might be of interest? Maybe somebody in the area who caught your attention? What about in recent days or weeks? Anybody around here who might have raised your suspicions? Or just given you one of those feelings. You know what I'm saying? A feeling right here."

He pointed at his gut, which she suspected used to be much more formidable than it was now. She based this on the sagging skin along his jaw. He used to be heavier.

"No," she said. "This is a quiet street. Certain types don't frequent this neighborhood. Now, the young man in the other apartment on my floor, he's a doctor at Bellevue. He smokes pot and must get it from somewhere, but I don't for a moment think he buys it right around here. More likely in the vicinity of the hospital, which isn't the nicest area. The woman in the apartment directly under this one, which, of course, faces the street just like mine. . . ."

"Neither one of them were here last night."

"She's not friendly, and I started to say that she has a boyfriend she fights with a lot. But he's been coming around for over a year, so I doubt he's a criminal."

"What about workmen, servicemen, anybody like that?"

"Now and then the cable company." She looked at the window behind her computer. "There's a satellite dish on top of the roof, which I have a good view of, and on occasion I've seen someone up there doing whatever it is they do."

He got up and looked out the window at the flat roof of the building where the police car was parked. His suit jacket was taut across his shoulders in back, and it wasn't even buttoned.

Without turning around, he said, "I see an old fire escape. Wonder if that's how the servicemen get up there? You ever seen anybody climbing up the fire escape? Don't know how you'd get a satellite dish up that ladder. Jeez. Not a job for me. Couldn't pay me enough."

He looked out the window, at the darkness. This time of year, daylight was gone by four.

"I don't know about the ladder," she said. "Can't think of a time I've seen anybody climbing it, and I suspect there's some other access to the roof. You're thinking the burglar got in through a roof access? If so, that's of great concern. Makes me worry about this building."

She looked up at her plaster ceiling, wondering what might be on the other side of it.

"I'm on the second floor, and that certainly would

make me vulnerable to an intruder, I should think. They must lock access doors."

She was working herself into quite a state over it.

"This building has an old fire escape, too, you know," she said.

"Tell me about the lady who gave you the puppy."

He sat down heavily, and the chair creaked as if it might snap in half.

"I know only her first name, Terri. She's very easy to describe because, and the proper way to say it is, she's a little person. Not the dwarf word. I've learned never to use that. There are a number of shows about little people, which I watch with great interest since I live across the street from one. And her boyfriend is a little person as well. Blond, handsome, a well-built man, although extremely short, of course. I happened to be returning from the market not so long ago, and saw him up close as he got out of his SUV, and I said hello and he said hello back. He was carrying a single long-stem yellow rose. I remember that vividly. Do you know why?"

The investigator's big face and glasses waited.

"Yellow suggests sensitivity. Not the same old red, red rose. It was sweet. It was the same yellow as his hair, almost. As if he were saying he was also her friend, not just her boyfriend, if you see what I mean. I remember it touched my heart. I've never had a yellow rose in my life. Not once. I would have liked yellow ones so much better than red on Valentine's Day. Not pink, mind you. Pink is anemic. Yellow is strong. It fills my heart with sunlight to see a yellow rose."

"When exactly was this?"

She thought hard. "I'd bought a half-pound of sliced honey-glazed turkey breast. Would you like me to dig up the receipt? Old habits die hard. My husband was an accountant."

"How 'bout a guess."

"Well, of course. He comes to see her on Saturdays, that I'm sure of. So it must have been this past Saturday, late afternoon. Although there are other times when I think I've spotted him in the area."

"You mean driving around? Walking around? Alone?"

"Alone. I've seen him drive by. A couple times in the last month. I go out at least once a day to get a little exercise, run errands. Unless the weather is impossible, I have to get out. Are you sure I can't get you anything?"

Both of them looked at her drink at the same time.

"Do you remember the last time you saw him in this area?" he asked.

"Christmas was on a Tuesday. I believe I actually saw him that day. And then a few days before that. Now that I'm thinking about it, I've spotted him three or four times over the past month, just driving by. So he's likely done it more than that, you know, when I didn't see him. Well, that was poorly worded. What I'm trying to . . ."

"Was he staring at her building? Was he going slow? Did he pull over at any point? And yeah, I get it. If you saw him once, he might have been here twenty other times when you didn't see him."

"He was driving slowly. And yes." She sipped. "You said it exactly the way I meant."

This investigator was far more intelligent than he looked and sounded. She wouldn't want trouble from him. He was the sort who caught people without them ever having the slightest premonition, and it entered her mind again. What if he were an agent investigating terrorist funding or who knows what? And that's why he was here?

"What time of day?" he asked her.

"Different times."

"You've been home throughout the holidays. What about your family?"

The way he said it made her suspect he already knew she had two daughters who lived in the Midwest, both of them very busy and disingenuous when they were attentive.

Shrew replied, "My two children prefer I go see them, and I don't like to travel, certainly not this time of year. They don't like to spend the money to visit New York. Certainly not these days. I never thought I'd live to see the Canadian dollar worth more than ours. We used to make jokes about the Canadians. Now I suspect they're making a few jokes about us. As I believe I mentioned, my husband was an accountant. I'm glad he's not one anymore. It would break his heart."

"You're saying you never see your daughters."

He'd yet to pick up on any comments about her husband and respond. But she felt sure the investigator knew about him, too. It was a matter of public record.

"I'm saying I don't travel," she said. "I see them now and again. Every few years, they come here for several days. In the summer. They stay at the Shelburne."

"The place near the Empire State Building."

"Yes. That lovely European-looking hotel on Thirty-seventh Street. Within walking distance of here. I've never stayed there."

"Why don't you travel?"

"I just don't."

"No big loss. Expensive as hell these days, the planes always late or canceled. Not to mention getting trapped in one on the runway and the toilet overflows. That ever happen to you? Because it happened to me."

She had completely shredded the tissue and felt foolish as she thought about the Shelburne and imagined times in her life when it would have been wonderful to stay there. Not now. She couldn't possibly get away from her work. And why bother?

"I just don't travel," she said.

"So you keep telling me."

"I like to stay put. And you're starting to make me uncomfortable, as if you're accusing me of something. And then being friendly to break me down, as if I have information. I don't. I don't have any. I shouldn't talk to you while I'm drinking."

"If I accused you of something, what might it be?" he said in that rough New Jersey accent of his, his glasses looking right at her.

"Ask my husband." Nodding at the recliner chair, as if her husband were in the room. "He'd look you squarely in the eye and with all seriousness want to know if nagging is a crime. If so, he'd tell you to lock me up and throw away the key."

"Well, now." The chair creaked as he leaned forward a little. "You don't seem like the nagging type. You seem like a nice lady who shouldn't be all alone over the holidays. Someone smart who doesn't miss a trick."

For some reason, she felt like crying, and she remembered the little blond man with the single long-stemmed yellow rose. But thinking about that made her feel worse.

"I don't know his name," she said. "Her boyfriend. But he must be pretty crazy about her. He's the one who gave her the puppy that she in turn gave to me. Apparently, he surprised her with it, and she couldn't possibly have one and the store wouldn't take it back. An odd thing to do, as I reflect on it. Someone you talk to now and then on the sidewalk, and out of the blue one day she appears at my door with a basket covered with a towel, as if bringing me something she'd just baked, which wouldn't have made sense, either, since, as I said, I didn't know her and she never made overtures like that to me. She said she had to find a home for a puppy, and wondered if I'd please take it. She knew I lived alone and didn't work outside of the apartment, and she didn't know where else to turn."

"When was this?"

"Around Thanksgiving. I told her it died. This was a week or so later, when I happened to bump into her on the street. She was upset about it and apologetic, and insisted on buying me another one as long as I picked it out myself. She said she'd give me the money, which I found rather impersonal. I can see the wheels turning in your head. You're wondering if I was ever inside her apartment, and I never was. I've never even been inside her building, and wouldn't have the foggiest notion as to what she owned that a burglar might have been after. Like jewelry, for example. I don't recall her wearing expensive-looking jewelry. Indeed, I don't recall her wearing any jewelry. I asked her why in the world I would want another puppy, warranty or not, from that same shop where her boyfriend got Ivy. She said there was no warranty and she had no intention of getting anything from that shop, but I shouldn't be judgmental. Not every place is as bad as that horrid Puppingham Palace. For example, she said the Tell-Tail Hearts chain of shops is wonderful, and she'd happily give me money if I wanted to get a puppy from there, from one of the shops here in New York or in New Jersey. I have read nice things about Tell-Tail Hearts, and I have been thinking seriously about trying again. Honestly, I just might in light of what's happened. Anything that barks or growls. Burglars don't break in if there's a dog."

"Except you have to take it out," Investigator Marino said. "Including in the middle of the night. Which leaves you wide open for getting mugged or having someone force his way inside your building and right into your apartment."

"I'm not naïve about security," Shrew said. "You don't have to take a dog out if it's small enough. Wee Wee Pads work fine. I had a Yorkie quite a long time ago and taught it to use the litter box. I could fit him in the palm of one hand, but talk about a bark. He would go for the ankles.

I had to pick him up whenever we were on an elevator or when people would come over. Until he got used to them. Obviously, I didn't take Ivy out. Not something that young and sickly on these filthy sidewalks. I've no doubt she already had the parvovirus when the boyfriend bought her at that dreadful Puppingham Palace."

"What makes you so certain her boyfriend bought the puppy?"

"Goodness," Shrew said.

She held her drink in both hands and contemplated what he was implying.

The recliner creaked as he waited.

"I'm jumping to conclusions," she said. "You're absolutely right."

"Here's what you do. What I tell every witness I talk to."

"Witness?"

"You knew her. You live across the street."

What was she a witness to? she asked herself as she shredded bits of tissue and stared up at the ceiling, hoping there was no access door beyond it.

"Pretend you're writing a movie," he said. "You got a pen and paper? Terri gives you little Ivy. Write me the scene. I'm going to sit right here while you write it up, then you're going to read it to me."

7

After Nine-Eleven, the city decided to build the Chief Medical Examiner's Office a fifteen-story DNA building that looked like a blue-glass office high-rise.

Technology, including STRs and SNPs and low-copy-number profiling, was so advanced, scientists could analyze a sample as small as seventeen human cells. There was no backlog. If Berger wanted DNA testing in a high-priority case, theoretically she could get results in a matter of hours.

"No smoking gun," Berger said.

She handed Benton a copy of the report as the waitress refilled their coffees.

"Just a hell of a lot of smoke," she said. "In fact, Terri Bridges's vaginal swabs are as confusing as I've seen in any case that comes to mind. No seminal fluid, and

DNA from multiple donors. I spoke to Dr. Lester about it, which wasn't helpful. I can't wait to hear what Kay has to say about this."

"Have all the profiles been run through CODIS?" Benton asked.

"One hit. It gets weirder. A woman."

"In the database for what reason?" Benton scanned the report.

It didn't tell him much—just that Dr. Lester had submitted swabs, and then the results that Berger was discussing.

"Vehicular manslaughter in 2002," Berger said. "Fell asleep at the wheel and hit a kid on a bicycle, convicted, sentence suspended. Not here, where we wouldn't be so nice, even if she is elderly and was stone-cold sober at the time of the accident. This was in Palm Beach, Florida, although she does have a Park Avenue apartment and is here, actually, even as we speak. But she was attending a New Year's Eve party last night at the time Terri Bridges was murdered, not that I have any reason to suspect for a nanosecond she had anything to do with it. Another reason the judge in Palm Beach was so forgiving? She broke her back when she hit the kid on the bike. So you got any brilliant ideas why a seventy-eight-year-old female paraplegic's DNA was in Terri Bridges's vagina along with a host of other people's?"

"Not unless there's some bizarre error in the sample or the analysis?"

"I'm told there's not a chance. In fact, to be on the safe side, since all of us have such deep respect for Dr.

Lester's competence, God, why did she have to be the one who did the damn autopsy? You are aware of that."

"Morales gave me a few things. I've seen her preliminary report. You know how I feel about her."

"And you know how she feels about me. Is it possible for a woman to be a misogynist? Because I believe she truly hates women."

"Envy or a feeling that other women might lower the person's status. In other words, sure. Women can be women-haters. We've seen plenty of that this political season."

"The labs went ahead and began running the DNA on every case autopsied in the morgue this morning, on the off chance Terri's swabs got contaminated or mislabeled somehow," Berger said. "Even gone so far as to make comparisons with everybody who works at the ME's office, including the chief, and, of course, all the cops who were at the scene last night—all of whom are already in the database for exclusionary reasons, obviously. Negative for the people in the morgue except for the ME who responded, which wasn't Dr. Lester. And for Morales, and both guys who transported the body to the morgue. DNA testing is so sensitive these days, you breathe at a scene and good chance your DNA turns up. Which is as bad as it's good."

"Has someone asked this Palm Beach lady if she knows Oscar Bane or has any connection with him?" Benton asked.

"I did the unpleasant deed and called her myself," Berger said. "Never heard of him before reading the *Post.*

To put it diplomatically, she was indignant and unhappy at the implication she might somehow be connected to him. She said, and I'm only loosely paraphrasing, that even if she's sitting in the same waiting room with a dwarf, she doesn't speak or look at him for fear she might make him self-conscious."

"Does she know why it would enter our minds to link her to Oscar? Did you mention her DNA?"

"Absolutely not. I said her name had come up. And she leapt to the conclusion that the parents of the sixteen-year-old Eagle Scout honor student she acciden-tally ran over in her Bentley are always trying to cause her problems. You know, shocking acts of aggression like lawsuits to pay medical bills that aren't covered by insurance, but how is that her fault? And she complained about the sob stories to the media. She supposed that the parents no doubt heard about the, and I quote, *Midget Murder,* and decided to somehow drag her through more public embarrassment."

"What a fucking bitch."

"I'm still thinking contamination," Berger said. "I can't see any other explanation for the DNA. Maybe Kay will have an insight that eludes me at the moment. And tomorrow, hopefully, we'll have Oscar's DNA. But we expect his DNA to be on everything. A positive result isn't likely to be helpful."

"What about his e-mail? His consent or not, you can access it, right? I'm assuming he e-mailed Terri," Benton said.

"We can access it, and we will. And no one's telling

him that. In summary, and I think we've established this clearly? He's really not as cooperative as he might seem. Unless we find probable cause for his arrest, that won't change. A very difficult position for me. I have to be extra-careful, yet I want to know what Kay knows. He's telling her something up there in the infirmary. Something he's not telling us and she's not allowed to divulge under the current circumstances. I'm sure I don't need to ask, but she has no history with Oscar Bane?"

"If she does, she didn't know about it, didn't remember it, or she would have said something the minute I mentioned his name when I called her earlier," Benton said. "But we're not going to find out unless Oscar is arrested or volunteers to waive doctor-patient confidentiality. I know Kay. She's not going to say anything improper."

"What about a connection with Terri Bridges? Possible?"

"Can't imagine it. If Oscar discusses Terri with her, and she realizes there's a connection, she'll immediately recuse herself or at least notify us so we could figure out what to do."

"Not a fun thing to put her through," Berger said. "Not fun for either of you, really. I imagine you're not used to it. Professional discussions are your dinner conversations. They're your dialogues on weekends, holidays. They're even the source of fights, perhaps." Her eyes on his. "Nothing off-limits unless you're expert witnesses for opposing counsel in the same court case, and that almost never happens. Quite the team, the two of you. No secrets. Always professionally inseparable. And now, personally inseparable. I hope it's going well."

"No, this isn't fun." He didn't like her personal references. "It would be easier if Oscar's charged with killing his girlfriend. That's a terrible thing to hope."

"We hope a lot of things we don't want to admit," she said. "But fact is, if he murdered Terri Bridges, we're not looking for someone else."

She remembered snow that stung like nettles, and she needed a pound of Breakfast Blend coffee, but she didn't feel like going out. Overall, there was nothing good she could say about that day.

She'd had a harder time than usual with a column she was supposed to post, an especially mean-spirited one titled "The Ex-File," which was a list of celebrities whose fans had turned on them and why. Certainly Shrew had to leave out that part as she wrote the scene for Investigator Marino. There was a lot she had to leave out. For example, she couldn't tell him her horror when her doorbell rang, and she let Terri in, not realizing the *Gotham Gotcha* website programming was as big as life on her twenty-four-inch computer screen.

Terri set the basket on the coffee table and walked right over to the desk, which was forward of her, now that Shrew thought about it as she wrote the scene on her pad of paper, leaving out what she was remembering right this minute.

Terri looked at what was on the screen, and Shrew

tried to figure out how to explain what was clearly a *Gotham Gotcha* column, formatted and embedded in actual programming language.

What's this? Terri was so short, she was eye level with the computer screen on top of the desk.

I confess I read Gotham Gotcha.

Why does it look like that? Are you a computer programmer? I didn't know you worked.

I have display codes on because I'm such a ninny. Please sit down. Shrew almost bumped her out of the way so she could exit the program. *No, I certainly don't work.* She was quick to clear that up.

Terri sat on the sofa and her feet stuck straight out from the edge of the cushion, because her legs were stunted. She said she used e-mail, but aside from that was computer-illiterate. Of course, she was familiar with *Gotham Gotcha,* because she saw ads for it everywhere and heard references to it all the time, but she didn't read it. Graduate school didn't allow her time to read for pleasure, although she wouldn't read a gossip column anyway. It wasn't her thing. In fact, she'd heard it was filth and lowbrow. And she wanted to know if Shrew thought so, too.

"I don't know how to write a movie script," Shrew said to Investigator Marino. "I believe they require a special language and formatting, and in fact, people who write them use special software. When I was at Vassar, I took a course in theater and read a number of scripts for plays and musicals, and I'm quite aware that scripts aren't written to be read. They're written to be acted, performed, sung, et cetera. I hope you won't be offended, but it's better I stick to plain prose. At any rate, let me read this to you."

She had a tickle in her throat. Memories and bourbon were making her emotional, and she sensed that Investigator Marino wouldn't be sitting in the recliner if he had nothing better to do. He did have better things to do. Asking her to write a movie scene and all the rest hinted that what had happened across the street was part of a much bigger, more threatening problem. The only other explanation would be the worst one of all. He was an undercover agent, perhaps for the federal government, and believed she was involved with terrorists because of unusual banking activity, such as wires from the UK and the fact that she didn't pay what she should in taxes, since on paper, it didn't appear she had an income beyond Social Security benefits and other monies she received in dribs and drabs.

She read from the pad of paper. "Terri set the basket on the coffee table and climbed up on the sofa with great agility and no hesitation, and it was quite clear she was accustomed to improvising and compensating for her short arms and legs. She managed in an effortless way, but I'd never seen her sit, so it did startle me a bit that her feet stuck out from the edge of the cushion like a cartoon character or a five-year-old. It's important to add that no matter what she said or did, from the instant I opened my door to her, I could tell she was immensely sad. Indeed, she seemed quietly frantic, and held the basket in a way that told me something unusual was in it that she neither wanted nor was comfortable with.

"I need to mention how she was dressed, because that, indeed, is part of a scene. She had on blue jeans and ankle boots, navy socks, and a navy blue cotton shirt. She was not wearing a coat, but had on blue dishwashing gloves, because she'd rushed out of her apartment as if it were on fire. No question, she was in the midst of a true crisis.

" 'What on earth has happened?' I said to her, and I offered her refreshment, which she declined.

" 'I know you love animals. Especially dogs,' she said, looking at all of the crystal and porcelain dogs placed about my apartment, gifts from my husband.

" 'It's true, but I don't know how you would know. I haven't had a dog since you moved in across the street.'

" 'When we chat on the sidewalk, you mention them and notice other people out walking them. I'm sorry. This is urgent. I don't know where else to turn.'

"I pulled back the towel and I thought my heart would break. Ivy was no bigger than a small flashlight, and so quiet, I thought at first she was dead. Terri said it was a gift, and she couldn't keep it, and her boyfriend had tried to get the shop to take it back. But it wouldn't. Ivy wasn't thriving, and right then a part of me knew she wouldn't make it. She didn't move until I picked her up to hold her against my heart, and she nuzzled her little head under my neck. I called her Ivy because she clung to me like . . ."

Shrew dried her eyes with a tissue and after a moment

said to Investigator Marino, "I can't. I'm sorry. It's as far as I got. It's too painful. And I'm still so angry about it. Why are you upsetting me like this? If you're toying with me, then I'll file a complaint against you with Jaime Berger's office. I don't care if you're the police. I'll complain about you all the same. And if you're some secret agent for the government, just come right out and say it and get it over with."

"I'm not toying with you, and I'm sure as hell not a secret agent," he said, and she detected kindness in his otherwise firm tone. "I promise I wouldn't be digging into all this if it wasn't important. Obviously, Terri's bringing the sick puppy over here's something I need to know about because it's unusual and isn't consistent with a few other things I'm aware of. I was inside her apartment earlier today. Went over there after talking to her parents. They live in Arizona. Maybe you knew that."

"I didn't know. I can't imagine what a mess her apartment must be."

"You told me you've never been inside it."

"Never."

"Let me put it to you this way. She's not a pet person. You could eat off her floors, and anybody as concerned about tidiness and cleanliness as she was wouldn't have pets. And she didn't have pets, and the reason I can say that with certainty is after I saw her apartment and noticed all the antibacterial soaps and the rest of it, I called her parents a second time and asked a few more questions. That's when the subject of pets came up. They said even as a child, she never had a pet and wouldn't have anything to do with other people's pets. She wouldn't touch a dog or cat, and was afraid of them, and hated the hell out of birds. Maybe if you think back to that scene you just described to me, you'll take a look at a couple of the details and see them in a different light. She didn't have on her coat, but she was wearing dish-washing gloves. You assumed she was washing the dishes when someone arrived with the sick puppy as a gift, and in a panic, she fled across the street to see you."

"Yes."

"Did you ask her why she had on dishwashing gloves?"

"I did. And that's what she told me. She seemed slightly embarrassed, and took them off and gave them to me to throw away."

"Did she touch the puppy after she took them off?"

"She never touched the puppy. She took the gloves off as she was leaving. I suppose I should make that clear. It was toward the end."

"That's right. She had the gloves on because she was afraid of germs. She wasn't wearing a coat because she didn't want the sick puppy's germs on it or germs from your apartment on it, and it's easier to wash a shirt than a coat. I bet she left the basket and towel in your apartment, too."

"She certainly did."

"She knew damn well the puppy was sick as hell and dying when she gave it to you."

"I told you I was angry."

"Damn right you are. She knew the puppy was going to die, so she dumps it on you. That was a pretty lousy thing to do. Especially to someone who loves animals. She took advantage of you because you have a tender heart, especially when it comes to dogs. But the big question is, where did she get Ivy? You see what I mean?"

"Exactly," Shrew said, feeling very angry now.

Those few days with Ivy were hell on earth. All Shrew did was cry as she held Ivy and tried to get her to drink water and eat something. By the time she got her to the vet, it was too late.

"No one who knew Terri would give her a puppy and think it was a nice thing to do," Investigator Marino said. "Certainly not a sick one. I can't imagine her boyfriend would do that, unless he's a mean son of a bitch and did it to hurt her, to make her suffer, to jerk her around."

"Well, she certainly was unhappy. Beside herself, really."

"It reminds me of dirty tricks little boys play on little girls in school. Remember? Scaring them with a spider, a snake in a shoe box. Whatever would make the little girl scream. Terri was afraid. She was afraid of germs and dirt, of sickness and death. So it was sick to give her a sick puppy."

"If what you're saying is true, it was diabolical."

"How long have you and Terri Bridges lived across the street from each other?" he asked, and leather creaked as he stretched his legs.

"She moved in about two years ago. I never knew her last name. We weren't friends, I need to make that clear. Other than running into her, really. Usually on the sidewalk when both of us were heading in and out, although I also want to make it clear I'm not aware that she was out a lot. I don't think she has a car. Walks like I do. Over the years I have run into her a few other places. Once in Lands' End, both of us like their shoes, turns out. She was getting a pair of Mary Jane Trekkers, I remember that. Once I ran into her near the Guggenheim. In fact, I believe it was the last time I went to the Guggenheim, for a Jackson Pollock exhibit. We ran into each other on the sidewalk and stopped to chat."

"She was going to a museum?"

"I don't believe so. I think she was just walking. But I do recall her face looked rather red and puffy, and she had on a hat and sunglasses, even though it was overcast. I wondered if she had gotten into something she was allergic to, or maybe had been crying. I didn't ask. I'm not a nosy person."

"Her last name's Bridges." He said it again. "It was in today's *Post*. So nobody's mentioned it."

"I don't read the *Post*. I get all the news I want on the Internet." Instantly, she regretted saying it.

The last thing she needed was for him to get nosy about what she did on the Internet.

"Well, TV, mostly," she added. "If you don't mind my asking, how bad was it? The break-in? It appears a police car's been there all day, and you've been over there, and I haven't seen her. I'm sure she went to stay with family, perhaps her boyfriend. I wouldn't sleep a wink after something like that. I've noticed you've used the past tense several times, as if she's not over there anymore. And you've talked to her family. So I assume it was bad. I don't know what her family in Arizona has to do with . . . Well, why you would talk to them. It's really bad, isn't it?"

He said, "I'm afraid it doesn't get any worse."

Something fluttered in her stomach like fingers about to grab.

Leather creaked loudly as he leaned forward in a chair not meant for him, and his face got bigger as he said to her, "Where'd you get the idea it was a burglary?"

"I just thought . . ." She could barely speak.

"I'm sorry to tell you it wasn't. Your neighbor was murdered last night. Kind of hard to believe you weren't aware of all the commotion out there, right across the street. Police cars, a van from the Medical Examiner's office."

Shrew thought about Dr. Scarpetta.

"A lot of flashing lights and car doors slamming shut, and people talking. And you didn't hear or see a thing," he said it again.

"Did Dr. Scarpetta show up at the scene?" she blurted out, wiping her eyes, her heart racing.

The look on his face—it was as if she'd just given him the finger.

"What the hell are you getting at?" he said, not nicely.

She realized it much too late. She hadn't made the connection, at least not consciously, before this instant. How could it be possible? P. R. Marino? As in Pete Marino, the same name in the column she herself had edited, formatted, and posted. It couldn't be the same person, could it? That Marino lived in South Carolina, didn't he? He didn't work for Jaime Berger, surely not. A woman like Ms. Berger wouldn't hire a man like that, would she? Shrew was about to panic, her heart beating so hard, her chest hurt. If this Marino was the same one the Boss had just written about, then he had no business sitting in Shrew's living room, in her husband's recliner. For all she knew, he was the maniac who murdered that defenseless little lady across the street.

This was exactly how the Boston Strangler got his victims. Pretended to be someone nice and responsible. Had a cup of tea and a pleasant conversation in the living room right before he . . .

"What about Dr. Scarpetta?" Investigator Marino looked at Shrew as if she had insulted him unforgivably.

"I worry about her," Shrew said as calmly as she could, her hands shaking so hard she had to lace them tightly in her lap. "I worry about all the publicity she gets and the nature of what she . . . well, the subject matter. It appeals to the ones who do the things she talks about."

She took a deep breath. She'd said just the right thing. What she mustn't do is make any allusion to having read anything about Dr. Scarpetta on the Internet, specifically in the very columns Shrew had posted today.

"I have a feeling you're thinking about something in particular," he said. "So get it out on the table."

"I think she might be in danger," Shrew said. "It's just a feeling."

"Based on what?" He looked stonily at her.

"Terrorists," she said.

"Terrorists?" He looked less stony. "What terrorists?" He didn't look as offended.

"It's what all of us are afraid of these days." Shrew tried that tactic.

"I tell you what." Pete Marino got up and was a giant towering over her. "I'm leaving my card for you, and I want you to do a lot of thinking. Anything that comes to mind, even if it seems trivial, you call me right away. I don't care what time it is."

"I can't imagine who would do something like that." She got up and followed him to the door.

"It's always the ones you don't imagine," he said. "Either because they knew the victim or they didn't."

8

Cyberspace, the perfect place to hide from ridicule.

Gotham was an online college, where students saw Dr. Oscar Bane's talents and intelligence and not the dwarfed vessel that contained them.

"It couldn't be a student or group of students," he said to Scarpetta. "They don't know me. My address and phone number aren't listed. There's no physical college where people go. The faculty meets several times a year in Arizona. And that's as much as most of us see each other."

"What about your e-mail address?"

"It's on the college website. It has to be. That's probably how it started. The Internet. Easiest way to steal your identity. I told the DA's office. I said that's probably how they got access to me. My speculations didn't matter. They didn't believe me, and I realized they might be part of the mind stealing. That's what's happening. They're trying to steal my mind."

Scarpetta got up from her chair. She tucked her notepad and the pen into her lab coat pocket.

She said, "I'm moving around to the other side of the table so I can look at your back. You must go out at least some."

"The grocery store, ATM, gas stations, doctors' offices, the dentist, the theater, restaurants. When it began, I started changing my patterns. Different places, different times, different days."

"What about the gym?"

She untied his gown and gently pulled it down to his hips.

"I work out in my apartment. I still power-walk outside. Four to five miles, six days a week."

There was a distinctive pattern to his injuries that didn't make her feel any better about him.

"Not the same walk or at the same time of day. I mix things up," he added.

"Groups, clubs, organizations you belong to or are involved with?"

"Little People of America. What's happening has nothing to do with the LPA, no way. Like I said, the electronic harassment just started maybe three months ago. As far as I know."

"Anything unusual happen three months ago? Anything change in your life?"

"Terri. I started dating Terri. And they started following me. I've got proof. On a CD hidden in my apartment.

If they break in, they won't find it. I need you to get it when you're in there."

She measured abrasions on his lower back.

"When you're inside my apartment," he said. "I gave my written consent to that detective. I don't like him. But he asked me, and I gave him my consent, my key, the information for the burglar alarm, because I've got nothing to hide, and I want you to go in. I told him I want you to go in with him. Do it right away before they go in there. Maybe they already have."

"The police?"

"No. The others."

His body relaxed as her gloved fingers touched him.

"I wouldn't put anything past them and their capabilities," he said. "But even if they've already gone in, they didn't find it. They won't find it. It's not possible. The CD's hidden in a book. *The Experiences of an Asylum Doctor* by Littleton Winslow. Published in 1874 in London. Fourth shelf of the second bookcase, left of the door in the guest bedroom. You're the only person who knows."

"Did you tell Terri you were being followed, spied on? Did she know about the CD?"

"Not for a long time. I didn't want her to worry. She has problems with anxiety. Then I had no choice. I had to tell her several weeks ago when she started mentioning she wanted to see my apartment, and I wouldn't let her. She started accusing me of hiding something from her, so I had to tell her. I had to make sure she understood it wasn't safe for me to bring her to my apartment because I was being electronically harassed."

"The CD?"

"I didn't tell her where it is. Just what's on it."

"Did she worry that knowing you might place her at risk, too? No matter where you saw her?"

"It's obvious they never followed me to her apartment."

"How is that obvious?"

"They tell me where they follow me. You'll see. I explained to Terri I was sure they didn't know about her and she was safe."

"Did she believe you?"

"She was upset, but she wasn't frightened."

"Seems a little unusual for someone who has a lot of anxiety," Scarpetta said. "I'm surprised she wasn't frightened."

"The communications from them stopped. It's been weeks, and they've stopped. I began to hope they weren't interested in me anymore. Of course, they were just setting me up for the cruelest thing of all."

"What are these communications?"

"E-mails."

"If they stopped after you told Terri about them, might that suggest the possibility they were from her? That she was sending you whatever these e-mails are that make you feel you're being harassed, spied on? And when you said something about it, she stopped sending them?"

"Absolutely not. She would never do something so heinous. Especially not to me. It's impossible."

"How can you be so sure?"

"She couldn't possibly do it. How would she know I took a detour when I was walking and ended up at Columbus Circle, for example, if I'd never told her? How could she know I went to the store for coffee creamer if I never mentioned it?"

"Is there any reason she might have to hire someone to follow you?"

"She wouldn't do that. And after what's happened, it makes no sense at all to think she had anything to do with it. She's dead! They killed her!"

The steel door moved slightly, and the guard's eyes appeared in the crack. "We okay in here?"

"We're fine," Scarpetta said.

The eyes vanished.

"But the e-mails stopped," she said to Oscar.

"Eavesdropping."

"You were raising your voice, Oscar. You need to stay calm or he'll come back in here."

"I made one backup copy of what I'd already gotten, and cleaned everything off my computer so they couldn't get in there and delete them or alter them to make it look as if I'm lying. The only record of the original e-mails is on the CD that's in the book. *The Experiences of an Asylum Doctor*. Littleton Winslow. I collect old books and documents."

Scarpetta took photographs of abrasions and clusters of fingernail marks, all in the same area of his right lower back.

"Psychiatry, topics related to it, mainly," he said. "A lot of them, including ones about Bellevue. I know more about this place than the people who work here. You and your husband would find my Bellevue collection of great interest. Maybe I'll get to show it to you someday. You're welcome to borrow it. Terri's always been interested in the history of psychiatry, fascinated by people. She really cares about people and why they do what they do. She says she could sit in an airport, a park, all day and watch people. Why are you wearing gloves? Achondroplasia isn't contagious."

"For your protection."

It was and it wasn't. She wanted a latex barrier between his skin and hers. He had crossed the line with her already. Before she'd even met him, he'd crossed it.

"They know where I go, places I've been, where I live," he said. "But not her apartment. Not Terri's brownstone. Not Murray Hill. I never had any reason to believe they knew anything about her. They've never shown that location when they let me know where I've been on any given day. So why wouldn't they show it? I go there every Saturday."

"Always the same time?"

"Five o'clock."

"Where in Murray Hill?"

"Not far from here. You could walk from here. Near Loews theater. We go to the movies sometimes and eat hot dogs and cheese fries when we're splurging."

His back trembled as she touched it. Grief welling up inside of him.

"Both of us are careful about our weight," he said. "I never had any reason to believe they'd followed me to Murray Hill, to any place we'd been together. I had no idea or I would have done something to protect her. I wouldn't have let her live alone. Maybe I could have convinced her to leave the city. I didn't do it. I would never hurt her. She's the love of my life."

"I've been meaning to ask." Berger's shrewd, pretty face studied Benton. "If Kay's Lucy's aunt, does that make you Lucy's uncle? Or are you a de facto uncle, an almost uncle? Does she call you Uncle Benton?"

"Lucy doesn't listen to her almost uncle or her aunt. I hope she'll listen to you." Benton knew damn well what Berger was doing.

She was sticking him, goading him. She wanted him to bring up that damn gossip column, to confess and surrender himself to the mercy of her court. But he had his mind made up. He wasn't going to volunteer anything because he'd done nothing wrong. When the timing was right, he could defend himself easily. He could explain his silence and justify it by reminding her that, legally, Marino had been neither charged nor accused of anything, and Scarpetta's privacy wasn't Benton's to violate.

"Does Lucy have the laptops?" he asked.

"Not yet. But she will. And as soon as she determines the details of the e-mail accounts, we'll go to the providers and get the passwords. Including Oscar's."

"When you met with her to discuss what she's going to—"

"I haven't met with her yet," Berger interrupted him.

"Only talked to her briefly over the phone. I'm surprised you never told me she'd moved to the city. On second thought, I shouldn't be surprised." She reached for her coffee. "I had to find out from several sources she'd recently moved here and started her own company. She's built a reputation rather quickly, which is why I decided to ask for her help in this particular case."

She drank coffee and set the mug back down, her every move thoughtful and deliberate.

"You have to understand that he and I don't routinely have contact with each other," she said.

She meant Marino. The cross-examination had begun.

"Knowing what I do, assuming there's any truth to it," she said, "I can't imagine Lucy told him she was here or has had any contact with him at all—or even knows that he's here. I'm wondering why you didn't tell her. Or am I making an unfair assumption? Have you told her?"

"No."

"That's quite something. She relocates to New York, and you've never told her he's here. Alive and well in my DA squad. And maybe his secret would have been safe a little longer if it wasn't his bad luck that he's the one who took Oscar's call last month."

"Lucy's still setting up shop, hasn't been involved in many cases yet," Benton said. "A couple in the Bronx and Queens. This will be the first in Manhattan, in other words, involving your office. Of course, at some point, she and Marino were going to find out about each other. I expected that to happen naturally and professionally."

"You didn't expect anything of the sort, Benton.

You've been in complete denial. You've made flawed and desperate decisions and not logically thought through the inevitable consequences. And now your two degrees of separation have begun to converge. Must be an indescribable feeling, moving people around like pawns only to wake up one day and realize that because of a banal gossip column, your pawns are now destined to confront each other and possibly knock each other off your game board. Let me try to recap what's happened."

With a slight movement of her fingers, she said no to the waitress and her coffeepot.

"Your original plan didn't include a residence in New York," Berger said.

"I didn't know John Jay was going to— "

"Ask both of you to be visiting lecturers, consultants? I bet you tried to talk Kay out of it."

"I thought it was unwise."

"Of course you did."

"She'd just been hired as chief, relocated her entire existence. I advised against her taking on more work, more stress. I told her she shouldn't do it."

"Of course you did."

"She was insistent. Said it would be good to help if we could. And she didn't want to be limited."

"That would be Kay," Berger said. "Always one to help anywhere she can and position herself accordingly. The world is her stage. You couldn't possibly coop her up in a corner of Massachusetts, and you couldn't push too hard because then you'd have to tell her why you didn't want her in New York. You found yourself with a problem on your hands. You'd already moved Marino to New York, and let's be honest, talked me into hiring him. And now Kay's going to be in and out of New York, and possibly end up helping in cases that will involve my office. Since both of you are going to be in and out of New York, why not? Lucy moves to the great city of opportunity, as well. What better place on the planet for her than the Village? How could you possibly have anticipated all this when you came up with your master design? And since you didn't anticipate it, you also didn't anticipate I'd find out the real reason you parked Marino in my office."

"I'm not going to say I never worried about it," Benton replied. "I simply hoped it wouldn't happen anytime soon. And it wasn't my place to discuss—"

She cut him off. "You've never told Marino, have you? About John Jay, about your apartment here?"

"I haven't told him Kay's in and out of New York. I haven't told him about Lucy's moving here."

"No, in other words."

"I can't remember the last time I talked to him, and have no idea what he might have found out on his own. But you're right. I never expected anything like this to happen when I recommended you hire him. However, it wasn't my place to divulge—"

She cut him off again. "Divulge? You divulged plenty, just not the whole truth."

"It would be hearsay. . . ."

"His was such a sad story. And savvy prosecutor that I am, I fell for it without question. Marino and his problem with alcohol. Quits his job because he can't deal with your engagement to Kay, and he's depressed and self-destructive. A month in a treatment center, good as new, and I should hire him. After all, he started out his career with NYPD, and he wasn't a stranger to me. I believe the phrase you used was *mutually beneficial*."

"He's a damn good investigator. At least give me credit for that."

"Did you really think—for even five minutes—that he'd never find out? That Kay and Lucy would never find out, for God's sake? At any given moment, Kay could be summoned to my office to go over an autopsy report that Marino has something to do with—which will probably happen, by the way. She's in and out of the morgue as a consultant. She's on CNN every other week."

"For all he knows, she does CNN by satellite from Boston."

"Oh, please. Marino hasn't had a lobotomy since you saw him last. But I'm starting to wonder if you have."

"Look," Benton said, "I hoped if enough time passed . . . Well, we'd deal with it. And I don't pass on tawdry stories that are, if we're honest, nothing more than rumors."

"Nonsense. What you wanted was to avoid dealing with reality, and that's how this entire mess has happened."

"I was putting off dealing with it. Yes."

"Putting it off until when? The next life?"

"Until I figured out what to do about it. I lost control of it."

"Now we're getting close to the facts of the case. This isn't about hearsay, and you know it. It's about your head in the sand," she said.

"All I wanted, Jaime, was to restore some civility. Restore something. To move on and do so without malice, without irrevocable damage."

"To magically make everybody friends again. Restore the past, the good ol' days. Happily ever after. Delusions. Fairy tales. I imagine Lucy hates him. Probably Kay doesn't. She's not the sort to hate."

"I don't know what the hell Lucy will do when she sees him. And she will. Then what? It's a big concern. It's not funny."

"I'm not laughing."

"You've seen her in action. This is serious."

"I was hoping she'd outgrown killing people in the line of what she considers duty."

"She's going to see him eventually, or know about it, at least," Benton said. "Since you've decided to avail yourself of her forensic computer skills."

"Which, by the way, I found out from the DA in Queens County and a couple of cops. Not from you. Because you didn't want me to know she was here, either, because you hoped I'd never use her—nice de facto uncle that you are. Because if I decided to use her, one day she'd show up at my office, and guess who she might run into?"

"When you talked to her on the phone, is that what happened?" Benton asked. "You said something about Marino?"

"To my knowledge, she doesn't know about him. Yet. Because no. I didn't mention him. I was too busy worrying about this woman who was murdered last night and what might be on her laptops and what Lucy could do to help. I was too busy thinking about the last time I saw Lucy in my own apartment after she'd come back from Poland, and you and I both know what she did over there. Brilliant, brash. A vigilante with no respect for boundaries. Now she's started this forensic computer investigation company. *Connextions*. Interesting name, I thought, as in *connections* and *What's next?* And we all know, whatever's next, Lucy will be there first. And what a relief. It didn't sound like the Lucy I once knew. Showed less of a need to overpower and impress, more thoughtful, more reflective. She used to be into all these acronyms, remember? When she was the wunderkind doing a summer internship at Quantico. CAIN. Criminal Artificial Intelligence Network. She designs a system like that when she's, what, still in high school? No bloody wonder she was so obnoxious, such a renegade, so out of bounds. And friendless. But maybe she's changed. When I talked to her—granted, over the phone, not in person—she sounded mature, not so grandiose and self-absorbed, and she appreciated my reaching out to her first. Certainly not the old Lucy."

Benton was rather stunned that she remembered so much about the old Lucy or seemed so fascinated by the new one.

"These were the things going through my mind when she was telling me that the programming she did way back when's now as obsolete as Noah's ark, and I'd be amazed by what's possible now," Berger said. "No. I didn't mention Marino. I don't think she has a clue he's currently assigned to my sex crimes unit and actively working the same case I just asked her to work. Obviously not. Or she would have reacted, said something. Well, she's about to know. I'm going to have to tell her."

"And that's still a good idea? Getting her involved?"

"Probably not. But I'm in a bit of a quandary, if I've not made that perfectly plain. I don't intend to un-invite her at this precise moment because, frankly, if her abilities are what they're cracked up to be, I need her. Internet crime is one of our biggest problems, and it's beating us. We're up against a world of invisible criminals who in many instances don't seem to leave evidence, or if they do, it's deliberately misleading. I'm not going to let Marino or a gossip column or your insecurities and marital issues derail what I've got in the works. I will do what's best for this case. Period."

"I know Lucy's capabilities. Frankly, you'd be foolish not to take advantage of her," Benton said.

"That's about the long and short of it. I'll have to take advantage of her. A city government budget can't afford someone like her."

"She'd probably do it for free. She doesn't need the money."

"Nothing's free, Benton."

"And it's true. She's changed. Not the same person you knew last time you saw her, when you could have had her brought up on—"

"Let's don't talk about what I could have done. Whatever she confessed to me that night five or so years ago, I don't remember. The rest of it, she never told me. As far as I'm concerned, she never went to Poland. However, I'm trusting there won't be a repeat of that sort of thing. And I sure as hell don't need another FBI, ATF situation."

Early in her career, Lucy basically had been fired by both.

"You'll get the laptops to her when?" Benton asked.

"Soon. I have the search warrant to go through the contents, all my ducks in a row."

"I'm a little surprised you didn't get on this right away, last night," he said. "Whatever's in her laptops may tell us what we need to know."

"Simple answer. We didn't have them last night. They weren't found on the first search. Marino came across them during a second one late this morning."

"News to me. I didn't realize Marino was that involved."

"And I didn't realize Oscar was the same person Marino talked to last month until Morales had already cleared the scene last night. Once I connected the dots, I called Marino. I said I wanted him involved because he's already involved."

"And because you need him to cover your ass," Benton said. "Perception will be that Oscar called your office for help a month ago and you dropped the ball. Marino dropped the ball. No one will work harder to cover your ass than a person who needs to cover his own. That's the cynical solution. But you're lucky. He also doesn't miss much. In fact, he's probably the best person you've got in your whole damn squad. You just haven't figured it out yet because he's easy to underestimate, and now you're biased. Let me guess. He took it upon himself to take a look at the scene, and he found what might be the most important piece of evidence. Her laptops. Where the hell were they? Under the floorboards?"

"Packed inside a piece of luggage in her closet. Obviously, something she planned to carry on the plane she was to take to Phoenix this morning. That and another packed suitcase," Berger replied.

"Who found out she was planning on flying to Phoenix this morning?"

"Oscar said nothing about it to you last night?"

"He didn't say anything to me about anything last night. He cooperated with the evaluation, and that's it, as I've said. So her travel plans weren't known last night? If not, who found out about them and how?"

"Well, that would be Marino, who's a good investigator and doesn't quit once he starts. All true. And he's a lone ranger because he's been out there long enough to know you don't divulge information just because the other person's a cop or even a prosecutor or a judge. People in criminal justice are the worst gossips and the least likely to keep their mouths shut when they should. You're right about him, and it's going to make him some enemies. I can see it coming, which is all the more reason what's surfaced about him is so unfortunate. Apparently, he tracked down Terri's parents in Scottsdale before anybody else—including Morales—did, and delivered the death notification. They mentioned she was planning to fly home to spend several days with them. That's what prompted him to go to her apartment."

"Let me guess," Benton said. "No plane ticket lying around that might have given the cops a heads-up last night. Because these days everything's done electronically."

"Right."

"That explains why I didn't see any luggage in the crime scene photos Morales gave me."

"Those photographs are from his search—the first search. I can see why the carry-on was missed last night. Not saying it's good that it was, but I can see it."

"You suspect it was deliberately hidden?"

"You mean, by someone like Oscar?"

"Wouldn't make a whole lot of sense." Benton thought about it. "If he's worried about her computers, why didn't he remove them from the scene? Why hide them in her closet?"

"People do a lot of things that don't make sense, no matter how meticulously they plan a crime."

"Then he's pretty disorganized. If he's the killer," Benton said. "But one thing Terri wasn't was disorganized, based on the photos of her apartment I've seen. She was extremely neat. A possible theory? She might have finished packing for her trip and put the luggage out of sight herself, because she was having company. I think it imprudent to assume Oscar planned any crime. I'm not ready to assume he killed her."

"You know the old saying, Benton. Don't search for unicorns. Start with the ponies. Oscar's the first pony on my list. The most obvious. Problem is, we have no evidence. Nothing yet."

"At least Oscar can't beat you to the draw when it comes to whatever's on Terri's computers. He doesn't have them, and he doesn't have access to the Internet on the ward," Benton said.

"And that was his choice. He doesn't have to be up there. And that continues to strike me as extremely suspicious and cause me great concern about his mental stability. Whether we found the laptops or not, he must know we'd gain access to her e-mail once we determined her username or usernames, her provider. And that would lead us to his e-mail, because I can't imagine he and Terri didn't e-mail each other regularly. Yet he doesn't seem to care. Were he not up here in isolation, he might have had a chance to rush home and start tampering. But he didn't try that. Why?"

"He may not feel it's necessary because he didn't do anything wrong. Or maybe he's not computer-savvy enough to tamper and get away with it. Or if he's the killer and premeditated her murder, he did his tampering in advance."

"Excellent point. Premeditation by someone who thinks he's smarter than we are. He tampers in advance, then checks into Bellevue because he's allegedly afraid the killer will get him next. In other words, he's manipulating the hell out of everyone. And probably having a good time doing it."

"I'm objectively presenting possibilities," Benton said. "Here's another one. He's not the killer but knows everyone will suspect he is, and by checking into Belle-vue, he earned the right to see me, to see Kay, and perhaps convince somebody who matters that he's inno-cent and in danger."

"Don't tell me that's what you really believe."

"What I believe is he thinks Kay is his sanctuary. No matter what he did or didn't do."

"Yes, he has her because he can't trust me. I believe my new moniker is 'superbitch.' " Berger smiled. "Or at least I hope it's new—the *super* part of it, anyway."

"In his mind, you dissed him."

"If you're referring to when he called my office a month ago—like half the crazies in the city do every day? True. I wouldn't talk to him. Nothing unusual about that. A lot of calls I never even hear about, much less take. He referred to me as a 'superbitch.' Adding if something bad happened, it would be my fault."

"And who was it he said this to?" Benton said. "Marino? During their phone conversation last month?"

"It's on tape," she said.

"Hope that never makes its way into the press."

"That certainly wouldn't be helpful. Because some-thing bad did happen. Very, very bad, indeed. There's no question we have to be careful with Oscar Bane. Ordi-narily, I'd be much more vigorous with someone in his situation. And by the way, I do suspect he murdered his girlfriend. It's what makes the most sense. And that cer-tainly would make his paranoia situational. He's afraid of being caught."

She picked up her briefcase as she pushed back her

chair, and her skirt hiked up enough for him to see the hollow between her slender thighs.

"Without proof," Benton said, "we shouldn't dismiss what Oscar says. It's possible he's being followed. We don't know for a fact he's not."

"That, Nessie, Bigfoot. Anything's possible. Seems to me, no matter what, I have a PR bomb ticking, a legal bomb ticking, because we didn't take him seriously when he called last month. And what I don't need is the Little People of America picketing One Hogan Place. I definitely don't need another problem. Seems I have more than my share. Which reminds me, and I'll just say it."

She paused to collect her coat, and they passed through the crowded cafeteria.

"If there's a scandal," she said, "do I need to worry that Kay might discuss it on CNN? Could that be why Oscar gave us no choice about getting her here? He wants the news coverage?"

Benton stopped at the cashier's desk to pay the bill.

When they were outside the cafeteria, he said, "She would never do that to you."

"I had to ask."

"Even if she were the type, she can't do it," Benton said as they walked toward the atrium. "She's either his physician or she ends up your witness."

"Not sure Oscar thought of all that when he demanded an audience with her, demanded she pay a house call," Berger said. "Maybe he thought he was giving her some grand pre-interview."

"I don't know what the hell he thought, but I shouldn't have talked her into it. I shouldn't have let anybody talk her into it."

"Now you're sounding like a husband. And by anybody, you obviously mean me."

He didn't answer.

Her high heels clicked on polished granite.

"If and when Oscar's charged," she said, "it may turn out that what he's telling Kay is the only information we ever get that might be remotely reliable. It's good she's examining him. Good for a number of reasons. We want him happy. We want him treated extremely well. We want him safe and everyone around him safe." She put on her coat. "When Marino interviewed him over the phone, Oscar started throwing around the term *hate crime*. He said he was a little person, made that point repeatedly to Marino, who of course didn't understand what a little person was. Had to ask him. Oscar, by now quite agitated, answered, 'Fucking dwarf.' Said that's why he was being followed, targeted. It was a hate crime in progress. . . ."

Berger's cell phone rang.

"Kay's going to have to be told Marino's here," she added as she put on her wireless earpiece.

She listened for a moment, and anger touched her face.

"We'll see about that," she said. "This is completely unacceptable. . . . Did I expect it? Well, it's become the pattern, now, hasn't it, but I hoped . . . No, no, no. I can't. Certainly not in this case . . . Well. I'd really

rather not . . . Yes, she is, but due to certain circumstances, I hesitate . . . Indeed, I did. Who the hell hasn't
seen it?" She looked at Benton. "Then maybe you understand why I don't want to do that . . . Uh-huh. I'm hearing you. I got it loud and clear the first time you said it.
I suppose I could find out if she's willing and get back
with you. But I wouldn't blame her for wanting to get
the hell out of here, catch the last shuttle to Logan. . . ."

She ended the call.

They were outside the hospital now, on the sidewalk.
It was almost four, and getting dark, and very cold, and
their breath was as thick as smoke.

"Marino doesn't mean to hurt people," Benton felt
compelled to say. "He didn't mean what happened."

"You're saying he didn't mean it when he raped Kay."
Matter-of-factly as she put on gray mirror-finished
glasses that hid her eyes. "Or is what's all over the Internet today untrue? I wish to hell you'd sent him to some
office other than mine. He's fully involved in this goddamn case, and there's no way to keep the two of them
apart indefinitely. You have to talk to her."

"What's in that gossip column gives a false impression."

"A forensic linguist would have a field day with that
statement. But I'll take your word for it. What's on the
Internet's a complete fabrication. Glad to hear it."

She pulled on kid-leather gloves and turned up the
collar of her shorn mink coat.

"I didn't say it was completely untrue," he replied.

He stared at the distant Empire State Building, lighted
red and green for the holidays, a warning beacon flashing

atop its spire to remind aircraft to stay clear. Berger placed her hand on his arm.

"Look," she said in a gentler tone. "You should have told me the real reason Marino left Charleston, left Kay, is because of what he did to her. I'm going to work very hard at being understanding. I know what it must have done to you. Of all people, I should know."

"I'll fix it."

"You won't fix anything, Benton. What you'll do is move forward. All of us have to move forward and be smart each step of the way."

She removed her hand from his arm, and it felt like rejection.

"It's astonishing you'd do anything to help him," Berger added. "You're quite the friend to him, I must admit. But if we're talking motive? My guess? You hoped if you helped him, covered up for him, it would make what he did untrue. But now the world knows. You want to guess how many calls I've had today? About that goddamn column?"

"You should ask him. He was drunk. Don't fire him."

"Every rapist I've locked up was drunk or on drugs or both or it was consensual or she started it or it didn't happen. I won't fire him unless he brings it upon himself. I've decided this is Kay's battle. Not yours. Not Lucy's. Although I fear Lucy's not likely to see it that way."

"Kay's dealt with it."

Hands in her pockets to ward off the cold, Berger said, "Really. Then why this big to-do about her not knowing he works for me? Why the secret? I thought it was all about his walking off the job, decompensating because of you and Kay, because he was jealous—which has always been as obvious as the Empire State Building you seem fixated on. He decided it was time to let her go and clean up his act. Stupid me. I never called Kay to corroborate your story. I didn't ask for references. Because I trusted you."

"He's tried. He's tried harder than anyone I know. That should be obvious to you. You're around him. You need to ask him about him. Let him tell you what he did," Benton said.

"For the record, you lied to me."

She was looking for a taxi.

"For the record, I didn't lie. And he didn't rape her."

"Were you there?"

"She said it didn't go that far. She never pressed charges. To her it's a private matter. It's not my place to talk about it with you or anyone. She didn't even tell me at first. Yes, fair enough. Delusion, my head in the sand. Poor judgment, probably. But what was in the gossip column this morning is distorted. Go ahead and ask Marino. I assume he's seen it. Or he will soon enough."

"And Lucy? Just so I know what to expect."

"She's seen the column, of course," he said. "She's the one who called me about it."

"I'm surprised she didn't kill him on the spot, as much as she adores her Aunt Kay."

"She almost did."

"Good to know. Not so long ago, she would have. You owe me a favor."

A taxi perilously swerved toward her and lurched to a halt.

"I need Kay to drop by the morgue tonight," she said. "And you're just the person to ask her."

She climbed inside the taxi.

"The phone call I got a few minutes ago?" She looked up at him and said, "I need Kay to examine the body, if she's willing. I'm afraid Dr. Lester's playing her usual games with me. We're tracking her down. She's getting her ass back to the morgue asap and will cooperate if I have to call the goddamn mayor."

She pulled the door shut. Benton stood on the sidewalk in the cold and watched Jaime Berger's yellow taxi speed away, cutting off two other cars to a cacophony of angry honks.

9

Scarpetta examined long, shallow abrasions on the left side of Oscar's upper back as he volunteered how he got them.

"He was already inside, and he attacked me," he was saying. "He ran off, and I found her. The police didn't believe me. I could see it on their faces. They think I got hurt because I struggled with her. You can tell, can't you? That I didn't struggle with her?"

"It would be helpful if you'd describe to me what you were wearing last night," she replied.

"You can tell these injuries aren't from my struggling with her. They won't find my DNA under her nails. She didn't scratch me. She didn't fight with me. We never fought. Maybe just an argument now and then. She was already dead."

Scarpetta gave him a moment, he was crying so hard.

When he was quieter, she repeated the question. "Last night. What were you wearing when you got into the struggle with—?"

"I couldn't see him."

"You're certain it was a him."

"Yes."

"Do you remember what time this was?"

"Five o'clock."

"Exactly?"

"I'm never late. All the lights were out. Even the entrance light was out. All her windows were dark. It didn't make sense. She was expecting me. Her car was there on the street. I parked behind it. There were empty spaces. Because it was New Year's Eve, and a lot of people were gone. I took my coat off and left it on the passenger's seat. I had on a T-shirt and jeans. She likes me to wear tight T-shirts, sleeveless ones. She loves my body. I work on it because she loves it and I'd do anything to please her. She loves sex. I couldn't be with a woman who doesn't love sex."

"Regular sex, rough sex, creative sex?" Scarpetta asked.

"I'm very considerate and gentle. I have to be. Because of my size."

"What about fantasies? Such as bondage. It's important I ask."

"Never! Never!"

"It's not a judgment. A lot of people do a lot of things, which is fine. As long as it's all right for both of them."

He was silent and uncertain. Scarpetta could tell he had a different answer than the one he wanted to give.

"I promise, there's no judgment," she said. "I'm trying to help. It doesn't matter what consenting adults do as long as it's all right for both of them."

"She liked me to dominate," he said. "Nothing painful. Just hold her down. To wrestle her down. She liked me to be strong."

"Hold her down how? I'm asking because any information can help us figure out what happened."

"Just hold her arms down on the bed. But I never hurt her. I never left a mark on her."

"Ever used any types of bindings? Handcuffs? Anything like that? I'm just making sure."

"Maybe her lingerie. She likes lingerie, to dress in very sexy ways. If I tie her hands with her bra, it's very loose and I never hurt her. It's just an idea, a suggestion, never real. I never spanked her or choked her or did anything real. We pretend, that's all."

"What about to you? Did she do these things to you?"

"No. I do them to her. I'm strong and powerful, and that's what she likes, to be taken advantage of, but only the idea of it, never for real. She's very, very sexy and exciting, and tells me exactly what she wants, and I do it, and it's always amazing. We always have amazing sex."

"Did you have sex last night? It's important I ask."

"How could I have? She was gone. It was so awful when I walked in and found her. Oh, God. Oh, God!"

"I'm sorry I have to ask you these questions. Do you understand why they're important?"

He nodded, wiping his eyes and nose with the backs of his hands.

"It was cold last night," Scarpetta said. "Why would you leave your coat in the car? Especially if all the lights were out and you were concerned."

"I took my coat off to surprise her."

"Surprise her?"

"She liked me in tight T-shirts. I already told you. I even thought about taking it off as she was opening the door. It was a sleeveless T-shirt. A white undershirt. I wanted her to open the door and see me in my undershirt."

Too much explanation. His coat was in the car for another reason. He was lying, and doing it badly.

"I have a key to her building," he said. "I went in and rang the bell to her apartment."

Scarpetta asked, "Do you have a key to her apartment, or only to the building's outer door?"

"Both. But I always ring the bell. I don't just walk in on her. I rang the bell and suddenly the door flew open and this person was all over me, attacking me, dragging me inside, and slamming the door shut. That's who killed her. It's the same person who's been following me, spying on me, tormenting me. Or he's one of them."

An interval of twenty-four hours was consistent with the age of Oscar's injuries. But that didn't mean he was telling the truth.

"Where's your coat now?" Scarpetta asked.

He was staring at the wall.

"Oscar?"

He stared at the wall.

"Oscar?"

He answered as he stared at the wall, "It's wherever they took it. The police. I said they could take my car, search it, do whatever they want. But they weren't going to lay a finger on me. I told them they had to get you here. I would never hurt her."

"Tell me more about your struggle with whoever was in her house."

"We were near the door and it was pitch-dark. He was hitting me with the plastic flashlight. He ripped my T-shirt. It's all ripped up and bloody."

"You said it was pitch-dark. How do you know it was a flashlight?"

"When he opened the door, he shone it in my eyes, blinding me, then started the attack. We struggled."

"Did he say anything?"

"All I heard was him breathing hard. Then he ran. He had on a big leather coat and leather gloves. He probably won't have any injuries. He probably won't have left his DNA or fibers. Things like that. He was smart."

Oscar was the one who was smart, offering explanations to unasked questions. And lying.

"I shut the door and locked it and turned on all the lights. I screamed for Terri. The back of my neck feels like a cat clawed me. Hope I don't get an infection. Maybe you should put me on an antibiotic. I'm glad you're here. You had to be here. I told them. It all happened so fast, and it was so dark . . ." Tears, and he began to sob again. "I screamed for Terri."

"The flashlight?" Scarpetta reminded him. "Was it on during your struggle?"

He hesitated, as if he'd never thought about that.

"He must have turned it off," he decided. "Or maybe it broke when he was hitting me. Maybe he's part of some kind of death squad. I don't know. I don't care how clever they are. There's no perfect crime. You always quote Oscar Wilde. 'Nobody ever commits a crime without doing something stupid.' Except you. You could get away with it. Only someone like you could commit the perfect crime. You say it all the time."

She couldn't recall ever quoting Oscar Wilde, and she'd never said she could commit the perfect crime. It would be a stupid and outrageously offensive thing to say. She checked a cluster of slivered moon-shaped nail marks on his muscular left shoulder.

"He made a mistake. He had to have made at least one mistake. I know you can figure it out. You always say you can figure out anything."

She never said that, either.

"Maybe it's your voice and the way you express yourself. Your lack of pretense. You're beautiful."

He clenched his fists in his lap.

"Now that I see you in person, I can tell it isn't from some makeup artist or perfect camera angle."

His blue-green eyes fastened to her face.

"A little bit like Katharine Hepburn, only you're blonde and not as tall."

His clenched hands trembled, as if he was trying with all his might not to do something with them.

"You look very good in slacks, same as her. Actually, she wore trousers, didn't she? Is there a difference? I don't mean anything inappropriate. I'm not coming on to you. I wish you would hug me. I need you to hug me!"

"I can't hug you. You understand why I can't?" she said.

"You always say you're very sweet with dead people. That you're considerate and touch them as if they're alive, talk to them as if they can feel and hear you. That people can still be attractive and desirable when they're dead, and that's why necrophilia's not as hard to understand as the public thinks, especially if the body's still warm. If you can touch dead people, why can't you touch me? Why can't you hug me?"

She'd never said she touched dead bodies as if they were alive, or talked to them as if they could feel and hear her. She'd never said dead bodies were desirable or that necrophilia was understandable. What the hell was he talking about?

"Did the person who attacked you try to choke you?" she asked.

The fingernail marks on the back of his neck were vertical. Perfectly vertical.

"At one point he had his hands around my neck, and he kept digging in his nails as I rolled around and managed to get myself free," Oscar said. "Because I'm strong. I don't know what would have happened if I weren't so strong."

"You said the spying started when you got involved with Terri. How did you meet her?"

"Online. She was one of my students, had been for a while. I know. You can't talk about it."

"I'm sorry?"

"Don't bother. I'll go along with it," he said. "She was enrolled in my history of psychiatry course. Wanted to be a forensic psychologist. Curious so many women want to be forensic psychologists. This ward's overrun with pretty young grad students from John Jay. Wouldn't you expect women, especially pretty ones, to be afraid of the patients up here?"

Scarpetta began examining his broad, hairless chest, measuring more shallow abrasions. She touched his wounds and he rested his manacled wrists over his groin, and his blue-green eyes were like hands trying to explore what was under her lab coat.

"Wouldn't you think women would be afraid to work in a place like this?" he said. "Are you afraid?"

When Shrew had gotten the cryptic phone call a year and a half ago, she'd had no idea how life-altering it would be.

The Italian-sounding man identified himself as an agent from a British trust company and said he had gotten her name indirectly because of the consulting group where she'd been a database marketing manager. In his bad English, he'd said he wanted to e-mail her a job description. Shrew had printed it out. It was still taped on her refrigerator to remind her of life's synchronicities:

> Webmaster: Must be able to take initiative, work
> unsupervised out of the home, have people skills and
> a flair for the dramatic. Limited technical experience
> required. Confidentiality utmost. Other requirements
> to be discussed. Great earning potential!

She had replied immediately, saying she was very interested but would like a little more information. In
response to certain questions, the agent explained in his
limited way that having people skills simply meant Shrew
had to be interested in them, period. She wasn't allowed
to talk to them but needed to know what appealed to
their "mostly basic instinct," which she realized soon
enough was voyeurism and taking immense pleasure in
other people's humiliation and extreme discomfort.

Shrew's e-mailed acceptance, formatted exactly like
the offer had been, was also taped to her refrigerator:

> I agree with all conditions and am honored. Can start
> this minute and have no problem with working when-
> ever needed, including weekends and holidays.

In a way, Shrew had become an anonymous cyber version by proxy of the comedian she adored, Kathy Griffin,
whose shows and stand-up routines Shrew watched
obsessively, always picking up a new pointer or two about
how to fillet the rich and famous and serve them up to
an insatiable audience that grew exponentially as the

world got worse. People were desperate to laugh. They were desperate to vent their frustrations, resentments, and fury at the golden scapegoats, as Shrew thought of the privileged untouchables who might be angered and annoyed but never really wounded by the slings and arrows of slights and ridicule.

After all, what damage could be done, really, to a Paris Hilton or a Martha Stewart? Gossip, savage insinuation, and exposés—even incarceration—only enhanced their careers and made people envy and love them all the more.

The cruelest of punishments was to be ignored, dismissed, made to feel invisible and nonexistent, exactly the way Shrew had felt when scores of computer technical assistance and marketing management jobs, including hers, were outsourced to India. She'd been pushed overboard with no notice and no parachute. She would never forget packing up her personal effects and carrying them out in a cardboard box, just like she saw in the movies. Miraculously, right about the time she feared she could no longer afford to live in Murray Hill and was asking around about more affordable housing that wasn't in the slums, the Boss's UK-based Italian agent called.

If Shrew had any chronic complaint now, it was a loneliness that unexpectedly had given her insight into serial killers and hit men, and caused her to feel slightly sorry for them. How burdensome and isolating it was to keep a secret when the stakes were so high, and she often imagined what people would do if they knew that the lady next to them in line at CVS or Whole Foods was largely responsible for the most popular Internet gossip column in history.

But she couldn't tell a soul, not even the police investigator who had just been here. She couldn't take credit. She couldn't have friends and run the risk she might make a slip. It was just as well she didn't confide in her daughters or have much contact with them. It was probably wise never to date or marry again. Even if she quit the website, she could never breathe a word of her former remarkable anonymous career. She'd signed enough nondisclosure and confidentiality agreements to send her to prison for life, land her in the poorhouse, or—and maybe she was getting silly—result in unnatural death if she committed even the smallest infraction. But what could she divulge?

She didn't know who *Gotham Gotcha* was. The columnist could be a man, a woman, old, young, American, or not. Or the website phenomenon could be a collection of people, maybe a bunch of young smart alecks from MIT or spies in China or a small pool of genius kids at a mega Internet search technology company. Shrew was paid well enough, and took enormous pride in being an anonymous celebrity by proxy, but the arrangement had begun to seriously wear on her in a way she hadn't seen coming. She was beginning to doubt her own raison d'être, which probably had something to do with why she had behaved like such a fool when Investigator Marino had stopped by.

Shrew was starved for interaction with flesh and

blood, for conversation and attention and validation, and had lost the art of having a substantive dialogue with a human being who was present. It had been an extraordinary event for her to have a living soul sit in her family room and notice the puppy hairs stuck in her rug, or bear witness to her wearing her red velour warm-up lounging suit that was splotched light pink in places from a mishap with bleach. She'd been sorry when he'd left, and at the same time relieved, but mostly sorry, the more she'd been thinking about it. She'd had no idea what desolate straits she was in. Now she knew and she could see why. She most certainly could. Who wouldn't be?

The invisible money wired to her bank account every two weeks, the impersonal and ungrateful e-mailed remarks and instructions she received now and then, may as well come from God, who Shrew also had never met and never seen a picture of, and whose real name was debatable. If Shrew needed encouragement, praise, gratitude, a holiday or birthday gift, maybe a raise, neither the Boss nor God was interested. Both remained silent and unseen.

She could forgive God, she supposed, who had a universe of employees and disciples to look after. But she was feeling less charitable about the Boss, who had only Shrew. Something about Investigator Marino's visit today had resulted in clarity. While Shrew was the first to acknowledge that the Boss had created her, although she was grateful, she realized she was resentful. Shrew had signed her life away. She had no dog and no friends, didn't dare travel or engage in candid conversations, and had no visitors, unless they were uninvited. The only person she could even have called an acquaintance had been murdered last night.

What awful terms Shrew had accepted for how to live her life. And life was short. It could end—and end horribly—in a blink. The Boss was a selfish user, uncaring, and completely unfair. Without Shrew, the Boss would not be able to populate the website with what Shrew chose from the thousands of gossipy e-mails and images and cranky, crude comments and mean mentions that were sent by fans. Shrew did all the work, and the Boss got all the credit, even if the fans didn't know who the Boss was.

Shrew sat at her desk in front of her computer, the curtains drawn so she didn't have to look at the building across the street and think of the horror that had happened. Shrew didn't want to look at the police car still parked in front of Terri's apartment, and have the policeman it belonged to report to Investigator Marino that the neighbor he had interviewed earlier was spying out her window. Although she would enjoy another visit, she couldn't afford one. Investigator Marino was suspicious of her already. She was certain he believed she'd seen something last night, and having done a little research on the Internet after he left, she could understand why.

Terri's death was quite a mystery, and a very ugly one. No one was saying how she died, only that the blond man with the yellow rose, whom Shrew had said hello to not long ago, was locked up at Bellevue just like the Son of Sam had been when he was caught, and the medical examiner who did Terri's autopsy had released no details. But they must be gruesome. The case must be of huge importance because Dr. Scarpetta had, indeed, been called in to help. That was the belief, based on her being spotted at both Logan and La Guardia airports this afternoon, then being sighted again at Bellevue, pulling a suitcase with a wobbly wheel, apparently on her way to meet her forensic psychologist husband on the men's prison ward, where the boyfriend was being held.

No doubt the Boss would get yet another column out of Dr. Scarpetta, and that was too bad. Blogs everywhere were responding to both of the columns posted today, and the opinions dramatically varied. While quite a number of people thought it a disgrace that any sexual violation of Scarpetta, whether by Investigator Marino or Sister Polly, was made public, there were plenty of other people who wanted more.

Details! Details!

Why would someone break a little kid's pencils?

Women like her ask for it. That's why they're attracted to crime.

I'm surprised about the investigator but not about the nun.

Shrew had been unusually unmotivated since Investigator Marino had left, and she'd better get with it and start weeding through the most recent information and images sent by fans, on the off chance there was something important she should post or move to the Boss's research folder.

She opened and deleted scores of banal, boring gossipy anecdotes, alleged sightings, and images taken with cell phone cameras until she came to an e-mail that had been sent several hours ago. Immediately, she was excited by the subject line but skeptical:

NEVER-BEFORE-SEEN PHOTO! MARILYN MONROE IN THE MORGUE

There was no message, only an attachment. Shrew downloaded the image, and as it appeared in high resolution on her screen, she felt a thrill that made her understand what people meant when they said their hair stood on end.

"My word," she muttered. "Oh, my dear Lord," she exclaimed.

Marilyn Monroe's nude body was stitched up like a rag doll on top of a shiny steel autopsy table, her blond hair wetly clumped around her dead face, which was a bit swollen, but recognizable. Shrew began zooming in on every detail, the mouse clicking like mad as she did exactly what the fans were bound to do. She gawked and enlarged and gawked some more at the puckering and flattening of the movie goddess's once gorgeous breasts caused by the dreadful railroad track of sutures that ran in a V from her collarbones to her cleavage, then all the way down her once gorgeous body, past old surgical scars, before disappearing in pubic hair. Her famous lips and blue eyes were shut, and at the highest magnification the software could muster, Shrew came upon the truth that the world had always wanted and certainly deserved.

Just like that, she knew, and could prove it.

It couldn't be more obvious.

The details were there. Evidence: The recently dyed blond hair without a hint of dark roots showing. The perfectly plucked eyebrows. The manicured finger- and toenails, and smoothly shaven legs. She was slender, not an unseemly ounce to spare.

Marilyn had been fastidiously attending to her grooming and pampering herself, and keeping a keen eye on her weight right up to her tragic last breath. And severely depressed people didn't do that. The photo was proof positive of what Shrew had always suspected.

She excitedly typed the copy. It had to be short. The Boss was the writer, not Shrew, and she was never allowed to craft more than fifteen words for a cutline or any sort of text on the site:

MARILYN MONROE MURDERED!
(VIEWER DISCRETION IS ADVISED)

AN ASTONISHING NEVER-BEFORE-SEEN AUTOPSY PIC PROVES WITHOUT A SHADOW OF A DOUBT THAT FILM GODDESS MARILYN MONROE WASN'T DEPRESSED AT THE TIME OF HER DEATH, AND DID NOT COMMIT SUICIDE.

DETAILS CLEARLY VISIBLE DURING THE AUTOPSY PERFORMED ON AUGUST 5, 1962, IN LOS ANGELES, REVEAL INDISPUTABLE EVIDENCE THAT EVIL—NOT AN ACCIDENT OR SUICIDE—ENDED MARILYN'S LIFE.

Shrew should stop at that, for heaven's sake. A word count of sixty-two, not including numbers and punctuation, almost five times the legal limit. But certainly the Boss would make an exception in this case and in fact would give Shrew a bonus and praise for once.

She jumped into the search window and easily found what purported to be the famous Dr. Thomas Noguchi's autopsy report and lab results. She read them carefully, not sure what many of the words and phrases meant. She looked up "fixed lividity," and "a slight ecchymotic area," and "no refractile crystals found in the stomach or the duodenum." She looked up a lot of things and got increasingly indignant.

How dare a bunch of powermongering, womanizing, selfish men do this to Marilyn! Well, the world could stop speculating about what really happened. Shrew's fingers flew over the keyboard.

HIGHLY CLASSIFIED INFORMATION FROM THE ACTUAL AUTOPSY REPORT IS COMPLETELY CONSISTENT WITH WHAT'S PLAINLY VISIBLE IN THIS REMARKABLE PHOTO. MARILYN MONROE, NUDE AND HELPLESS, WAS FORCIBLY HELD DOWN ON HER BED (EXPLAINING BRUISES ON HER LEFT HIP AND LOWER BACK) WHILE HER KILLERS ADMINISTERED AN ENEMA HEAVILY LACED WITH BARBITURATES.

SHE CERTAINLY DIDN'T DIE FROM A SUICIDAL OVER-DOSE OF NEMBUTAL, OR THERE WOULD HAVE BEEN AT LEAST A TRACE OF PILL CAPSULES AND A YELLOWISH RESIDUE IN HER STOMACH AND DUODENUM—AND THERE WASN'T. ADDED TO THAT IS THE DISCOVERY THAT HER COLON WAS DISCOLORED AND DISTENDED—JUST AS ONE WOULD EXPECT IT TO BE AFTER A POISONOUS ENEMA!

AND BY THE WAY, IF SHE GAVE HERSELF THE ENEMA AS OPPOSED TO OTHERS DOING IT, WHERE WERE ALL THOSE EMPTY PILL CAPSULES? WHERE WAS THE EMPTY ENEMA BOTTLE?

ONCE THE DRUGS WERE IN HER SYSTEM, COMMON SENSE WOULD TELL YOU SHE COULDN'T POSSIBLY HAVE RUN OUT OF HER HOUSE TO DISPOSE OF THE EVIDENCE, THEN RETURNED, TAKEN OFF HER CLOTHES, CLIMBED BACK IN BED, AND TUCKED THE COVERS NEATLY UNDER HER CHIN. AFTER THAT ENEMA, SHE WOULD HAVE BEEN INCAPACITATED, UNCONSCIOUS, AND DEAD, FAST. IN FACT, SHE NEVER EVEN MADE IT TO THE BATHROOM! AT DEATH, HER BLADDER WAS FULL! IT SAYS SO ON THE AUTOPSY REPORT!

MARILYN WAS MURDERED BECAUSE SHE WOULDN'T KEEP HER MOUTH SHUT—NO MATTER WHO GAVE THE ORDER!

10

The view from Jaime Berger's office was of rampant lions carved in bas-relief on the granite building across from her eighth-floor office window.

She happened to have been gazing out that same window when American Airlines Flight 11 roared abnormally loud and low in a clear blue sky and slammed into the north tower of the World Trade Center. Eighteen minutes later, the second plane hit the south tower. In disbelief, she watched the symbols of power she had known much of her life burn and collapse, and rain ash and debris over lower Manhattan, and she was sure the world had come to an end.

Since then, she wondered what would be different had she not been in New York that Tuesday morning, sitting in this same office, talking on the phone with Greg, who was in Buenos Aires without her because she had yet another big trial—one she could scarcely recall now.

There were always extremely important, and later hard to recall, big trials requiring her to stay in the city while Greg squired his two children from a previous marriage to wondrous spots around the world. He decided he liked London best and took a flat there, and then it turned out what he'd really taken there was a mistress, a young English barrister he'd met several years earlier while she was spending a few weeks at Berger's office during an excessively stressful trial.

Berger had never thought twice about it when the young barrister and Greg had dinner together while Berger worked until the hands fell off the clock. As he used to put it.

She remained in a state of conjugal unconsciousness until Greg dropped by her office unannounced one day last winter to take her to lunch. They walked to Forlini's, a favorite hangout of criminal-justice potentates and politicians, and husband and wife sat across from each other, surrounded by dark paneling and heavy oil paintings of the Old Country. He didn't tell her he was having an affair and had been for years, just that he wanted out, and at that time and of all things, Berger's thoughts shifted to Kay Scarpetta. There was a logical reason.

Forlini's named booths after influential patrons, and the booth where Berger and Greg sat, coincidentally, was named for Nicholas Scoppetta, now the fire commissioner. Seeing the name Scoppetta on the wall made Berger think of Scarpetta, who Berger felt sure would have gotten up from that damn dusky rose leather booth and stalked out of the restaurant, instead of subjecting herself to, if not encouraging, blatant lies and humiliation.

But Berger didn't move or lodge a protest. She was her usual poised, controlled self listening to Greg make the insane bullshit point that he didn't love her anymore. He had stopped loving her after Nine-Eleven, probably because he was suffering post-traumatic stress disorder, even though he was well aware he wasn't in the country when the terrorist attack happened, but the constant replays on the news made it almost as bad as being there.

He said what had happened to America, and was continuing to happen—especially to his real-estate investments and the plummeting value of the dollar—was unbearably traumatizing, and therefore he was moving to London. He wanted a discreet divorce, and the more discreet and uncontested it was, the better off everyone would be. Berger asked if another woman might discreetly have something to do with it, just to see if he might have it in him to be honest. He'd said the question was irrelevant when a couple wasn't in love anymore, and then made a not-so-subtle accusation that Berger had other interests, and he didn't mean professional ones. She didn't object, redirect, or even offer proof that she'd never violated the terms of their marital contract, even if she'd thought about it.

Berger was now discreetly divorced, discreetly rich, and discreetly isolated. Her office floor was vacant this late afternoon. It was, after all, a holiday, or a sick day, depending on how enthusiastically one had brought in the New

Year. But Berger had no incentive to stay home. There was always work to be done. So with her former husband across the Pond, his children grown, and none of her own, she was alone in this cold stone Art Deco building not far from Ground Zero, nobody here to even answer the phone.

When it rang at exactly five p.m., exactly twenty-four hours after Oscar Bane said he had arrived at Terri Bridges's brownstone, Berger picked up the receiver herself, already knowing who it was.

"No. Not the conference room," she said to Lucy. "It's just the two of us. We'll do it in my office."

Oscar stared at the clock built into a plastic case on the wall, and then covered his face with his cuffed hands.

At this time yesterday afternoon, Terri should have been opening her door to him, and maybe she did. Or maybe what he claimed was true, and by this time yesterday she was already dead. The minute hand on the wall clock twitched ahead to one past five.

Scarpetta asked, "Did Terri have any friends?"

"Online," Oscar said. "That's how she connected with people. That's where she learned to trust them. Or realize she couldn't. You know that. Why are you doing this? Why can't you admit it? Who's stopping you?"

"I don't know what it is you want me to admit."

"You've been instructed."

"What makes you think I've been instructed? And instructed to do what?"

"Okay, fine," Oscar said testily. "I'm getting very

tired of this game. But I'll tell you anyway. I have to believe you're protecting me. I have to believe that's why you're so evasive. I'll accept it and answer your question. Terri met people online. If you're a little person and a woman, you're much more vulnerable."

"At what point did the two of you get together, start seeing each other?"

"After a year of exchanging e-mails. We discovered both of us were going to a meeting in the same location at the same time. Orlando. The LPA. That's when we realized we both have achondroplasia. After Orlando, we began seeing each other. I told you. Three months ago."

"Why her apartment from the very start?"

"She liked to be in her own place. She's very neat, obsessively neat and clean."

"She worried your apartment might be dirty?"

"She worried most places were dirty."

"Was she obsessive-compulsive? Phobic of germs?"

"When we'd go out somewhere, she'd want both of us to shower when we got back to her place. At first I thought it was about sex, which was fine. Showering with her. Then I realized it was about being clean. I had to be very clean. I used to have long hair, but she made me cut it short because it's easier to keep clean if it's short. She said hair collects dirt and bacteria. I was a good sport but said there was one place I was keeping my body hair. Nobody was coming near me down there."

"Where do you get your hair removal done?"

"A dermatologist on East Seventy-ninth. Laser removal. Other painful things I'll never bother with again."

"What about Terri? Did she go to this same dermatologist?"

"She referred me to her. Dr. Elizabeth Stuart. She has a big practice and is well respected. Terri's been going to her for years."

Scarpetta wrote down Dr. Stuart's name and asked about any other doctors or other practitioners Terri might have seen, and Oscar said he didn't know or he didn't remember, but he was sure there would be records of that type of information in Terri's apartment. She was impeccably well organized, he said.

"She never threw anything away that might be important, but everything has its proper place. If I draped my shirt over a chair, she was going to hang it up. I could barely finish eating before the dishes were in the dishwasher. She hated clutter. Hated things out of place. Her pocketbook, her raincoat, her snow boots, whatever it was, she tucked it out of sight even if she planned to use it again five minutes later. I realize that's not normal."

"Is her own hair cut short like yours?"

"I keep forgetting you never saw her."

"I'm sorry, but I didn't."

"She didn't cut her hair short, but she keeps it very clean. If she went somewhere, the minute she got back inside, she'd take a shower and wash her hair. Never a bath. Because you're sitting in dirty water. That's what she says, constantly. She uses a towel once, and then it went into the wash. I know it's not normal. I told her she might want to talk to someone about her anxiety, that she's obsessive-compulsive, not severely but has some of the symptoms. She didn't wash her hands a hundred times a day or walk around the cracks in the sidewalk or refuse take-out food. Nothing like that."

"What about when you had sex? Any extra precautions because of her vigilance about cleanliness?"

"Just that I'm clean. We shower afterwards, wash each other's hair, and usually have sex again in the shower. She likes having sex in the shower. She calls it *clean sex*. I wanted to see her more than once a week. But that was all. Once a week. Always the same day, exact same time. Probably because she's so organized. Saturday at five. We'd eat and make love. Sometimes we'd make love the minute I got there. I didn't sleep there. She likes to wake up alone and get started on her work. My DNA's all over her house."

"But you didn't have sex with her last night."

"You already asked me that!"

He clenched his fists and the veins stood out in his muscular arms.

"How could I!"

"I'm just making sure. You understand why I have to ask."

"I always use condoms. You'll find them in the drawer by her bed. My saliva would be on her."

"Because . . .?"

"Because I held her. I tried mouth-to-mouth. When I knew she was gone, I kissed her face. I touched her. I had her in my arms. My DNA's on her."

"This and this." Scarpetta touched bruises on his sternum. "When he hit you with the flashlight?"

"Some of them. Maybe some from hitting the floor. I don't know."

Bruises change color with time. They can indicate the shape of the object that caused them. His were reddish-purple. There were two on his chest, one on his left thigh, all about two inches wide and slightly curved. The most Scarpetta could say was they were consistent with a flashlight's rim, and that he had been struck with what appeared to be moderate force around the same time he'd received his other injuries.

She took close-up photographs, aware of how easy it would be for him to throttle her with his forearm. She wouldn't be able to scream. In minutes she would be dead.

She felt his body heat and smelled him. Then the air between them was cool again as she stepped back and returned to the counter, and began documenting injuries and making other notes while he watched her back. She could feel his mismatched eyes, only they weren't as warm. They felt like cool drops of water. His devotion, his idealization, was beginning to chill. To him she wasn't bigger than life on CNN. She was a woman, a real person who was disappointing him, betraying him. Almost without exception, that was the path of hero worship, because it was never really about the object of it.

"Nothing's any better than it was thousands of years ago," Oscar said to her back. "The fighting, the ugliness, the lies and hatefulness. People don't change."

"If you believe that," she asked, "why would you want to go into psychology?"

"If you want to figure out where evil comes from, you have to follow where it goes," he said. "Did it end up in a stab wound? Did it end up in the decapitated head of a hiker? Did it end up in discrimination? What part of our brain remains primitive in a world where violent aggression and hatred are counterproductive to survival? Why can't we knock out that part of our genetic coding the way we knock out genes in mice? I know what your husband's doing."

He talked fast and in a flinty tone while she retrieved a silicone casting extruder gun and a polyvinylsiloxane refill cartridge from her crime scene case.

"The research he's doing into that sort of thing. At his Harvard hospital, McLean. Using MRI. Functional MRI. Are we any closer to figuring it out? Or will we just keep tormenting, torturing, raping and killing and starting wars and committing genocide and deciding some people don't deserve basic human rights?"

Locking the cartridge in place, she removed the pink cover cap and pressed the trigger, squeezing the white base and clear catalyst on a paper towel until there was a steady flow. She attached the mixing tip and returned to the table, explaining she was going to use a silicone compound on his fingertips and his injuries.

"This is very good for taking elastic impressions of rough or smooth surfaces, such as your fingernails and even your fingerprint pads," she said. "There are no harmful side effects, and your skin should have no reaction to it. The scratches and nail marks are scabbed over and this shouldn't hurt them, but if at any point you want me to stop, just tell me. I'm confirming I have your consent to do this."

"Yes," he said.

He went very still as she touched his hands, careful of his injured thumb.

"I'm going to very gently clean your fingers and your injuries with isopropyl alcohol," she said. "So your own body secretions don't interfere with the curing process. This shouldn't hurt. At the most, a little sting. You let me know if you want me to stop."

He fell silent, watching her clean his hands, one finger at a time.

"I'm trying to figure out why you'd be familiar with Dr. Wesley's research study at McLean," she said. "Since he hasn't published anything yet. But I know the recruitment for subjects has been going on for a while and has been heavily advertised and publicized. I suppose that's the answer?"

"It doesn't matter," Oscar said, staring down at his hands. "Nothing changes. People know why they're hateful, and it changes nothing. You won't change feelings. All the science in the world won't change feelings."

"I don't agree," she said. "We tend to hate what we fear. And we hate less when we're less afraid."

She squeezed the odorless compound over his fingertips, the extruder gun clicking each time she pressed the trigger.

"Hopefully, the more enlightened we are, the less we fear and the less we hate. I'm covering each finger to the first knuckle, and when the compound is dry, it will roll off like one of those rubber fingertips people wear when counting money. This material is excellent for microscopic evaluation."

She used a wooden spatula to spread and smooth, and by the time she'd finished covering his multiple scratches and nail marks, the compound on his fingertips had begun to cure. It was interesting that he didn't ask her why she'd want to get impressions of his fingertips, especially his fingernails, and also of the scratches and nail marks allegedly made by a stranger he said had attacked him. Oscar didn't ask because he probably knew, and she didn't really need these impressions for microscopic study as much as she needed him to see her taking them.

"There. If you can just hold your hands up," she said.

She met his blue-green stare.

"It's cool in here," she said. "I'm guessing sixty-eight degrees. It should set in about four minutes. I'm going to pull your gown back up for now so you'll be more comfortable."

She smelled the pungent sweat of fear and confinement. She smelled unbrushed teeth and a trace of cologne. She wondered if a man would bother with cologne if his intention was to murder his lover.

11

Lucy hung her leather jacket on the coatrack and, without invitation, moved a chair next to Berger and opened a MacBook Air.

"Excuse me," Berger said, "I'm accustomed to people sitting on the other side of my desk."

"I need to show you something," Lucy said. "You're looking well. The same."

She openly appraised Berger.

"No, I'm wrong," Lucy decided. "You look better, maybe even better than the first time we met eight years ago when you had two more skyscrapers several blocks from here. When I'm flying the helicopter and the skyline first comes in view, it still looks like the city's had its two front teeth knocked out. Then along the Hudson at maybe eight hundred feet and I pass Ground Zero, and it's still a hole."

"It's not something to make light of," Berger said.

"I'm definitely not making light of it. I just wish it would change. You know. So I don't keep feeling like the bad guys won?"

Berger couldn't recall ever seeing Lucy in anything but tactical wear, and the tight threadbare jeans and black T-shirt she had on wouldn't hide any type of weapon. The way she was dressed didn't hide much at all, least of all that she had money. Her wide belt was crocodile with a Winston saber-toothed tiger buckle handcrafted of precious metals and stones, and the thick chain around her neck and its turquoise skull pendant was a Winston as well, and considered fine art and as expensive as such. She was remarkably fit and strong, and her mahogany hair with its shades of rose gold had been cut quite short. She could easily pass for a pretty boy model were it not for her breasts.

Berger said, "Terri Bridges's laptops."

She pointed to a table near the closed door, to the package wrapped in brown paper and neatly sealed with red evidence tape.

Lucy glanced at the package as if its presence couldn't have been more obvious.

"I assume you've got a search warrant," she said. "Anybody looked to see what's on the hard drives yet?"

"No. They're all yours."

"When I find out what e-mail accounts she has, we're going to need legal access to those as well. Quickly. And likely others, depending on who she was involved with—besides the boyfriend at Bellevue."

"Of course."

"Once I locate her e-mail hosting provider, check out her history, I'll need passwords."

"I know the drill, believe it or not."

"Unless you want me to hack." Lucy started typing.

"Let's refrain from using that word, please. In fact, I never heard you use it."

Lucy smiled a little as her agile fingers moved over the keyboard. She began a PowerPoint presentation.

Connextions—The Neural Networking Solution

"My God, you're really not going to do this," Berger said. "You have any idea how many of these things I see?"

"You've never seen this." Lucy tapped a key. "You familiar with computational neuroscience? Technology based on neural networking? Connections that process information very much the way the brain does."

Lucy's index finger tap-tapped, a bulky silver ring on it. She had on a watch that Berger didn't recognize, but it looked military, with its black face and luminous dial and rubber strap.

Lucy caught Berger looking at it and said, "Maybe you're familiar with illumination technology? Gaseous tritium, a radioactive isotope that decays and causes the numbers and other markings on the watch to glow so they're easy to read in the dark? I bought it myself. You buy your Blancpain yourself? Or was it a gift?"

"It was a gift to myself from myself. A reminder that time is precious."

"And mine's a reminder that we should utilize what other people fear, because you don't fear something unless it's powerful."

"I don't feel compelled to prove a point by wearing a radioactive watch," Berger said.

"A total, at most, of twenty-five millicuries, or an exposure of maybe point-one micro sievert over the period of a year. Same thing one gets from normal radiation. Harmless, in other words. A good example of people shunning something because they're ignorant."

"People call me a lot of things, but not ignorant," Berger said. "We need to get started on the laptops."

"The artificial system I've developed—am developing, actually," Lucy said, "because the possibilities are infinite, and when considering infinity, one has to ask if by its very nature it transforms what's artificial into something real. Because to me, artificial is finite. So to me, it follows that infinite will no longer be artificial."

"We need to get into this dead lady's laptops," Berger said.

"You need to understand what we're doing," Lucy said.

Her green eyes looked at Berger.

"Because it will be you explaining everything in court, not me," Lucy said.

She started moving through the PowerPoint. Berger didn't interrupt her this time.

"Wet mind, another bit of jargon you don't know," Lucy said. "The way our brain recognizes voices, faces, objects, and orients them into a context that's meaningful, revealing, instructive, predictive, and I can tell you're not looking at any of this or even listening."

She removed her hands from the keyboard and studied Berger as if she were a question to be answered.

"What I want from you is straightforward," Berger said. "To go through e-mail, all files of any description, re-create all deletions, recognize any patterns that might tell us the slightest thing about who, what, when, where. If she were murdered by somebody she knew, chances are good there's something in there." She indicated the packaged evidence on the table by the door. "Even if this is a stranger killing, there may be something she mentioned somewhere that could clue us in as to where this person might have come across her or where she came across him. You know how it works. You've been an investigator more years than you're old."

"Not exactly."

Berger got up from her desk.

"I'll receipt these to you," she said. "How did you get here?"

"Since you don't have a helipad, I took a cab."

Lucy had closed the office door when she'd come in. They stood in front of it.

"I assumed one of your troops would give me a lift back to the Village and up the stairs, straight into my office," Lucy said. "And I'll sign the appropriate paperwork. Pro forma, maintaining the chain of evidence. All those things I learned in law enforcement one-oh-one."

"I'll take care of it."

Berger made the phone call.

When she hung up, she said to Lucy, "You and I have one last thing to discuss."

Lucy leaned against the door, hands in the pockets of her jeans, and said, "Let me guess. That gossip column. Pedestrian programming, I might add. Do you believe in the Golden Rule? Do unto others?"

"I'm not talking specifically about *Gotham Gotcha*," Berger said. "But it raises an important issue I need to tell you about. Marino works for me. I'm taking for granted you can and will handle that."

Lucy put on her jacket.

"I need your assurance," Berger said.

"You're telling me this now?"

"Until earlier this afternoon, I didn't know there was a reason to have this conversation. By then, you and I had already agreed to meet. That's the chronology of things. That's why I'm bringing it up right now."

"Well, I hope you screen other people better than you did him," Lucy said.

"That's a topic for you and Benton, since he's the one who referred Marino to me last summer. What I read today is the first I'd heard of why Marino really left Charleston. I'll reiterate what matters right now, Lucy. You have to handle it."

"That's easy. I don't intend to have anything to do with him."

"It's not your choice to make," Berger said. "If you want to work for me, you'll have to handle it. He takes priority over you because—"

"Glad to know your definition of justice," Lucy interrupted. "Since I'm not the one who feloniously assaulted someone and then took a job under false pretenses."

"That's not legally or literally true, and I don't want to argue about it. The fact is, he's completely involved in this investigation and I can't remove him without repercussions. The fact is, I don't want him off the case for a number of reasons, not the least of which is he already has a history with it since he took a complaint from the victim's boyfriend a month ago. I'm not going to get rid of Marino because of you. There are other forensic computer experts. Just so we're clear."

"There's no one else who can do what I can. Just so we're clear. But I'd rather end this before it starts. If that's what you want."

"It's not what I want."

"Does he know my aunt's here?"

"To use your aviation language, it seems I'm an air traffic controller at the moment," Berger said. "Doing my best to keep things moving without people crashing into each other. My goal is strategic, gentle landings."

"What you're saying is he knows she's here."

"I'm not saying that. I haven't talked to him about it, but that doesn't mean others haven't. Especially since he's suddenly headline news. At least on the Internet. He may have known for a long time that Kay's in and out of New York, but in light of their sullied past, it doesn't surprise me he's never mentioned anything about her to me."

"And you've never said anything about her to him?"

Lucy's eyes were shadowed by anger. "Like, how's Kay? How's she like working for CNN? How's married life treating her? Gee, I really should try to have coffee with her some time when she's in the city."

"Marino and I don't chat. It's never been my desire to be his new Scarpetta. I'm not Batman, and I don't need a Robin. No insult toward Kay intended."

"Lucky for you, now that you know what Robin did to Batman."

"I'm not entirely sure what happened," Berger said as her phone rang. "I believe your car's here."

Scarpetta peeled off the hardened silicone and placed it in plastic evidence bags. She opened a cabinet and found antiseptic wipes and antibacterial ointment, then untied Oscar's gown in back and lowered it around his waist again.

"You're sure it was a flex-cuff?" she asked.

"You see them on TV," Oscar said. "The police, the military, use them to tie people up like bags of garbage."

"This shouldn't hurt."

Oscar didn't move as she began cleaning his wounds again and gently applying ointment.

"They had no right to touch her," he said. "I was already holding her, so what difference did it make if it had been me who picked her up and put her on the stretcher? Instead of those assholes putting their hands all over her. They took the towel off her. I saw them. When they were making me leave the bathroom. They took the towel off her. Why? You know why. Because they wanted to see her."

"They were looking for evidence. For injuries."

She carefully pulled up his gown and tied it in back.

"They didn't need to take the towel off," he said. "I told them there wasn't any blood except the scratches on her legs. It's like he hit her with something. Maybe a board. I don't know where he got a board. Or where they got one. I didn't see anything that might have made those scratches on her legs. Her face was dark red. There was a line around her neck. As if he strangled her with a rope or something. Whatever it was, it wasn't around her neck anymore. The police didn't need to take the towel off to see that, to take her pulse, to look at her wrists. You could look at her and see she was dead. I'm cold. Is there a blanket in here?"

Unable to find one, Scarpetta took off her lab coat and draped it over his shoulders. He was shivering. His teeth were chattering.

"I sat on the floor next to her, petting her hair, her face, talking to her," he said. "I called nine-one-one. I remember feet. Black ankle boots and dark pants moving in the doorway. I had the towel over her and was holding her."

He stared at the wall.

"I heard voices telling me to get away from her. They grabbed me. I started screaming I wasn't going to leave her. But they made me. They wouldn't let me see her even one more time. I never saw her again. Her family lives in Arizona, and that's where she'll go, and I'll never see her again."

"You said your online college is based in Arizona."

"Her father's the dean," he said to the wall. "That's why she ended up going there. They call it Gotham College as if it's here in New York, but it's really nowhere except there's a building in Scottsdale, probably because it's a nice place to live, much cheaper to live there. Her parents have a big house near Camelback Mountain. We never went to Scottsdale together because the next meeting isn't until March. She's not on the faculty, but she would have gone. . . . Well, she was supposed to fly there early this morning, to be in Scottsdale for a few days."

"When you were in her apartment last night, did you see her luggage? Was she packed?"

"Terri doesn't leave things out unless she's about to use them. And she knows it upsets me to see her suitcase if I'm not going with her. It would have ruined our night."

"Were you invited to go to Scottsdale with her?"

"She wanted a chance to tell them about me first."

"After three months, they didn't know she was seeing you?"

"They're very protective of her. Stiflingly controlling." He continued to face the wall, as if he was talking to it. "She didn't want to tell them unless she was sure. I told her it was no wonder she was obsessive-compulsive. It's because of them."

"What did she feel she needed to be sure of?"

"Of me. That we're serious. I fell harder for her than she did for me."

He continued mixing up tenses, the way people often do when someone they love has just died.

"I knew right away what I wanted. But her parents . . . Well, if it didn't work out, she didn't want to explain. She's always been afraid of them, afraid of their disapproval. It says a lot about her that she finally had the courage to move out. They have two other children who aren't little people, and they went to universities and do what they want. But not Terri. She's the smartest one in the family. One of the smartest people I know. But not her. They kept her at home until she was twenty-five, until she couldn't take it anymore because she wanted to amount to something. She got into a fight with them, and she left."

"How could she afford New York?"

"It was before I knew her. But she said she had money in savings, and they continued to help her some, not much, but some. Then she made amends with them, and I think they came to see her once and didn't like where she lived. They increased whatever it is they give her, and she moved into the apartment where she is now. That's what she told me. To give them credit, they've supported her, at least financially."

His face turned very red with anger, and his short gold hair seemed as bright as metal.

"With people like that, there are always strings attached," he then said. "I suspect they started controlling her long distance. I watched her obsessive-compulsiveness get worse. I began to notice an increasingly anxious tone to her e-mails. Even before we'd met. And over the past few months it's just gotten worse and worse. I don't know why. She can't help it. I have to see her. Please let me see her. I have to say good-bye! I hate the police. Fuck them."

He wiped his eyes with his cuffed hands.

"Why did they have to be so cold? Shouting and shoving. And on their radios. I couldn't make sense of what was happening. I hate that detective. . . ."

"The same one you invited to go through your apartment?" Scarpetta said.

"I don't get to pick them! He was shouting, ordering me to look at him when he spoke to me, and I tried to explain I couldn't hear him if I looked at him. Asking me things in the living room, demanding answers. Look at me, look at me! I was trying to help at first. I said someone must have come to the outer door and rung the bell and she thought it was me. Maybe she thought I was early and forgot my keys. There had to be a reason she felt it was safe to let the person in."

"You keep telling me how anxious Terri was. Was she unusually cautious?"

"It's New York, and people don't just open their doors, and she's always been incredibly cautious. People our size are cautious. That's one of the reasons her parents are so protective, practically kept her locked up in the house when she was growing up. She wouldn't open her door unless she felt safe."

"What do you think that means, then? How did the intruder get in, and do you have any idea why someone would want to harm Terri?"

"They have their motives," he said.

"When you were in her apartment, did you notice any signs of robbery? Might that have been a motive?"

"I didn't notice anything missing. But I didn't look."

"What about jewelry? Did she wear a ring, a necklace, anything that was missing?"

"I didn't want to leave her. They had no right to make me leave her, to make me sit in that detective's car as if I were a murderer. He looks more like a murderer than I do, with his gang clothes and braided hair. I refused to talk."

"You just said you did. Inside the house."

"They had their minds made up. I hate the police. I've always hated them. Driving by in their patrol cars, talking, laughing, staring. Someone keyed my car and smashed all the windows. I was sixteen. And this cop says, 'So, are we having a *little* problem?' And he sat in my car and put his feet on the extended pedals, and his knees were on either side of the steering wheel, while the other cop laughed. Fuck them."

"What about other people? Have they mistreated you, made fun of you?"

"I grew up in a small town, and everybody knew me. I had friends. I was on the wrestling team and made good grades. I was the class president my senior year. I'm realistic. I don't take stupid chances. I like people. Most people are all right."

"Yet you've chosen a career where you can avoid them."

"It's predicted most students will go to college online

eventually. The police think everybody's guilty of something. If you look different or have some sort of disability. There was a boy with Down syndrome across the street from me. The cops always suspected him of something, always assumed he was going to rape every girl in the neighborhood."

Scarpetta began packing her crime scene case. She was done with him. Comparing the silicone impressions of his fingernails and the scratches and nail marks, and relying on measurements and photographs were only going to corroborate what she already knew. He would realize that already, he must, and she wanted him to realize it.

She said, "You understand what we can tell from all that I've done today, don't you, Oscar? The silicone impressions of your fingertips and wounds. The photographs and precise measurements."

He stared at the wall.

She continued to bluff, slightly. "We can study these impressions under the microscope."

"I know what you can do," he said. "I know why you made the silicone casts. Yes, I know that now you'll look at them under a microscope."

"I'll let the police labs do that. I don't need to. I think I already have the information I need," she said. "Did you do this to yourself, Oscar? The scratches, the bruises? They're all within your reach. All angled the way they would be if they were self-inflicted."

He didn't say anything.

"If you really have this mythical notion that I can solve the perfect crime, would there have been a doubt in your mind that I would figure out you injured yourself?"

Nothing. Staring at the wall.

"Why?" she asked him. "Was it your intention for me to come here and determine you'd done this to yourself?"

"You can't tell anyone. You can't tell your husband. You can't tell Detective Morales. You can't tell Berger or that asshole in her office who didn't believe me last month."

"Under the current circumstances, what's gone on between us is confidential. But that could change," she reminded him.

"It's the only way I could get you here. I had to be injured."

"The attacker at her door?" she said.

"There was no one. I got there and the lights were out. Her door was unlocked. I ran inside calling out her name. And found her in the bathroom. The light was on in there, as if he wanted me to be shocked. You can't see that light from where I parked because the bathroom's in the back. I removed the flex-cuffs with scissors from the kitchen. That's when I cut my thumb. Just a small cut, not sure how it happened, but I was grabbing for the scissors, and the block of knives fell over, and one of them must have nicked me, so I wrapped a paper towel around my thumb and ran out to my car and threw my coat inside. I sat with her on the bathroom floor and ripped my shirt and hurt myself. There's blood on my shirt. I called the police."

"The flashlight? You hit yourself with it?"

"I found it in the kitchen drawer. I wiped it off and left it on the living room floor. Near the door."

"Why did you bother to wipe it off if your fingerprints and DNA are all over her house and all over her body?"

"So I could tell the police the intruder was wearing gloves. That would corroborate my story. The gloves wiped off any prints on the flashlight. Leather gloves, I told them."

"And the scissors from the kitchen? What did you do with those after you cut off the flex-cuff?"

His face twitched, and she could almost see him re-creating that scene, and he began to breathe hard, rocking back and forth.

His voice wavered when he said, "Her hands were this awful deep bluish red. Her fingernails were blue. I rubbed her wrists and her hands to get the circulation going. I tried to rub the grooves away, these deep grooves."

"Do you remember what you did with the scissors?"

"That flex-cuff was so tight. It had to hurt. I left the scissors on the bathroom floor."

"When did you decide to injure yourself because, as you just told me, it was the only way to get me here?"

"I was on the bathroom floor with her. I knew I'd be blamed. I knew if I got to your husband, I could get to you. I had to get to you. I trust you, and you're the only one who cared about her."

"I didn't know her."

"Don't lie to me!" he screamed.

12

Shrew had resumed drinking Maker's Mark, the same thing the Boss drank. She poured herself a tumbler full, on the rocks, the same way the Boss drank it.

She picked up the remote to the forty-inch flat-screen Samsung TV, just like the Boss used to have, according to the columns, but apparently not anymore. If what Shrew read was true, the Boss had gotten a new fifty-eight-inch plasma Panasonic. Unless that was nothing more than another paid endorsement. It was hard to know what was real and what was made up for money, because the business part of *Gotham Gotcha* was as hidden from Shrew as everything else.

Terrorists, she thought.

What if that's where the money went? Maybe terrorists had killed her neighbor, gotten the buildings mixed up, and were really after Shrew because they sensed she was on to them? What if government agents who were after terrorists had tracked the website to Shrew and had gotten the apartments confused? It would be easy enough to do. Shrew's and Terri's apartments were directly across the street from each other, except Shrew's was one floor higher. Governments took out people all the time, and Marilyn Monroe was probably one of them because she knew too much.

Maybe Shrew knew too much, or the wrong people thought she did. She was working herself into such a state of panic, she picked up the business card Investigator Pete Marino had left for her. She drank bourbon and held the card, and was within an inch of calling him. But what would she say? Besides, she wasn't sure what she thought of him. If what the Boss had written about him was true, he was a sex maniac and had gotten away with it, and the last thing she needed inside her apartment right now was a sex maniac.

Shrew placed a dining room chair in front of her door, wedging the back of it under the knob, like she saw in the movies. She made sure all of her windows were locked and that no one was on the fire escape. She checked the TV guide to see if she could find a good comedy, and didn't, so she played her favorite DVD of Kathy Griffin.

Shrew settled in front of her computer and drank her bourbon on the rocks and used her password to get into the website's programming, or under the hood, as she thought of it.

She was astonished by what she discovered and not sure she believed it.

The Marilyn Monroe photo and Shrew's accompanying sensational story had already gotten more than six hundred thousand hits. In less than an hour. She thought back to the video footage of Saddam Hussein being taunted and hanged, but no. That hadn't gotten even a third as many hits the first hour it was up. Her amazement turned to pride, even if she was slightly terrified. What would the Boss do?

Shrew would justify her civil and literary disobedience by pointing out that if she hadn't written the story about Marilyn's murder, the world wouldn't know the truth. It was the right and moral thing to do. Besides, the Boss never posted breaking news, so why should the Boss care if Shrew did? The Boss wasn't particularly concerned about breaking anything except the hearts and spirits of whoever was on the radar.

Shrew logged out of the website and started surfing television channels, certain that somebody had picked up her startling revelation. She expected to see Dr. Scarpetta on CNN talking about it with Anderson Cooper or Wolf Blitzer or Kitty Pilgrim. But no sign of the famous medical examiner whom the Boss seemed to hate, and no mention of Marilyn Monroe. It was early yet. She drank bourbon, and fifteen minutes later logged back in to the website programming to check the numbers again, and was dumbfounded to discover that almost a million people had clicked on the morgue photo of Marilyn

Monroe. Shrew had never seen anything like this. She logged out of the programming and on to the actual site.

"Oh dear God," she said out loud as her heart seemed to stop.

The home page looked demon-possessed. The letters spelling *Gotham Gotcha!* continuously rearranged themselves into **OH C THA MAGGOT!** and in the background, the New York skyline was blacked out, and behind it the sky flashed blood-red, then somehow the Christmas tree from Rockefeller Center was upside down in Central Park, and ice skaters were twirling inside the Boathouse restaurant while diners ate at tables on the ice of Wollman Rink, and then a heavy snow began to fall, and thunder clapped and lightning illuminated a horrendous rainstorm that ended up inside FAO Schwarz before turning into a sunny summer's flight along the Hudson, where the Statue of Liberty suddenly filled the screen and deconstructed as if the helicopter had flown right into it.

On and on, over and over again, the banner was caught in a crazy loop that Shrew couldn't stop. This is what millions of fans were seeing, and she couldn't click her way out of it. All of the icons were unresponsive— dead. When she tried to access this morning's column, or the more recently posted bonus column, or any column archived, she got the dreaded spinning color wheel. She couldn't send an e-mail to the site or enter **Gotham Gossip**, where fans chatted and had spats and said terrible things about people they didn't know.

She couldn't visit the Bulletin Bored, or Sneak Peeks, or the Photo Swap Shop, or even the Dark Room, where one could see Sick Pics or Celebrity Overexposures or the wildly popular Gotham Gotcha A.D., where Shrew posted photographs taken after death, including the most recent one of Marilyn.

How could hundreds of thousands of fans be opening that photo and Shrew's accompanying story when the website was locked up and haywire? *A conspiracy,* she thought. The Mafia, it occurred to her with horror as she thought about the mysterious Italian agent who had hired her over the phone. The government! Shrew had spilled the beans and the CIA or FBI or Homeland Security had sabotaged the site so the world wouldn't know the truth. Or maybe it really was all about terrorists.

Shrew frantically clicked on every icon, and nothing happened, and the banner continued its infernal loop as *Gotham Gotcha* rearranged itself nonstop:

> . . . GOTHAM GOTCHA! OH C THA MAGGOT!
> GOTHAM GOTCHA!

Benton was waiting outside the infirmary, and in the space of the closing door, Oscar's mismatched eyes stared at Scarpetta before disappearing behind beige steel. She heard the clanks and clicks of restraints being removed.

"Come on," Benton said, touching her arm. "We'll talk in my office."

Tall and slender, he seemed to dominate any space he

was in, but he looked tired, as if he was coming down with something. His handsome face was tense, his silver hair a mess, and he was dressed like an institutional employee in a bland gray suit, white shirt, and nondescript blue tie. He wore a cheap rubber sports watch and his simple platinum wedding band. Any sign of affluence was unwise on a prison ward, where the average stay was less than three weeks. It wasn't uncommon for Benton to evaluate a patient at Bellevue and a month later see the same person on the street, rooting through garbage for something to eat.

He took the crime scene case from her, and she held on to envelopes of evidence and said she needed to receipt them to the police.

"I'll get someone to stop by my office before we leave," Benton said.

"It should go straight to the labs. They should analyze Oscar's DNA and get it into the database as soon as possible."

"I'll call Berger."

They walked away from the infirmary. Two linen carts rolling by sounded like a train, and a barrier door slammed shut as they passed cells that would have been spacious by prison standards were they not crammed with as many as six beds. Most of the men were in ill-fitting pajamas, sitting up and engaged in loud conversations. Some gazed through mesh-covered windows at the dark void of the East River, while others watched the ward through bars. One patient thought it a fine time to use the steel toilet, smiling at Scarpetta as he peed and telling her what a great story he'd be. His cell mates began bickering about who would look better on TV.

Benton and Scarpetta stopped at the first barrier door, which never opened fast enough, the guard in the control room on the other side busy with the rhythm of gatekeeping. Benton loudly announced that they were coming through, and they waited. He called out again as a man mopped a corridor that led to the recreation room, where there were tables and chairs, a few board games, and an old home gym with no detachable parts.

Beyond that were interview rooms, and areas for group therapy, and the law library with its two typewriters, which like the televisions and the wall clocks were covered with plastic to prevent patients from disassembling anything with components that could be fashioned into a weapon. Scarpetta had gotten the tour the first time she was summoned up here. She was confident nothing had changed.

The white-painted steel door finally slid open and slammed shut behind them, and a second opened to let them through. The guard inside the control room returned Scarpetta's driver's license, and she surrendered her visitor's pass, the exchange made mutely through thick bars as officers escorted in the newest patient, who wore the blaze-orange jumpsuit of Rikers Island. Prisoners like him were temporary transfers, brought here only if they needed medical attention. Scarpetta never ceased to be dismayed by what malingerers would do to themselves to earn a brief stay at Bellevue.

"One of our frequent flyers," Benton said as steel

slammed. "A swallower. Last visit it was batteries. Triple A, double A. Can't remember. About eight of them. Rocks and screws before that. Once it was toothpaste, still in the tube."

Scarpetta felt as if her spirit were unzipped from her body like the lining of a coat. She couldn't be who she was, couldn't show emotion, couldn't share her thoughts about Oscar or a single detail he had told her about himself or Terri. She was chilled by Benton's professional distance, which was always the most extreme on the ward. It was here where he entertained fears he wouldn't confess, and didn't need to, because she knew him. Ever since Marino had gotten so drunk and out of control, Benton had been in a quiet, chronic panic he refused to admit. To him, every male was a potential beast who wanted to carry her off to his lair, and nothing she did or said reassured him.

"I'm going to quit CNN," she said as they headed to his office.

"I understand the position Oscar's just put you in," Benton said. "None of this is your fault."

"You mean, the position you've just put me in."

"It's Berger who wanted you here."

"But you're the one who asked."

"If I had my way about it, you'd still be in Massachusetts," he said. "But he wouldn't talk unless you came here."

"I just hope I'm not the reason he's here."

"Whatever the reason, you can't hold yourself responsible."

"I don't like the way that sounds," she said.

They passed shut office doors, no one around. It was just the two of them, and they didn't disguise their tense tones.

"I hope you're not hinting it's possible some obsessed fan pulled a horrific stunt so he could have an audience with me," she added. "I hope that's not what you're implying."

"A woman's dead. That's no stunt," Benton said.

She couldn't talk to him about Oscar's conviction that he was being spied on and that whoever was behind it was Terri Bridges's killer. Maybe Benton already knew, but she couldn't ask. She couldn't reveal that Oscar's injuries were self-inflicted, that he'd lied to the police and everyone else about how he'd gotten them. The most she could do was speak in generalities.

"I have no information that might justify my discussing him with you," she said, implying Oscar had confessed to nothing, nor indicated he was a threat to himself or others.

Benton unlocked his office door.

"You spent a long time with him," he said. "Remember what I always tell you, Kay. Your first cue is your gut. Listen to what your gut tells you about this guy. And I'm sorry if I seem strung out. I've had no sleep. Actually, things are rather much a fucking mess."

The work space the hospital had allotted Benton was small, with books, journals, clutter piled everywhere as neatly as he could manage. They sat, and the desk between them seemed a solid manifestation of an emotional barrier she could not get past. He did not want sex, at least not with her. She didn't believe he was having it with anybody else, but the benefits of marriage seemed to include shorter and more impersonal conversations, and less time in bed. She believed Benton had been happier before they'd gotten married, and that sad fact she wasn't going to blame on Marino.

"What did your gut tell you?" Benton asked.

"That I shouldn't be talking to him," she replied. "That I shouldn't be prevented from talking to you. My head tells me otherwise."

"You're an associate, a consultant here. We can have a professional discussion about him as a patient."

"I don't know anything about him as your patient. I can't tell you anything about him as mine."

"Before now you'd never heard of him? Or Terri Bridges?"

"That much I can say. Absolutely not. And I'm going to ask you not to cajole me. You know my limitations. You knew them when you called this morning."

Benton opened a drawer and pulled out two envelopes. He reached across the desk to hand them to her.

"I didn't know what might happen by the time you got here," he said. "Maybe the cops would have found something, arrested him, and we probably wouldn't be having this conversation. But you're right. At the moment, your priority has to be Oscar's well-being. You're his physician. But that doesn't mean you have to see him again."

Inside one envelope was a DNA report, and inside the other, a set of crime scene photographs.

"Berger wanted you to have a copy of the DNA analysis. The photographs and police report are from Mike Morales," Benton said.

"Do I know him?"

"He's relatively new to the detective division. You don't know him, maybe won't have to. Candidly speaking, I think he's a jerk. Photos he took at the crime scene, his preliminary report. The DNA's from swabs Dr. Lester took from Terri Bridges's body. There's a second set of photos I haven't gotten yet. From a second search earlier this afternoon when luggage in her closet was checked, and it turned out Terri's laptops were in it. Apparently, she was supposed to fly to Arizona this morning to spend a few days with her family. Why her luggage was packed and out of sight in her closet, no one knows."

Scarpetta thought about what Oscar had told her. Terri didn't leave luggage out. She was obsessively neat, and Oscar didn't like good-byes.

Benton said, "One possible explanation is she was extremely neat. Perhaps obsessively so. You'll see what I mean in the photos."

"I'd say that's a very plausible explanation," she commented.

He held her gaze. He was trying to determine if she'd just given him information. She didn't break their eye contact or the silence. He retrieved a number from his cell phone contact list and reached for the landline. He asked Berger if she could send someone by to pick up evidence Scarpetta had collected from Oscar Bane.

He listened for a moment, then looked up at Scarpetta

and said to Berger, "I completely agree. Since he can leave whenever he wants, and you know how I feel about that. And no, I haven't had a chance . . . Well, she's right here. Why don't you ask her?"

Benton moved the handset to the middle of the desk and held out the receiver to Scarpetta.

"Thanks for doing this," Jaime Berger said, and Scarpetta tried to remember the last time they'd talked.

Five years ago.

"How was he?" Berger asked.

"Extremely cooperative."

"Do you think he'll stay put?"

"I think I'm in an awkward position." Scarpetta's way of saying she couldn't talk about her patient.

"I understand."

"All I can comfortably tell you," Scarpetta said, "is if you can get his DNA analyzed quickly, that would be a good thing. There's no downside to that."

"Fortunately, there are plenty of people in the world right now who love overtime. One of them, however, isn't Dr. Lester. While I've got you, I'll ask you directly and let Benton off the hook, unless he's already said something. Would you mind looking at Terri Bridges's body tonight? Benton can fill you in. Dr. Lester should be on her way in from New Jersey. Sorry to subject you to something so unpleasant, and I don't mean the morgue."

"Whatever's helpful," Scarpetta replied.

"I'm sure we'll talk later. And we should get together. Maybe dinner at Elaine's," Berger said.

It seemed to be the favorite line of professional women like them. They would get together, have lunch, maybe dinner. She and Berger had said it to each other the first time they met eight years ago, when Berger was brought to Virginia as a special prosecutor in a case that was one of the most stressful ones in Scarpetta's life. And they'd said it to each other last time they met, in 2003, when both of them had been concerned about Lucy, who had just returned from a clandestine operation in Poland that Scarpetta still knew very little about, except that what Lucy had done wasn't legal. It certainly wasn't moral. In Berger's penthouse apartment here in the city, the prosecutor had sat down with Scarpetta's niece, and whatever had gone on between them had remained between them.

Oddly, Berger knew far more about Scarpetta than almost anybody she could think of, and yet they weren't friends. It was unlikely they would get together and do anything except work, no matter how many times they suggested lunch or a drink and meant it. Their disconnection wasn't simply due to the vicissitudes of very busy lives that collide and then resume their separate paths. Powerful women tended to be loners, because it was their instinct not to trust one another.

Scarpetta handed the receiver back to Benton.

She said, "If Terri were obsessive-compulsive, her body might offer a few hints. It seems I'll have a chance to look for myself. Coincidentally."

"I was about to tell you. Berger asked me earlier to see if you would."

"Since Dr. Lester's on her way back into the city, I guess I agreed to it before I knew about it."

"You can leave afterwards, stay out of it," Benton said. "Unless Oscar gets charged. Then I don't know how it will involve you. That will be up to Berger."

"Please don't tell me this man killed someone to get my attention."

"I don't know what to tell you about anything. At this point, I don't know what to think about anything. The DNA from Terri's vaginal swabs, for example. Take a look."

Scarpetta removed the lab report from an envelope and read it as he described what Berger had told him about a woman in Palm Beach.

"Well?" he said. "Can you think of any reason?"

"What's not here is Dr. Lester's report of what samples she took. You said vaginal."

"That's what Berger told me."

"Exactly what they were and from where? Not here. So no. I'm not going to venture a guess about the unusual results and what they might mean."

"Well, I will. Contamination," he said. "Although I can't figure out how an elderly woman in a wheelchair factors into that."

"Any chance she has a connection with Oscar Bane?"

"I'm told no. Berger called her and asked."

His phone rang. He answered, listening for a long silence, his closed face giving away nothing.

"Don't think it was such a great idea," he finally spoke to whoever was on the line. "Sorry that happened . . . Of course I regret it in light of . . . No, I didn't want to tell you for this very reason . . . Because, no, hold on. Listen to me for a minute. The answer is, I have . . . Lucy, please. Let me finish. I don't expect you to understand, and we can't get into it now. Because . . . You don't mean that. Because . . . When someone has nowhere else to turn . . . We'll deal with it. Later, all right? Calm down and we'll talk later," and he got off the phone.

"What the hell was that about?" Scarpetta asked. "What was Lucy saying? What are you sorry about, and who has nowhere else to turn?"

Benton's face was pale but impassive, and he said, "Sometimes she has no sense of time and place, and what I don't need right now is one of her rages."

"Rage? Over what?"

"You know how she gets."

"Usually when she has good reason to get that way."

"We can't get into it now." He said the same thing to her that he'd said to Lucy.

"How the hell am I supposed to concentrate after overhearing a conversation like that? Get into what?"

He was silent. She never liked it when he stopped to think after she'd asked him a question.

"Gotham Gotcha," he said, to her surprise and annoyance.

"You're not really going to make a big deal out of that."

"You read it?"

"I started reading it in the cab. Bryce said I needed to."

"Did you read all of it?"

"I was interrupted by being thrown out on the street."

"Come look."

He typed something as she moved next to him.

"That's odd," Benton said, frowning.

The *Gotham Gotcha* website had a massive programming error or had crashed. Buildings were dark, the sky flashing red, and Rockefeller Center's huge Christmas tree was upside down in Central Park.

Benton impatiently scooted the mouse around on its pad and clicked it repeatedly.

"The site's down for some reason and completely fucked up," he said. "However, unfortunately, I can pull up the damn column anyway."

Typing, he executed a search, hitting keys vigorously.

"It's all the hell over the place," he said.

The screen filled with references to *Gotham Gotcha* and Dr. Kay Scarpetta, and he clicked on a file and opened a copy of not one column but two that someone had cut and pasted on a forensic fan site. The unflattering photograph of Scarpetta filled the screen, and she and Benton looked at it for a moment.

"You think it was taken in Charleston?" he asked. "Or your new office? Do the scrubs tell you anything? The color? Don't you wear cranberry scrubs in Watertown?"

"Depends on what we get from the medical linen service. They pick up and deliver, and one week it might be teal-green, the next week purple, different shades of blue, cranberry. That's true at most morgues in recent years. The most I might specify is I don't want something cute like SpongeBob, the Simpsons, Tom and Jerry. Literally true. I know pathologists who wear them, as if they're pediatricians."

"And you have no recollection of someone taking a picture of you during an autopsy? Maybe using their cell phone?"

She thought back, thought hard, and said, "No. Because if I saw it happen, I would have made the person delete it. I would never permit such a thing."

"Most likely it happened since you moved and started with CNN. The celebrity factor. A cop. Someone from a funeral home, a removal service."

"That would be bad," she said, thinking about Bryce. "That would make me worry about someone on my staff. What's this about Sister Polly? Who's Sister Polly?"

"Don't know. Read this. Then we'll get to that."

He moved the cursor to the first column that had been posted today, to the part he wanted her to see:

> . . . yet beneath that impenetrable façade is a
> dirty secret she hides pretty well. Scarpetta may
> live in a world of stainless steel but she's certainly
> no woman made of steel. She's weak, a disgrace.
>
> Guess what, she can be raped.
>
> That's right. Just like any other woman, only
> you can blame the victim this time. She brought
> it upon herself. Pushed away, mistreated, and
> belittled her investigative partner in crime
> until one drunken night in Charleston when he

couldn't take it anymore. You have to feel a little
sorry for poor Pete Marino. . . .

Scarpetta returned to her chair. Gossip was one thing. This was another.

"I won't ask why people are so hateful," she said. "I learned a long time ago not to ask. Finally figured out the why part might give insight, but really doesn't matter. Just the end result. That's what matters. If I find out who this is, I'll sue."

"I won't tell you not to let it get to you."

"I believe you just told me by not telling me. What happened was never in the news. I never reported it. It's not accurate. This is slander. I'll sue."

"Sue whom? An anonymous piece of shit in cyberspace?"

"Lucy could find out who."

"Speaking of, I'm not sure it's coincidental the site crashed," he said. "That's probably the best remedy. Maybe it will stay crashed forever."

"Did you ask her to crash the site?"

"You just heard me on the phone with her. Of course not. But you know her, as do I. Sure as hell is something she'd do, and much more effective than a lawsuit. There's no slander. You can't prove that what this person's written is a lie. You can't prove what happened. And what didn't."

"You say that as if you don't believe what I've told you."

"Kay." He met her eyes. "Let's don't turn this into a fight between us. What you need to brace yourself for, obviously, is the exposure. The public didn't know, and now it does, and you're going to be asked. Same thing with this. . . ." He read some more. "This other bullshit. Parochial school. Sister Polly. That's a story I'm not familiar with."

Scarpetta barely read it, didn't need to, and she replied, "There's no Sister Polly, and what was described didn't happen, not like that. It was a different nun, and there certainly was no salacious whipping in the bathroom."

"But some truth."

"Yes. Miami, the scholarship to parochial school. And my father's protracted, terminal illness."

"And his grocery store. Did the other girls in school call you a Florida cracker?"

"I don't want to talk about this, Benton."

"I'm trying to determine what's true and who would know it. What's already out there? Any of this?"

"You know what's out there. And no. None of this, true or false, is out there. I don't know where the information came from."

He said, "I'm not as concerned about what's false. I want to know what's out there that's true, and if there's a publicized source for what's in these columns. Because if there isn't, as you seem to be suggesting, then someone close to you is leaking information to whoever this hack writer is."

"Marino," she reluctantly said. "He knows things about me that other people don't."

"Well, obviously the Charleston information. Although I can't imagine him using that word."

"What word, Benton?"

He didn't answer.

"You can't bring yourself to say it, can you? The word *rape*. Even though that's not what happened."

"I don't know what happened," he said quietly. "That's my problem. I only know as much as you've let me know."

"Would you somehow feel better if you'd watched?"

"Jesus Christ."

"You need to see every detail, as if that will give you closure," Scarpetta said. "Who's the one always saying there's no such thing as closure? I believe that would be both of us. And now this columnist, and whoever is leaking information to him or her, wins. Why? Because we're sitting here upset, not trusting each other, estranged. Truth is, you probably know far more about what happened than Marino does. I sincerely doubt he remembers much of what he did or said that night. For his sake, I hope I'm right."

"I don't want to be estranged, Kay. I don't know why this bothers me more than it seems to bother you."

"Of course you know why, Benton. You feel even more powerless than I did because you couldn't stop it, and at least I stopped some of it. I stopped the worst of it."

He pretended to read the two columns again. What he was really doing was composing himself.

"Would he know the Florida information?" he asked. "What did you tell him about your childhood? Or let me restate the question. The part that's true"—he indicated what was on the computer—"is that from information you gave him?"

"Marino's known me for almost twenty years. He's met my sister, my mother. Of course he knows some details about my life. I don't remember everything I've said to him, but it's no great secret among those close to me that I grew up in a not-so-nice Miami neighborhood, and we had no money, and my father lingered with cancer for many years before dying. And that I did pretty well in school."

"The girl who broke your pencils?"

"This is ridiculous."

"I take that as a yes."

"There was a girl who did that. A bully. I don't remember her name."

"Did a nun slap you across the face?"

"Because I confronted the girl, and she tattled on me, not the other way around, and one of the sisters punished me. That was it. No titillating bathroom scene. And it's absurd we're having this conversation."

"I thought I knew all your stories. It doesn't feel good that I don't and had to find out from the Internet. Absurd or not, details like this will be bounced around all over the place, probably already are. You can't escape it, not even on CNN, where you have friends. When you're on the set, someone will be obliged to ask. I guess you'll have to get used to it. I guess we both will."

She wasn't thinking about the exposure or getting used to it. She was thinking about Marino.

"That's what Lucy was talking about when she called you a little while ago," Scarpetta said. "She was saying something about him."

Benton said nothing. That was his answer. Yes, Lucy had been talking about Marino.

"What did you mean about him having nowhere else to turn? Or were you talking about somebody else? Don't keep anything from me. Not now."

"What he did. Hit-and-run. That's how Lucy thinks of it," Benton said, and she had gotten better at knowing when he was being evasive. "Because he disappeared, and I've explained until I'm blue in the face that when someone feels he has no place to turn, he looks for an out. This isn't new. You know the story. And you know Lucy."

"What story? I've never known the story. He disappeared, and I never believed he killed himself. That's not Marino. He wouldn't have the nerve or the stupidity, and most of all he's afraid of going to hell. He believes there really is a physical hell located somewhere in the molten core of the earth, and if he ends up there he'll be on fire for all eternity. He confessed that to me on another drunken occasion. He's wished hell on half the planet because he's terrified of it for himself."

The look in Benton's eyes was unutterably sad.

"I don't know what story you're talking about, and I don't believe you," she said. "Something else has happened."

They held each other's eyes.

Benton said, "He's here. He's been here since last July. The first weekend in July, exactly."

He went on to tell her that Marino worked for Berger, who found out from the gossip column the real reason Marino had left Charleston, a sordid detail she certainly didn't know when she hired him. Now Lucy knew about Marino because Berger had just met with her and had told her.

"That's why Lucy called," he said. "And knowing you as well as I do, I suspect you would have wanted me to help Marino, despite it all. And you would have wanted me to honor his wish that he go into treatment and basically start his life again without your knowledge."

"You should have told me a long time ago."

"I couldn't divulge details about him to anyone. Any more than you can tell me what Oscar told you. Doctor-patient confidentiality. Marino called me at McLean not long after he disappeared from Charleston and asked me to get him into a treatment center. He asked me to confer with his therapist up there, to oversee, to intervene."

"And then get him a job with Jaime Berger? And that's a secret, too? What's that got to do with doctor-patient confidentiality?"

"He asked me not to tell you."

Benton's voice said he'd done the right thing, but the look in his eyes belied his certainty.

"This isn't about doctor-patient confidentiality or your even being decent," Scarpetta said. "You know what it's about. Your reasoning is completely irrational because there's no way he could work for Jaime Berger and I wouldn't find out, eventually. Which is exactly what's happened."

She started flipping through the police report because she didn't want to look at him. She felt someone behind her before the person spoke, and turned around, startled by the man in Benton's doorway.

In his baggy gang clothing, thick gold chains, his hair in cornrows, he looked as if he'd just escaped from the prison ward.

"Kay, you and Detective Morales haven't met, I don't think," Benton said, and he wasn't particularly friendly about it.

"I bet you don't remember, but we almost met once," Morales said as he brazenly walked in and looked her over.

"I'm sorry." Meaning she didn't remember, and she didn't offer to shake his hand.

"Last Labor Day weekend. In the morgue," he said.

He had an unsettling energy that made her edgy and uncomfortable, and she imagined that whatever he did was thought out quickly and done in a hurry, and that it was his nature to dominate whatever he touched.

"A couple of tables away from where you were busy looking at that guy found in the East River, floating off the shore of Ward's Island?" he said. "I can tell you don't remember me. Question was whether he was tired of life and jumped off the footbridge, or someone hastened his journey to the Great Beyond, or maybe he'd had a heart attack and fell off the embankment. One of Pester Lester's cases. Turns out, she failed to connect the dots—didn't recognize the telltale fern-like pattern on his torso was—guess what? Arborization from being struck by lightning, which she had ruled out because she didn't find any burns in his socks, the bottom of his shoes, shit like that. You used a compass to show his belt buckle was magnetized, which is typical in lightning strikes, right? Anyway, you wouldn't remember me. Was in and out, grabbing a couple bullets that needed to go to the labs."

He pulled an evidence form out of the back pocket of his half-mast voluminous jeans, unfolded it, and started filling it out, leaning over the desk, so close to her his elbow brushed against her shoulder as he wrote, obliging her to move her chair. He handed her the form and the pen, and she filled out the rest and signed it. Then he took the envelopes of Oscar Bane's evidence and left.

"Needless to say," Benton remarked, "Berger's got her hands full with him."

"He's in her squad?"

"No, that might make it easier. Then maybe she could control him, at least a little," Benton said. "He's rather ubiquitous. Whenever a case is high-profile, he somehow manages to show up. Such as the lightning death he mentioned. And by the way, he probably won't forgive you for not remembering him, which is why he had to point it out three times."

13

Benton leaned back in his fake leather chair and was quiet as Scarpetta scanned paperwork on the other side of the small scarred desk.

He loved the straight bridge of her nose, the strong lines of her jaw and cheekbones, and the deliberate but graceful way she moved when she did the slightest thing, such as turning a page. In his mind, she looked no different than the first time they'd met, when she'd appeared in the doorway of her conference room, her blond hair out of place, no makeup on, the pockets of her long white lab coat filled with pens, tissues, pink telephone slips for calls she had no time to return but somehow would.

He'd recognized on the spot that for all of her strength and seriousness, she was thoughtful and kind. He'd seen it in her eyes during that first encounter, and he saw it in them now, even when she was preoccupied, even when he had hurt her yet again. He couldn't imagine not having her, and felt a pang of hatred pierce him, hatred of Marino. What Benton had immersed himself in all of his adult life was now inside his home. Marino had let the enemy in, and Benton didn't know how to make it leave.

"What time did the police arrive at the scene? And why are you staring at me?" Scarpetta asked without looking up at him.

"About quarter past six. I messed things up. Please don't be angry with me."

"Notified how?" She turned a page.

"Nine-one-one. He claims he found Terri's body around five, but he didn't call nine-one-one until six. Nine minutes past six, to be exact. The police were there within minutes. About five minutes."

When she didn't answer him, he picked up a paper clip, started unbending it. He didn't used to fidget.

"They found the outer door locked," he said. "There are three other apartments in the building, no one home, no doorman. The police couldn't get into the building, but her apartment's on the ground floor, so they went around to the back, to the windows, and through a gap in the curtains they saw Oscar in the bathroom, cradling a woman's body. She was covered by a blue towel. He was crying hysterically, holding her, stroking her. The cops rapped on the glass until they got his attention and he let them in."

He was talking in choppy sentences, his brain sluggish and slightly disorganized, probably because he was extremely stressed. He worked on the paper clip. He watched her.

After a lengthy silence, she looked up at him and said, "Then what? Did he talk to them?"

She's comparing notes, he thought. *Wants to line up what I know with what Oscar said to her. She's being clinical, impersonal, because she's not going to forgive me,* he thought.

"I'm sorry. Please don't be angry with me," he said.

She held his gaze and said, "I'm wondering why she had nothing on but a bra and a robe. If a stranger was at her door, would she answer it like that?"

"We can't work through it now." Benton meant their relationship, not the case. "Can we put it on a shelf?"

It was the way they phrased it when private matters presented themselves in the wrong place, at the wrong time. Her lingering gaze and the way her eyes turned a deeper shade of blue told him she would. She would put it on a shelf for now because she loved him, even if he didn't deserve it.

"It's a good question. The way she might have been dressed when she answered the door," he said. "I have a few observations, when we get to that part."

"What exactly did Oscar do when the police were inside the apartment with him?" she asked.

"He was sobbing, knees buckling, yelling. So insistent on returning to the bathroom that two officers had to hold on to him while they tried to get him to talk. He said he cut off the flex-cuff. It was on the bathroom floor near a pair of scissors he said he'd removed from the cutlery block in the kitchen."

"Did he call it a flex-cuff at the scene? Or is that what

the police called it? Where did the term *flex-cuff* come from? It's important we know who said it first."

"Don't know."

"Well, someone knows."

Benton bent the paper clip into a figure-eight as what they'd placed on the shelf kept falling off. At some point they would talk, but talking didn't fix broken trust any more than it fixes broken bones. Lies and more lies. The necessary axis of his life was lies, all well intended or professionally and legally necessary, which was why, in fact, Marino was a threat. The foundation of Marino's relationship with her had never been lies. When he forced himself on her, he wasn't showing contempt or hate or trying to humiliate. Marino was taking what he wanted when she wouldn't give it, because it was the only way he could kill an unrequited love he could no longer survive. His betrayal of her was actually one of the most honest things he'd ever done.

"And we don't know what's become of the ligature she was strangled with," Benton said. "It appears the killer removed it from her neck after she was dead and left with it. Police suspect it was another flex-cuff."

"Based on?"

"Would be unusual to bring two different types of ligatures to the scene," Benton said.

He worked the straightened paper clip back and forth until it broke.

"And of course it's assumed the killer brought the flex-cuff—or cuffs—with him. Not exactly the sort of thing most people have lying around the house."

"Why remove the flex-cuff from her neck and leave with it, and not bother with the one around her wrists? If that's what happened," she said.

"We don't know this person's mind. Not much to go on except circumstances. I suspect it comes as no surprise to you they think Oscar did it."

"Based on?"

"Either the killer had a key or she must have let him in, and as you pointed out, she was wearing a bathrobe, not much else. So let's talk about that. Why was she so comfortable, so trusting? How did she know who was buzzing the outer door? There's no camera, no intercom. The implication, in my opinion, is she was expecting someone. She unlocked the outer door after dark when the building was empty, then she unlocked her apartment door. Or someone did. Violent offenders love holidays. Lots of symbolism, and nobody's around. If Oscar killed her, last night was an ideal time to do it and stage it as something else."

"That's what the police believe happened, I assume you're saying."

She's making comparisons again, Benton thought. *What does she know?*

"To them it makes the most sense," he replied.

"When the police arrived, was her apartment door locked or unlocked?"

"Locked. Oscar locked the apartment door at some point after he was inside. What's a little peculiar is after he called nine-one-one, he didn't unlock the apartment building's outer door, maybe prop it open. And he didn't unlock the apartment door. I don't know how he thought the police would get in."

"I don't find that peculiar in the least. No matter what he did or didn't do, he probably was afraid."

"Of what?"

"If he didn't kill her, he was likely afraid the killer might come back."

"How would the killer get back into the building? If he didn't have a key?"

"People don't always think about every detail when they're afraid. Your first impulse when you're afraid is to lock the doors."

She's checking out Oscar's story. He must have told her he locked Terri's apartment door because he was afraid.

"What did he say when he called nine-one-one?" she asked.

"I'll let you listen for yourself," Benton said.

The CD was already in his computer, and he opened an audio file and turned up the volume:

911 OPERATOR: "Nine-one-one, what is your emergency?"

OSCAR (hysterical): "Yes! Police . . . ! My girl-friend . . . !"

911 OPERATOR: "What's the problem, sir?"

OSCAR (almost inaudible): "My girlfriend . . . when I walked in . . . !"

911 OPERATOR: "Sir, what's the problem?"

OSCAR (screaming): "She's dead! She's dead! Someone killed her! Someone strangled her!"

911 OPERATOR: "She was strangled?"

OSCAR: "Yes!"

911 OPERATOR: "Do you know if the person who strangled her is still in the house?"

OSCAR (crying, almost inaudible): "No . . . She's dead . . . !"

911 OPERATOR: "We have units en route. Just stay where you are, okay?"

OSCAR (crying, unintelligible): "They . . ."

911 OPERATOR: "They? Is someone with you?"

OSCAR: "No . . ." (inaudible)

911 OPERATOR: "Stay on the line. The police are almost there. What happened?"

OSCAR: "I got here and she was on the floor . . ." (unintelligible)

Benton closed the file and said, "Then he hung up and wouldn't answer when the operator called him back. If he'd stayed on the line, it would have been easier and quicker for the police to get inside the apartment. Instead of them having to go around back and bang on the window."

"He sounded genuinely terrified and hysterical," Scarpetta said.

"So did Lyle Menendez when he called nine-one-one to report his parents had been murdered. And we know how that story ended."

"Just because the Menendez brothers—" she started to say.

"I know. I know it doesn't mean Oscar killed Terri Bridges. But we don't know he didn't," Benton said.

"And your explanation for why he said *they*? As if implying more than one person killed her?" Scarpetta asked.

"His paranoia, obviously," Benton said. "Which I do think he genuinely feels. But that isn't necessarily to his advantage in terms of how the police view it. Paranoid people commit murder because of their paranoid delusions."

"And that's what you're really thinking?" Scarpetta said. "That basically this is a domestic homicide?"

She doesn't believe it, Benton thought. *She believes something else. What did Oscar say to her?*

He answered, "I can understand why the police think it. But I'd like some real evidence."

"What else do we know?"

"What he said."

"At the scene or when he was in the detective's car, Morales's car?"

"Oscar wasn't cooperative with him once they were out of the apartment," Benton said.

He tossed the bits of paper clip into his wastepaper basket, and they binked against empty metal.

"By that point," Benton said, "all he wanted was to go to Bellevue. Said he wouldn't talk unless it was to me. Then he demanded that you come here. And here we are."

He started on another paper clip. She watched him work on it.

"What did he tell the police while he was still inside the apartment?" she asked.

"Said when he arrived at the building, all the lights were out. He unlocked the outer door. Then he rang her apartment bell, and the door swung open and he was attacked by an intruder. Who quickly fled. Oscar locked the front door, turned on the lights, looked around, and found her body in the bathroom. He said there was no ligature around her neck, but he saw a reddish mark."

"And he knew she was dead, yet waited to call the police. Because? What was his reason, in your opinion?" Scarpetta asked.

"He had no concept of time. He was beside himself. Who knows what's true? But no probable cause for arrest. Doesn't mean the cops weren't more than happy to grant his request and lock him up. Doesn't help he's a muscle-bound dwarf who for the most part lives and works in cyberspace."

"You know about his profession. What else?"

"We know everything about him except what he chooses not to tell us. How about you?" Maiming the paper clip. "Any thoughts?"

"I can speak theoretically."

He gave her silence so she would fill it.

"I've had numerous cases when the police weren't called right away," she said. "When the killer needed time to stage the crime scene to look like something else. Or whoever found the body attempted to cover up what really happened. Embarrassment, shame, life insurance. Asphyxiophilia, for example—sexual hanging that turns

tragic and the person dies of asphyxiation. Usually accidental. Mother walks in, sees her son in black leather,
a mask, chains, nipple clips. Maybe cross-dressing. He's
hanging from a rafter, pornography everywhere. She
doesn't want the world to remember her son like that
and doesn't call for help until she's gotten rid of the
evidence."

"Another theory?"

"The person's so bereft, so unwilling to let his loved
one go, he spends time with the body, stroking it, holding it, covering it if it's nude, removing restraints. Restor-
ing his person to the way she was, as if somehow that will
bring her back."

"Rather much what he did, isn't it," Benton said.

"I had a case where the husband found his wife dead
in bed, an overdose. He climbed in next to her, held her,
didn't call the police until rigor was fully developed and
she was cold."

Benton looked at her for a long moment and said,
"Remorse in domestic cases. Husband kills wife. Child
kills mother. Overwhelming remorse, grief, panic.
Doesn't call the police right away. Holds the body, strokes
it, talks to it, cries. Something precious that's broken and
can't be fixed. Forever changed, forever gone."

"A type of behavior more typical with impulse
crimes," she said. "Not premeditated ones. This murder doesn't seem impulsive. When an offender brings
his own weapon, his own bindings, like duct tape or
flex-cuffs, that's premeditated."

Benton accidentally poked his fingertip with the

twisted paper clip and watched a bead of blood form. He sucked the blood away.

She said, "No first-aid kit in my crime scene case, which probably isn't very smart, now that I think of it. We should clean that up, find a Band-Aid. . . ."

"Kay, I don't want you in the middle of this."

"You're the one who put me in the middle of it. Or at least permitted it." She stared at his finger. "It would be good if you let it bleed as much as possible. I don't like puncture wounds. They're worse than cuts."

"I didn't mean to put you in the middle of it, wasn't my choice."

He started to say he didn't make choices for her, but that would be another lie. She reached across the desk and handed him several tissues.

"I hate it," he said. "Always hate it when you're in my world, not yours. A dead body doesn't get attached to you, have feelings for you. You don't have a relationship with someone dead. We're not robots. A guy tortures someone to death, and I sit across a table from him. He's a person, a human being. He's my patient. He thinks I'm his best friend until he hears me testify in court that he knew the difference between right and wrong. He ends up in prison for the rest of his life or, depending on the jurisdiction, on death row. Doesn't matter what I think or believe in. I'm doing my job. I've done what's right in the eyes of the law. Knowing that doesn't make me feel any less haunted."

"We don't know what it is not to feel haunted," she said.

He squeezed his finger, staining the tissue brilliant red. He looked at her on the other side of his desk, at the squareness of her shoulders, at her strong, capable hands, and the lovely contour of her body beneath her suit, and he wanted her. He felt aroused just doors away from a prison, and yet when they were alone at home, he scarcely touched her. What had happened to him? It was as if he'd been in an accident and had been pieced back together wrong.

He said, "You should go back to Massachusetts, Kay. If he gets indicted and you're subpoenaed, then you'll come back and we'll deal with it."

"I'm not going to run from Marino," she said. "I'm not going to avoid him."

"That's not what I'm saying." But it was exactly what he was saying. "It's Oscar Bane I'm worried about. He could walk out of Bellevue right now. I'd like you as far away from him as possible."

"What you want is for me to be as far away from Marino as possible."

"I don't know why you'd want to be around him." His feelings went flat, his voice hard.

"I didn't say I wanted it. I said I wasn't going to run from it. I'm not the one who ran like a coward. He did."

"Hopefully my part in this will be over in a few days," Benton said. "Then it's NYPD's responsibility. God knows I'm way behind at McLean. Only halfway through my research study, although I'm not sure about the journal article anymore. You don't have to do the consultation at the damn morgue. Why should you pull Dr. Lester's feet out of the fire again?"

"That's not what you really want. For me to be a no-show? For me to walk off the job after Berger's asked me to help? The last shuttle's at nine o'clock. I'd never make it. You know that. Why are you talking like this?"

"Lucy could take you in her helicopter."

"It's snowing at home. The visibility's probably two feet."

She watched his face, and it was hard for him to keep his feelings out of his eyes, because he wanted her. He wanted her now, in his office, and if she knew what he was feeling, she would be repulsed by him. She would decide he'd spent too many years wallowing through every form of perversion imaginable, and had finally been infected.

"I keep forgetting the weather's different there," he said.

"I'm not going anywhere."

"Then that's the way it will be. You certainly packed as if you aren't going anywhere."

Her luggage was by the door.

"Food," she said. "As much as you'd love to take me out for a romantic dinner tonight, we're eating in. If we ever get home."

They looked into each other's eyes. She had just asked him the question she'd been wanting to ask but hadn't.

He answered her, "My feelings about you haven't changed. If you knew how I felt sometimes. I just don't tell you."

"Maybe you'd better start telling me."

"I am telling you."

He wanted her right then, and she sensed it, and she didn't recoil. Maybe she felt the same way. It was so easy for him to forget there was a reason she was so polished and precise, that science was just the lead she looped around the neck of the wild animal so she could walk with it, so she could understand it and handle it. What she'd chosen to expose herself to in life couldn't be more naked or primitive or powerful, and nothing shocked her.

"I believe a very important element in this case is why Terri Bridges was murdered in the bathroom," she said. "And what makes us so sure she was?"

"The police found no evidence she was killed in any other area of the house. Nothing to suggest her body was moved into the bathroom after the fact. What food?"

"What we were going to have last night. When you say nothing suggests her body was moved, what does that mean? What might have suggested it?"

"I only know that Morales says nothing suggested it."

"And likely nothing would in this case," Scarpetta said. "If she'd been dead less than two hours, her body wasn't going to tell anybody much of anything. Livor, rigor usually take at least six hours to be fully developed. Was she warm?"

"He said when he got there, he felt for a pulse. She was warm."

"Then if Oscar didn't kill her, whoever did must have left her apartment shortly before he got there and found her dead. Coincidence, amazing good luck for the killer that he wasn't interrupted. He was just minutes away from Oscar walking in on him. Assuming the killer and Oscar aren't one and the same."

"If they aren't," Benton said, "you have to wonder why someone else would assume Terri would be home alone on New Year's Eve. Unless it was random. Her lights were on in an otherwise dark building, and this time of year, most people who are home have their lights on all day, or at least by four, when the sun is going down. Question is whether she was a victim of opportunity."

"What about an alibi? Oscar have one that you know of?"

"He have one that you know of?"

She watched him squeeze as much blood from his finger as he could.

"I'm trying to remember the last time you had a tetanus shot," she said.

14

It hadn't been difficult searching the NYPD's Real Time Crime Center and finding the two cases Morales had mentioned. What took a little longer was getting a response from the investigators who had worked them.

Marino was unbuttoning his coat inside his apartment when his cell phone rang at six-twenty. The woman identified herself as Bacardi, like the rum he used to drink mixed with Dr Pepper. He called her back on his landline and gave her a synopsis of the Terri Bridges case, asking if she'd ever heard of Oscar Bane, or if someone fitting his description had been spotted in the area when the homicide in Baltimore had occurred in the summer of 2003.

"Before we go galloping off together on some great big manhunt," Bacardi said, "what makes you think the cases are connected?"

"First, let's start with it wasn't my idea. This other detective's name is Mike Morales, and he got hits on our computer system. You know him?"

"Not off the top of my head. So you're not taking credit. Must be shit, what you got."

"Maybe, maybe not," Marino said. "There are similarities in the MOs between yours and mine. Same thing in the Greenwich case, which I assume you're aware of."

"Went over it until my eyes fell out. Broke up my marriage. He died of cancer last year. Not my ex-husband, the Greenwich investigator. Where are you from? You sound like a Jersey boy."

"Yeah, from the bad part. I'm sorry about the Greenwich detective. What kind?"

"Liver."

"If I still had one, that would be what gets me."

"Here one day, gone the next. Just like my ex and last two boyfriends."

Marino wondered how old she was and if she was making sure he knew she was single.

"The case here, Terri Bridges?" he said. "She had a gold bracelet on her left ankle. A thin gold chain. I saw it in the pictures. I haven't actually seen the body. I didn't go to the scene or the morgue."

"Real gold?"

"Like I said, I've only seen photographs, but on the report it says ten-karat. Must be stamped on the clasp. Don't know how else you'd know."

"Hon, I can tell just by looking at it. I can tell you anything you want to know about jewelry. Real, fake, good, bad, expensive, cheap. I used to work property crimes. Plus, I like stuff I can't afford and would rather have nothing than crap. You know what I mean?"

Marino was aware of his cheap knockoff Italian designer suit, made in China. He felt sure if he got rained on, he'd leave a trail of black dye-stained water, like a squid. He struggled out of the jacket and tossed it over the back of a chair. He yanked off his tie and couldn't wait to put on jeans, a sweater, and that old fleece-lined leather Harley jacket he'd had forever and had refused to hand over at the bazaar.

"Can you e-mail me a picture of the ankle bracelet Terri Bridges had on?" Bacardi asked him.

Her voice was melodic and happy, and she seemed interested in what she did and interested in him. Talking to her was waking him up in a way he hadn't felt in a very long while. Maybe it was because he'd forgotten how nice it was to be treated like an equal, or, more important, with the respect he deserved. What had changed in the last few years to make him feel so bad about himself?

Charleston had been an accident waiting to happen, and that was the fact of the matter. It wasn't about a so-called disease one poured out of a bottle. When he'd come to that realization, he and his therapist Nancy got into their biggest disagreement, an ugly argument. This was right before he'd finished his treatment program. She'd started it by saying that everything dysfunctional in his life was rooted in his alcoholism, and as drunks and junkies got older, they became exaggerated versions of themselves.

She'd even drawn a chart for him when they were alone in the chapel that sunny June afternoon, and all the windows were open, and he could smell the sea air and hear the gulls screaming as they swooped over the rocky coastline on the North Shore, where he ought to have been fishing or riding a motorcycle, or better yet, sitting with his feet propped up, drinking booze instead of blaming his life on it. Nancy had shown him in black and white how after he and beer had become "best friends" when he was twelve, his life had begun a slow deterioration peppered with traumas that she inked heavily and labeled:

Fighting
Poor Perf. in School
Isolation
Sexually Promix.
FX relationships
Risk/boxing/guns/police/motorcy.

Nancy had charted his fuckups for the better part of an hour, using abbreviations that required deciphering. What she basically demonstrated to him was that ever since his first beer, he'd been on an angry, dangerous path of aggression, sexual promiscuity, fractured friendships, divorce, and violence, and the older he got, the closer together his traumas were spaced, because that was the nature of the Disease. The Disease took you over, and as you got older, you physically couldn't resist its having its way with you, or something like that.

Then she had signed and dated his chart, and even drew a smiley face under her name, and handed the damn thing to him, all five pages, and he said, *What do you want me to do? Tape it on my fucking refrigerator?*

He'd gotten up from the pew and walked over to the window, and looked out at the ocean crashing against black granite, and spray shooting up and gulls screaming as if whales and birds were gathering and rioting right in front of him, trying to break him out of the joint.

Do you see what you just did? Nancy said to his back, from her pew, while he looked out at the most beautiful day he'd ever seen, wondering why he wasn't outside in the middle of it. *You just pushed me away, Pete. That's the alcohol talking.*

The hell it is, he replied. *I haven't had a fucking drink in a fucking month. That was me talking.*

Now as he talked to a woman he'd never met who had a name that made him happy, he realized he hadn't been doing all that badly, really, until he'd stopped being a real cop. When he'd finally left Richmond PD, and had gone to work as a private investigator for Lucy, and then as a death investigator for Scarpetta, he'd lost enforcement powers and all self-respect. He couldn't arrest anybody. He couldn't even have some asshole's car ticketed or towed. All he could do was muscle his way into situations and issue empty threats. He might as well have had his dick cut off. So what did he do last May? He had to show Scarpetta he still had a dick, because what he was really doing was proving it to himself and trying to take his life back. He wasn't saying what he'd done was right or should be excused. He'd never said that, and he sure as hell didn't think it.

"I'll get you whatever you need," he said to Bacardi.

"That'd be great."

He took perverse pleasure in imagining Morales's reaction. Marino was talking to the Baltimore homicide investigator, doing whatever he wanted.

Fuck Morales.

Marino was a sworn NYPD cop. More than that, he worked for the elite DA squad, and Morales didn't. What made that poor man's Puff Daddy in charge? Just because he was on duty last night and responded to the scene?

Marino said to Bacardi, "You sitting in front of your computer?"

"Home alone, Happy New Year. Fire away. You watch the ball drop in the Big Apple? Me? I ate popcorn and watched *The Little Rascals*. Don't laugh. I got the complete set of originals."

"When I was a kid, you could name something Buckwheat and not have Al Sharpton up your ass. I had a cat named Buckwheat. Guess what. She was white."

He opened a big envelope and pulled out his copies of the police and autopsy reports, and then opened the envelope of photographs, which he pushed around on the Formica countertop, covering a couple of cigarette burns and pot rings, until he found what he wanted. Cordless phone tucked under his chin, he inserted a photograph into the scanner attached to his laptop.

"You should know there's some political bullshit here," he said.

"You only got some?"

"Point being, just you and me need to be talking about this right now, and nobody else involved. So if anybody besides me gets in touch—I don't care if it's the NYPD police commissioner—I'd appreciate it if you'd not mention me, but let me know. And I'll handle it. Not everybody in the mix is—"

"You're telling me the grass is green and the sky is blue. No worries, Pete."

It felt good to hear her call him Pete. He went into his e-mail to attach the scanned photograph as an image.

"I get any calls," she said, "I'll let you know first and foremost. I'd appreciate the reciprocation. There are a lot of people running around who'd love the credit for solving my lady here in Baltimore and the kid in Greenwich. Did I mention how weird people are about getting credit? See, my theory? That's what led up to the mortgage crisis. Everybody wants credit. I'm not being a comedian."

"Especially if Morales calls," Marino added. "I'm surprised he hasn't. But then, he doesn't seem to be a follow-up kind of guy."

"Yup. What I call fuck and run. Shows up for the big moment, then disappears, lets everybody else clean up after him or finish what he started. Sort of like a deadbeat dad."

"You got kids?"

"Not in the house anymore, happy to report. They turned out pretty good, considering. I'm looking at the picture now. And nobody seems to know why the victim there, Terri Bridges, was wearing the bracelet?"

"That's the story. Her boyfriend, Oscar, said he'd never seen it before."

"A bracelet's not rocket science, but I'm not one of those who ignores circumstantial evidence," she said. "I guess you can tell I'm over forty and superstitious about putting my entire case in a lab coat pocket. All the young ones? Shit. It's *Forensic Let's Make a Deal*. Behind door number one is a videotape of someone raping and murdering a woman he's kidnapped. Behind door number two is DNA from a cigarette butt found at the driveway. Which do they choose?"

"Don't get me started."

"Yeah, you and me together. I tell them, you know what CSI stands for? It stands for Can't Stand It. Because when I hear that term or acronym or whatever the hell it is, I think to myself, I can't stand it. I really can't stand it. You tell me, Pete. When you was getting started, was there such a thing as a CSI?"

"TV invented it. They was crime scene techs in the real world. Or most times, people like you and me got out our fingerprint kit, camera, measuring tape, and all the rest, and did it our damn self. I didn't need a friggin' laser to map a crime scene and get all the dimensions right. Luminol works just as good as all these new chemicals and fancy crime scene lights. Been mixing up luminol in a spray bottle and using it all my life. I don't need the Jetsons to work a homicide."

"I won't go that far. A lot of the new stuff? So much better, there's no comparison. I can work a scene without totally trashing the place, if nothing else. You know, some old lady gets burglarized, and no more ruining everything she owns with black dusting powder. Technology at least lets me be considerate. But I don't have a magic box. You got one?"

"I keep forgetting to recharge it," he said.

"You ever come to Baltimore, Pete?"

"Hadn't heard that expression in a while," Marino said. "The case-in-a-lab-coat-pocket thing you said. So guess what? I'm over forty. You have some files landing. You checking your e-mail as we complain? You ever come to New York?"

He was scanning pages of the police report, and Dr. Lester's preliminary autopsy findings.

"It's not the way I started," Bacardi said. "I still believe in talking to people and looking at motive, the old-fashioned way. Sure, I come to New York. Or I can. No big deal. We should exchange yearbook pictures first. But I promise I look better since I had my face transplant."

Marino grabbed a Sharp's out of the refrigerator. He had to meet this one. She was something.

"I'm looking at the photograph of the bracelet right now. Jesus—money," Bacardi said. "It's the same as the others. All three of them ten-karat. A herringbone design, really thin. Based on the scale in this photo, it looks like your bracelet—just like the other two—is ten inches long. Sort of thing you'd buy in a mall kiosk or on the Internet for forty, fifty bucks. One interesting difference that strikes me right off the bat is in my case and Greenwich, the bodies weren't indoors. It appears the victims were out looking to score drugs for sex, and got picked up by someone cruising for an opportunity. Your victim—Terri Bridges—have a history of drug abuse or a secret life that might have left her open for that kind of thing happening to her?"

"No information to make me think she was into oxys or anything else. All I can tell you is what you're looking at. Her STAT alcohol was negative. Too early for drug screens, but no evidence of drugs at her apartment. We also don't know that in her case, the killer wasn't cruising for victims. Assuming the boyfriend didn't do it. Or even if he did, it was New Year's Eve. She was the only person home in her apartment building. Nobody directly across the street, either, except one lady who wasn't looking out her window about the time we suspect Terri was murdered. Supposedly. And this same lady had a couple stories that got my antenna going. Like this weird one about a puppy. Who would give a sick puppy to someone as a present? Knowing it's going to die."

"Ted Bundy."

"That's what I'm thinking."

"So maybe the guy's driving around, sees an opportunity last night," Bacardi said.

"I don't know," Marino said. "I need to get a better feel for the neighborhood, plan to go back out in a minute, prowling. But I can tell you already it was pretty deserted last night. That's New York. Weekends and holidays, and people who live here get the hell out of Dodge. And after all my years of doing this, one thing I've learned. There's never a formula. Maybe our guy was on good behavior and had a relapse. Maybe that guy is Oscar Bane. Maybe it's somebody else. There's the small problem of timing. Your two cases was five friggin' years ago."

"No figuring out why people do what they do. Or when. But *relapse* is a good word for it. I think serial killers have a compulsion just like drinking and drugging."

The refrigerator sucked open as Marino got another Sharp's.

"Maybe there's a reason it's under control for a while," her friendly voice said in his ear. "Then stress, a breakup, you get fired, get in financial trouble, and off the wagon you go."

"In other words, everything."

"Yeah. Everything can do it. I'm looking at what you just sent and right off I'm wondering why the ME's pended the case. This Dr. Lester isn't sure it's a homicide?"

"She and the DA don't get along."

"Sounds like you got a problem with the boyfriend, if there's no homicide."

"No shit," Marino said. "Kind of hard to charge someone with pending. But Berger's brought in another ME for a second opinion. Dr. Scarpetta."

"You're lying." Bacardi sounded like a fan.

Marino wished he hadn't brought up Scarpetta. Then he reasoned it wasn't right to withhold information, and having Scarpetta involved was important. Whenever she showed up, everything changed. Besides, if Bacardi was going to turn on him, now was a good time to do it and get it over with.

He said, "She's all over the Internet at the moment. Not in a good way. I'm only telling you because you're going to hear about it."

A long pause and Bacardi replied, "You're the guy who worked with her in Charleston. It was on the news here this morning. Heard it on the radio."

It had never occurred to Marino that Internet gossip might end up on the news, and he felt sucker-punched.

"No mention of names," Bacardi said, and she didn't sound as friendly. "Just that she was supposedly assaulted by a colleague while she was chief down there. An investigator she worked with for a long time. These shock jocks were talking about it, saying the expected bullshit, mostly making fun of her and getting off on imagining whatever was done to her. I was pretty disgusted."

"Maybe if you and me are ever sitting down face-to-face, I'll tell you the story," he surprised himself by saying.

He'd never told anybody the story, except Nancy. He'd told her as much as he could remember, and she'd listened with that sincere look on her face that started to annoy the living shit out of him after a while.

"You don't need to explain yourself to me," Bacardi said. "I don't know you, Pete. What I do know is people say all kinds of things, and you don't know what's true until you decide to make it your mission. It's not my mission to know what's true about your life, okay? Just what's true about what happened to my lady, the kid in Greenwich, and now your lady in New York. I'll send you my files electronically, what I've got, anyway. You ever want to dig through all of it, you'll need a week locked up in a room with a case of Advil."

"I'm told there's no DNA in your case and the kid," Marino said. "No sign of sexual assault."

"That's what's called the nightmare of multiple choice."

"Maybe we'll have some crab cakes in Baltimore, and I'll tell you," he said. "Don't draw conclusions from gossip. Or when you come here. You like steak houses?"

She didn't answer.

It was as if someone had tethered his emotions to a cinder block, he felt so depressed. He was ruined. That *Gotham Gotcha* asshole had ruined him. He meets a nice woman named after his favorite rum, and now she's acting as if he's got smallpox and spits when he talks.

"These VICAP forms, shit like that?" Bacardi said. "Check the boxes, multiple choice like school when there's more than one answer? Literally, no sign of sexual assault, except in both cases there was evidence of a lube job. Some Vaseline-type stuff that was negative for sperm. Vaginally in my lady. Anally in the Greenwich boy. A mixture of DNA, contaminated as hell. No hits in CODIS. We figure since they were found nude and dumped outdoors, all kinds of contaminants stuck to the petroleum jelly or whatever it was. Imagine how many people's DNA would be in a Dumpster? Plus dog hairs, cat fur."

"Kind of interesting," Marino said. "Because the DNA's messed up in this case, too. We got a hit on an old lady in a wheelchair who ran over some kid in Palm Beach."

"She ran him over in her wheelchair? She was speeding, busted a red light in her wheelchair? I'm sorry. Did somebody put in a different movie and not tell me?"

"What's also interesting," Marino said, walking toward the bathroom with the cordless phone, "the DNA from your cases are in CODIS. And the DNA from our case was just run in CODIS. So guess what that means?"

He covered the mouthpiece with his hand while he peed.

"I'm still hung up on the wheelchair," Bacardi said.

"What it means," he said, when it was safe to talk again, "is there's a different mixture of DNA profiles. In other words, you didn't get a hit on the old lady from Palm Beach, because her DNA wasn't on your victims. For whatever reason. I think you should come up here and sit down with everyone. As soon as possible, like tomorrow morning," Marino said. "You got a car?"

"Whenever you guys need. I can be there in a few hours."

"It's my belief," Marino said, "when things are this different, they got something in common."

15

"Nobody's accusing anybody of anything," Benton said on the phone, talking to Scarpetta's administrative assistant, Bryce. "I was just wondering when you looked at it first thing, what might have entered your mind . . . Really . . . That's a very good point . . . Well, that's interesting. I'll tell her."

He hung up.

Scarpetta was only halfway paying attention to whatever he and Bryce had been discussing. She was far more interested in several photographs of Terri Bridges's master bathroom, and had placed them in a row on a space she'd cleared on Benton's desk. They showed a spotless white ceramic-tile floor and a white marble countertop. Next to a sink with ornate gold fixtures was a built-in vanity arranged with perfumes, a brush, and a comb.

Attached to the rose-painted wall was a gold-framed oval mirror, and it was askew, but so slightly it was barely perceptible. As far as she could tell, it was the only thing in the bathroom that looked even remotely disturbed.

"Your hair," Benton said to her as his printer woke up.

"What about it?"

"I'll show you."

Another close-up of the body, this one taken from a different angle after the towel had been removed. Terri's achondroplastic features were more typical than Oscar's. She had a somewhat flattened nose and pronounced forehead, and her arms and legs were thick and about half the length they ought to be, her fingers thick and stubby.

Benton swiveled around and removed a sheet of paper from the printer, and handed it to her.

"Do I have to look at that again?" she said.

It was the photograph from this morning's *Gotham Gotcha* column.

"Bryce said for you to take a good look at your hair," Benton said.

"It's covered," she said. "All I can see is a little fringe of it."

"His point. It used to be shorter. He showed the photo to Fielding, who shares his opinion."

She ran her fingers through her hair, realizing what Bryce and Fielding meant. Over the past year, she'd let her hair grow out another inch.

"You're right," she said. "Bryce—Mr. Hygiene—is always nagging me about it. It's that in-between length where I can't completely cover it, and yet it's not long enough to tuck in. So there's always a little fringe of it exposed."

"He and Fielding both say the same thing," Benton said. "This photograph was taken recently. As recently as the past six months, because both of them believe this was taken since they started working for you. They're basing this on the length of your hair, the watch you're wearing, and the face shield is the same type you use."

"It's just a face shield. Not like our fancy safety glasses with different neon-colored frames to cheer up the place."

"Anyway, I'm inclined to agree with them," Benton said.

"That says something. Because, obviously, if it was taken in Watertown, they're on the list of suspects. And they don't recall noticing anybody else taking it?"

"That's the difficulty," Benton said. "Everybody and their brother who's through your place, as I pointed out earlier, could have done it. You can tell from your demeanor, the expression on your face, that you had no idea it was being taken. A quick picture taken with a cell phone. That's my guess."

"It wasn't Marino, then," she said. "He's certainly not been within camera range."

"I suspect he hates having that column on the Internet even more than you do, Kay. It wouldn't make any sense to think Marino's behind this."

She looked through more photographs of Terri Bridges's body on the bathroom floor, perplexed by the thin gold chain around her left ankle. She handed a close-up to Benton.

"Oscar told the police he'd never seen it before," he said. "And since you don't seem to know where it came from, I'm going to conclude that either Oscar told you he knew nothing about it or he didn't mention it at all."

"Suffice it to say, I don't know anything about it," she said. "But it doesn't look like something she'd wear. For one thing, it doesn't fit. It's much too tight. Either she'd had the bracelet for a long time and had gained weight, or someone gave it to her without realizing or even caring what size she needed. I don't think she bought it for herself, in other words."

"So I'll make my sexist comment," Benton said. "A man is more likely to make a mistake like that than another woman. Had a woman bought this for her, she likely would be aware that Terri has thick ankles."

"Oscar knows all about dwarfism, of course," Scarpetta said. "He's extremely body-conscious. He's less likely to buy the wrong size because he's intimately familiar with her."

"That, and he denied having ever seen the bracelet before."

"If the person you were in love with would see you only once a week at a predetermined time and place of her choosing, what might enter your mind after a while?" Scarpetta said.

"She's seeing someone else," Benton said.

"Another question. If I'm asking about the bracelet, what does that imply?"

"Oscar never mentioned it to you."

"I suspect Oscar has a deep-seated fear that Terri was seeing someone," Scarpetta replied. "To consciously deal with that would be to inflict an injury he can't endure. I don't care how shocked he was when he discovered her body, if that's really what happened. He should have noticed the ankle bracelet. His not bringing it up says far more than if he had volunteered it, in my opinion."

"He fears it was a gift from someone else," Benton said. "Of interest to us, of course, is if she really was seeing someone else. Because that person could be her killer."

"Possibly."

"It could also be argued that Oscar killed her because he discovered she was seeing someone else," Benton said.

"Do you have any reason to think she was?" she asked.

"I'm going to accept that you don't know the answer, either. But if she was, and he gave her a piece of jewelry, why would she wear it when Oscar was coming over?"

"I suppose she could say she bought it herself. But I don't know why she'd wear it at all. It didn't fit."

She looked at another photograph of clothing in the tub, as if dropped there: pink bedroom slippers, and a pink robe slit open from the collar to the cuffs, and a red lacy bra, unhooked in front with the straps cut.

She leaned across the desk, handing the photograph to him.

"Most likely her wrists were already bound behind her back when the killer removed her robe, her bra," she said. "That would explain cutting the straps, cutting open the sleeves."

"Suggesting she was quickly subdued by her assailant," he said. "A blitz attack. She didn't see it coming. Whether it was after she opened her door, or after he was already inside her apartment. He bound her so he could control her. Then he dealt with getting her clothing off."

"He didn't need to cut her clothing off if his goal was to sexually assault her. All he had to do was open the front of her robe."

"To induce terror. Total domination. All consistent with a sadistic sexual homicide. Doesn't mean it wasn't Oscar. Doesn't mean it was."

"And the absence of her panties? Unless they're simply not mentioned in the report. Rather unusual to have a bra on under your robe, but no panties. I'm assuming they'll check the scissors for fibers to see if that's what was used to cut off her clothing. As for any fibers that might be on whatever Oscar was wearing? One would expect fibers from her body, from the towel, to have been transferred to him while he was sitting in there, holding her."

She found several photographs of kitchen scissors on the floor next to the toilet. Nearby was the flex-cuff, or disposable restraint, that had bound her wrists. It was severed through the loop. Something about it bothered her. She realized what it was, and she handed the photograph to Benton.

"Notice anything unusual?" she asked.

"Back in my early days with the FBI, we used handcuffs, not flex-cuffs. And needless to say, we would never use flex-cuffs on patients."

It was his way of admitting he wasn't an expert.

"This one's colorless, almost transparent," she said. "Every flex-cuff I've ever seen is black, yellow, or white."

"Just because you haven't seen it . . ."

"Of course. Doesn't necessarily mean anything."

"Possibly there are new versions of them and new companies making them all the time, especially since we've got a war going on. Cops, the military, carry them in clip cases on their belts, have dozens in their vehicles. Great for rapid application to multiple prisoners. Like most things these days, easy to get on the Internet."

"But extremely difficult to remove," Scarpetta said. "That's the point I'm about to make. You couldn't cut through flex-cuffs with kitchen scissors. Requires special cutters with compound leverage, like a Scarab."

"Why didn't Morales say anything?"

"Maybe he's never tried to cut through flex-cuffs with scissors," Scarpetta said. "Good chance a lot of cops haven't. First time I got in a body bound in flex-cuffs, it took a damn rib cutter to get them off. Now I keep a Scarab in the morgue. Homicides, deaths in custody, suicides with flex-cuffs around wrists, ankles, necks. Once you pull the strap through the locking block, there's no going back. So either the kitchen scissors were staged to make it appear they were used to cut off the flex-cuff, when in fact something else was used, or this colorless strap on the bathroom floor isn't a flex-cuff. Did the police find any other straps like this one in her house?"

Benton's hazel eyes watched her closely.

"You know as much or as little as I do," he said. "Whatever's in the report and evidence inventory. But clearly, any other straps would have been collected and documented unless Morales is the worst cop on the planet. So I think the answer's no. Which brings us back to premeditation. The killer brought flex-cuffs to the apartment. Maybe he used the same thing around her neck, maybe not."

"We can say *he* all we want," Scarpetta said. "But Terri Bridges was very small. It's possible a woman could have subdued her easily. For that matter, a kid could have, male or female."

"An unusual crime, if a female did it. But it could explain why Terri felt safe opening her door. Unless, once again, Oscar staged the scene to look like a sexual homicide, when in fact it's something else."

"The missing ligature," Scarpetta said. "That doesn't feel staged. It feels as if the killer took it for a reason."

"Maybe a souvenir," Benton said. "The ligature, an item of lingerie such as her panties. A mechanism for the actualization of violent fantasy after the fact. He winds back the tape, replays what he did, because it gives him sexual gratification. A type of behavior rarely associated with domestic homicides. Souvenirs usually indicate a sexual predator who objectifies his victim, a stranger or distant acquaintance. Not a boyfriend, a lover. Unless we're talking about staging." He made that point again. "Oscar's extremely bright. He's calculating and quick."

Calculating and quick enough to return to his car and toss in his coat, making sure his story about being attacked as he was entering her house, and his torn T-shirt and injuries, was plausible to the police. But when did Oscar do that, assuming it was true? Scarpetta guessed it was after he raked his nails over his own flesh and struck himself with the flashlight, then realized it wasn't possible to explain the injuries if they were inflicted while he was wearing a coat.

"Souvenirs," Scarpetta said. "Maybe a killer who takes souvenirs and leaves one. If we consider the possibility that the ankle bracelet was put on the body by the killer, possibly after the murder. Like the silver rings in that case you had in California years ago. Four coeds, and in each homicide, the killer put a silver ring on the victim's wedding finger. But the symbolism of a silver ring strikes me as completely different from an ankle bracelet."

"One is possession—as in, with this ring, I make you mine," Benton said. "The other is control—as in, I'm putting a shackle around your ankle. I own you."

More photos: a table set for two. Candles, wineglasses, linen napkins in blue napkin rings, and dinner and bread plates and salad bowls. In the center of the table, a flower arrangement. Great attention to details, everything perfectly appointed, perfectly matched, and centered and straight but lacking in imagination and warmth.

"She was obsessive," Scarpetta observed. "A perfectionist. But she went to trouble for him. I think Oscar mattered to her. Was there music playing when the police arrived?"

"Nothing in the report."

"The television on? There's one in the living room, but it's off in the photograph. Any hint as to what she might have been doing when someone arrived at her door? Other than cooking at some point during the afternoon?"

"What you see in the photos, what's in the reports, is pretty much all we know." He paused. "Because you're the only one Oscar would really talk to."

She scanned the report out loud. "Oven set at two hundred, a whole chicken inside, suggesting it was cooked. She was just keeping it warm. Fresh spinach in a pot, hadn't been cooked yet. Stove off."

Another photo: a black plastic flashlight on the carpet near the front door.

Another photo: clothing neatly laid out on a bed. A low-cut sweater, red. Looked like cashmere. Red pants. Looked like silk. Shoes? No sign of them. No sign of her panties.

Another photo: no sign of makeup on Terri's suffused face.

Scarpetta reconstructed: Terri was going to dress festively and provocatively in bright red that was soft to the touch. She had on a sexy bra, a not-so-sexy robe and slippers, perhaps waiting until shortly before Oscar arrived to put on makeup and finish getting dressed, alluringly, in red. Where were her shoes? Maybe she didn't always wear them indoors, especially in her own apartment. Where were her panties? Some women don't wear panties. Maybe she was one of them. But if so, Scarpetta found that inconsistent with what Oscar had told her about Terri's obsession with cleanliness, with "germs."

"Do we know if she had a habit of not wearing panties?" she asked Benton.

"Got no idea."

"And shoes. Where are they? She'd gone to so much trouble to pick out what she was going to wear, but no shoes? Three possibilities. She hadn't picked them out yet. The killer took them. Or she didn't wear shoes in the house. And that's curious and a little hard for me to accept. Someone obsessive-compulsive about neatness, cleanliness, isn't likely to walk around barefoot. And when she was in her robe, she had on slippers. Wasn't barefoot then. Someone obsessive-compulsive about dirt and bacteria is likely to wear panties."

"I wasn't aware she was obsessive-compulsive," Benton said.

Scarpetta realized she'd revealed something she shouldn't have.

"Oscar didn't talk about her when I evaluated him, as you know." Benton wasn't going to let go of her indiscretion. "I didn't pick up on anything that might indicate Terri was obsessive-compulsive, or overly vigilant about cleanliness, neatness. Beyond what you see in the photos. And yes, you can tell she's very organized and tidy. That's been suggested, but not to the degree of a compulsion. So if she wasn't likely to walk around bare-foot and without panties, we're back to the possibility of a killer who took souvenirs. That points away from Oscar. For him to remove those from the scene, then hurry back to be there when the police arrived, strikes me as far-fetched."

"I'm inclined to agree."

"You don't think Oscar did it, do you?" Benton said.

"I think the police had better not make the assumption that the killer is a, quote, deranged little person safely locked up here on the prison ward. That's what I think," she said.

"Oscar isn't crazy—not a nice word, but I'm using it. He doesn't have a personality disorder. Isn't socio-pathic, narcissistic, borderline. His SCID revealed an inclination toward anger and avoidance, and it appears something triggered paranoia and reinforced his feeling that he needs to disaffiliate himself from others. In sum-mary, he's afraid of something. He doesn't know who to trust."

Scarpetta thought of the CD Oscar claimed to have hidden in his library.

In Murray Hill, Marino walked along a dark, tree-lined street, looking through the eyes of a predator.

Terri Bridges's brownstone was tucked between a playground and a doctor's office, both closed last night. Across the street, on either side of her peculiar neighbor's two-story building, were a French bistro and a bakery, also closed last night. He had checked, had carefully researched the area, and had come to the same conclusion that Morales had: When Terri opened her door to her killer, there was no one watching.

Even if someone happened to walk past, the person probably had no idea what he was looking at when a lone figure climbed the steps and buzzed the front door, or opened it with a key. Marino suspected the truth of the matter was the perpetrator had stayed out of sight until he was sure no one was in the area, and that returned Marino's thoughts to Oscar Bane.

If his intention was to kill Terri last night, it didn't matter if he was spotted. He was her boyfriend. He was supposed to have dinner with her, or people would assume he was, and parking his Jeep Cherokee right out front was smart because that would be the normal thing to do if he had no violent intentions. After talking to Bacardi, there was no doubt about what type of crime Marino was dealing with. This was exactly what it appeared to be—a sexually motivated premeditated act committed by someone whose murder kit included bindings, a lubricant, and a ten-karat-gold ankle bracelet.

Either Oscar was innocent or he was going to be hard as hell to catch, because he had every reason to show up at Terri's house late yesterday afternoon. By all appearances, Terri was expecting him for dinner. By all appearances, she was expecting a romantic evening with him. The crime scene so far seemed virtually useless, because remnants of Oscar would be everywhere, including on

Terri's dead body. The perfect crime? Maybe, were it not for one oddball thing: Oscar's insistence, which predated Terri's death by a month, that he was being spied on, brainwashed, that his identity had been stolen.

Marino thought about Oscar's ranting and raving over the phone. Unless he was psychotic, why would he draw attention to himself like that if he were a serial killer who had already murdered at least two people?

Marino felt guilty and worried. What if he had listened to Oscar more carefully, maybe encouraged him to come to the DA's office and sit down with Berger? What if Marino had even halfway given him the benefit of the doubt? Would he still be walking down this dark sidewalk on this cold, windy night?

His ears were getting numb, his eyes watering, and he was furious with himself for drinking so many Sharp's. As Terri's building came into view, he noticed her apartment lights were on, the drapes drawn, and a marked car was parked in front. Marino imagined the cop sitting inside the apartment, securing the scene until Berger decided to release it. He imagined the poor guy bored out of his mind. What Marino wouldn't give to borrow the bathroom, but you don't borrow anything at a crime scene.

At the moment, the only public bathroom was the great outdoors. Marino kept his scan going, looking for a good spot as he walked closer to Terri's building. He noticed that the lanterns at either side of the entryway were on, and recalled from Morales's report that they had been off last night when the police had arrived shortly after six.

Marino thought of Oscar Bane again. It made no difference if anyone had seen him well enough to identify him later. He was Terri's boyfriend, had keys to her building, and he was expected. If the outside lights weren't on when he arrived, then why not? By five p.m., when he allegedly arrived, it would have been completely dark out.

Marino supposed it was possible that the lights had been on when he'd arrived, and for some reason, he'd turned them off as he'd entered the building.

Marino stopped half a block away from the brownstone, staring at the entrance on East 29th. He imagined himself the killer, imagined what it would have been like to approach Terri's apartment building. What would he have seen? What would he have felt? Yesterday had been cold and damp, and extremely windy with gusts up to twenty-five miles an hour, making it very unpleasant for people to be out walking, about as unpleasant as it was right now.

By three-thirty in the afternoon, the sun was below the buildings and trees, and the entryway would have been cast in shadows. It was unlikely the lanterns would have been on that early, whether they were on a timer or not. By mid-afternoon, anybody inside the apartment building probably would have had his lights on, making it obvious to a predator which tenant might be home.

Marino hurried to the playground. He was relieving himself against the dark front gate when he spotted a dark, bulky shape on the brownstone's flat roof. The shape was near the faint silhouette of the satellite dish, and then the shape moved. Zipping up his pants, he reached into his coat pocket for his gun and crept around to the west side of Terri's apartment. The fire escape was a narrow ladder, straight up, and much too small for Marino's hands and feet.

He was sure it would pull away from the building and send him plummeting backward to the earth. His heart pounded, and he was sweating profusely beneath his Harley jacket, his Glock forty-caliber pistol in hand as he climbed, one rung at a time, his knees shaking.

He never used to have a fear of heights but had developed one after leaving Charleston. Benton had said it was the result of depression and accompanying anxiety, and had recommended a new treatment that involved an antibiotic called D-cycloserine, just because it had worked on rats in a neuroscience research project. Marino's therapist, Nancy, said his problem was "an unconscious conflict," and he'd never determine the exact nature of that conflict unless he stayed sober.

Marino had no doubt about the source of his conflict. At this very moment, it was a goddamn narrow ladder bolted to a brownstone. He pulled himself onto the roof, and his heart lurched and he grunted in surprise as he found himself eye to eye with the barrel of a gun held by a dark figure lying on his belly in a sniper's position. For a moment, neither of them moved.

Then Mike Morales holstered his pistol as he sat up and whispered furiously, "You stupid fuck! What the hell are you doing?"

"What the hell are you doing?" Marino whispered back. "I thought you were a fucking serial killer."

He scooted on his butt until he was a safe distance from the roof's edge.

"You're lucky I didn't shoot your fucking head off," Marino added.

He tucked the Glock back into his coat pocket.

"We just had this conversation," Morales said. "You don't get to run around and not tell me what the hell you're doing. I'm going to get your ass fired. Berger's probably going to do it anyway."

His face was almost indistinguishable in the dark, and he wore dark, loose clothing. He looked like a homeless person or a drug dealer.

"I don't know how I'm going to get back down from here," Marino said. "You know how old that ladder is? Probably a hundred years old, that's how old. Back then when people were half the size they are now."

"What's the matter with you? You trying to prove something? Because the only thing you're proving is you ought to go work security in a fucking mall or something."

The rooftop was concrete, with a boxy HVAC and the satellite dish. In the building across the street where Marino had been earlier today, the only lighted windows were those of the second-floor neighbor's apartment, and the drapes were drawn across them. Across the street from the back of Terri's building, there were more people home, and two of them seemed to assume that nobody could see them. An older man was typing on a computer, clueless that he was being watched. One floor below him, a woman in green pajamas was sitting on her living room couch, gesturing as she talked on a cordless phone.

Morales was chewing out Marino for screwing up everything.

"The only thing I'm screwing up is you being a Peeping Tom," Marino retorted.

"I don't have to peep to see whatever I want, whenever I want," Morales replied. "Not saying I wouldn't look if there's something to look at."

He pointed at the dish antenna, angled up about sixty degrees and facing south of Texas where somewhere high in the night sky was a satellite that Marino couldn't envision.

"On the mounting foot's a wireless camera I just installed," Morales said. "In case Oscar shows up. Maybe tries to get back inside her apartment. You know, the old returning-to-the-scene-of-the-crime shit. Or if anybody decides to drop by, for that matter. I'm keeping an open mind. Maybe it's not Oscar. But my money's on him. My money's on him killing the other two."

Marino wasn't in the mood to relay his conversation with Bacardi. Even if he weren't on top of a roof and extremely unhappy about it, he wouldn't be in the mood.

"The officer securing her apartment know you're up here?" he asked.

"Shit, no. And you tell him, you'll find out what a

long way down it is, because I'll throw your ass off the roof. Quickest way to fuck up a surveillance is to tell other cops about it. Including you."

"Occur to you his marked unit's right in front like a billboard ad for the NYPD? Maybe you should have him move it, if you're hoping the killer will come sneaking back here."

"He's gonna move it. It was fucking stupid to park there to begin with."

"Usually the bigger worry is regular people and the media thinking they can poke around. But no marked car? Okay. There goes your deterrent. Have it your way. You got any idea why the entrance lights weren't on last night?" Marino said.

"I only know that they weren't. It's in my report."

"They're on now."

Gusts of wind hit them like invisible waves of a stormy surf, and Marino felt as if he was about to be washed off the roof. His hands were stiff, and he pulled his sleeves over them.

"Then my guess would be the killer turned them off last night," Morales said.

"Kind of a strange thing to do once he's already inside the building."

"Maybe he turned them off when he was leaving. So nobody would see him, in case someone was walking by, driving by."

"Then you're probably not talking about Oscar doing it. Since he never left."

"We don't know what he did. Maybe he was in and

out getting rid of shit. Like whatever was used around her neck. Where'd you park?" Morales asked.

"Couple streets away," Marino said. "Nobody saw me."

"Yeah, you're real subtle, bro. Sounded like a three-hundred-pound cat climbing up the side of the building. Too bad you didn't get here a little earlier," Morales said. "See that lady on the phone?"

He indicated the apartment where the woman in green pajamas was still on her couch, gesturing and talking.

"Amazing how many people don't pull down their shades," Morales said.

"That's probably the real reason you're up here," Marino said.

"The window to the left? Lights are off now, but maybe thirty minutes ago, blazing as bright as a movie premier, and there she was."

Marino stared at the dark window as if it would suddenly light up again and show him what he'd missed.

"Out of the shower, off came the towel. Nice tits, I mean real nice," Morales said. "Thought I would fall off the fucking roof. God, I love my job."

Marino would forgo seeing fifty naked women if it would spare him having to climb back down the ladder. Morales got to his feet, as comfortable up here as a pigeon, while Marino started scooting back toward the edge, his heart thudding again, and as he inched his way, he wondered what had gotten into him. All those years he flew on Lucy's helicopters and jets. He used to love glass elevators and expansion bridges. Now he hated climbing up a stepladder to change a lightbulb.

He watched Morales walk off in the direction of the satellite dish and got a weird feeling about him. Morales had gone to fancy schools. He was a doctor, or could be one, if he wanted. He was nice-looking, even if he went out of his way to make people think he was the leader of a street gang or some Latino gangster. He was one big contradiction, and it didn't make sense he would climb up here to install a camera, with a cop sitting two floors below, securing a homicide scene, and not say anything. What if the cop had heard him up here?

And Marino remembered what the neighbor had mentioned about a roof access, about seeing service people near the satellite dish. Maybe Morales hadn't climbed up the ladder. Maybe he'd gotten up here another way—an easy way—and was too much of an asshole to let Marino in on the secret.

Cold steel bit into his bare hands as he gripped the rungs and made his way down slowly. He didn't know he had reached the ground until he felt it beneath his shoes, and he leaned against the side of the brownstone for a moment to calm down and catch his breath. He walked to the entrance and stood at the bottom of the steps, looking up to see if Morales was watching. Marino couldn't see him.

Attached to his keys was a small tactical light, and he directed the powerful beam at the lanterns on either side of the brownstone's ivy-covered entrance. He checked the brick steps, the landing, then swept the beam over bushes and trash cans. He called the dispatcher and indicated he needed the officer inside Terri Bridges's apartment to go

to the building's front door and let him in. He waited
a minute, and the front door opened, and it wasn't the
same uniformed cop who had let him in earlier today.

"Having fun yet?" Marino asked, moving past him
into the foyer and shutting the door.

"It's starting to stink in there," the officer said, and he
looked all of sixteen. "Remind me never to eat chicken
again."

Marino found two light switches to the left of the
door. He tried them. One was for the outside lights, the
other for the foyer.

"You know if these are on a timer?" he asked.

"They're not."

"So how'd the entrance lights get on tonight?"

"I turned them on when I got here maybe two hours
ago. Why? You want 'em off?"

Marino looked at the dark wooden stairs leading up
to the second floor.

He said, "No, leave them on. You been up there?
Looks like the other residents aren't back."

"I haven't been anywhere. Stuck on my ass inside the
door." He nodded at the apartment door, which he'd left
open a crack. "Nobody's been inside the building. If it
was me, I'd sure take my time coming back, especially if I
was a woman living alone."

"No other women living alone," Marino said. "Just
the one whose apartment you're babysitting. This one
here." He indicated the door on the other side of the
foyer. "Two guys, both of them bartenders. Probably
never here at night. Upstairs? Right above Terri Bridges,

a guy who goes to Hunter College, supports himself walking dogs. The apartment on the other side, some Italian consultant with a British financial company that's the actual tenant. In other words, one of those corporate rentals. The guy's probably never here."

"Anybody talked to them?"

"Not me, but I've run their backgrounds. Nothing jumps out. I get the impression from talking to her parents that she wasn't the friendly type. She never talked about the other residents and didn't seem to know them or have any interest. But hey, this ain't the South. People don't bake cakes for their neighbors so they can stick their nose into their business. Don't mind me. I'm going to poke around up there for a few minutes."

"Just be careful because Investigator Morales is up on the roof."

Marino stopped on the bottom step and said, "What?"

"Yeah, he went up there maybe an hour ago."

"He tell you why?"

"I didn't ask."

"He tell you to move your car?"

"What for?"

"Ask him," Marino said. "He's the big investigator with all the big ideas."

He climbed the steps, and on the second floor, in the ceiling between the two apartments, was a stainless-steel access hatch with an inside T-handle. Under it was an aluminum stepladder with slip-resistant treads, a fold-up safety bar, and a work tray with several screwdrivers in it. Nearby, a utility closet door was wide open.

"Son of a bitch," he muttered.

He imagined Morales on the roof, laughing as he'd listened to Marino struggling down the fire escape, when all he'd had to do was direct him to the roof access. Marino could have climbed down five sturdy ladder steps inside a lighted building instead of thirty narrow rungs outside in the frigid dark.

Marino folded the ladder and returned it to the closet.

He was halfway back to his car when his cell phone rang. The display said *Unknown,* and he was sure it was Morales, pissed as hell.

"Yo," he answered cheerfully as he walked.

"Marino?" It was Jaime Berger. "I've been trying to get hold of Morales."

There was a lot of background noise, what sounded like traffic, and he knew when she was irritated.

"I just saw him," he said. "He's sort of unreachable this very minute."

"If you happen to talk to him, you might mention I've left three messages. I won't leave a fourth. Maybe you can take care of my problem. Eighteen passwords so far."

"For just her?" He meant Terri Bridges.

"All the same e-mail provider, but different usernames. For whatever reason. And her boyfriend's got one. I'm getting out of a taxi now."

Marino heard her driver say something, and then Berger did, and then the taxi door shut and he could hear her better.

"One second," he said. "Let me get to my car."

His unmarked dark blue Impala was parked just ahead.

"Where are you and what are you doing?" she said.

"Long story. Morales mention anything to you about a case in Baltimore and one in Greenwich, Connecticut?"

"I think I just made the point that I haven't talked to him."

He unlocked his driver's door and climbed in. He started the engine and opened the glove box, looking for a pen and something to write on.

"I'll e-mail some stuff to you, think I can do it from my BlackBerry," he said. "And Benton should get it."

Silence.

"If that's all right with you, I'll e-mail what I've got to him, too."

"Of course," she said.

"You don't mind me saying it, nobody's talking to each other. An example of what I mean? You got any idea if the cops looked upstairs in Terri's building last night? Like maybe checked the roof access and the ladder in the utility closet?"

"I have no idea."

"That's what I'm saying. Nothing in the report. No photographs," Marino said.

"That's interesting."

"The roof would have been an easy way to get in and out, and nobody sees you. There's a fire-escape ladder on the west side of the brownstone—like I said, nobody sees you."

"Morales should know the answer to that."

"Don't worry. I'm sure the subject will come up. And one other thing. We need Oscar's DNA run through

CODIS right away. Because of Baltimore and Greenwich. Have you gotten my e-mails?"

"Should already be in the works. I've asked for answers tonight. Yes, I've gotten your e-mails," Berger said. "Nice of Morales not to bother alerting me about two other possible cases."

"Meaning Oscar's in CODIS or will be soon," Marino said. "I'm sure Morales was going to get around to it."

"I'm sure," Berger said.

"I'll leave word about the DNA with the investigator in Baltimore I hooked up with," Marino said. "Not that I'm holding my breath we're going to get a hit with Oscar on those other two cases. I don't know. Something's not right about it. Doesn't work for me thinking he did those. And his girlfriend."

Marino always knew when Berger took somebody seriously. She didn't interrupt or change the topic of conversation. He kept talking because she kept listening, both of them careful about being too specific, since he was on a cell phone.

"These other two cases I've sent you info on?" Marino said. "The part I left out is what I was just told over the phone. They got junk DNA. A mixture of other people's DNA."

"Like we did in this one here?" Berger asked.

"I don't want to go into all this now for security reasons," Marino said. "But if you could maybe get a message to Benton. I know he's here. I know he's in the city. Morales says he is and that they're going to the morgue later. We can all keep hoping we don't bump into each other. I'm just going ahead and saying it. No point in running around the fat-ass elephant in the room."

"They're not at the morgue yet. Dr. Lester's been delayed."

"That's the only kind of laid she's ever been," Marino said.

Berger laughed.

"I'd say within the hour everyone will be there," she said, and her tone was entirely different.

As if she found him interesting and amusing, and maybe didn't hate him.

"Benton and Kay," she added.

She was letting Marino know, and in doing so, it was her way of saying she wasn't his enemy. No, it was better than that. She was telling him she might just trust and respect him.

"But it would be helpful if all of us got together," he said. "Have a case discussion. I asked the investigator from Baltimore to come. She should be here in the morning. She can be here whenever we want."

"That's fine," Berger said. "What I want right now is for you to get me the passwords and account histories associated with the usernames I'm about to give you. I've already faxed a letter instructing the provider to put a freeze on the accounts so they stay active. And one other thing. If anybody else calls for this info, they don't get it. You make that clear to whoever you talk to. I don't care if it's the White House, the passwords aren't to be given to anybody else. I'm on my cell."

She must be referring to Oscar Bane. Marino couldn't

imagine who else would know what Terri's and Oscar's usernames and e-mail providers were, and without them, one couldn't get the passwords. The car's interior light was off, and he left it off. An old habit. He used his flashlight to write down the usernames and other information she gave him.

Marino said, "Is Oscar still on the ward?"

"Obviously, that's one concern." She didn't sound as all-business as she usually did.

She sounded almost friendly, and maybe curious, as if she'd never given Marino much thought, and now she was.

"I don't think for much longer," she added. "And there are some other developments. I'll be at a forensic computer group called Connextions, which I have a feeling you're familiar with. Here's the number."

She gave it to him.

"I'll try to grab the phone before Lucy does," Berger said.

16

Jet Ranger was almost deaf and quite lame, and was seriously compromised in the potty department. Lucy's elderly bulldog was not a native New Yorker.

His dislike of concrete and asphalt posed a serious problem in a city where soulless people were known to sprinkle red pepper in sparse patches of dirt or grass that might surround an occasional tree. The first time Jet Ranger got a snootful when sniffing for just the right spot, Lucy figured out correctly that the shop nearest the puny maple was to blame, and handled the matter swiftly and without reprimand or explanation.

She'd walked in early the next morning, flung twenty ounces of crushed red pepper all over the shop, and in case the dumbstruck owner missed the point, dumped a generous dose in the urine-stinking back room on her way out the back door. Anonymously, she reported Save My Sole shoe repair to PETA.

She walked her slow, arthritic bulldog a good half-hour before success, and as a result was late. When she reached her building, a Baggie of poop in hand, Berger was silhouetted in the waving gaslight of lanterns against old brick and iron railings, waiting by the three steps that led up to Lucy's heavy oak front door.

"They make colorful ones in the little dispensaries," Berger's shadowy face said as it looked at the Baggie. "Ones that aren't transparent."

Lucy dropped Jet Ranger's job well done into a trash barrel.

She said, "Hope you haven't been waiting long. He's not a city boy. Must have had a real grass yard with a white picket fence in an earlier life. His name's Jet Ranger, as in the first helicopter I ever owned. Jet Ranger, meet Jaime. He doesn't know any tricks, like shaking hands or high-fives or hovering. He's pretty simple, aren't you, boy?"

Berger squatted to rub Jet Ranger's neck, not seeming to care that her long shorn mink coat spilled around her on the dirty sidewalk and she was blocking foot traffic. People detoured around her in the cold dark as she kissed the top of the bulldog's head, and he licked her chin.

"That's impressive," Lucy said. "He doesn't like most people. Funny thing about living with an asshole. I don't mean me. Whoever owned him before me. I'm sorry," she said to her dog, petting him and touching Berger's shoulder as she did. "I shouldn't openly discuss your painful and private past or use the word *owned*. That was rude of me. I don't really own him," she said to Berger. "In fact, I have to pay him a considerable sum to let me feed him, pet him, take him out, sleep with him."

"How old?" Berger asked.

"Not sure." Lucy massaged Jet Ranger's spotted ears. "Not long after I moved here, I was leaving the West Thirtieth heliport after flying in from Boston, and saw him trotting along the West Side Highway. You know that panicky look, when a dog's lost? He was limping."

Lucy covered Jet Ranger's ears so he wouldn't hear the rest.

"No collar," she said. "Obviously dumped out of a car, probably because he's old, got bad hips, half blind. You know, not fun anymore. They usually don't live past ten. He's probably pretty close."

"People suck," Berger said, getting up.

"Come on," Lucy said to her dog. "Don't be upset by Jaime's coat. I'm sure every one of those poor little minks died of natural causes."

"We should have the passwords soon," Berger said. "Maybe that will help explain the rest of it."

"I don't know what the rest of it is, since I barely know the first of it. We're just getting started," Lucy said. "But there's enough for me to be worried about my aunt. And I'm worried."

"I got that when you called."

Lucy inserted an interactive key into a Mul-T-Lock Mortise cylinder, and the alarm system began to beep as she opened the front door. She entered a code on the keypad and the beeping stopped, and she shut the door behind them.

"When you see what I'm talking about, your first impulse will be to fire me," Lucy said. "But you won't."

Shrew considered herself a crackerjack Web administrator, but she was no programmer. She was no information technology expert.

She sat at her computer, watching the *Gotham Gotcha* home page continue its maniacal loop while a technician from the Web hosting company told her over the phone that the problem was a buffer overflow. He explained that the number of users attempting to access certain information on the site had exceeded the server's enormous capacity and at this moment the situation was so out of control, millions of people per minute were clicking on a photograph in the dark room, and this, in the technician's opinion, could mean but one thing: "A worm," he said. "Or basically, a virus. But nothing I've ever seen. It's really more of a mutant worm."

"How could a worm, mutant or otherwise, have infiltrated the programming?" Shrew asked.

"It's likely that a remote unprivileged user somehow executed arbitrary code and exploited the buffer overflow vulnerabilities of the Web proxy server. Whoever did this is extremely sophisticated."

He went on to say that typically what happened was someone sent an attachment containing a worm that wasn't recognized by any virus-detection program known to the industry. This worm mimicked users opening an image that took up a lot of space, "such as a photograph," he said, adding that "this self-replicating worm mimics millions of people opening the same image at the same time, which causes the server to run out of memory, and in addition, it would appear that this worm is also performing the malicious action of destroying data. In other words, it's an odd mutation of a worm, a macro virus. And possibly a Trojan horse if, for example, it's also spreading the virus to other programs, which is what I fear."

He repeatedly emphasized that the saboteur was someone who really knew what he was doing, as if the technician was secretly envious of whoever was clever enough to create such destruction.

Shrew innocently asked which image was the culprit, and he replied unequivocally that the worm was launched by a photograph of Marilyn Monroe. As he continued to explain the havoc caused by the mutant worm, Shrew was imagining the conspiracy behind it. Whoever was involved in Marilyn Monroe's murder almost half a century ago still had a vested interest in the public's not knowing the truth.

That pointed at the government, which implied politics and organized crime. Maybe there were terrorists back then, she considered. Maybe these people were somehow connected and had their eye on Shrew, all because she'd been foolish enough to take a job she knew nothing about and served at the behest of anonymous people who might be criminals.

For all she knew, the technician on the phone was a criminal, a terrorist, or a government agent, and this business about the Marilyn Monroe photograph launching the mutant worm was an attempt to muddy the waters so Shrew didn't figure out what was really going on: The website had self-destructed like those tape recorders in *Mission: Impossible,* because without intending to, Shrew had inserted herself into the middle of a massive plot against a world power or an Evil Empire.

She felt extremely confused and overwhelmed by anxiety.

"You realize, I hope," she said to the alleged technician, "that I have no idea what's going on. I want no part of it, and never intended to be part of it. Not that I know anything. Because I certainly don't."

"It's complicated," he said. "Even for us. I'm trying to tell you this is a very sophisticated code someone's written. Has to be. By *code* I mean a computer program that's embedded in something that seems innocuous, such as a data file or an attachment."

She didn't care what he meant, and she didn't care that the mutant worm couldn't be stopped and that all attempts to shut down and restart the system had failed. She glazed over as the technician suggested they could attempt loading an archived earlier version of the *Gotham Gotcha* site, but his only other available servers didn't have much disk space and were much slower, and that also could cause a crash. Possibly, they should purchase a new server, but that couldn't happen instantly, and he'd have to clear it with the "business office," and in the UK it was five hours later than it was here, so he wasn't going to get anyone.

He pointed out that loading an earlier version would also mean Shrew would have to repopulate the website and repost all the latest information, and fans would need to be alerted that e-mails and images they had sent should be resent. The fixes required of Shrew would take days, maybe weeks, and the public was going to be angry, and those who most recently had joined the site wouldn't be in the older version of the database and would be deeply offended. The website could be down for days. It could be weeks.

When the Boss found out the worm had been launched by the Marilyn Monroe morgue photo, at the very least, Shrew would be out of work. She had no backup plan. It would be like a year and a half ago, only this time there would be no windfall from a job offer made by anonymous strangers. This time she really would have to give up the apartment, which was the same thing as giving up what little she had left of who she used to be. Only worse. Life for virtually all decent people had only gotten harder. She didn't know what on earth she would do.

She thanked the technician and got off the phone.

She checked to make sure all the blinds were closed, and poured herself another bourbon and gulped it down as she paced, half mad with fear, and near tears, as she thought about what likely would happen next.

The Boss wouldn't fire her directly but rather would have that UK agent who barely spoke English do it. If the Boss was really tied in with some terrorist sect, then

Shrew's life was in danger. An assassin could find his way inside her apartment while she slept, and she'd never hear him.

She needed a dog.

The more bourbon Shrew drank, the more depressed, scared, and lonely she got. She contemplated the column she'd posted several weeks before Christmas that mentioned the same chain of pet stores Terri had recommended after Ivy had died and she'd offered to pay for a replacement.

Shrew went on the Internet to check.

The Tell-Tail Hearts pet shops' flagship location happened to be the one nearest her, and it stayed open until nine.

The loft was an expansive open space of exposed beams and brick, and floors of polished tobacco wood, all pristinely restored and modernized. Other than work stations, black swivel chairs, and a glass conference room table, there was no furniture. There was no paper, not a single sheet of it.

Lucy had invited Berger to make herself at home. She had emphasized that Berger was safe and secure. All of the phones were wireless and equipped with scrambling devices, and the alarm system was probably better than the Pentagon's. Somewhere in here Lucy probably had guns and other lethal weapons that were illegal enough to hang her from the Tappan Zee Bridge like a pirate. Berger didn't ask, and she didn't feel safe or secure. Nor did she make an effort to change that. She simply fretted, reflected, and deliberated.

Annie Lennox was playing in the background, and Lucy was in her glass cockpit, surrounded by three video displays as large as most living room flat screens. In the soft light, her profile was well defined, her brow smooth, her nose aquiline, her face intense, as if there was nothing she'd rather do than navigate through what was already giving Berger a headache. A real one. The kind that always ended the same way, with her lying down in a dark room, holding hot compresses over her eyes.

She stood next to Lucy's chair, rifling through her briefcase, hoping a Zomig might be lurking somewhere, because that was the only medication that worked. The blister pack she found tucked between the pages of a legal pad was empty.

Lucy was explaining more than Berger really wanted to know about what the neural networking program was acquiring from one of the laptops found in Terri Bridges's apartment, and the technology involved. Berger was frustrated that Lucy refused to start on the second laptop—one that apparently had been solely dedicated to the Internet. She was anxious for Marino to call with the e-mail passwords. The question was whether she would still be here when he did. The bigger question was why she was here at all. A part of her knew, and she was unsettled by everything and nothing, and didn't know what to do. She and Lucy had a striking problem on their hands. They had more than one.

"Ordinarily, when you delete a file in an operating

system, you've got a good chance of getting the data back if the recovery is attempted quickly," Lucy was saying.

Berger sat back down next to her. Bright white bits and pieces of text, fractured sentences and words, reconnected in the blackness of electronic space. She thought about putting on her tinted sunglasses. She had a feeling it wouldn't help. This was going where it was going, and she wasn't going to stop it.

Had she sincerely intended to stop it, she wouldn't have taken a taxi to the Village tonight, no matter the crisis, the urgency, and the logic in what Lucy had told her over the phone, when she'd called to suggest Berger take a look at what was developing. She'd been alone with Lucy before, but that was years ago, when Scarpetta's astonishingly complicated and high-risk niece was too young and Berger had been too married. One thing she didn't do was violate contracts or lose cases because of technicalities.

She had no contract now, and Lucy was older, and the only technicality was whatever Berger decided to manufacture.

"But it doesn't appear Terri ever had a reason to recover anything she deleted," Lucy said, "which is why you're seeing some fairly large chunks of intact text mixed with fragments of all sizes, many so small they're nothing but shards. The longer one waits to recover deleted or corrupted data, the more opportunity for newly created data to occupy areas on the hard disk freed up by the deletions. And that makes it harder for the software to locate what was originally there."

What they were seeing, in summation, were bits

and pieces of a thesis that offered, in part, a historical perspective on forensic science and medicine, and psychiatry, which wasn't necessarily surprising. Records searches and information from Terri Bridges's parents indicated she was enrolled at Gotham College, where her father was the dean, and was working on a master's degree in forensic psychology. Berger watched forensic words and phrases stream by as the familiar pain heated up in her temples and crept toward the backs of her eyes.

She noted references to the Body Farm, and to Bellevue and Kirby psychiatric hospitals, and the names of numerous forensic experts well known in their fields, including Dr. Kay Scarpetta. Repeatedly, there were references to her, and that was why Lucy had made the comment earlier that Berger might be tempted to fire her. She was more than tempted. For a number of reasons, that would be the wisest course of action.

For one thing, it appeared that Terri—or whoever had been using this particular laptop—had collected hundreds of articles, video clips, photographs, and other published media pertaining to Scarpetta. That meant a conflict of interest, and a very serious one, which was further compounded by another problem that probably had been there from day one.

Berger remembered being startled by Lucy the first time they'd met eight years ago in Richmond, startled in a way Berger had found as exciting as it was, realistically speaking, unfortunate back then. Foolishly back then—when she was in her late thirties and had almost convinced herself she'd gotten beyond certain temptations, as evidenced by the life she had prescribed for herself. She could answer *no*. The fact was—and at age forty-six, she was quite clear about this—she wouldn't have needed to answer anything had there not been a question.

"The laptops are installed with what I call over-the-counter security software, the settings preprogrammed, preloaded." Lucy had wandered off on that subject. "Not something I'd use because it recognizes only known viruses, spyware, et cetera. And the known ones aren't the ones I worry about. She's got anti-virus, anti-spyware, anti-spam, anti-phishing, firewall, and wireless PC protection."

"Unusual?" Berger rubbed her temples.

"For your average user, yes. She was security-minded, or someone was. But not security-minded the way people like you or I would be. What she's got here is the type of protection I see with people who are worried about hacking, identity theft, but aren't real programmers and have to rely on prefab software, a lot of which is expensive and not necessarily what it's cracked up to be."

"It may be that she and Oscar Bane had paranoia in common," Berger said. "They feared someone was out to get them. We know he fears that, at any rate. He certainly made a case for it when he called last month and had a rather unfortunate conversation with Marino. Not really Marino's fault. Were the same scenario to happen all over again, I still wouldn't take Oscar Bane's call."

"I wonder if it would have changed anything had you taken it," Lucy said.

"On the surface it wasn't any different from all the other nutty calls we get every day," Berger said.

"It's still too bad. Maybe you could have made a difference."

Lucy's hands were strong but graceful on the keyboard. She closed a programming window she had opened on the screen, and once again the deep space was restored and fragmented text streamed through it, moving, finding its missing parts. Berger tried not to look.

"If I played the recording for you, you'd completely understand," she explained. "He sounds like a nutcase. Almost hysterical, and he goes on and on about somebody or a group of people taking over his mind electronically, and thus far he's resisted being controlled by them, but they know every breath he takes. At the moment, I feel somebody's doing the same thing to me. I apologize in advance. On rare occasions I get these headaches. I'm trying like hell not to get this one."

"You ever gotten cybersick?" Lucy asked.

"I'm not sure what that is," Berger said.

"What about motion sickness?"

"I do know what that is, and yes. I can't look at anything in a moving car, and as a kid I always threw up in amusement parks. And I don't want to think about it right now."

"Guess you won't be flying with me."

"Police helicopters don't bother me. As long as they don't take the doors off."

"Disoriented, nauseated, vertigo, even seizures and migraines," Lucy said. "Usually associated with virtual reality, but any computer display of motion can do it. Such as watching all this shit. I happen to be one of the lucky ones. Doesn't affect me. You can throw me into full-scale crash simulation all day long, and it doesn't bother me a bit. I could be a test dummy at Langley. It's probably what I should have done in life."

She leaned back in her chair and tucked the tips of her fingers into the front pockets of her jeans, her physical openness an invitation, somehow, and Berger's eyes were drawn to her the same way they were to a provocative painting or a sculpture.

"So here's what you're going to try," Lucy said. "You're going to look at the monitors only when I think you should see something. If you continue to feel bad, I'll spool off the data I want you to see, and you can look at it in static word-processing format. I'll even break my rule and print stuff. Anyway, don't look at the monitor. Let's go back to what I was saying about what software protections are loaded on the laptops. I was suggesting we should see if we find the same software loaded on Oscar's home computer. See if we find evidence he's the one who purchased it. Can we get into his apartment?"

Lucy continued to say *we*, and Berger didn't see how there could be a *we*.

It was completely reckless for there to be a *we*, Berger kept telling herself, kept trying to talk herself out of it, only to talk herself right back into it.

She shut her eyes and rubbed her temples and said, "It's easy to assume it was Terri who was researching Kay. But how do we know Oscar wasn't? Maybe these are his computers and he had them at Terri's apartment for some reason. And no, right now we can't get into his computer or computers. Whatever computers he has in his apartment. We don't have his consent, and we don't have probable cause."

"His fingerprints on these laptops?"

They were on a nearby desk, both of them connected to a server.

"Don't know yet," Berger replied. "But that wouldn't necessarily prove anything, since he was in and out of her apartment. Theoretically, we don't know whose work this is. But what's certain is Kay is a focus. You've made that point."

"She's more than a focus. Don't look, but what's happening right now? It's sorting by footnotes. Ibid. this and that, and dates. Footnotes that seem to correlate with quotations from my aunt."

"You're saying Terri interviewed her?"

"Someone did, supposedly. Keep your eyes shut. The computer doesn't need your help or approval. It's sorting by references, thousands of them in parentheses, from multiple drafts of the same thesis. And hundreds of these parenthetical references pertain to interviews conducted at different times. Alleged interviews with my aunt."

Berger opened her eyes and saw fragmented words and sentences streaming by and reattaching.

"Maybe they're transcripts of interviews on CNN or newspaper interviews," she suggested. "And you're right. Next time I'll ask. That just made me dizzy. I don't know what's wrong with me. I should leave."

"Can't be transcripts," Lucy replied. "Not all of them or even most. Chronologically, that can't be right. *Scarpetta, November tenth,* and *Scarpetta, November eleventh,* then the twelfth and thirteenth. No way. She didn't talk to her. Nobody talked to her. This is bullshit."

It was indescribably strange, looking at her looking at the monitors and bickering with her computer creation as if it were her best friend.

Berger realized Jet Ranger was under the desk, snoring.

"References to four different interviews that took place back-to-back, four days in a row," Lucy said. "And again here. Three days in a row. See, that's exactly what I mean. She doesn't come to the city and go on TV every day of the week, and she rarely does newspaper interviews. And this one right here? No fucking way."

Berger considered getting out of her chair and saying goodnight. But the thought of riding in the back of a taxi right now was unbearable. She would be sick.

"Thanksgiving Day? Impossible." Lucy seemed to be arguing with the data. "We were together in Massachusetts Thanksgiving Day. She wasn't on CNN, and she sure as hell wasn't giving an interview to a newspaper or some graduate student."

17

The cold wind was biting, and the half-moon was high and small, illuminating nothing as Scarpetta and Benton walked to the morgue.

The sidewalk was almost deserted, the few people they passed seeming aimless with very little in life. A young man was rolling a joint. Another young man leaned against a wall, trying to stay warm. Scarpetta felt eyes on their backs, and she felt vaguely unsettled. She felt exposed and uneasy for reasons that were too layered for her to readily identify. Yellow taxis sped by, most of their lighted rooftop signs advertising banks and finance and loan companies, typical after Christmas, when people face the consequences of their holiday cheer. A bus boasted a banner ad for *Gotham Gotcha,* and anger touched Scarpetta like the tip of a spear.

Then she felt fear, and Benton seemed to sense it and he found her hand, and he held it as they walked.

"It's what I get," she said, thinking about the gossip column. "I did a pretty good job avoiding the limelight for twenty-something years. Now CNN and now this."

"It's not what you get," he said. "It's just the way things are. And it's not fair. But nothing is. That's why we're headed where we are. We're the experts in *unfair*."

"I won't complain even one more time," she said. "You're absolutely right. It's one thing to walk into the morgue. It's another thing to be carried in."

"You can complain all you want."

"No, thank you," she said, pulling his arm against her. "I'm all done."

Lights from passing cars grazed the empty windows of Bellevue's old psychiatric hospital, and across a side street from its iron gates was the blue-brick Medical Examiner's office, where two white vans with blacked-out glass were parked along the curb, waiting to be sent on their next sad mission. Benton rang the buzzer as they stood in the cold on the top step at the entrance. He rang again and again, his patience fraying.

"She must have left," he said. "Or maybe she decided not to show up."

"That wouldn't be as much fun," Scarpetta said. "She likes to make people wait."

Cameras were everywhere, and she imagined Dr. Lenora Lester watching them on a monitor and enjoying herself. Several more minutes, and just as Benton was determined to leave, Dr. Lester appeared behind the glass front door and unlocked it to let them in. She was wearing a long green surgical gown and round steel-rimmed glasses, her graying hair pinned up. Her face was plain and unlined except for the deep furrow that ran from the top of her nose halfway up her forehead, and her dark eyes were small and darted like squirrels dodging cars.

Inside the tired lobby, a photograph of Ground Zero filled most of a wall, and Dr. Lester told them to follow her, as if they had never been here before.

As usual, she talked to Benton.

"Your name came up last week," she said, walking slightly ahead of them. "The FBI was here on a case. A couple agents, and one of their profilers from Quantico. Somehow we got on the subject of *Silence of the Lambs,* and I was reminded you were the head of the Behavioral Science Unit way back then. Weren't you the main consultant for the film? How many days did they spend at the Academy? What were Anthony Hopkins and Jodie Foster like?"

"I was working a case somewhere," he said.

"That's a shame," she said to him. "Back then Hollywood's interest in us was rather refreshing. It was a good thing in many respects, because the public had such ridiculous stereotypes of what we're like and what we do."

Scarpetta refrained from saying that the movie hadn't exactly helped dispel morbid myths, since the famous scene with the moth took place in a funeral home and not a modern autopsy suite. She didn't point out that if anyone fit the unfortunate Grim Reaper stereotype of a forensic pathologist, it was Dr. Lester.

"Now? Not a day goes by I don't get a call to consult about this show or that movie. Authors, screenwriters, producers, directors. Everybody wants to see an autopsy and tromp all over a crime scene. I'm so sick of it, I can't tell you."

Her long gown flapped around her knees as she walked in quick, clipped steps.

She said, "This case? Already I've had, must be a dozen phone calls. I suppose because it's a dwarf. My first, actually. Very interesting. Mild lumbar lordosis, bowed legs, some frontal bossing. And megalencephaly, which is enlargement of the brain," she explained, as if Scarpetta wouldn't know what that was. "Common in people with achondroplasia. Doesn't affect intelligence. In the IQ department, they're no different than the rest of us. So it's not as if this lady was stupid. Can't blame what happened on that."

"I'm not sure what you're implying," Benton said.

"There very well may be more to this case than meets the eye. It may not be what you think it is. You've taken a look at the scene photographs, I hope, and I'm about to give you a set of the ones taken during the autopsy. Typical asphyxia by ligature strangulation. Assuming this is a homicide."

"Assuming?" Benton said.

"In an unusual case like this, you have to keep every option open. As small as she was, she was more vulnerable to things going awry that might not have with someone else. Four-foot-one. Eighty-nine pounds. If it's an accident—rough sex, let's say—she was more at risk for things going too far."

Scarpetta said, "In several photographs, I noticed blood and contusions on her legs. How might that fit with your suggestion of rough sex?"

"Possibly spanking that got out of control. I've seen it before. Whippings, kicking, other types of punishment that go too far."

They were on the administrative floor now. Old gray linoleum tiles and bright red doors.

"I found no defensive-type injuries," Dr. Lester went on. "If she was murdered, then whoever did it managed to subdue her instantly. Maybe with a gun, a knife, and she did what she was told. But I can't dismiss the possibility that she and her boyfriend or whoever she was with last night were engaging in some sort of sex game that didn't turn out exactly as planned."

"What evidence, specifically, are you referring to that makes you think we're possibly dealing with a sex game, as you call it?" Benton asked.

"First of all, what was found at the scene. I understand she liked to play a role, shall we say. And more important, generally, in an attempted rape, the perpetrator makes the victim undress." Dr. Lester talked without ever slowing her pace. "That's part of his gratification, forcing her to undress and anticipating what he's going to do to her. Then he might bind her. To bind her first and then go to all the trouble to cut off her robe and bra sounds more like sex play to me. Especially if the victim enjoyed sexual fantasy, and based on what I'm told, she liked sex."

"Actually," Benton said, "cutting her clothing off after she was bound would have been far more terrifying than making her disrobe first."

"This is the quibble I have with forensic psychology, profiling, whatever you want to call it. It's based on personal opinion. What you assume is terrifying might be exciting, depending on the individual."

"I'll let you know if something I say is based on my personal opinion," Benton said.

Berger was aware of Lucy's arm brushing against her, of near touch as she made notes on a legal pad. Bright white fragmented data streamed by, and when she looked, it hurt her eyes, and the real pain followed.

"Do you think we'll get most of it back?" she asked.

"Yes," Lucy replied.

"And we're sure these drafts go back about a year?"

"At least. I'll be able to tell you specifically when we're done. We have to get to the very first file she saved. I'll keep saying she, even though I realize we really don't know who wrote this."

Lucy's eyes were very green, and when she and Berger looked at each other, it was lingering and intense.

"It doesn't appear she saved files the same way I do," Berger observed. "In other words, doesn't appear she was very careful for someone who has all this security software, over-the-counter or not. Every time I work on a brief, for example, I make a copy and give it a new name."

"That's the right way to do it," Lucy said. "But she didn't bother. She continued to revise and save the same file, overlaying one on top of another. Stupid. But half the world does it. Fortunately, every time she made a change and saved that same file, it got a new date stamp. Even though you can't see it when you look at her list of documents, it's in here, scattered all the hell over the place. The computer will find the dates, and sort by them, and do a pattern analysis. For example, how many times in one day did she or someone revise and save the same file? In this instance, the master's thesis file. What days of the week did this person work on it? What time of day or night?"

Berger made notes and said, "Might give us an idea of where she was and when. Her habits. Which might possibly lead to who she was with. If, for example, she spent most of the time in her apartment working, except on the Saturday nights she saw Oscar. Or did she go to other places to do her writing? Perhaps even another person's residence. Did she have some other person in her life we don't know about?"

"I can get you a timeline right up to the last keystroke she ever made," Lucy said. "But not where she worked. E-mail can be traced to an IP address, saying, for example, she did e-mail off-site, such as in an Internet café. But there's nothing to trace when we're talking about her word-processing files. We can't say for a fact that she always worked on her thesis at home. Maybe she used a library somewhere. Or Oscar might know if she always worked in her apartment. Assuming anything he says is true. For all we know, he's the one writing this thesis. I'll continue to remind you of that."

"The cops didn't find research materials in Terri's apartment," Berger said.

"A lot of people have electronic files these days. They don't have paper. Some people never print anything out unless it's absolutely necessary. I'm one of them. I'm not a fan of paper trails."

"Kay will certainly know how much of what Terri or someone was collecting and writing is accurate," Berger said. "Can we completely re-create every draft?"

"I wouldn't put it quite like that. Better to say I can recover what's here. Now the computer's sorting by bibliography. Every time Terri made a new entry or revised or altered anything, a new version of the same file was created. That's why you see so many copies of what appears to be the same document. Well, you're not seeing it. I assumed you're not looking. How are you feeling?"

Lucy looked over at her, looked right at her.

"I'm not entirely sure," Berger said. "I probably should leave. We have to figure out what we're going to do about this."

"Instead of trying so hard to figure out everything, why don't you wait and see what we're dealing with. Because it's too early to know. But you shouldn't leave. Don't."

Their chairs were side by side, and Lucy moved her

fingers on the keyboard and Berger made notes, and Jet Ranger's big head appeared between their chairs. Berger began to pet him.

"More sorting," Lucy said. "But now by different forensic science disciplines. Fingerprints, DNA, trace evidence. Copied and routed into a folder called Forensic Science."

"Files that were replaced," Berger said. "One file copied over another. I've always been told that when you copy one file on top of another, the old copy's gone for good."

The office phone rang.

Berger said, "It's for me."

She placed her hand on top of Lucy's wrist to stop her from answering it.

18

Inside Dr. Lester's office, everywhere she could fit them, were framed degrees, certificates, commendations, and photographs of herself wearing a hard hat and a white protective suit, excavating The Hole, as those who worked there referred to what was left of the World Trade Center.

She was proud to have been part of Nine-Eleven, and seemed to be personally unfazed by it. Scarpetta hadn't fared quite as well after spending almost six months at the Water Street recovery site, hand-scanning thousands of buckets of dirt like an archaeologist, screening for personal effects, body parts, teeth, and bone. She had no framed photographs. She had no PowerPoint presentations. She didn't like to talk about it, having felt physically poisoned by it in a way that was unlike anything she had ever felt before. It was as if the terror those victims had experienced at their moment of certain death had been suspended and fixed in a miasma that enveloped wherever they had been, and later, where remnants of them were recovered and bagged and numbered. She couldn't quite explain it, but it was nothing to flaunt or brag about.

Dr. Lester retrieved a thick envelope from her desk and gave it to Benton.

"Autopsy photos, my preliminary report, the DNA analysis," she said. "I don't know how much of it Mike gave to you. Sometimes he gets distracted."

She mentioned Mike Morales as if they were close friends.

"The police are calling it a homicide," Benton said.

He didn't open the envelope but gave it to Scarpetta, making a point.

"They aren't the ones who make the determination," Dr. Lester answered him. "I'm sure Mike isn't calling it that. Or even if he is, he knows where I stand."

"And what does Berger say?" Benton asked.

"She doesn't make the determination, either. People have such a hard time waiting their turn in line. I always say the doomed ones who end up down here aren't in a hurry, so why should the rest of us be? I'm pending the manner of death for now, especially in light of the DNA. If I was unsure of this case before, well, now I'm completely in limbo."

"So you don't foresee determining a manner of death in the near future," Benton said.

"There's nothing more I can do. I'm waiting on everybody else," she said.

It was exactly what Scarpetta didn't want to hear. Not only was there no evidence that warranted Oscar's arrest, legally there was no crime. She might be bound to secrecy with him for a very long time.

They left her office, and Dr. Lester said, "For example, she had some sort of lubricant in her vagina. That's unusual for a homicide."

"This is the first anyone's mentioned a lubricant," Scarpetta said. "It's not in any of the preliminary reports I've seen."

Dr. Lester replied, "You realize, of course, these DNA profiles in CODIS are nothing but numbers. And I've always said, all you need is an error in the numbers, which would result in a totally different chromosomal position. One thing off in a marker or maybe more than one marker, and you've got a serious problem. I think it's possible that what we have here is a very rare false positive due to computer error."

"You don't get false positives, not even very rarely," Scarpetta said. "Not even if there is a mixture of DNA, such as in cases where more than one person sexually assaulted a victim or there's cross-contamination from multiple people having contact with an item or a substance, such as a lubricant. A mixture of DNA profiles from different people won't magically be identical to the profile of a woman in Palm Beach, for example."

"Yes, the lubricant. Which raises another possible explanation," Dr. Lester said. "Cross-contamination, such as you yourself just suggested. A prostitute who didn't leave semen, meaning the prostitute could be male or female. What do we know about anybody's private life until they end up here? That's why I'm not so quick to call something a homicide, suicide, accident. Not until all the facts are in. I don't like surprises after I've committed myself. I'm sure you saw in the lab report that the presence of seminal fluid was negative."

"Not unheard of," Scarpetta said. "Not even unusual. Nor is it unheard of for a lubricant to be used in a sexual assault, by the way. K-Y jelly, Vaseline, sunblock, even butter. I could make you a long list of what I've seen."

They were following Dr. Lester through another corridor that dated back to earlier decades, when forensic pathologists were crudely called *meat cutters*. It wasn't all that long ago that science and the dead had little in common beyond ABO blood-typing, fingerprints, and X-rays.

"No evidence of seminal fluid in or on her body or on the clothing found in the tub," Dr. Lester said. "Or at the scene. Of course, they used UV light, as did I. Nothing fluoresced the distinctive bright white that seminal fluid does."

"In sexual assaults, some perpetrators wear condoms," Scarpetta said. "Especially these days, because everybody knows about DNA."

Fractured data streamed across dark screens, reattaching at mind-numbing speed, as if it were fleeing and being caught.

Maybe Berger was getting acclimated to cyberspace. Her headache had mysteriously vanished. Or maybe adrenaline was the cure. She was feeling aggressive because she didn't like being bucked. Not by Morales. Certainly not by Lucy.

"We should get started on the e-mail," Berger said, and it wasn't the first time she'd said it since Marino had called.

Lucy didn't seem the least bit interested in Marino or what he was doing, and she wasn't listening to Berger's insistence that they turn their attention to e-mail. They had the passwords right in front of them, but Lucy refused to change her focus until she had a better idea why her aunt's name continued to appear with alarming frequency in the fragmented revisions of the thesis Terri, or perhaps Oscar, had been writing.

"I'm afraid your interest is too personal," Berger said. "And that's exactly what I'm worried about. We need to look at e-mails, but you'd rather look at what's been written about your aunt. I'm not saying it isn't important."

"This is where you have to trust that I'm doing things the right way," Lucy said, not budging.

The legal pad with the passwords written on it remained where it was, on the desk, next to Lucy's keyboard.

"Patience. One thing at a time," Lucy added. "I don't tell you how to run your cases."

"Seems that's exactly what you're telling me. I want to get into their e-mails, and you want to keep reading this thesis or whatever the hell it is. You're not helping me."

"Helping you is exactly what I'm doing—by not deferring to you or allowing you to tell me how to do my job. I can't allow you to have any influence over me and direct me, that's the point. I know what I'm doing, and there's a lot you don't understand yet. You need to know exactly what we're doing and why and how, because if this becomes the big deal I'm sure it will, you're going to be asked and attacked. It won't be me in front of the judge and jury explaining the forensic computer part of this investigation, and you probably won't be able to call me in as an expert witness for at least one obvious reason."

"We have to talk about that," Berger said bluntly.

"The relationship issue," Lucy said.

"You would be discredited." Berger seized the opportunity to voice her misgivings and maybe put a stop to things.

Or maybe that's what Lucy was about to suggest. Maybe Lucy was about to quit and put a stop to things.

"Frankly, I'm not sure what to do," Berger added. "If you could be objective about it, I'd ask you for a suggestion. You started something not knowing it personally involved you. Now what? You probably don't want to continue with this, either. I suspect you're realizing it's a bad idea and we should shake hands and walk away, and I'll find another company."

"Now that we know my aunt's involved? Are you kidding? The worst idea of all would be to quit and walk away," Lucy said. "I'm not quitting. You probably want to fire me. I warned you that you would. I also told you there is no other company. We've been through that."

"You could let someone else finish running your program."

"My proprietary software? Do you have any idea what it's worth? That's like letting someone else fly my helicopter with me sitting in the back or letting somebody else sleep with my lover."

"Does your lover live with you? Do you live in this loft?" Berger had noticed stairs leading to a second level. "It's risky working where you live. I'm assuming this person doesn't have access to highly classified—"

"Jet Ranger doesn't have a password to get into anything, don't worry," Lucy said. "What I'm saying, literally, is nobody's touching my software. It's mine. And I wrote the code. Nobody's going to figure it out, and that's deliberate on my part."

"We have a major conflict neither you nor I anticipated," Berger said.

"If you want to make it one. I don't want to quit, and I won't."

Berger scanned data rolling by at a dizzying rate. She looked at Lucy and didn't want her to quit.

"If you fire me," Lucy said, "you'll hurt yourself in a way that isn't necessary."

"I have no intention of hurting myself. Or you. I have no intention of hurting the case. Tell me what you want to do," Berger said.

"I want to teach you a few things about recovering overwritten files, because as you pointed out, people don't realize it's possible. You can expect opposing counsel to go after you on this one. As you've noticed,

I find analogies helpful. So here's one. Let's say you visited your favorite vacation spot. Sedona, for example. Let's say you stayed in a certain hotel with a certain person. For the sake of simplicity, let's say you stayed with Greg. Images, sounds, smells, emotions, tactile sensations are captured in your memory, much of it not conscious."

"What are you doing?" Berger asked.

"A year later," Lucy went on, "you and Greg take the same flight to Sedona on the same weekend, rent the same car, stay in the same room of the same hotel, but the experience isn't going to be identical. It's altered by what has gone on in your life since then, altered by your emotions, your relationship, your health, his health, by what preoccupies you, preoccupies him, altered by the weather, the economy, road detours, renovations, every detail right down to the flower arrangements and chocolates on your pillows. Without being aware of it, you're overlaying old files with new ones that aren't identical, even if consciously you don't notice the difference."

"I'll state this clearly," Berger said. "I don't like people snooping into my life or violating my boundaries."

"Read what's out there about you. Some nice, some not so nice. Read Wikipedia." Lucy held her gaze. "I'm not saying anything that isn't public information. You spent your honeymoon with Greg in Sedona. It's one of your favorite places. How is he, by the way?"

"You have no right to research me."

"I have every right. I wanted to know exactly what I'm dealing with. And I think I do. Even though you haven't offered much in the way of honesty."

"What have I said that you think is dishonest?"

"You haven't said. You haven't said anything," Lucy replied.

"You have no reason to distrust me, and you shouldn't," Berger said.

"I'm not going to abort what I'm doing because of boundaries or a possible conflict of interest. Even if you order me to," Lucy said. "I've downloaded everything onto my server, so if you want to take the laptops and walk out of here, go right ahead. But you won't stop me."

"I don't want to fight with you."

"It wouldn't be smart."

"Please don't threaten me."

"I'm not. I understand how threatened you might feel and how reason might dictate that you should try to remove me from this case, from everything. But the fact is, you don't have the capabilities to stop me from what I'm doing. You really don't. Information about my aunt was inside an apartment where a woman was just murdered. A thesis that Terri or someone was constantly working on and revising. I'd use the word *obsessively*. That should be what you and I are worried about. Not what other people think or whether they're going to accuse us."

"Accuse us of what?"

"Of having a conflict of interest. Because of my aunt. Because of anything."

"I care what people think far less than you imagine," Berger said. "Because I learned it's better to make them think what I want them to think than to care about it. I'm pretty good at that. I've had to be. I've got to be certain Kay isn't even remotely aware of what's going on. I need to talk to her."

"She would have told Benton," Lucy said. "She would have told you. She never would have agreed to examine Oscar Bane if she was somehow acquainted with him or with Terri Bridges."

"When I requested that she examine him, she was given virtually no information about the case. Including the name of the victim. So maybe she was acquainted with Terri but didn't realize it until she got in that room with Oscar."

"I'm telling you, by now she would have said something."

"I don't know about you," Berger said, "but I find it unusual that a student didn't make at least some effort to contact sources for a master's thesis or doctoral dissertation. Terri Bridges was writing about Kay and never contacted her or tried? Are we sure? Maybe she did, and Kay just doesn't remember because she wasn't interested."

"She would remember and at the very least would have politely declined. Aunt Kay didn't know this lady."

"Do you really think you can be objective? That you can handle this? Or that you want to?"

"I can. And I want to," Lucy said, her attention suddenly distracted by what was on a video screen.

SCARPETTA by Terri Bridges streamed by, the same words repeatedly, in different fonts and different sizes.

"It's begun sorting by title page," Lucy said. "Was she fucking crazy?"

19

The morgue was located at the lowest level, where it was convenient for vans and rescue vehicles to park in the bay as they brought in the dead and took them away.

The smell of industrial deodorizer was heavy on the air in a silent passageway of abandoned gurneys. Behind locked doors they passed were stored skeletal remains and specimens of brains, and then the grim conveyance of a dull steel elevator that lifted bodies upstairs, where they could be looked at from behind glass. Scarpetta had a special sympathy for those whose last image of someone they loved was that. In every morgue she'd ever managed, glass was unbreakable, and viewing rooms were civilized, with hints of life such as prints of landscapes and real plants, and the bereft were never unchaperoned.

Dr. Lester led them to the decomp room, usually

restricted to remains that were badly decomposed, radioactive, or infectious, and a faint, lingering stench reached out to Scarpetta as if a special brand of misery was inviting her inside. Most doctors weren't eager to work in there.

"Is there a reason you've got this body in isolation?" she said. "If so, now would be a good time to let us know."

Dr. Lester flipped a switch. Overhead lights flickered on, illuminating one stationary stainless-steel autopsy table, several surgical carts, and a gurney bearing a body covered by a disposable blue sheet. A large flat-screen monitor on a countertop was split into six quadrants that were filled with rotating video images of the building and the bay.

Scarpetta told Benton to wait in the corridor while she stepped into the adjoining locker room and retrieved face masks, shoe and hair covers, and gowns. She pulled purple nitrile gloves from a box as Dr. Lester explained she was keeping the body in the decomp room because its walk-in refrigerator happened to be empty at the moment. Scarpetta barely listened. There was no excuse for why she hadn't bothered to roll the gurney a brief distance away into the autopsy suite, which was much less of a biohazard and had no odor.

The sheet rustled when Scarpetta pulled it back, exposing a pale body with the long torso, large head, and stunted limbs that were characteristic of achondroplasia. What she noticed immediately was the absence of body hair, including pubic hair. She suspected laser removal, which would have required a series of painful treatments, and this was consistent with what Oscar Bane had said about Terri's phobias. She thought about the dermatologist he had mentioned.

"I'm assuming she came in like this," Scarpetta said, repositioning one of the legs to get a better look. "That you didn't shave her."

She, of course, couldn't repeat information Oscar had given to her, and her frustration was acute.

"I certainly didn't," Dr. Lester said. "I didn't shave any part of her. There was no reason."

"The police say anything about it? They find anything at the scene, find out anything from Oscar, maybe from witnesses, about her hair removal or any other procedures she might have been getting?"

"Only that they noticed it," Dr. Lester said.

Scarpetta said, "So there was no mention of someone she may have gone to, an office where she got this done. A dermatologist, for example."

"Mike did say something about that. I have the name written down. A woman doctor here in the city. He said he was going to call her."

"He found out about this doctor how?" Benton asked.

"Bills inside the apartment. As I understand it, he carried out a lot of bills, mail, things like that, and started going through them. The usual things. And it goes without saying, that leads to another speculation, that the boyfriend's a pedophile. Most men who want a woman to remove all her pubic hair are pedophiles. Practicing or not."

"Do we know for a fact the hair removal was the boy-friend's idea?" Benton said. "How do you know it wasn't her idea, her preference?"

"It makes her look prepubescent," Dr. Lester said.

"Nothing else about her looks prepubescent," Benton said. "And pubic hair removal could also be about oral sex."

Scarpetta moved a surgical lamp closer to the gurney. The Y incision ran from clavicle to clavicle, intersecting at the sternum, and ending at the pelvis, and had been sutured with heavy twine in a pattern that always reminded her of baseballs. She repositioned the head to get a better look at the face, and felt the sawed skull cap move beneath the scalp. Terri Bridges's complexion was a dark dusky red, the petechiae florid, and when Scarpetta opened the eyelids, the sclera were solid red from hemorrhage.

She had not died mercifully or fast.

Ligature strangulation affects the arteries and veins that carry oxygenated blood to the brain and deoxygenated blood away. As the ligature had been tightened around Terri's neck, occluding the veins that drain blood away, blood continued to flow into her head but had nowhere to go. Increasing pressure ruptured blood vessels, resulting in congestion and masses of tiny hemorrhages. The brain was starved of oxygen, and she died of cerebral hypoxia.

But not right away.

Scarpetta retrieved a hand lens and a ruler from a cart and studied abrasions on the neck. They were

U-shaped, high under the jaw, and angled up behind her head, sharply up on either side of it, and she noted a subtle pattern of linear marks overlapping one another. Whatever was used to strangle her was smooth, with no distinct edges, and its width ranged from three-eighths to five-eighths of an inch. She had seen this before when the ligature was an article of clothing or some other elastic material that became narrower as it was pulled hard, and wider as it was released. She indicated for Benton to come closer.

"This looks more like a garroting," she said to him.

She traced the partially abraded horizontal marks around the neck and where they stopped just behind the jawbones.

"The angle indicates her assailant was positioned behind and above her, and didn't use a slipknot or some type of handle to twist the ligature tighter," she said. "He held the ends of it and pulled back and up with force, and did so multiple times. Rather much like a car moving backwards and forwards when it's stuck in the snow. It's running over its own tracks, but not a perfect overlay, and you may or may not be able to count how many times this went on. Note the tremendous florid petechiae and congestion, also consistent with garroting."

He looked through the lens, his gloved fingers touching the marks on the neck, moving it from one side to the other to get a better view. Scarpetta felt him against her as they looked on together, and she was distracted by an argument of odors and sensations. The chilly, unpleasant dead air contrasted palpably with the warmth of him, and she felt the tension of life in him as she continued to make her case that Terri Bridges had been garroted multiple times.

"Based on the marks I'm seeing—three times, at least," she added.

Dr. Lester stood back from the other side of the gurney, her arms folded, her face uneasy.

"How long before she was unconscious each time he did it?" Benton asked.

"Could have occurred in as few as ten seconds," Scarpetta replied. "Death would have followed in minutes unless the ligature was loosened, and that's what I believe happened. The killer allowed her to regain consciousness, then strangled her into unconsciousness again, and repeated his routine until she could no longer survive it. Or perhaps he got tired of it."

"Or possibly was interrupted," Benton suggested.

"Maybe. But this repetitive ritual explains the profound congestion of her face, the abundance of pinpoint hemorrhages."

"Sadism," he said.

Dr. Lester stepped closer and said, "Or S-and-M that went too far."

"Did you check her neck for fibers?" Scarpetta asked her. "Anything that might give us a clue as to the type of ligature we're dealing with?"

"I recovered fibers from her hair and other areas of her body, sent them to the labs for trace evidence. No fibers from the abrasions on her neck."

Scarpetta said, "I would expedite everything you can.

This isn't S-and-M gone bad. The reddish, dry deep furrows on her wrists indicate they were lashed together very tightly in a single loop with a binding that had sharp edges."

"The flex-cuff will be checked for DNA."

"These marks weren't made by a flex-cuff," Scarpetta said. "Flex-cuffs have rounded edges to prevent injury. I'm assuming you've already sent—"

Dr. Lester cut her off. "Everything went to the labs. Of course, the binding was brought here first. Mike showed it to me so I could correlate it with the furrows on her wrists and possibly with the marks around her neck, then he took it. But there are several photographs included in the ones I gave you."

Scarpetta was disappointed. She wanted to see the actual binding, see if it reminded her of anything she'd ever come across before. She found the photographs, and the close-ups told her nothing more than the scene photographs had. The binding Oscar allegedly cut from Terri's wrists was a colorless nylon strap exactly one-quarter of an inch wide, and twenty and one-half inches long from the pointed tip to the ratchet case lock. One side was scored, the other smooth, the edges sharp. There was no serial number or any other type of marking that might indicate a manufacturer.

"Looks like a cable tie of some sort," Benton said.

"It's definitely not a flex-cuff or PlastiCuff, anything that would be used as a type of handcuff," Scarpetta said.

"Except a lot of cable ties are black," Benton pondered as he looked at several photographs. "Anything that would be outdoors and could be degraded by UV is going to be black. Not clear or a light color."

"Possibly a single-use bag tie of some sort," Scarpetta speculated. "For indoors, since it's colorless. But we're talking a large, sturdy bag. This isn't a typical trash-bag tie."

She looked across the room at a biohazard waste bag, bright red with the universal symbol, attached to a stainless-steel holder next to a sink.

"Actually," she said. "Where I have seen this type of tie is right there. For those."

She pointed to the biohazard waste holder.

"Ours use a twist tie," Dr. Lester snapped, as if Scarpetta was actually suggesting the binding used on Terri Bridges had come from the morgue.

"What's important in this," Scarpetta said, "is people into S-and-M generally don't bind each other so tightly as to cut off circulation, and they aren't likely to use sharp-edged straps or mechanical restraints that can't be easily loosened or removed with a key. And this type of tie"—she indicated the photograph—"can never be loosened once it's applied. It can only be pulled tighter. She would have been in pain. There was no way to free her without forcing a knife or some other sharp instrument under the ligature. And you can see a small cut here by her left wrist bone. That might be how it happened. Could be from the kitchen scissors, if it's true that's what was used. Was there any blood on her body when she was brought in, besides blood from the injuries on her legs?"

"No." Dr. Lester's dark eyes stared at her.

"Well, if she was dead when the binding was removed and that's when she was cut, she wouldn't have bled, or at least not much," Scarpetta said. "This was no game. There was too much pain for this to be a game."

"Seems to me pain is the point of S-and-M."

"No pleasure was derived from this pain," Scarpetta said. "Except by the person inflicting it."

The title page belonged to a revision dated about three weeks ago, December 10.

"A really big file that we're far from completely recovering yet," Lucy said. "But this partial chapter gives you the picture."

She had spooled it into a text file, and Berger began reading to Lucy's tap-taps of the down-arrow key:

. . . While I've got my hands in a dead body, I imagine how I could have killed the person better. With all I know? Of course I could commit the perfect crime. When I'm with my colleagues and throw back enough whiskey, we love to come up with scenarios that we'd never present at professional meetings or mention to family, friends, certainly not to our enemies!

I asked her what her favorite whiskey is.

Maybe a toss-up between Knappogue Castle single-malt Irish whiskey and Brora single-malt Scotch.

Never heard of either.

Why would you? Knappogue is probably the finest Irish whiskey in the world and costs close to seven hundred dollars. And Brora is so rare and exquisite, each bottle is numbered and costs more than your schoolbooks in a year.

How can you afford to drink such expensive whiskey, and don't you feel guilty when there are so many people losing their homes and unable to fill their cars with gas?

My turning down a magnificent Irish whiskey isn't going to fill your car with gas—assuming you have a car. It's a fact that the finer labels—whether it's a Château Pétrus, a single-malt whiskey, or very fine pure agave tequila—are less damaging to your liver and brain.

So wealthy people who drink the good stuff aren't as affected by alcohol abuse? That's something I've never heard.

How many human livers and brains have you seen and sectioned?

How about some other examples from the dark side? What else do you say behind the scenes, especially when you're with your colleagues?

We brag about famous people we've autopsied (all of us secretly wish we'd done Elvis or Anna Nicole Smith or Princess Diana). Listen, I'm no different from anybody else. I want the case nobody else gets. I want the Gainesville serial murders. I want to be the one who arrives at the scene and finds the severed head on a bookshelf staring at me when I walk through the door. I would have loved to have been cross-examined by Ted Bundy when he represented himself at his own murder trial. Hell, I would have loved to have done his autopsy after he was executed.

Share some sensational cases you have worked.

I've been fortunate to have a number of them. For example, lightning strikes, where nobody else could figure out the cause of death, because you've got this body lying in a field, her clothes ripped off and scattered. First thought? Sexual assault. But no sign of injury at autopsy. Dead giveaways, excuse the pun? The branching pattern known as the Lichtenberg figures or electrical treeing. Or if the person was wearing anything ferrous, such as a steel belt buckle, it would have become magnetized, or the wristwatch might have stopped at the time of death—I always check for things like that. Most medical examiners don't because they're inexperienced or naïve or just not very good at what they do.

You don't sound as compassionate as I expected.

Let's face it. Dead is dead. I can show all the empathy in the world and move any jury to tears. But do I really feel that my heart has been snatched out of my chest when the latest tragedy's rolled in? Do I really care when the cops make comments that the public never hears?

Such as?

Typically, comments with sexual overtones. The size of the deceased's penis—especially if it's small or huge. The size of the deceased's breasts—especially if they're what I'd call centerfold material. I know plenty of medical examiners who take souvenirs. Trophies. An artificial hip from someone famous. A tooth. A breast implant, and it's always the men who want those. (Don't ask me what they do with them, but they're usually within easy reach.) A penile implant—those are amusing.

Have you ever kept a souvenir?

Only one. This was twenty years ago, a case early in my career, serial murders in Richmond, where I was the brand-new chief. But the trophy wasn't from a dead body. It was from Benton Wesley. The first time we met was in my conference room. When he left, I kept his coffee cup. You know, one of these tall foam cups from a 7-Eleven? I was totally in lust with him the first minute I saw him.

What did you do with his coffee cup?

I took it home with me and ran my tongue along the rim of it, as if by tasting it, I was tasting him.

But you didn't actually sleep with him until, what? About five years later?

That's what everybody thinks. But that's not what really happened. I called him after that first meeting and invited him over for a drink—allegedly so we could continue discussing the cases in private, and the instant my front door shut behind us, we were all over each other.

Who started it?

I seduced him. That made it less of a moral struggle for him. He was married. I was divorced and not seeing anyone. His poor wife. Benton and I had been lovers for almost five years before he finally admitted it to her, feigning that his adultery had just begun because their marriage had gotten stale, lifeless.

And nobody knew? Pete Marino? Lucy? Your secretary, Rose?

I've always wondered if Rose suspected it. Just something about the way she'd act when Benton would show up for yet another case discussion, or when I was on my way

to Quantico for yet another consultation. She died of cancer
last summer. So you can't ask her.

**Doesn't sound as if working with the dead makes
you sexually inhibited.**

Quite the opposite. When you've explored every inch of
the human body so many times that you haven't the least
bit of self-consciousness or revulsion about it, there isn't
anything out of bounds sexually, and there's plenty of experi-
mentation to be had. . . .

"Can you forward this to Kay?" Berger said when the
section of text abruptly stopped. "So when she gets a
chance, maybe she can give it her attention. Maybe she'll
have thoughts, insights we don't."

"Supposedly from one of the interviews this past
Thanksgiving," Lucy said. "Which I know she didn't
give. Not that she'd ever talk like this to anyone."

"I'm noticing a creative use of fonts. Your opinion?"

"The writer, Terri or whoever, does a lot with fonts,"
Lucy agreed.

She was doing her best to be calm, but she was out-
raged. Berger sensed it, and she was waiting. In the past,
Lucy's anger was something to be feared.

"And in my opinion, there's symbolism involved,"
Lucy was saying. "In this phony interview, for example,
when Terri's asking questions, I'm going to say it's Terri,
the font is Franklin Gothic and it's in bold. Arial in
smaller type for my aunt's phony answers."

"Then symbolically, Terri has superseded Kay in
importance," Berger said.

"It's worse than that. For your purists in the word-processing world, Arial has a very bad rep." Lucy studied text as she talked. "It's been called homely, common, lacking in character, and is considered a shameless imposter. There are plenty of articles about it."

She avoided Berger's eyes.

"An imposter?" Berger prodded her. "As in plagiarism, copyright violation? What are you talking about?"

"It's considered a rip-off of Helvetica, which was developed in the nineteen-fifties and became one of the most popular typefaces in the world," Lucy said. "To the untrained eye, there's no difference between Helvetica and Arial. But to a purist, a professional printer or print designer, Arial's a parasite. The irony? Some young designers think Helvetica is based on Arial instead of the other way around. Do you see the significance symbolically? Because it's scary, at least to me."

"Of course I see it," Berger said. "It could suggest that Terri and Kay have switched places in terms of their being world-renowned forensic experts. Rather much what Mark David Chapman did before he killed John Lennon. He was wearing a name tag with Lennon's name on it. Rather much what Sirhan Sirhan did when he allegedly made the comment that by assassinating Bobby Kennedy, he'd become more famous."

"The change in fonts is a progression," Lucy said. "The more recent the drafts, the more pronounced it is, the prominence of Terri's name and an implied negativity toward my aunt."

"A change that suggests Terri's emotional attachment

to Kay was turning hostile, dismissive. I should say the author. But for the sake of simplicity, I'll keep saying Terri," Berger speculated. "Rather much what happened between Kay and Marino, now that I think of it. He worshipped her. Then wanted to destroy her."

"It's not that simple, and it's not the same," Lucy said. "Marino had a reason to be in love with my aunt. He knew her. Terri didn't have a reason to feel anything about her. It was delusional."

"We're assuming she was an aficionado of typefaces. Let's go back to that," Berger said, continuing her assessment.

Lucy was different—genuinely so. Fiery, yes. But not reactive the way she used to be, and in Berger's opinion, Lucy used to teeter on the edge of violence. That used to be her default, and it had made her completely unsafe.

"I definitely think she was well versed in fonts," Lucy said. "She uses different ones for footnotes, the bibliography, chapter headings, table of contents. Most people don't do that when they're writing a thesis. They might change point size and use italics but not all this artsy use of fonts. In fact, the most common typeface is usually the default on a number of word-processing packages, including the one Terri was using. For the most part, the actual text is in Times New Roman."

"Examples," Berger said, writing on her legal pad. "What fonts does she use, and for what and why? Theoretically."

"For footnotes, Palatino Linotype, which is highly legible both on a computer screen and when printed. For the bibliography, Bookman Old Style. Also legible.

Chapter headings, she picked MS Reference Sans Serif, which is typically used in headlines. Again, it's rare to find this many different typefaces, especially in an academic paper. What it suggests to me is her writing was highly personalized. It wasn't just about the writing."

Berger looked at her for a long moment.

"How the hell do you know all this off the top of your head?" she said. "Fonts? I never even pay attention to them. I can't even tell you what font I use when I'm writing my briefs."

"You use the same default for text that Terri did. Times New Roman, designed for the London *Times*. A typeface that's narrow, so it's economical, but very readable. I saw printouts on your desk when I was in your office earlier today. In forensic computer work, what seems the most trivial detail might be significant."

"Which may be the case here."

"I can tell you this much with certainty," Lucy said. "These different fonts were deliberate choices, because she had to select them. Now whether she attached symbolism to them in terms of how she felt about herself or someone else, such as my aunt? Don't know. But my opinion? The whole thing is sick, and it was well on its way to becoming sicker. If Terri really is the author and she were still around, I would consider her dangerous to my aunt. Maybe even physically dangerous. At the very least, she's defaming someone she never even met."

"Kay would have to prove it was untrue. And how would she prove that the anecdote about the coffee cup isn't true, for example? How do you know it isn't true?"

"Because she would never do anything like that."

"I don't believe you're in a position to know what Kay does in private," Berger said.

"Of course I'm in a position to know." Lucy met her eyes. "So are you. Ask anyone if she's ever made fun of dead bodies or allowed anyone else to. Ask anyone who's ever been in the morgue with her or at a crime scene if she enjoys gruesome cases and wishes she'd autopsied people like Ted Bundy. I hope this doesn't all come out in court."

"I was talking about the coffee cup. Why does it disturb you to imagine Kay as a sexual person? Have you ever allowed her to be human? Or is she the perfect mother, or worse, one who isn't perfect enough?"

"I admit I used to have a problem with that, competing for her attention, not allowing her to have flaws or real feelings," Lucy said. "I was a tyrant."

"No more?"

"Maybe Marino was the final radiation, the last dose of chemo. Unintentionally, he cured something somewhat malignant in me, and actually, my aunt and I are better off. I realized she has a life quite apart from mine, and that's fine. It's more than fine. It's better. It's not that I didn't know it before. But in retrospect, I didn't feel it. And now she's married. If Marino hadn't done what he did, I don't think Benton would have gotten around to getting married."

"You act as if the decision was his alone. She had no input?" Berger studied her.

"She's always let him be what he is. She would have

continued to. She loves him. She probably couldn't be with anybody else, in truth, because there are three things she can't abide and won't tolerate. Being controlled, betrayed, or bored. Any one of them, and she'd rather be alone."

"Sounds like a few other suspects I know," Berger said.

"Probably true," Lucy said.

"Well," Berger said, returning her attention to what was on the computer screen. "Unfortunately, what's on these laptops is evidence, and people involved in the case will read it. And yes, it could become public."

"It would destroy her."

"It won't destroy her," Berger said. "But we've got to find out where this information came from. I don't think it was fabricated from whole cloth. Terri, or whoever wrote this, knows too much. Benton and Kay's first meeting in Richmond twenty years ago, for example."

"They didn't start their affair then."

"How can you know that?"

"Because I was staying in her house that summer," Lucy said. "Benton never came over, not once. And when she wasn't at the office or at a scene, she was with me. I was a screwed-up pudgy little brat, mad as hell and desperate for her attention. In other words, just looking to get into trouble, and not in a position to really understand that the kind of trouble she dealt with caused people to end up raped and murdered. She didn't run around and leave me alone, not for a minute, not with a serial killer terrorizing the city. I never saw a Seven-Eleven coffee cup, just so you know."

"It means nothing that you didn't see one," Berger said. "Why would she show it to you, much less explain why she'd carried it home from her office conference room?"

"She wouldn't have," Lucy said. "But I'm sort of sorry I didn't see one. She was really all alone back then."

20

Scarpetta turned Terri Bridges's body on its side to look at it, front and back.

Other than the marks on the neck and a small cut on one wrist, the only injuries Scarpetta saw began mid-thigh, anteriorly, or on the front. These were long, narrow bruises with multiple linear abrasions that would have bled, most of them horizontal, as if she had been struck with something like a board that had a flat surface with an edge.

Her knees were badly bruised and abraded, as were the tops of her feet, and under the magnification of the hand lens, Scarpetta discovered tiny blondish splinters as fine as hair embedded in each. The vivid redness and lack of swelling of the wounds indicated all of them had been inflicted close to the time of death. That could have been minutes. It could have been an hour.

Dr. Lester's response to the discovery of the splinters anteriorly, on the knees, on the feet, was that perhaps, at some point, the body was dragged, and only those areas of it had been in contact with a wooden surface, a floor. Scarpetta remarked that few wooden floors were rough enough to cause splinters, unless the wood was untreated.

"You aren't going to get me to rule out an accident yet," Dr. Lester stubbornly asserted. "Bondage, beatings, whippings, severe spanking. And sometimes things go too far."

"What about a struggle?" Benton said. "Does that also factor into your theory that this might be an accident?"

"Writhing, screaming in pain. I've seen it on videotapes that profilers like you show at meetings," Dr. Lester said, and the crease between her eyebrows seemed deeper, like a crevice dividing her forehead. "Couples turn the camera on, never knowing their perverted rituals will end in death."

"If you could go through the photographs," Scarpetta said to Benton. "The ones from the scene. Let's look at a few things."

He retrieved an envelope from a counter and together they arranged photos of the bathroom. She pointed to one that showed the vanity, and directly above it, the oval mirror that was slightly askew.

Scarpetta said, "The injuries to her legs were caused by moderate to severe blunt force with an object that is flat and has an edge. The edge of the vanity and the underside of its drawer, maybe? If she'd been seated in front of the vanity? That could explain why all of her injuries are anterior and from the mid-thigh down. Nothing posterior, or on any area of her upper body. Nothing on her back or buttocks, which are usually the preferred target for spanking."

"You know if police found any weapon at the scene that might have caused these bruises and abrasions?" Benton asked Dr. Lester.

"Not that I've been told," she replied. "That doesn't surprise me. If whoever she was with left the scene with whatever was used around her neck, maybe he also left with whatever was used to beat her. If she were beaten. Frankly, I'd lean more toward homicide if she'd been raped. But there's no evidence of that. No inflammation, no lacerations, no seminal fluid . . ."

Scarpetta returned to the gurney and moved the surgical lamp over the pelvis.

Dr. Lester watched her and said, "As I've told you, I took swabs."

She was beginning to sound unnerved and defensive.

"I also took the initiative to make several slides, which I examined microscopically for sperm," she said. "Negative. And samples went to the DNA lab, and you're aware of those results. Doesn't seem likely intercourse occurred, in my opinion. Doesn't mean that wasn't the intention. I think we have to at least be sure she wasn't planning something consensual, and the foreplay involved bondage."

"Was there lubricant at the scene? Something, perhaps, in her bathroom or by her bed that might indicate the source of it might have been the victim? I didn't see anything like that listed in the police report, as I've said," Scarpetta said.

"They say no."

"Well, that's extremely important," Scarpetta said. "If there's no source of it in her apartment, that might suggest whoever she was with brought it with him. And there are a plethora of reasons intercourse could have occurred or been attempted and there's no sperm or semen. The most obvious is erectile dysfunction, which isn't uncommon in rape. Other possible scenarios? He'd had a vasectomy, or suffered from azoospermia, resulting in a complete absence of sperm cells. Or a blocked ejaculatory duct. Or retrograde ejaculation, when the sperm and semen flow backward into the bladder instead of out of the penis and into the vagina. Or medications that interfere with the formation of sperm."

"Again, I'll remind you of what I said earlier. Not only is there no sperm, but under UV, nothing fluoresced that might indicate the presence of semen, either. Whoever she was with, it doesn't appear he ejaculated."

"Depends on if the semen was deep in the vaginal canal or rectum," Scarpetta said. "Without dissection or some type of forensic fiber-optic technology that can incorporate UV, you're not going to see anything. Did you try the light source on the inside of her mouth? You did swab her rectum and her mouth?"

"Of course."

"Fine. I'd like to take a look."

"Help yourself."

The more determined Scarpetta got, the less combative and self-assured Dr. Lester sounded.

Scarpetta opened a cabinet and found a speculum still in its wrapper. She put on fresh gloves and went through the same procedure with the body that a gynecologist did during a routine pelvic exam. She inspected the external genitalia and saw no injury or abnormalities, then, with the speculum, spread open the vaginal canal, where she found enough lubricant for several swabs, which she smeared on slides. She swabbed the rectum. She swabbed the inside of the mouth and throat, because it's not uncommon for a victim to aspirate or swallow seminal fluid while being orally sodomized.

"Stomach contents?" Scarpetta asked.

"A small amount of brownish fluid, about twenty cc's. She hadn't eaten for hours, at least," Dr. Lester said.

"You kept it?"

"No point. I'm having the usual body fluids screened for drugs."

"I wasn't thinking about drugs as much as the possibility of semen," Scarpetta said. "If she was orally sodomized, you might find semen in the stomach. Might even find it in the lungs. Unfortunately, we have to think creatively."

She retrieved a scalpel from a cart and snapped in a new blade. She began incising contusions on Terri's knees, and could feel the broken patellae beneath the abraded skin. Each kneecap was fractured into several pieces—a typical injury in car accidents where knees impact the dashboard.

"If you'll make sure I have electronic images of all X-rays," she said.

She incised contusions on the thighs and discovered ruptured blood vessels more than an inch deep, all the way to muscle. Using a six-inch ruler as a scale, she got Benton to help with photographs, and she made notes on body diagrams she retrieved from cubbyholes above the counter.

With forceps, she removed splinters from the knees and the tops of the feet and placed them on several dry slides. Seating herself before the compound microscope, she manipulated light and contrast and moved the slide on the stage. At a magnification of 100X, she could see the tracheids, the water-conducting cells of the wood, and determine that areas of them had been roughly crushed at bondline surfaces where veneers had been glued together with a very strong adhesive.

The splinters had come from abrasively planed plyboard. She and Benton looked again at the eight-by-ten photograph of Terri's nude body on the bathroom floor. In the background was the white marble countertop that included the built-in vanity and a small gold metal chair with heart-shaped back and black satin–upholstered bottom. On top of the vanity was a mirrored tray of perfumes, a brush, and a comb. Everything was perfectly neat and straight except for the oval mirror, and as Scarpetta looked closely at the photo and studied it under a lens, she confirmed that the edge of the countertop was squared off where the vanity was built in. It was sharp.

She looked through more photographs of the bathroom, taken from different angles.

"It's all one unit." She showed a photograph to Benton. "The counter built around the sink, cabinets, and the vanity with its drawer are one unit. And if you look here, this picture taken at floor level, you can see the counter has a white-painted plyboard back that's against the tile wall. Very similar to desks built into kitchen counters. However, often with plyboard built-ins, the underside that's not visible isn't painted. It's possible the underside of the vanity drawer isn't, in other words. Microscopically, we can tell the splinters recovered from her knees and the tops of her feet are from unpainted plyboard. We need to go to the scene."

Dr. Lester was behind them, looking on silently.

Scarpetta explained, "I think it's possible he forced her to sit in the chair and watch herself in the mirror while he garroted her, and when she struggled—kicking violently—her legs struck the edge of the counter, causing the linear abrasions, the deep contusions on her thighs. Her knees struck the underside of the vanity so violently her patellae were shattered. If the underside of the vanity is unpainted plyboard, that would explain the splinters in the knees, and also the tops of her feet. As short as her legs are, her feet wouldn't have reached the wall. They would have struck the underside of the drawer."

"If you're right," Dr. Lester conceded, "it will have a bearing. If she was kicking and struggling that hard, and someone was making her sit and look in the mirror, that's a different story."

"An important question is what the bathroom was like when Oscar first got there and found the body," Benton said. "Assuming his story is true."

"I think we can get some measurements and figure out if his story is true," Scarpetta said. "Depending on the chair. If Terri was sitting in it and Oscar was standing behind her, I don't believe he could have pulled up high enough with the ligature to achieve the angle of the mark on her neck. But we need to go to the scene. We need to go there quickly."

"First thing I'm going to do is outright ask him," Benton said. "Maybe he'll talk to me if he thinks new evidence has turned up and it's in his best interest to cooperate. I'll call the ward, see if he'll be reasonable."

Lucy was going through e-mail as Scarpetta explained over speakerphone why she wanted swabs from Terri Bridges's orifices, and an entire chair, to be flown to the National Security Complex in Oak Ridge, Tennessee.

"I have friends at Y-Twelve," Scarpetta said to Berger, whose approval she wanted. "I think we could get a very rapid turnaround on this. Once they have the evidence, it's just a matter of hours. The longest part will be vacuuming down the chamber, because that's going to be slower than usual. The petroleum-based lubricant has a lot of moisture."

"I thought they made nuclear weapons," Berger said. "Didn't they process the uranium for the first atomic bomb? You're not suggesting Terri Bridges had connections that might have to do with terrorism or something like that?"

Scarpetta said that while it was true that Y-12 produced components for every weapon in the United States' nuclear arsenal and also had the largest stockpile of enriched uranium, her interest in the place was because of its engineers, chemists, physicists, and especially its materials scientists.

"Are you familiar with their Visitec Large Chamber Scanning Electron Microscope?" she asked.

"I assume what you're getting at is we don't have one here," Berger said.

"I'm afraid at present there's no forensic lab on the planet that has a ten-ton microscope with a magnification of two hundred thousand X, and detectors for EDX and FTIR, energy dispersive X-ray detection, and Fourier transform infrared spectroscopy," Scarpetta said. "One-stop shopping to get the morphology, and elemental and chemical compositions, of a sample as small as a macromolecule or as large as an engine block. It's possible I might want to put an entire chair in the chamber. But we need to see. I'm not going to ask Lucy if she'll let us borrow her jet and have police fly evidence down to Tennessee and receipt it to one of my scientist friends in the middle of the night unless I'm sure there's a reason."

"Tell me more about the chair," Berger said. "Why you think it's so important?"

"From her bathroom," Scarpetta said. "I believe she was sitting in it when she was murdered—a theory at this point that I can't begin to verify without a hands-on examination. I have reason to believe she was nude when she was sitting on it, and since we know the lubricant is contaminated with an admixture of DNA, it may be contaminated with traces of other organic and inorganic substances as well. We don't know what the lubricant originally was used for, where it came from, or what's in it. But the LC-SEM might help tell us, and tell us quickly. I'd like to go to the scene, to Terri's apartment, as soon as possible."

"There's an officer in her apartment around the clock," Berger said. "So it's not a problem getting you inside. But I'd like an investigator with you. I also need to ask you again if you had any prior connection to Terri or Oscar."

"None."

"We're finding things on a computer from her apartment that make it appear you did. At least with her."

"I didn't. We'll be finished up here in fifteen, twenty minutes," Scarpetta said. "Then all we have to do is drop by Benton's office to pick up a few things. If someone could meet us in front of the hospital."

"How would you feel if that someone is Pete Marino?" Berger was deliberately bland.

"If what I'm considering might have happened to Terri Bridges is right," Scarpetta said, and she was bland, too, as if she had been expecting Berger to suggest what she did, "we're dealing with a sexual sadist who may have killed before. Possibly two other people in 2003. Benton's gotten e-mails, the same ones you've seen, from Marino."

"I haven't looked at my e-mail in the past few hours," Berger said. "We're actually just getting started on Terri Bridges's e-mail right now. Hers and Oscar Bane's."

"If my suspicion's correct, I don't see how he could have done what I'm thinking the killer did. Of course, his DNA hasn't been run through CODIS yet. But what I can say is if he was standing behind Terri while she was sitting, they would have been almost the same height. Unless he was standing on top of something like a step stool, and for him to maintain his balance while doing all the rest of it would have been difficult, if not impossible."

"What did you just say?"

"Because of their achondroplasia," Scarpetta said. "Their torsos are a normal length but their arms and legs aren't. I'll have to show you with measurements, but if someone suffering achondroplasia is four-foot-one, let's say, and is sitting in front of someone standing who's about the same height, their heads and shoulders will be almost level with each other."

"I don't understand what you're saying. It sounds like a riddle."

"Does anybody know where he is? Someone should check on him, to make sure he's safe. He may have good reason to be paranoid if he's not the killer, and I'm having my doubts. Serious doubts."

"Jesus," Berger said. "What do you mean 'where he is'? Don't tell me he's left Bellevue."

Scarpetta said, "Benton just called the prison ward. I assumed you knew."

21

Tell-Tail Hearts's flagship pet store was on Lexington Avenue, a few blocks west of Grace's Marketplace, and as Shrew walked through the blustery dark, she kept thinking of the column she'd posted several weeks ago.

She recalled descriptions of cleanliness, and a staff in lab coats who offered the highest level of care, whether it was a nutritious diet, medical attention, or affection. All of the chain's pet shops were open seven days a week, from ten in the morning until nine at night, ensuring that the puppies, in particular, with their delicate constitutions, weren't left alone for long periods. After hours, the heat or air-conditioning wasn't turned down to save on oil or electricity, and music was piped in to keep the little babies company. Shrew had done plenty of research after Ivy died and knew how critical it was for puppies to be kept hydrated and warm, and not to languish from loneliness.

When the store came in view just up on the left, it wasn't at all what Shrew expected, much less what had been described in the column the Boss had written. The display window was filled with untidy shredded newspaper, and a red plastic fire hydrant was precariously tilted to one side. There were no puppies or kittens in the window, and the glass was dirty.

Tell-Tail Hearts was sandwiched between In Your Attic, which by the looks of it sold junk, and a music store called Love Notes, which was having a going-out-of-business sale. A sign hanging on the pet store's dingy white front door read *Closed,* but all the lights were blazing, and on the counter was a big foil bag of take-out barbecue from Adam's Ribs, three doors down. Parked in front was a black Cadillac sedan, with a driver in it and the engine on.

The driver seemed to be watching Shrew as she opened the front door and walked into an invisible fog of air freshener, the spray can on top of the cash register.

"Hello?" she called out, not seeing anyone.

Puppies began to bark and stir and stare at her. Kittens snoozed in beds of wood shavings, and fish fluttered lazily in tanks. A counter wrapped around three walls, and behind it, reaching almost to the water-stained ceiling, were wire cages filled with tiny representatives of every breed of pet imaginable. She avoided making eye contact with any of them. She knew better.

Eye contact led straight to the heart, and the next

thing she knew, she was carrying someone home she hadn't intended to get, and she couldn't have all of them. And she wanted all of them, the poor, pitiful things. She needed to research her selection intelligently, ask questions, and be convinced of what would be the best choice before anyone removed a puppy from its cage and placed it in her arms. She needed to talk to the manager.

"Hello?" she called out again.

She walked tentatively toward a door in back that was slightly ajar.

"Anybody here?"

She opened the door the rest of the way. Wooden stairs led down to the basement, where she could hear a dog barking, then several others began barking. She started down, one slow step at a time, careful because the lighting was poor and she'd had too much bourbon. Walking all the way here had helped a little but not nearly enough. Her thoughts were dull and sluggish, and her nose felt numb the way it got when she was tipsy.

She found herself in a storage area that was thick with shadows and stunk like sickness, feces, and urine. Amid piled boxes of pet supplies and bags of dry food were cages filled with filthy shredded paper, and then she saw a wooden table with glass vials and syringes, and red bags with *Biohazard Infectious Waste* stamped on them in black, and a pair of heavy black rubber gloves.

Just beyond the table was a walk-in freezer.

Its steel door was open wide, and she saw what was inside. A man in a dark suit and a black cowboy hat and a woman in a long gray frock coat had their backs to her, their voices muffled by loud blowing air. Shrew saw what they were doing, and she wanted to get out as fast as she could, but her feet seemed stuck to the concrete floor. She stared in horror, and then the woman saw her and Shrew turned around and ran.

"Hold on!" a deep voice yelled after her. "Whoa now!"

Heavy footsteps sounded after her, and she missed a step on the stairs and whacked her shin hard. A hand grabbed her elbow, and the man in the cowboy hat was escorting her back into the bright lights of the store. Then the lady in the gray frock coat was there, too. She glared disapprovingly at her but looked too worn-out to do anything about Shrew's transgression.

The man in the cowboy hat demanded, "What the hell do you think you're doing sneaking around in here like that?"

His eyes were dark and bloodshot in his dissipated face, and he had big white sideburns and plenty of flashy gold jewelry.

"I wasn't sneaking," Shrew said. "I was looking for the manager."

Her heart pounded like a kettledrum.

"We're closed," the man said.

"I came in to buy a puppy," she said, and she started to cry.

"There's a closed sign in the door," he said while the woman mutely stood by.

"Your door's unlocked. I came downstairs to tell you. Anybody could walk right in." Shrew couldn't stop crying.

She couldn't stop envisioning what she'd seen in the freezer.

The man looked at the woman, as if demanding an explanation. He walked over to the front door and checked, then muttered something. It probably dawned on him that Shrew had to be telling the truth. How else would she have gotten in?

"Well, we're closed. It's a holiday," he said, and she guessed him to be about sixty-five years old, maybe seventy. He had a Midwest drawl that seemed to crawl off his tongue.

She had a feeling he'd been doing the same thing she was a little earlier, drinking, and she noticed that the big gold ring he wore was shaped like a dog's head.

"I'm sorry," she said. "I saw the lights on and came in, thinking you were open. I really am sorry. I thought I might buy a puppy, and some food and toys and things. Sort of a New Year's present to myself."

She picked up a can of food off a shelf.

Before she could stop herself, she said, "Wasn't this banned in that Chinese-import melamine scare?"

"Believe you have that confused with toothpaste," the man said to the woman in the gray frock coat, who had a lifeless jowly face and long dyed black hair straying from a barrette.

"That's right. Toothpaste," she said, and she had the same accent. "A lot of people got liver damage from it. Of course, they never tell you the rest of the story. Like maybe they were alcoholics, and that's why they had liver damage."

Shrew wasn't uninformed. She knew about the toothpaste that had killed several people because it had diethylene glycol in it, and the man and woman knew that wasn't what Shrew was talking about. This was a bad place—maybe the worst in the world—and she'd come at a bad time, the worst time imaginable, and she'd seen something so awful she'd never be the same.

What was she thinking? It was the evening of New Year's Day, and no pet store in the city was going to be open, including this one. So why were they here?

After being down in the basement, she knew why they were here.

"It's important to clear up confusion," the man said to Shrew. "You had no business down there."

"I didn't see anything." A clear indication she'd seen everything.

The man in the cowboy hat and gold jewelry said, "If an animal dies from something contagious, you do what you got to do, and you got to do it fast to make sure the other animals don't catch it. And once you do the merciful thing, you have to deal with temporary storage. Do you understand what I'm getting at?"

Shrew noticed six empty cages with their doors open wide. She wished she'd noticed them when she first walked in. Maybe she would have left. She remembered the other empty cages in the basement, and what was on the table, and then what was in the freezer.

She started to cry again and said, "But some of them were moving."

The man said to her, "You live around here?"

"Not really."

"What's your name?"

She was so scared and upset, she stupidly told him, and then stupidly said, "And if you're thinking I'm some kind of inspector for the Department of Agriculture or some animal group?" She shook her head. "I just came in to get a puppy. I forgot it's a holiday, that's all. I understand about pets getting sick. Kennel cough. Parvovirus. One gets it, they all get it."

The man and woman silently looked at her as if they didn't need to talk to come up with a plan.

He said to Shrew, "Tell you what. We're getting a new shipment tomorrow, all kinds to choose from. You come back and pick out whatever you want. On the house. You like a springer spaniel, a shih tzu, or what about a dachshund?"

Shrew couldn't stop crying, and she said, "I'm sorry. I'm a little drunk."

The woman retrieved the can of air freshener from the top of the cash register and headed back to the basement door. She closed it behind her, and Shrew could hear her on the stairs. Shrew and the man in the cowboy hat were alone. He took her arm and walked her out of the shop, where the black Cadillac sedan was parked. The driver in his suit and cap got out and opened the back door for them.

The man in the cowboy hat said to Shrew, "Get in and I'll drop you off. It's too cold to be walking. Where do you live?"

Lucy wondered if Oscar Bane was aware that his girlfriend had eighteen e-mail usernames. He was far less complicated and probably more honest. He had only one.

"Each of hers was for a specific purpose," Lucy was telling Berger. "Voting in polls, blogging, visiting certain chat rooms, posting consumer reviews, subscribing to various online publications, a couple of them for getting online news."

"That's a lot," Berger said, glancing at her watch.

Lucy could think of few people she knew who had a harder time being still. Berger was like a hummingbird that never quite landed, and the more restive she got, the more Lucy slowed things down. She found that quite the irony. Almost always it was the other way around.

"It's really not a lot these days," Lucy said. "Her e-mail service, like most of them, was free as long as she didn't want additional options. But basic accounts? She could open as many as she wanted, all virtually untraceable because she didn't need a credit card, since there's no fee, and she wasn't required to divulge any personal information unless she chose to. All anonymous, in other words. I've come across people who have hundreds, are a one-person crowd, their aliases talking to each other, agreeing, disagreeing, in chat rooms, comments sections. Or maybe they're ordering things or buying subscriptions they don't want easily linked to them, or who knows what. But with rare exception, no matter how many aliases a person has, usually there's just one that's really them, so to speak. The one they use for their normal correspondence. Oscar's is Carbane, rather straightforward—as it's the last part of Oscar appended to his surname, unless his hobby is organic chemistry and he's referencing the systematic analogue of the mononuclear hydride CH-four, or he builds airfield models and is alluding to the carbane struts mounted to biplane wings. Which I sort of doubt. Terri's is Lunasee, and we should look at those e-mails first."

"Why would a forensic psychology graduate student pick a username like that?" Berger said. "Seems extremely insensitive to make an allusion to lunatics or lunacy or any other disparagement from the Dark Ages. In fact, it's worse than insensitive, it's cold-blooded."

"Maybe she was an insensitive, cold-blooded person. I'm not one to deify the dead. A lot of murder victims weren't necessarily nice people when they were alive."

"Let's start with mid-December and work our way up to the most recent ones," Berger directed.

There were one hundred and three e-mails since December 15. Seven were to Terri's parents in Scottsdale, and all the rest were between Terri and Oscar Bane. Lucy sorted them by time and date, without opening them, to see if there was a pattern of who wrote most often and when.

"Far more from him," she said. "More than three times as many. And it looks like he wrote her at all hours. But I'm not seeing any e-mails from her that were sent later than eight p.m. And in fact, most days of the week, nothing from her after four in the afternoon. That's really strange. You'd think she had a night job."

"It could be they talked on the phone. Hopefully, Morales has already started on phone records," Berger said. "Or he should have. Or maybe he went on vacation and didn't tell me. Or maybe he'd better start looking for a new career. I like the last option best."

"What's his problem, anyway? And why do you put up with it? He treats you with complete disrespect."

"He treats everyone with complete disrespect and calls it prioritizing."

"What do you call it?" Lucy continued opening e-mails.

"I call it cocky and irritating as hell," Berger said. "He thinks he's smarter than everyone, including me, but what makes it complicated is he *is* smarter than most people. And he's good at what he does if he chooses to be. And in most cases, his priorities end up making sense and he gets things done in a fraction of the time it takes someone else. Either that or somehow he manages to get people to do the work for him, then finagles accolades for it while managing to get that person into trouble. Which is probably what he's doing now."

"To Marino," Lucy said.

It was as if she had decided it was easiest to think of Marino as just another detective she really didn't know. Or maybe she didn't hate him as much as Berger had assumed.

"Yes, he's putting Marino out on a limb," Berger said. "Marino seems to be the only one doing anything that matters."

"He married?" As Lucy opened e-mails. "Obviously, I'm not talking about Marino."

"He's not exactly the commitment type. Screws anything that stands still. Maybe even if it doesn't stand still."

"I've heard rumors about the two of you."

"Oh, yes. Our famous Tavern on the Green tryst," Berger said.

They skimmed through the typical mundane electronic exchanges that people fire back and forth.

"That murder in Central Park last fall," Lucy said. "The marathon runner raped and strangled. Near the Ramble."

"Morales drove me to the scene. Afterwards, we stopped by Tavern on the Green for coffee and to talk about the case. Next thing, it's all over the city that we're an item."

"That's because it was in *Gotham Gotcha*. One of the infamous sightings. Including a photograph of the two of you looking cozy," Lucy said.

"Don't tell me you have search engines chugging after me morning, noon, and night."

"My search engines don't chug," Lucy said. "They're a little faster than that. The source of information for that gossip column is mainly what the readers send in. Almost always anonymously. How do you know he didn't?"

"That would have been pretty clever of him. Taking a photograph of both of us while we were sitting across the table from each other."

"Or getting somebody else to," Lucy said. "Quite a feather in his cap. The superstud detective having a cozy tryst at Tavern on the Green with the superstar DA. Be careful of him."

"In case you missed the important point, we weren't having a tryst," Berger said. "We were having coffee."

"I have a funny feeling about him. Maybe recognize certain traits even though I haven't met him. Someone who should have complete power over him, outranks him, outclasses him, and he, quote, prioritizes. He makes you wait your turn in line? Makes himself the center of your attention in a negative way, because he aggressively trips you up at every chance? Who's got the power? A tried-and-true trick. Assert dominance, be disrespectful, and next thing, the big boss is in your bed."

"I didn't realize you're such an expert," Berger said.

"Not that kind of expert. When I've had sex with a guy, it's never been because he dominated me. It's always been because I made a mistake."

"I'm sorry. I shouldn't have said what I did," Berger said.

She skimmed through e-mails. Lucy fell silent.

"I apologize," Berger again said. "Morales makes me angry because, you're right, I can't control him and I can't get rid of him. People like him shouldn't go into policing. They don't blend with the rank and file. They don't take orders. They're not team players, and every-body hates them."

"That's why I had such a stunning career with the Feds," Lucy said quietly, seriously. "Difference is, I don't play games. I don't try to overpower and belittle people so I can get what I want from them. I don't like Morales. I don't have to know him. You should be careful of him. He's the sort of person who could cause you real trouble. It worries me that you never really know where he is or what he's doing."

She got interested in four e-mails on a split screen—e-mails between Terri and Oscar.

"I don't think they were talking on the phone," she then said. "Sent at eight-forty-seven, sent at nine-ten, sent at ten-fourteen, sent at eleven-nineteen. Why would he be writing her almost every hour if he's talking to her on the phone? Notice that the ones from him are long, while hers are short. Consistently."

"One of those instances when what isn't said matters more than what is," Berger observed. "No references to phone calls, to any responses from her, any contacts with her. He's saying things like *I'm thinking of you. Wish I were with you. What are you doing? You're probably working.* There doesn't seem to be any back-and-forth between them."

"Exactly. He's writing to his lover several times a night. She's not writing back."

"He's obviously the more openly romantic of the two," Berger said. "Not saying she wasn't in love with him, because I don't know. We don't know. We may never know. But her e-mails are less demonstrative, more reserved. He's comfortable making sexual references that are almost pornographic."

"Depends on your definition of pornographic."

Berger went back to an e-mail Oscar had written to Terri not even a week ago.

"Why is that pornographic?" Lucy asked.

"I think what I meant was sexually explicit."

"You work sex crimes?" Lucy said. "Or do I have you mixed up with a Sunday-school teacher? He's writing about exploring her with his tongue. He's writing about how writing about it arouses him."

"I think he was trying to have cybersex with her. And she was rebuffing him by not responding. He's getting angry with her."

"He was trying to tell her how he felt," Lucy pointed out. "And the less she responded, maybe the more he persisted out of insecurity."

"Or anger," Berger emphasized. "And his increased sexual references are manifestations of his anger and aggression. That's not a good combination when the person these feelings are directed at is about to get murdered."

"I could see how working sex crimes might take its toll. Maybe make it difficult to tell the difference between erotica and pornography, between lust and lewdness, between insecurity and rage, and accept that some instant replays are a celebration and not a degradation," Lucy said. "Maybe you're jaded because everything you see is disgusting and violent, and therefore all sex is always a crime."

"What I don't see is any allusion whatsoever to rough sex, bondage, S-and-M," Berger said as they read. "And I'd appreciate it if you'd refrain from analyzing me. Amateurishly, I might add."

"I could analyze you, and it wouldn't be amateur-ishly. But you'd have to ask me first."

Berger didn't ask, and they kept reading.

Lucy said, "So far, no allusions to anything, quote, kinky, I agree. Nothing rough. Not a hint of handcuffs, dog collars, all that good stuff. Certainly no allusion to anything like the lubricant Aunt Kay told you about a little while ago. No body lotions, massage oils, nothing like that, and by the way, I text-messaged my pilots, and they'll be waiting at La Guardia if there's evidence to be flown to Oak Ridge. What I was saying, though, is lubricants aren't compatible with oral sex unless they're, bluntly put, edible. And what Aunt Kay described sounds more like a petroleum-based lubricant, which most people aren't going to apply if they plan on having oral sex."

"The other puzzling part? The condoms in Terri's nightstand," Berger said. "Lubricated ones. So why would Oscar use a petroleum-type lubricant, saying he did?"

"Do you know what type she had in her nightstand?"

Berger opened her briefcase and pulled out a file. She looked through paperwork until she found a list of evi-dence collected from the scene last night.

"Durex Love Condoms," she said.

Lucy Googled it and reported, "Latex, twenty-five per-cent stronger and a larger size than standard condoms, easy to roll on with one hand, good to know. Extra head-room with a reservoir tip, also good to know. But not compatible with a petroleum-based lubricant, which can weaken latex and cause it to break. That and the fact that no petroleum-based lubricant was found in her apartment, and you can read my mind. You ask me, everything keeps pointing away from Oscar and toward someone else."

More e-mails, getting closer to the day Terri was murdered. Oscar's frustration and unrequited sexual love were becoming increasingly apparent, and he was beginning to sound more irrational.

"A lot of excuses," Lucy said. "Poor guy. He sounds miserable."

Berger read more and commented, "It's almost annoying, makes me not like her very much and feel rather sorry for him, I must confess. She doesn't want to rush into anything. He needs to be patient. She's overwhelmed by work."

"Sounds like someone who has a secret life," Lucy said.

"Maybe."

"People in love don't see each other only one night a week," Lucy said. "Especially since neither of them had physical workplaces outside the home. That we know of. Something's not right. If you're in love, in lust, you don't sleep. You can hardly eat. You can't concentrate on your work, and you sure as hell can't stay away from each other."

"As we get closer to her murder, it gets worse," Berger said. "He's sounding paranoid. Really upset with how little time they spend together. Seems to be suspicious of her. Why will she see him only once a week? And only on Saturday nights, and why does she basically kick him out of bed before dawn? Why does she suddenly want to see his apartment when she's never been interested in the past? What is it she thinks she'll find in there? It's not a good idea, he says. He would have told her yes in the beginning. But not now. He loves her so much. She's the love of his life. He wishes she hadn't asked to see his apartment because he can't tell her why the answer's no. One day in person he'll tell her. God. This is weird. After three months of dating each other, sleeping with each other, she's never set foot inside his apartment? And now suddenly she wants to go in there? Why? And why won't he let her? Why won't he explain it unless he does so in person?"

"Maybe the same reason he never tells her where he's been or what he's doing," Lucy said. "He doesn't tell her his plans—if he's going to run errands on a given day, for example. He says he walked x number of miles but doesn't give specifics as to where or when he plans to do it next. He writes the way one would if he's worried that someone else might be reading his e-mails or watching him."

"Jump back earlier to last fall, last summer or spring," Berger said. "And let's see if the pattern's similar."

They skimmed for a while. Those e-mails between Terri and Oscar weren't at all like the recent ones. Not only were they less personal, but the tone and content of his were much more relaxed. He mentioned libraries and bookstores that were his favorites. He described where he liked to walk in Central Park, and a gym he'd tried a few times, but a lot of the machines weren't the right fit.

He included a number of details that revealed information he wouldn't have been open about were he worried that someone else was reading his e-mails or, in other words, spying on him.

"He wasn't scared back then," Berger said. "What Benton's concluded seems right. He says Oscar is afraid of something now—right now. A perceived threat—right now."

Lucy typed Berger's name into a search field and said, "I'm curious to see if there's any mention anywhere of his phone call to your office last month. His fears of being under electronic surveillance, followed, his identity stolen, and so on."

She got a hit on Jaime Berger's name, but the e-mail in question had nothing to do with Oscar's recent phone call to the DA's office:

```
Date: Mon, 2 July 2007 10:47:31
From: "Terri Bridges"
To: "Jaime Berger"
CC: "Dr. Oscar Bane"
Subject: "Interview with Dr. Kay Scarpetta"
Dear Ms. Berger,
   I'm a graduate student writing a master's
thesis on the evolution of forensic science
and medicine from earlier centuries to mod-
ern times. It's tentatively titled "Forensic
Follies."
   In brief: We've come full circle, gone
from the ridiculous to the sublime, from the
```

quackery of phrenology, physiognomy, and the
image of the murderer captured by the retina
of the victim's eye to the "magic tricks" of
modern movies and TV dramas. I'll happily
explain further if you might be so gracious
as to answer me. E-mail is preferable. But
I'm including my phone number.

   I'd love your thoughts, of course, but
my real reason for writing is I'm trying to
contact Dr. Kay Scarpetta—who better for the
topic, I'm sure you agree! Perhaps, if nothing else, you'll give her my e-mail address?
I've tried to contact her several times at
her office in Charleston, but with no success.
I know you've had professional connections
in the past, and assume you're still in touch
with each other and friends.
Sincerely,
Terri Bridges
212-555-2907

"Obviously, you never got this," Lucy said.

"Sent to New York City Government-dot-org from someone who called herself Lunasee?" Berger replied. "I wouldn't get that in a million years. A more important question to me is why Kay didn't know Terri was trying to get hold of her. Charleston isn't exactly New York City."

"It may as well have been," Lucy said.

Berger got out of her chair and collected her coat, her briefcase.

"I have to go," she said. "We'll probably have a meeting tomorrow. I'll call you when I know the time."

"Late last spring, early summer," Lucy said. "I can see why my aunt never got Terri's message, if that's what happened. And likely, it is."

She got up, too, and they walked through the loft.

"Rose was dying," Lucy said. "Mid-June to early July, she lived in my aunt's carriage house. Neither of them went to the office anymore. And Marino wasn't there. Aunt Kay's new practice was small. She was only about two years into it. There really was no other staff."

"No one to take a message, and no one to answer the phone," Berger said as she put on her coat. "Before I forget, if you'd forward that e-mail to me so I have a copy. Since you don't seem to print things around here. And if you find anything else I should know about?"

"Marino had been gone since early May," Lucy said. "Rose never knew what happened to him, which was really unfair. He vanished into thin air, and then she died. No matter what, she cared about him."

"And you? Where were you while the phones rang and no one picked up or noticed?"

"It all seems like a different life, as if I wasn't there," Lucy said. "I almost can't remember where I was or what I did toward the end, but it was awful. My aunt put Rose in the guest room and stayed with her around the clock. She spiraled down really quickly after Marino disappeared, and I stayed away from the office and the labs. I'd known Rose all my life. She was like the cool grandmother everyone wants, just so cool in her proper suits with her hair pinned up, but a piece of work and not afraid of anything whether it was dead bodies or guns or Marino's motorcycles."

"What about dying? Was she afraid?"

"No."

"But you were," Berger said.

"All of us were. Me most of all. So I did a really brilliant thing and suddenly got busy. For some reason it seemed urgent that I do a refresher in advanced executive protection training, attack recognition and analysis, tactical firearms, the usual. I got rid of one helicopter and found another, then went to the Bell Helicopter school in Texas for several weeks when I really didn't need to do that, either. Next thing I knew, everybody had moved up north. And Rose was in a cemetery vault in Richmond, overlooking the James, because she loved the water so much, and my aunt made sure she'd have a water view forever."

"So somehow what we're dealing with now, in a way, started back then," Berger said. "When nobody was paying attention."

"I'm not sure what started," Lucy said.

They stood near the front door, neither one of them particularly keen to open it. Berger wondered when they would be alone again like this, or if they should be, and what Lucy must think of her. She knew what she thought of herself. She had been dishonest, and she couldn't leave it like that. Lucy didn't deserve it. Neither of them did.

"I had a roommate at Columbia," Berger said, fastening her coat. "We shared this slum of an apartment. I didn't have money, wasn't born with it, married into it, and you know all that. During law school we lived in this most God-awful place in Morningside Heights, it's a wonder both of us weren't murdered in our sleep."

She tucked her hands into her pockets while Lucy's eyes held hers, both of them leaning their shoulders against the door.

"We were extremely close," Berger added.

"You don't owe me any explanations," Lucy said. "I completely respect who you are and why you live the way you do."

"You don't know enough to respect anything, actually. And I'm going to give you an explanation, not because I owe it but because I want to. She had something wrong with her, my roommate. I won't say her name. A mood disorder, which I had no understanding of at the time, and when she got ugly and angry I thought she meant it. I fought with her when I shouldn't have, because that made matters only worse, unbelievably worse. One Saturday night, a neighbor called the police. I'm surprised you didn't dig that up somewhere. Nothing was done about it, but it was rather unpleasant, and both of us were drunk and looked like train wrecks. If I ever run for office, you can imagine, if there are stories like that."

"Why would there be?" Lucy asked. "Unless you plan on getting in fights when you're drunk and looking like a train wreck."

"There was never a threat of that with Greg, you see. I don't think we ever yelled at each other. Certainly never threw anything. We coexisted without rancor or much of anything. A relatively pleasant détente, much of the time."

"What happened to your roommate?"

"I suppose it depends on how you measure success," Berger said. "But nothing good, in my opinion. It will only get worse for her because she lives a lie, meaning she doesn't live at all, and life is very unforgiving if you don't live it, especially as you get older. I've never lived a lie. You may think so, but I haven't. I've simply had to figure things out as I've gone along, and I've respected decisions I've made, right or wrong, no matter how hard that's been. Many things remain irrelevant as long as they remain theoretical."

"Meaning there wasn't someone and hasn't been when there shouldn't have been," Lucy said.

"I'm no Sunday-school teacher. Far from it," Berger said. "But my life is nobody's business, and it's mine to mess up, and I don't intend to mess it up. I won't let you mess it up, nor do I intend to mess up yours."

"Do you always start with disclaimers?"

"I don't start," Berger said.

"This time you're going to have to," Lucy said. "Because I'm not. Not with you."

Berger slid her hands out of her coat pockets and touched Lucy's face, then reached for the door but didn't open it. She touched Lucy's face again and kissed her.

22

Nineteen floors below the prison ward, in the parking lot across East 27th, Marino was a lone figure obscured by hydraulic lifts, most of them empty at this hour, no valet in sight.

He watched them in the bright green field of a long-range night-vision monocular, because he needed to see her. He needed to look at her in person, even if it was covertly and from a distance and for only a moment. He needed to somehow feel reassured that she hadn't changed. If she was still the same, she wouldn't be cruel to him when she saw him. She wouldn't disgrace or humiliate or shun him. Not that she would have in the past, no matter how much he deserved it. But what did he know about her anymore, except what he read or saw on TV?

Scarpetta and Benton had just left the morgue and were

taking a shortcut through the park, back to Bellevue. It was dizzying to see her again, and unreal, as if she'd been dead, and Marino imagined what she'd think if she knew how close he'd come to dying. After what he'd done, he hadn't wanted to be here anymore. While he lay in the guest bed of her carriage house the morning after he'd hurt her, he'd started going through a list of possibilities, intermittently fighting off nausea while the worst headache of his life hammered his brain to pulp.

His first thought was to drive his truck or maybe his motorcycle off a bridge and drown himself. Then again, he might survive, and he was terrified of not being able to breathe. That meant smothering wasn't a good choice, either, using a plastic bag, for example, and he couldn't stomach the thought of hanging, of twisting and thrashing after kicking the chair out from under himself and then changing his mind. He'd briefly considered sitting in a bathtub and slashing his throat, but with the first spurt of blood from his carotid, he'd want to take it back and it would be too late.

As for carbon monoxide poisoning? It gave him too much time to think. Poison? Same thing, and it was painful, and if he chickened out and called 911, he'd end up with his stomach pumped and a complete loss of respect from all who knew about it. Jumping off a building? Never. His luck, he'd survive and be maimed beyond recognition. Last on the list was his nine-millimeter pistol. And Scarpetta had hidden it.

As he'd lain in her guest room bed trying to figure out where she might have tucked it out of sight, he decided he'd never find it, was too sick to find it, and he could always shoot himself later because he had a couple extra guns in his fishing shack, but it would have to be a precision shooting because the worst scenario of all was to end up in an iron lung.

When he'd eventually contacted Benton at McLean and confessed all this, Benton matter-of-factly informed him that if an iron lung was the only thing stopping him, he had no worries unless he tried to kill himself with polio. That was exactly what he'd said, adding that most likely, if he did a bad job shooting himself, he'd end up with brain damage that profoundly compromised him but left him vaguely aware of why he'd wanted to off himself in the first place.

What would be really shitty luck, Benton had said, was an irreversible coma that became a discussion among Supreme Court justices before someone got the go-ahead to pull the plug. While he'd said it wasn't likely Marino would have any awareness that this was going on, no one knew for sure. You'd have to be the person who was brain-dead to know for sure, he'd said.

You mean I could hear people saying they were going to take me off that . . . ? Marino had asked.

Life support, Benton had said.

So it wouldn't breathe for me anymore, and I might be aware of it but nobody knows I am?

You wouldn't be able to breathe anymore. And it's within the realm of possibility you might be aware that you were about to be taken off the respirator. Have the plug pulled, in other words.

Then I could literally watch the person walk to the wall and pull it out of the socket.

It's possible.

And I'd instantly start smothering to death.

You wouldn't be able to breathe. But hopefully loved ones would be there helping you through it, even though they wouldn't know you were aware of them.

Which brought Marino right back to his fear of smothering, and the grim reminder that the only loved ones he had were the very people he'd just fucked over, most of all, her, Scarpetta. It was at this point in a motel room near the Boston Bowl Family Fun Center where he and Benton had been having this discussion that Marino decided not to kill himself but to take the longest vacation he'd ever had in his life, at the treatment center on Massachusetts's North Shore.

If he showed improvement once the alcohol and the male-performance-enhancement drugs had been completely flushed out of his system, and if he stuck with therapy and was sincere about it, then the next step would be finding him a job. So here he was, about half a year later, in New York, working for Berger and hiding in a parking lot just to catch a glimpse of Scarpetta before she got into his car and they drove to a crime scene, business as usual.

He watched her move silently, eerily in bright green, her gestures familiar as she talked, every detail vivid but so far removed from him, he felt as if he were a ghost. He could see her but she couldn't see him, and her life had gone on without him, and knowing her as well as he did, he was sure that by now she had gotten over what he'd done to her. What she wouldn't have gotten over was his disappearing the way he did. Or maybe he was giving himself too much importance, he decided. It could very well be that she never thought about him anymore, and when she saw him, it wouldn't matter. She wouldn't feel anything, would scarcely remember the past.

So much had happened since. She'd gotten married. She'd left Charleston. She was the chief of a big office just outside Boston. She and Benton actually lived together like a couple, for the first time, in a beautiful old house in Belmont that Marino had driven past at night once or twice. Now they had a place in New York, too, and sometimes he walked along the Hudson several blocks west of Central Park and stared at their building, counting the floors until he was pretty sure he knew exactly which apartment was theirs, and he imagined what it must look like inside and the beautiful view they must have of the river, and of the city at night. She was on television all the time, was really famous, but whenever he tried to envision people asking her for her autograph, he drew a blank. That part he didn't get. She wasn't the type to like that sort of attention, or at least he hoped she wasn't, because if she was, she had changed.

He watched her through the powerful night-vision scope that Lucy had given to him for his birthday two years ago, and was lonely for the sound of Scarpetta's voice. He recognized her mood by the way she moved, shifting her position, slightly gesturing her dark-gloved hands. She was understated. People said that about her all the time, that she said and did less, rather than more, and because of it made her point more loudly, so to speak. She wasn't histrionic. That was another word Marino had heard. In fact, he remembered, Berger had said it when describing how Scarpetta conducted herself on the witness stand. She didn't need to raise her voice or flail away but could just sit there calmly and shoot straight with the jurors, and they trusted her, believed her.

Through the scope, Marino noticed her long coat and the shape of her neatly styled blond hair, a little longer than she used to wear it, a little bit over her collar and brushed straight back from her forehead. He could make out her familiar strong features, so hard to compare to anyone he could think of, because she was pretty and she wasn't, her face too sharply defined to be of beauty-pageant quality or to fit in with the sticklike women in designer clothes who cruised the runways of fashion shows.

He thought he might throw up again, just like he had that morning in her carriage house. His heart began to pound as if it were trying to hurt itself.

He longed for her but as he hid in his rust-smelling, filthy shadowy space, he realized he didn't love her the way he once did. He had driven the stake of self-destruction into the part of him where hope had always hidden, and it was dead. He no longer hoped she would fall in love with him someday. She was married, and hope was dead. Even if Benton was out of the picture, hope was dead. Marino had killed hope and killed it savagely, and he had never done anything like that in his life, and he had done it to her.

On his most disgusting, drunken dates, he had never forced himself on a woman.

If he kissed her and she didn't want his tongue in her mouth, he withdrew. If she pushed his hands away, he didn't touch her again uninvited. If he had a hard-on and she wasn't interested, he never pushed himself against her or shoved her hand between his legs. If she noticed his soldier wouldn't settle down, he'd make his same old jokes. *He's just saluting you, baby. He always stands up when there's a lady in the room. Hey, babe, just 'cause I got a stick shift don't mean you gotta drive my car.*

Marino might be a crude, poorly educated man, but he wasn't a sex offender. He wasn't a bad human being. But how was Scarpetta supposed to know? He didn't fix it the morning after, didn't make even a feeble attempt at it when she appeared in the guest bedroom with dry toast and coffee. What did he do? He faked amnesia. He complained about the bourbon she kept in her bar, as if it was her fault for having something in her house that could cause such a wicked hangover and a blackout.

He acknowledged nothing. Shame and panic had made him mute because he wasn't exactly sure what he'd done, and he wasn't going to ask. Better if he figured it out on his own, and over weeks and months of investigating his own crime, he finally fit the pieces together. He couldn't have gone but so far, because when he awakened the next morning, he was fully dressed, and the only body fluid detectable was his cold, stinking sweat.

With clarity, he remembered only fragments: pushing her against the wall, hearing the ripping of fabric, feeling the softness of her skin, her voice saying he was hurting her, and she knew he didn't want that. He clearly remembered she didn't move, and now he understood it and wondered how her instincts could have been so right. He was completely out of control, and she was smart enough not to incite him further by fighting. He remembered nothing else, not even her breasts, except his vague recollection that he had been surprised by them but not unpleasantly. Rather, after decades of elaborate fantasies, they didn't look quite the way he had envisioned them. But then, no woman's did.

It was a realization that came with maturity and had nothing to do with intuition or common sense. As a horny little boy whose only point of reference was the dirty magazines his father hid in the tool shed, Marino couldn't possibly know what he eventually discovered. Breasts, like fingerprints, have their own individual characteristics that aren't necessarily discernible through clothes. Every breast he'd ever been intimate with had its own unique size, shape, symmetry, slope, with the most obvious variable being the nipple, which really was what the timeless attraction was about. Marino, who considered himself a connoisseur, would be the first to say that big was better, but once he got beyond the ogling and fondling, it was all about what he put in his mouth.

In the green field of the night-vision monocular, Scarpetta and Benton walked out of the park, onto the sidewalk. She had her hands in her pockets, wasn't carrying anything, meaning she and Benton would be making at least one stop, most likely his office. He noticed they weren't talking much, and then, as if they read Marino's thoughts, they held hands and Benton leaned down and kissed her.

When they reached the street, so close that he didn't need light intensification to make out their faces, they were looking at each other as if they'd meant the kiss and that there would be more to come, Marino thought. They reached First Avenue and faded out of sight.

Marino was about to abandon his safe haven of triple-stacked hydraulic lifts when he noticed another figure appear in the park, walking briskly. Then he saw yet another figure enter the park from the direction of the DNA building. In the bright green field of the night-vision monocular, Investigator Mike Morales and Dr. Lenora Lester sat next to each other on a bench.

They said things Marino couldn't hear, and she gave him a large envelope. Probably information about Terri Bridges's autopsy. But it was a peculiar handoff, as if they were spies. He entertained the notion that the two of them were having an affair, and his stomach flopped as he imagined her grim, pinched face, imagined her bird-like body naked on a wad of sheets.

That couldn't be it.

It was far more likely that Dr. Lester had called Morales as fast as she could so she could take credit for whatever Scarpetta had discovered in the morgue. And he would want the information before anybody else got it, including Marino and, most of all, Berger. That must mean Scarpetta had found out something important. Marino watched until Dr. Lester and Morales got up from the bench. He disappeared around a corner of the DNA building, and she headed in Marino's direction, toward East 27th, walking her fast walk, her eyes on the BlackBerry in her bare hands.

She hurried through the cold wind toward First Avenue, where she would probably catch a cab, then take the ferry back home to New Jersey. It appeared she was text-messaging someone.

Museum Mile used to be Shrew's favorite walk. She'd set out from her apartment with a bottle of water and a granola bar, and choose the Madison Avenue route so she could window-shop as anticipation built and accelerated her feet.

The highlight was the Guggenheim, where she was thrilled by Clyfford Still, John Chamberlain, Robert Rauschenberg, and of course Picasso. The last exhibition she'd seen there was Jackson Pollock Paintings on Paper, and that had been two years ago this spring.

What had happened?

It wasn't as if she had a time clock to punch, or a life, really. But after she'd gone to work for the Boss, little by little she'd stopped going to museums, to the theater, to the galleries, to newsstands or Barnes & Noble.

She tried to remember the last time she'd tucked herself into the pages of a good book or outsmarted a crossword puzzle or patronized musicians in the park or been mindless in a movie theater or drunk on a poem.

She'd become a bug in amber, trapped in lives she

didn't know or care about. Gossip. The tawdry, banal goings-on of people who had the heart and soul of paper dolls. Why did she care what Michael Jackson wore to court? What difference did it make to her or anyone else that Madonna had fallen off her horse?

Instead of looking at art, Shrew had started looking into the toilet of life, taking delight in other people's shit. She began to realize a number of truths as she thought about her dark ride home along the River Styx of Lexington Avenue in the black Cadillac sedan. The man in the cowboy hat had been nice to her, even patted her knee as she'd gotten out of his car, but he'd never given her his name, and common sense had warned her not to ask.

She'd walked right into evil tonight. First Marilyn Monroe, then the worm, then the basement. Maybe God had just administered spiritual electroshock therapy of sorts, by showing her the truth about the heartless way she lived, and she looked around her rent-controlled one-bedroom apartment, and possibly for the first time since her husband was no longer in it, she saw what it really looked like, and that it hadn't changed.

The corduroy sofa and matching chair were unpretentious and comforting, and the worn nappy texture brought her husband back to the living room. She saw him sitting in the recliner, reading the *Times,* chewing on the butt of a cigar until it was slimy, and she smelled the smoke that used to saturate every molecule of their lives. She smelled it now as if she'd never brought in professional cleaners.

For several seasons, she couldn't muster up the

courage to clear out his clothes and tuck away items she couldn't bear to look at or part with.

How often had she lectured him not to cross the street just because the white man on the traffic signal assured him it was fine?

How was that any less stupid than standing on the sidewalk because the red hand forbade him to walk, even though the cross street was barricaded, not a car in sight?

In the end, he'd been beckoned to by the white man instead of listening to Shrew, and one day she had a husband she was constantly nagging about cigars and not picking up after himself, and the next day and the ones after that she had nothing but his odors and his clutter, and the memory of the last words they'd exchanged on his way out the door.

How we doing for coffee cream? As he put on his silly wool deerstalker's cap.

She'd bought it for him in London several decades back, and he'd never figured out she didn't really mean for him to wear it.

I don't know how we're doing for coffee cream, since you're the only one who drinks coffee with cream in it. That was what she'd said.

The last words of hers in his ears.

The words of a shrew who had come to live with them that same cruel month of April, when they'd outsourced her job to someone in India and the two of them were knee-to-knee inside their small place, day after day, and worried sick about money. Because he was an accountant, and he had done the math.

She'd scripted their last moment together on this earth, revised it every way imaginable, wondering if there was something she could have done or mentioned that might have altered fate. If she'd said she loved him and would he like his favorite lamb chops and a baked sweet potato for dinner, and had she bought a potted hyacinth for the coffee table, might his mind have been on one or the other or all of it instead of whatever it was on when he didn't look both ways?

Was he irritable and distracted because of her shrewish remark about the coffee cream?

What if she'd sweetly reminded him to be careful, would that have saved him and her and them?

She fixed her attention on the flat-screen TV and imagined him smoking his cigar, watching the news with that skeptical look on his face, a face she saw every time she closed her eyes or saw something in the corner of them—a shadow or laundry piled on a chair or she didn't have her glasses on. And she would see him before he was gone. And she would remember he was gone.

He would look at her fancy TV and say, *Dearest, why the TV? Who needs a TV like that? It probably wasn't even made in America. We can't afford a TV like that.*

He would not approve. Oh, Lord, not of anything she'd done and gotten since he'd been gone.

The recliner was empty, and the worn spot made by him caused her to feel such despair as more memories rushed back at her:

Reporting him missing.

Feeling as if she were living a scene in a hundred

movies as she clutched the phone and begged the police to believe her.

Believe me. Please believe me.

She told the oh-so-politic female police officer that her husband didn't go to bars or wander off. He wasn't having a little memory problem or a little affair. He always came right back like a Boy Scout, and if he'd gotten "adventurous" and "ornery," he would have called Shrew.

And simply told me to fuck off, that he'd be home when he got around to it, just like he'd done last time he'd gotten goddamn adventurous and ornery, Shrew had said to the politic police officer, who'd sounded like she was chewing gum.

Nobody was in a panic except Shrew.

Nobody cared.

The detective, yet someone else in the landmass of the NYPD, who finally called with the news was regretful.

Ma'am, I'm very sorry to inform you . . . At around four p.m. I responded to a scene. . . .

The policeman was polite but quite busy and said he was sorry several times, but didn't offer to escort her to the morgue the way a well-behaved nephew might escort his stricken aunt to a wake or a church.

The morgue? Where?

Near Bellevue.

Which Bellevue?

Ma'am, there's only one Bellevue.

There most certainly isn't. There's the old one. And then there's the new one. What Bellevue is the morgue near?

She could go there at eight a.m. and identify the body, and she was given the address, lest she confuse the location of one Bellevue with the other, and she was given the name of the medical examiner:

Dr. Lenora Lester, LL.B., M.D.

Such an unfriendly, unpleasant woman for all her education, and how unfeeling she was when she hurried Shrew into that little room and drew back the drape.

His eyes were closed, and he was covered up to his chin with a papery blue sheet.

No sign of any injury, not a scratch, not a bruise, and for an instant Shrew hadn't believed anything had happened.

There's nothing broken. What happened? What really happened? He can't be dead. There's nothing wrong with him. He looks fine. Just pale. He's so pale, and I'll be the first to agree he doesn't look well. But he can't be dead.

Dr. Lester was a stuffed dove under glass and her mouth didn't move as she explained, very briefly, that he was a textbook pedestrian fatality.

Hit from behind while upright.

Thrown over the hood of the taxi.

Struck the back of his head on the windshield.

He had massive fractures of the cervical vertebrae, the doctor's stiff white face had said.

The severity of the impact had fractured both of his lower extremities, the stiff white face had said.

Extremities.

Her beloved's legs that wore socks and shoes, and on this cruel April afternoon, corduroy slacks almost the same tawny brown as his recliner and the couch. Slacks that she had picked out for him at Saks.

The stiff white face said in that small room: *He looks pretty good because his most profoundly mutilating injuries are to the lower extremities.*

Which were covered—the lower extremities, his lower extremities—by the papery blue sheet.

Shrew left the morgue, and she left her mailing address, and later she wrote the check and got a copy of Dr. Lester's final report after it had been pended for about five months, awaiting toxicology. The official autopsy results were still sealed inside their official envelope, in a bottom drawer of her desk, under a box of her husband's favorite cigars that she'd sealed in a freezer bag because she didn't want to smell them, yet she couldn't bring herself to toss them out.

She put another glass of bourbon next to the computer and sat down, working later than usual and not wanting to go to bed anytime soon or ever again. It occurred to her that all had been bearable until she'd opened that Marilyn Monroe photograph earlier today.

She thought of a punishing God as she envisioned the man with the mutton-chop sideburns and flashy jewelry, and his offer of a free dachshund or a shih tzu or a springer spaniel puppy, and then the ride home. He was trying to silence her through the bribery of a kindness that hinted what it would be like if he weren't inclined to be kind at all. She'd caught him red-handed, and they both knew it, and he wanted her to feel friendly toward him. For their own good.

She went on the Internet and searched until she found

a story that had run in the *Times* just three weeks ago, the very same week that the Boss had written such nice things about Tell-Tail Hearts's main pet shop on Lexington Avenue. The article was accompanied by a photograph of the white-haired man with the big sideburns and dissipated face.

His name was Jake Loudin.

This past October, he had been charged with eight counts of animal cruelty after one of the pet shops he owned in the Bronx was raided, but several weeks ago, in early December, he'd gotten off scot-free:

CHARGES AGAINST PUPPY MILL KING DROPPED

The New York County District Attorney's office has dropped eight counts of aggravated animal cruelty against a Missouri businessman who animal-rights activists call "The Puppy Pol Pot," comparing Jake Loudin to the Khmer Rouge leader responsible for the slaughter of millions of Cambodians.

Loudin could have received up to sixteen years in prison had he been convicted and given the maximum sentence for all eight felony counts. "But there just wasn't a way to prove the eight deceased animals discovered in the pet store's freezer were alive when placed there," said Assistant District Attorney Jaime Berger, whose recently formed animal-cruelty task force raided the shop last October. She added that the judge didn't feel the police had supplied sufficient evidence to prove a lack of justification for the euthanization of these same eight companion animals, all of them puppies ranging from three to six months in age.

Berger said it is commonly known that some pet shops "eliminate" dogs, cats, and other pets if they can't sell them, or if for some reason they become a commercial liability.

"A sick puppy, or one that's three or four months old, loses its 'doggie in the window' appeal," she said. "And far too many of these stores are notoriously negligent in supplying medical care or even the most basic necessities such as warm, clean cages and sufficient water and food. One of the reasons I started this task force is because the people of New York have had enough, and I am making it my mission to bury some of these offenders under the jailhouse." . . .

It was the second time tonight Shrew called 911.

Only she was drunker and more unraveled now.

"Murderers," she said to the operator, repeating the Lexington address. "The little ones being locked in there—"

"Ma'am?"

"He forced me into his car after the event, and my heart was under my feet. . . . He had a red sullen face and a frosty silence."

"Ma'am?"

"You've tried to put him in jail before, for the same thing! Hitler! Yes, Pol Pot! But he got away. Tell Ms. Berger. Please. Right away. Please."

"Ma'am? Would you like an officer to respond to your residence?"

"Someone from Ms. Berger's dog squad, please. Oh, please. I'm not crazy. I promise I'm not. I took a picture of him and the freezer with my cell phone."

She hadn't.

"They were moving!" she cried. "They were still moving!"

23

The dark blue Impala was waiting at the hospital's entrance when Benton and Scarpetta walked out into the night.

She recognized the fleece-lined leather jacket, then realized it was Marino who was wearing it. The trunk popped open, and he took the crime scene case from Benton and started talking about coffees he'd picked up for them, that the two coffees were in the backseat.

That was how he said hello after all this time, after all that had happened.

"I stopped at Starbucks," he was saying, shutting the trunk. "Two Ventis," which he didn't pronounce correctly. "And some of those sweeteners in the yellow wrapper."

He meant Splenda. He must have remembered that Scarpetta didn't touch saccharin or aspartame.

"But no cream because it's in those pitchers, so I couldn't get it. I don't think either of you drink it with cream, unless that's changed. They're in the console in back. Jaime Berger's up front. You might not be able to see her, it's so dark, so don't start talking about her."

Trying to be funny.

"Thank you," Scarpetta said as she and Benton got into the car. "How are you?"

"I'm doing good."

He slid behind the wheel, his seat back so far it was touching Scarpetta's knees. Berger turned around and said hello, and she didn't act as if the situation was unusual. That was better. It was easier.

Marino pulled away from the hospital, and Scarpetta looked at the back of his head, at the collar of the black leather bomber-style jacket. It was classic *Hogan's Heroes*, as Lucy used to tease him, with its half-belt, sleeve zippers, and plenty of antique brass hardware. On and off over the twenty years Scarpetta had known him, he'd get too big to wear it, especially around the gut, or more recently, too bulked up from the gym and, in retrospect, probably steroids.

During the interim without Marino in her life, she'd had a lot of space to think about what had happened and what had led up to it. Insight came to her one day not that long ago, after she'd reconnected with her former deputy chief, Jack Fielding, and hired him. Fielding had practically ruined his life with steroids, and Marino had been witness to much of it, but as he had gotten more disgruntled and frightened about a growing sense of powerlessness that Scarpetta couldn't seem to do anything about, he'd become obsessed with his own physical strength.

He'd always admired Fielding and his bodybuilding physique, all the while critical of the illicit and destructive means he used to obtain it. She was convinced Marino began taking steroids several years before the more recent sexual-performance drugs, which would help explain why he turned aggressive and, frankly, mean, long before his violent eruption in her carriage house last spring.

The sight of him pained her in ways she hadn't anticipated and probably couldn't explain, bringing back memories of the long span of their lives spent together when he'd let his graying hair grow long and would comb it over his baldness, Donald Trump–style, only Marino wasn't the sort to believe in gels or hairspray. The slightest stir and long strands would drift below his ears. He'd started shaving his head and wearing a sinister-looking do-rag. Now he had fuzz shaped like a crescent moon, and he wasn't wearing an earring and didn't look like a hard-riding Outlaw or Hells Angel.

He looked like Marino, only in better shape but older, and on forced good behavior, as if he was taking the parole board on a drive.

He turned onto Third Avenue, toward Terri Bridges's apartment, which was only a few minutes from the hospital.

Berger asked Scarpetta if she remembered Terri contacting her Charleston office last spring or early summer—or ever.

Scarpetta said no.

Berger fooled around with her BlackBerry and muttered something about Lucy's opposition to paper, and then read an e-mail Terri had written to Berger last year, asking for assistance in contacting Scarpetta.

"July second," Berger said. "That's when she sent this e-mail to the Bermuda Triangle of New York City government's general e-mail address, hoping it would get to me because she hadn't been able to get to you. It appears she never got to either of us."

"I'm not surprised, with a username like Lunasee," Benton replied from the dark backseat while he looked out his window at the quiet neighborhood of Murray Hill, where so far Scarpetta had seen only one person out, a man walking a boxer.

"I wouldn't be surprised if the username was the Pope's," Berger replied. "But I didn't get it. Question is, Kay, are you absolutely sure you don't recall her calling your office in Charleston?"

"I'm absolutely sure I was never aware of it," Scarpetta said. "But last spring and early summer my office was rather much of a Bermuda Triangle, too."

She didn't want to elaborate, not with Marino sitting directly in front of her. How was she supposed to talk about what it had been like for her after he disappeared without a word or a trace, and then Rose had gone into such a rapid decline that she no longer had the proud stubbornness to resist Scarpetta's moving her and taking care of her, eventually spoon-feeding her, changing her gowns and sheets when she soiled the bed, and then the morphine and oxygen at the very end when Rose decided she'd suffered enough, and death was in her eyes?

How would Marino feel if he knew how angry Rose was with him for abandoning everyone in his life, especially her, when he knew she wasn't long for this world? Rose had said it was wrong of him, and would Scarpetta please tell him that someday.

Rose had said, *You tell him for me I'll box his ears.*

As if she'd been talking about a two-year-old.

You tell him for me I'm mad at Lucy, too, just mad as hell at both of them. I blame him for what she's doing right now. Up there at Blackwater or some training camp like that, shooting guns and kneeing huge men in the kidneys as if she's Sylvester Stallone, because she's too scared to be home.

Those last weeks Rose got disinhibited, her talk wild and loose, but nothing she said was utter nonsense.

You tell him when I'm on the Other Side it will only be easier for me to find him and take care of business. And I'm going to take care of it. You watch.

Scarpetta had set up a portable hospital bed, and had the French doors open so they could look at the garden and the birds, and hear the stirring of live oaks that had been there since before the Civil War. She and Rose would talk in that lovely old living room with its view, while the bracket clock on the mantel tick-tocked like a metronome measuring the final rhythm of their days together. Scarpetta never did go into detail about what Marino had done, but she did tell Rose something important about it, something she'd not told anyone.

She'd said, *You know how people say if they could live something again?*

You don't hear me saying it, Rose had replied, propped up in bed, the morning light turning the sheets very white. *Doesn't do a damn bit of good to say something silly like that.*

Well, I wouldn't say it because I wouldn't mean it, you're exactly right. I wouldn't live that night again if offered the chance, because it wouldn't change anything. I can try to rewrite it all I want. Marino would still do what he did. The only way I could stop him would be to start the process years earlier, maybe a decade or two earlier. My culpability in his crime is I didn't pay attention.

She'd done to him what he and Lucy had done to Rose in the end. Scarpetta hadn't looked, had pretended not to notice, had absented herself by suddenly being busy and preoccupied or even in the midst of some crisis, instead of confronting him. She should have been more like Jaime Berger, who wouldn't hesitate to tell some big cop with the appetites and insecurities that Marino had to stop looking down her blouse or up her skirt—to get over it because she wasn't going to have sex with him. She wasn't going to be his whore, his madonna, his wife, or his mother, or all of the above, and all of the above was what he'd really always wanted, what most men have always wanted because they don't know any better.

She could have told Marino something to that effect when she'd first been appointed chief in Virginia and he'd gone out of his way to give her such a hard time, acting like a nasty little boy with a crush. She'd been so afraid of hurting him, because ultimately her biggest flaw was her overriding fear of hurting anyone, and so she'd hurt the hell out of him and herself and all of them.

What she'd finally admitted was she was selfish.

Scarpetta had said to Rose, *I'm the most selfish person there is. It goes back to feeling shamed. I was different, not like other people. I know what it is to feel ostracized and shunned and shamed, and I've never wanted to do it to anyone else. Or have it done to me again. And the last thing I just said is what's most important. It's about my not wanting discomfort more than it's really about anyone else. What a dreadful thing to know about yourself.*

You're the most different person I've ever met, Rose had said, *and I can see why those girls didn't like you, and why most people didn't like you and maybe still don't. It's about people being small and your reminding them of it without trying to, and so they go out of their way to make you small as if that will somehow make them bigger. You know exactly how all that works, but who has the wisdom to figure it out while it's going on? I would have liked you. If I'd been one of those nuns or one of the other girls, you would have been my favorite.*

I probably wouldn't have been.

You certainly would have. I've been following you around for twenty damn years, almost. And not because of the plush work conditions and all the jewelry and furs you give me and exotic vacations you take me on. I'm crazy about you. Was the first time you walked in that office. Do you remember? I'd never met a woman medical examiner and assumed the obvious. What a strange and difficult and unpleasant person you must be. Why else would a woman do this for a living? I hadn't seen a picture of you and was sure you'd look like some creature that had just climbed out of a black lagoon or a plague pit. I'd already been planning on where I might go, maybe the medical college. Somebody over there would hire me. Because I didn't think for a minute I'd stay with you, until I met you. Then I wouldn't have left you for the world. I'm sorry I'm doing it now.

"I'm sure we could go back and check phone records, the office e-mail," Scarpetta said in the car, to Benton, to Marino, to Berger.

"Not a priority this moment," Berger said, turning around. "But Lucy's been forwarding information to you that you're going to want to look at when you get the chance. You need to see what Terri Bridges was writing, or we might assume it was her. Hard to say, since Oscar Bane could just as easily have a hand in it, or even be Lunasee, for all we know."

"I got a list of evidence collected that corresponds to markers inside," Marino said as he drove. "And scene diagrams. A set for each of you so you know what was where."

Berger handed back two copies.

Marino turned onto a dark neighborhood street with lots of trees and old brownstones.

Benton observed, "Not well lit, and a lot of people appear to still be out of town for the holidays. Not a high-crime area."

"Nope," Marino said. "Nothing around here. Last complaint before the murder was someone playing music too loud."

He parked behind an NYPD cruiser.

"One new wrinkle in this," Berger said. "Based on some of the e-mails Lucy and I have been looking at, one has to wonder if Terri might have been seeing someone else."

"Looks like nobody's bothering to hide their damn police car," Marino said, turning off the engine.

"Hide it?" Berger asked.

"Morales said he didn't want them in plain view. In case the bogeyman came back. Guess he forgot to tell anyone who matters."

"You mean cheating on Oscar," Benton said, opening his door. "That maybe Terri was cheating on Oscar? I think we should leave our coats in the car."

Blasts of cold air grabbed at Scarpetta's suit and hair as she took off her coat, and then Marino climbed out, talking on his cell phone, obviously alerting the officer who was stationed inside the apartment that they had arrived. It was still an active crime scene and should be in the exact condition it was in when the police left shortly after one a.m., according to the reports Scarpetta had read.

The building's front door opened, and Marino, Benton, Berger, and Scarpetta climbed up five steps and entered the foyer, where a uniformed officer was very serious about his assignment.

Marino said to him, "I see your car's parked in front. I thought the latest order from headquarters was not to have your unit in plain view."

"The other officer wasn't feeling good. I think the smell, which isn't much until you sit there for a while," said the officer. "When I relieved him, I didn't get instructions about not parking in front. You want me to move it?"

Marino said to Berger, "You got an opinion? Morales didn't want it to look like there's a police presence. Like I said. In case the killer returns to the crime scene."

"He installed a camera on the roof," the officer said.

"Glad it's such a big friggin' secret," Marino said.

"The only person who could return to this apartment," Benton said, "would be Oscar Bane, unless there are other people running around who have keys. And I have a hard time believing, as paranoid as he is, that he would show up here and try to get in."

"Someone in his state of mind is more likely to show up at the morgue, in hopes of getting a last look at their person," Scarpetta said.

She'd decided she'd had enough of being completely close-mouthed. There were ways to communicate necessary information without breaking patient-physician confidentiality.

Marino said to the officer, "Maybe it would be a good idea to step up patrol around the area of the ME's office. In case Oscar Bane shows up, but do me a favor and don't transmit nothing about him over the air so some reporter hears it, okay? We don't need every dwarf on the East Side being stopped and questioned."

As if the area around the Medical Examiner's office was a popular hangout for little people.

"You need to get something to eat or do whatever, this is a good time," Marino said.

"As much as I'd like to take you up on that, no, thank you," the officer said, glancing at Berger. "My orders are to stay here. And I'll need you to sign the log."

"Don't be so damn professional. Nobody bites, even Ms. Berger doesn't," Marino said. "And we need a little elbow room. You can hang out in the foyer, suit yourself. Or you can make a pit stop. I'll give you a fifteen-minute heads-up before we're ready to leave. Just don't go to Florida or nothing."

The officer opened the apartment door, and Scarpetta smelled cooked chicken that was well on its way to turning ripe. He collected his jacket from the back of a folding chair, and a copy of Philipp Meyer's *American Rust* from the oak floor under it. Beyond that point the officer wasn't allowed to venture for any reason, and should he be tempted, the small blaze-orange cones marking locations where evidence had been collected were a bright reminder. Didn't matter if he needed water or food, or was desperate to use the bathroom, he had to call for a backup to cover for him while he took care of himself. He couldn't even sit unless he brought his own chair.

Scarpetta opened her crime scene case just inside the door and retrieved a digital camera and a notepad and pen, and gave each person a pair of gloves. She took her usual survey without moving closer or speaking, noticing that except for the evidence markers, there was nothing out of place, and not the slightest indication that anything remotely violent had happened. The apartment was impeccable, and everywhere she looked, she saw traces of the rigid, obsessive woman who had lived and died here.

The floral upholstered couch and side chair in the living room straight ahead were perfectly arranged around a maple coffee table, and on top of it were magazines impeccably fanned, and in a corner a standard-size Pioneer flat screen that looked new and was precisely positioned to face the exact center of the sofa. Inside the fireplace was an arrangement of silk flowers. The ivory Berber rug was straight and clean.

Other than the cones, there was barely a hint that the police had been all over this place. In this new age of crime scene management, they would have been suited up in disposable clothing, including shoe covers. Electrostatic dust lifters would have been used to recover any impressions from the polished wood floors, and forensic lights and photography would have taken precedence over messy black powders. In sophisticated departments such as the NYPD, crime scene scientists neither created nor destroyed.

The living room flowed into the dining area and kitchen, the apartment small enough that Scarpetta could see the table set for dinner, and the makings of it on a countertop near the stove. No doubt the chicken was still in the oven, and God knows how long it would stay there, didn't matter how rancid anything got by the time the landlord or Terri's family were allowed free access to the place. It wasn't the responsibility or the right of law enforcement to clean up the gore left in the wake of a violent death, whether it was blood or an uneaten holiday dinner.

"Let me ask the obvious question," Scarpetta said to no one in particular. "Is there any possibility she wasn't the intended victim? Even remotely possible? Since there's another apartment across from this one, and what? Two more upstairs?"

"I always say everything's possible," Berger replied. "But she opened the doors. Or if someone else did, he or she had keys. There would seem to be a connection between her and the person who killed her." To Marino she said, "You mentioned the roof access? Anything new about that?"

"A text message from Morales," he replied. "He said when he got to the scene last night, the ladder was exactly where he found it after installing the roof camera. In the utility closet."

Marino had a look on his face as he said that, as if he knew a joke he wasn't about to share.

"I'm assuming nothing new. Nobody of interest in terms of a possible suspect or witness among the other tenants?" Berger asked Marino, continuing the conversation just inside the apartment door.

"According to the landlord, who lives on Long Island, she was a real quiet lady except when she had a complaint. One of those who had to have everything just right," Marino said. "But what's a little interesting is, it was something she couldn't take care of herself, she'd never let the landlord in to fix it. She'd say she'd get someone to take care of it. He said it was like she was making notes of all the problems in case he got any ideas about raising the rent."

"Sounds like the landlord might not have been too fond of her," Benton said.

"He called her demanding more than once," Marino said. "Always e-mailed him, though. Never called, as if she was building a court case, is the way he put it."

"We can get Lucy to locate those e-mails," Berger said. "We know which of her eighteen usernames she used for complaining to the landlord? I don't think it was Lunasee, unless we just didn't come across anything to or from him while I was with Lucy a little while ago. And by the way, I've asked her to forward anything to me she might find. So all of us are rather much online with her while she continues to go through the laptops removed from this apartment."

"It's the one called Railroadrun, like running her railroad. My interpretation," Marino said. "The landlord said that's the e-mail address he's got for her. Anyway, point being, it appears she was a royal pain in the butt."

Scarpetta said, "Also appears she had somebody who helped her when she needed something fixed."

"Well, I have my doubts it was Oscar," Berger said. "No references to anything like that in the e-mails we've seen so far. Nothing—such as her asking him to come over and unstop the toilet or change a lightbulb in the ceiling. Although his height might have made at least a few tasks rather difficult."

"There's the ladder in the closet upstairs," Marino said.

Scarpetta said, "I'd like to wander through alone first."

She found the tape measure in her crime scene case and slipped it into her suit jacket pocket, and looked at the evidence inventory that told her which cone corresponded to which item that had been removed from the scene. Some six feet inside the door, to her left, was cone number one, and this was where the flashlight had been found, described as a black metal Luxeon Star with two Duracell lithium batteries, and in working condition. It wasn't plastic, as Oscar had described, which may or may not be of any consequence, except that a metal flashlight would be a serious weapon, suggesting Oscar hadn't struck himself very hard at all to cause the bruises she'd examined.

The cones numbered two through four corresponded to shoe prints lifted from the hardwood floor, described only as having a running shoe–type tread pattern with the approximate dimensions of six and a half by four inches. That was small, and as Scarpetta scanned the list, she noted that a pair of sneakers had been removed from Terri's closet. Size five, women's Reeboks, white with pink trim. A size-five woman's shoe would not be six and a half inches from heel to toe, and as Scarpetta recalled looking at Terri's feet in the morgue, she remembered them as smaller than that, because of her disproportionately short toes.

She suspected the shoewear impressions recovered near the door were Oscar's, and likely had been left when he'd gone in and out of the apartment, back to his car, to leave his coat and do whatever else he might have done after discovering the body.

That was assuming his story was true, for the most part.

Other impressions lifted from the floor were of interest because they had been left by bare feet, and Scarpetta recalled seeing several photographs that had been taken in oblique lighting. She had assumed the bare footprints were Terri's, and the location of them was significant.

All were clustered just outside the master bathroom where Terri's body had been found, and Scarpetta wondered if Terri had put on body lotion or oil, perhaps after her shower, and that's why the bare footprints had been visible on the hardwood floor, all in close proximity to one another. She wondered what it might mean if Terri hadn't taken her slippers off until she'd been about to enter the area of the apartment where she was murdered. Had she been attacked the instant she'd opened her front door, and had she resisted or been forced to the master bedroom in back, wasn't there a good chance her slippers would have come off earlier?

In all of her years working homicide scenes, it had been Scarpetta's experience that bedroom slippers, one or both, rarely stayed on once the violent encounter occurred. People literally were scared out of them.

She walked as far as the dining room, and from here the smell of cooked chicken was stronger and more unpleasant, the kitchen just ahead, and then the guest-room/office, according to the detailed computer-aided drafting or CAD of the apartment's interior and its dimensions that was included in the paperwork Marino had assembled.

The dining room table was meticulously set, blue-rimmed plates on two starchy spotless blue mats opposite each other, the stainless flatware shiny and exact in its placement, everything just right to the extreme of fussiness, of obsessiveness. Only the flower arrangement was less than perfect, the button poms beginning to hang their heads, and petals had fallen from the larkspur like tears.

Scarpetta pulled out chairs, checking the blue-velvet cushions for indentations left by someone kneeling to compensate for a dramatically shortened reach. If Terri had climbed up to set the table, she had groomed the nap afterward. All of the furniture was the standard size, the apartment not handicap-equipped. But as Scarpetta began opening closets and cupboards, she found a step stool with a handle, a grabbing tool, and another tool similar to a fireplace poker that Terri probably had used for prodding and pulling.

In the kitchen, there was chaos in the corner beneath the microwave, drips of blood and smears that had dried a blackish-red, presumably from Oscar cutting his thumb while grabbing a pair of kitchen shears that were no longer here. The wooden block of knives was gone and, like the shears, most likely sent to the labs. On the stove was the pot of uncooked spinach, the handle turned inward, the way people do when they are safety-minded. The chicken in the oven smelled pungent and was stuck to the bottom of the deep aluminum pan, grease coagulated around it like yellow wax.

Cooking utensils and pot holders were in a neat line on

the counter, as were basil, a set of salt and pepper mills, and cooking sherry. In a small ceramic bowl were three lemons, two limes, and a banana that was turning a speck-led brown. Nearby was a cork pump, which Scarpetta considered a gadget that ruined the ritual and romance of opening a bottle, and an unopened chardonnay, a decent one for the money. Scarpetta wondered if Terri might have removed the wine from the refrigerator an hour or so before Oscar was due to arrive, again assuming she had been killed by someone other than him. If she had, a pos-sible explanation was she'd done some research and knew that white wine should be served cool, not cold.

Inside the refrigerator was a bottle of champagne, also a decent one for the money, as if Terri had followed every recommendation she could find, possibly on the Inter-net, as if her Bible was *Consumer Reports*. Apparently, no purchase she made was based on passion or playfulness. Whether it was a TV or stemware or china, all of it was the selection of a well-informed shopper who did noth-ing in a hurry or on a whim.

In refrigerator drawers were fresh broccoli, peppers, onions, and lettuce, and deli packages of sliced turkey and Swiss cheese that according to their labels had been purchased from a grocery store on Lexington Avenue, several blocks from here, on Sunday, along with the food for last night's dinner. Salad dressings and condiments in the refrigerator door were low-calorie. In cupboards were crackers, nuts, soups, all low-sodium. The liquor, like everything else, was the best brand for the price: Dewar's. Smirnoff. Tanqueray. Jack Daniel's.

Scarpetta removed the rim from the trash can, not surprised it was brushed steel, which would neither rust nor show finger smudges. To open its lid, one stepped on a pedal and didn't have to touch anything that might be dirty. Inside the custom-fit white polyethylene bag were wrappers from the roaster chicken and the spinach, and an abundance of crumpled paper towels, and the green paper from the flowers on the table. She wondered if Terri had used the kitchen shears to snip off about three inches of the stems, which were still bound in their rubber band, then cleaned the shears and returned them to the cutlery block.

There was no receipt because the police had found it last night, and it was listed in the inventory. Terri had bought the flowers for eight dollars and ninety-five cents yesterday morning at a local market. Scarpetta suspected the rather pitiful little spring bouquet had been an afterthought. She found it sad to think of someone so lacking in creativity, spontaneity, and heart. What a hellish way to live, and what a shame she had done nothing about it.

Terri had studied psychology. She certainly would have known she could have been treated for her anxiety disorder, and had she chosen that course, it might have changed her destiny. It was likely her compulsions had led, even if indirectly, to the reason strangers were now inside her apartment and investigating every aspect of who she was and how she had lived.

Beyond the kitchen, on the right, was the small guest room that was an office. There was nothing in it but a desk, an adjustable chair, a side table with a printer, and, against a wall, two filing cabinets that were empty. Scarpetta stepped back out into the hallway and looked toward the apartment door. Berger, Marino, and Benton were in the living room, examining the evidence inventory and discussing the significance of the small orange cones.

"Does anybody know if these filing cabinets were empty when the police got here?" Scarpetta asked.

Marino flipped through his list and said, "Mail and personal papers, is what it says they took. A file box of stuff like that was removed from the closet."

"Meaning nothing was taken from actual filing cabinets," Scarpetta supposed. "That's rather interesting. There are two of them in here with nothing in them, not even an empty folder. As if they've never been used."

Marino came toward her and asked, "What about dust?"

"You can look. But Terri Bridges and dust weren't compatible. There's no dust, not a speck."

Marino entered the guest room office and opened the filing cabinets, and Scarpetta noted the indentations his booted feet left in the deep-pile dark blue wall-to-wall carpet. She realized there were no other indentations at all, except those left by her when she'd walked in, and that was odd. The police might be fastidious about not tracking dirt and evidence in and out of a scene, but they weren't about to bother brushing the carpet when they were done.

"It's as if no one was in here last night," she said.

Marino closed file drawers.

He said, "Doesn't look to me like anything was in there, unless someone wiped down the bottom of the drawers. No dust outline of any hanging files that might have been there. But the cops was in here."

He finally met her eyes, and his were tentative.

"You can see on the list the file box was taken out of the closet in here." He frowned, looking at the carpet, apparently noticing the same thing she had. "Well, that's fucking weird. I was in here this morning. That closet there"—he pointed—"is where her suitcases were, too."

He opened the closet door, where draperies in dry-cleaning bags hung from the rod and more luggage was neatly upright on the floor. Everywhere he stepped, he flattened the pile of the carpet.

"But it's like nobody walked in here or else came in after the fact and swept the carpet," he said.

"I don't know," Scarpetta said. "But what I'm hearing you say is nobody has walked through this apartment since last night except you. When you came in earlier today."

"Well, maybe I lost weight, but I don't float off the ground," Marino said. "So where the hell are my footprints?"

On the floor near the desk, a magnetic power connecter was plugged into the wall, and Scarpetta found this curious, too.

"She packed her laptops for the trip home to Arizona and left a power connecter behind?" she said.

"Somebody's been in here," Marino said. "Probably that fucking Morales."

24

Lucy was alone in her loft, her old bulldog asleep by her chair.

She read more e-mails from Terri and Oscar as she talked to Scarpetta over the phone:

```
Date: Sun, 11 November 2007 11:12:03
From: "Oscar"
To: "Terri"
See, I told you Dr. Scarpetta wasn't that
kind of person. Obviously, she just didn't
get your earlier messages. Amazing how
what's under your nose and obvious some-
times works. Are you going to copy me on the
e-mails?
```

```
Date: Sun, 11 November 2007 14:45:16
From: "Terri"
To: "Oscar"
No. That would be a violation of her Privacy.
This project has now risen to the stars. I'm
in awe! So happy!
```

"What's under her nose and obvious? It's like she tried something, or he did, and got what he or she or both of them wanted," Lucy said into her jawbone wireless earpiece. "What the hell's she talking about?"

"I don't know what was under her nose, but she's mistaken. Or not being truthful," Scarpetta replied.

"Probably untruthful," Lucy said. "Which was why she wouldn't let Oscar see e-mails from you."

"There can't be any e-mails from me," Scarpetta said again. "I need to ask you about something. I'm standing in the middle of Terri Bridges's apartment, and it's not a good place for us to be having this conversation. Especially over cell phones."

"I got you your cell phone. Remember? It's special. You don't have to worry. Neither do I. Our phones are secure."

Lucy talked as she opened each e-mail account and looked in the e-mail trash for anything useful that might have been deleted.

She said, "May have given Oscar a reason to resent you as well. His girlfriend's obsessed with her hero, who finally has answered her—he's led to believe. And she won't let him see the e-mails. Sounds like you might have created a problem you didn't know anything about."

"Or have anything to do with," Scarpetta said. "What type of power supplies do her laptops use? That's my simple question."

One of Terri's e-mail accounts was empty, and Lucy had saved that one for last, assuming Terri had created it but simply never gotten around to using it. As Lucy opened the trash folder, she was stunned by what she found.

"Wow," Lucy said. "This is unbelievable. She deleted everything yesterday morning. One hundred and thirty-six e-mails. She deleted them one right after another."

"Not a USB but a magnetized power cord? What was deleted?" Scarpetta asked.

"Hold on," Lucy said. "Don't go anywhere. Stay on with me and we'll look at this together. You might want to get Jaime, Benton, Marino in there and put me on speakerphone."

All of the deleted e-mails were between Terri and another user with the name Scarpetta612.

Six-twelve—June 12—was Scarpetta's birthday.

The Internet service provider address was the same as that of the eighteen accounts that were assumed to be Terri's, but Scarpetta612 wasn't listed in the history. It hadn't been created on this laptop, nor was that account accessed by this laptop or—based on the dates of the e-mails Lucy was already seeing—Scarpetta612 would be listed in the history along with the other eighteen accounts.

It would be in the history if Terri had created Scarpetta612. But there was no evidence she had, not so far.

"Scarpetta six-twelve," Lucy said, scrolling through text. "Someone with that username was writing to her—to Terri, I'm presuming. Can you get Jaime and Marino so we can get the password to that account?"

"Anybody could come up with some permutation of my name, and my date of birth is no big secret, if anybody cares," her aunt said.

"Just give Jaime the username. Scarpetta appended to the numbers six one two."

Lucy gave her the e-mail service provider and waited. She could hear Scarpetta talking to someone. It sounded like Marino.

Then Scarpetta said to Lucy, "It's being taken care of."

"Like right now," Lucy said.

"Yes, right now. I was asking if either of the laptops you have might use a magnetized power supply."

"No," Lucy said. "USB, recessed five pin port, eighty-five-watt. What you're talking about wouldn't be recognized by Terri's laptops. The IP for Scarpetta six-twelve traces to eight-ninety-nine Tenth Avenue. Isn't that John Jay College of Criminal Justice?"

"What IP? And yes. What's John Jay got to do with anything? Jaime and Marino are still here. They want to listen to what you're saying. I'm putting you on speakerphone. What's Benton doing?" she asked them.

Lucy could hear Berger's voice in the background

say something about Benton being on the phone with Morales. It bothered Lucy to hear Berger say anything about Morales, and she wasn't sure why unless it was her sense that he was interested in Berger, that he wanted her sexually, and maybe it seemed he had a way of getting what he wanted.

"Whoever was writing to Terri and saying she was you was doing so from that IP address, from John Jay," Lucy said.

She continued going through deleted e-mails sent by someone who was clearly impersonating her aunt.

"I'm going to forward some of these," she said. "Everybody should look at them, then I need the password, okay? This most recent one was sent by Scarpetta six-twelve to Terri four days ago, December twenty-eighth, at close to midnight. The day after Bhutto was assassinated, and you talked about it on CNN, Aunt Kay. You were here in New York."

"I was, but that's not me. That's not my e-mail address," Scarpetta insisted.

The e-mail read:

Date: Fri, 28 December 2007 23:53:01
From: "Scarpetta"
To: "Terri"
Terri,
Again, I owe you an apology. I'm sure you
understand. Such a terrible tragedy, and I
had to get to CNN. I wouldn't blame you for
thinking I don't keep my word, but I don't

have much say about my schedule when some-
body dies or other inconveniences interfere.
We'll try again! —Scarpetta
P.S. Did you get the photograph?

Lucy read it over the phone and said, "Aunt Kay? When did you leave CNN that night?"

"Other inconveniences?" Berger's voice talking to Scarpetta. "As if you would refer to an assassination or any other act of violence as an inconvenience? Who the hell is doing this? Sound like anybody you might know?"

"No." Scarpetta's voice answering Berger. "Nobody."

"Marino?" Berger again.

His voice. "Got no idea. But she wouldn't say nothing like that," as if Scarpetta needed him to stick up for her character. "I don't think it's Jack, if that's entered anybody's head."

He meant Jack Fielding, and it was unlikely he would have entered anybody's head. He was a solid forensic pathologist and meant well and in the main was loyal to Scarpetta, but he was a musclebrain with ragged moods and an assortment of physical problems such as high cholesterol and skin disorders from his years of pumping iron and pumping himself full of anabolic steroids. He didn't have the energy to parade as Scarpetta on the Internet, and he wasn't cunning or cruel, and to give Terri Bridges the benefit of the doubt, if she wasn't Scarpetta612, then it was cruel of somebody to lead her on. In the beginning, at least, she'd idolized Scarpetta. She'd tried hard to get in touch with her. If she finally thought Scarpetta was responding to her, that had to be a thrill until her hero started to diss her.

Lucy said, "Aunt Kay? You left CNN on the night of December twenty-eighth and were within two blocks of John Jay. And you walked back to the apartment, just like you always do?"

The apartment was on Central Park West, and very close to CNN and John Jay.

"Yes," Scarpetta said.

Another e-mail, this one dated yesterday. Again, the IP traced to John Jay.

```
Date: Mon, 31 December 2007 03:14:31
From: "Scarpetta"
To: "Terri"
Terri,
I'm sure you realize my time in NY is unpre-
dictable and I have so little control over
the OCME because I'm certainly not the
chief, just a low-level consultant there.
    I was thinking, why not meet in Watertown
where I make the rules? I'll give you a tour
of my office, and no problem about seeing an
autopsy or anything else you need. Happy New
Year and look forward to seeing you soon.
—Scarpetta
```

Lucy forwarded it to all of them as she read it out loud.

"I wasn't in New York yesterday afternoon," Scarpetta said. "I couldn't have e-mailed this from John Jay.

Not that I would have. And I don't give tours of the morgue."

"The emphasis about your not being the chief here in New York," Berger said. "Someone is belittling you with your own lips, so to speak. Of course, I'm wondering about Terri being Scarpetta six-twelve and sending the e-mails to herself as if they're from Scarpetta. Think what a coup that would be for her thesis. My question, Lucy, is do you see any reason we should completely dismiss the possibility that the imposter was Terri?"

As Lucy listened to Berger's voice, she thought she heard a special warmth in it.

It had happened so swiftly, and Berger had been surprisingly sure of what she wanted. She had been surprisingly bold. Then the bitter wind had rushed in as Berger had opened the door and left.

Lucy said over the phone to her aunt, "These e-mails to Terri, allegedly from you, would explain why she quoted you in her thesis and seemed to think she knew you."

"Kay? Did you get any indication of this from Oscar?" Berger asked.

"I can't tell you what he said to me. But I won't deny that I got such an indication."

"So you did." Berger's reply. "So he definitely knew about this correspondence. Whether he saw it or not is another matter."

"If Terri's not the imposter," Marino said, "who deleted all of the e-mails? And what for?"

"Exactly," Berger said. "Right before she was

murdered. Right before Oscar was supposed to come over for dinner. Or did someone else make the deletions and put the laptops in the closet?"

Lucy said, "If Terri made the deletions because she was worried about someone seeing them, she should have emptied the damn trash. Even an idiot knows you can recover deleted files from the trash, especially if the deletions are recent."

"This much I think we can be sure of," Scarpetta said. "No matter why she or someone else deleted the e-mails, Terri Bridges wasn't expecting to be murdered last night."

Lucy said, "No. She couldn't have been expecting her own death. Unless she planned to commit suicide."

"And then removed the ligature from her neck after the fact? I don't think so," said Marino, as if he'd taken Lucy literally.

"There was no ligature to remove," Scarpetta said. "She was garroted. Nothing was tied or locked around her neck."

Lucy said, "I have to find out who Scarpetta six-twelve is, and which photograph this person supposedly sent. There are no photographs, no JPEG images in the trash. It's possible she deleted it before she deleted all these other e-mails, and flushed her cache."

"Then what?" Berger's voice.

"Then we'll have to try recovering it from this laptop the same way we're recovering her text files from the other one," Lucy said. "Do the same thing you were watching earlier when you were here with me."

"Any other possible explanation about the photograph?" It was Scarpetta who asked.

Lucy said, "If she, assuming we're talking about Terri, accessed an attached e-mailed photograph from a different device—such as a BlackBerry or another computer somewhere—then it won't be on the laptop she used for the Internet."

"That's what I've been trying to tell you," Scarpetta said. "There's a power cord in her office that doesn't go to either of the laptops you have. There must be another one somewhere."

"We should go from here to Oscar's apartment." Marino's voice, to the others. "Morales had the key. He's still got it?"

"Yes," Berger said. "He has it. Oscar could be there. We don't know where he is."

"I don't believe for a minute he's there." Benton's voice now.

"You were just talking to Morales? What did he want?" Berger asked him.

"He suspects Oscar figured he was about to get arrested—said one of the guards told him that Oscar didn't do well after Kay left. Morales said, and remember to consider the source, that Oscar feels betrayed by Kay. Feels lied to and disrespected, and he's glad Terri didn't witness how abusive Kay was to Oscar during the examination. She supposedly put chemicals on Oscar and caused him a lot of pain."

"Abuse?" Scarpetta asked.

They were having this conversation as if they'd

forgotten Lucy was on the phone. She continued to search through deleted e-mails.

"That was the word Morales used," Benton's voice.

"I certainly wasn't abusive, and whoever this Morales is, he knows damn well I can't say what went on in there." Scarpetta talking to Benton. "He knows Oscar's not under arrest. So I really can't defend myself if he starts tossing around words like that."

"I don't believe Oscar made those comments," Benton said. "He knows you can't repeat anything. So if he really didn't trust you, he would assume that you would defend yourself if he did start misrepresenting you. He would assume you would breach confidentiality because you have no integrity. And I'll talk to the guard, myself."

"I agree," Berger said. "Morales is probably the source of the comments."

"He's a shit stirrer," Marino said.

"He has a message for you," Benton said.

"Yeah, I bet he does," Marino said.

"The witness you interviewed earlier today, the woman across the street?" Benton said, and it seemed they had forgotten that Lucy was listening.

"I hadn't talked to him about it," Marino said.

"Well, he knows about it," Benton said to him.

"I had to get the dispatcher to talk the lady into letting me in. She thought I was an ax murderer and called nine-one-one. Maybe he heard about it that way."

"Apparently, she called nine-one-one again," Benton told him. "Just a little while ago."

"She's scared shitless," Marino said. "Because of what happened to Terri."

"To report animal abuse," Benton said.

"Don't tell me. Because of her dead puppy?"

"What?"

"That's what I'm asking," Marino said. "What are you talking about?"

"Apparently, the woman told the nine-one-one operator to pass on the message to Jaime that it was the same man who, quote, got off the hook earlier this month. And she, the lady who called, said she took a picture with her cell phone and can prove he's at it again."

"Jake Loudin," Berger said. "Who's this claiming she took a picture of him?"

"All I know is the nine-one-one operator passed on the message to Morales. I guess because of his connection with Jaime."

Lucy popped open a Diet Pepsi, listening and reading as Jet Ranger snored.

"What damn connection?" Marino sounded angry. "Tavern on the goddamn Green? I'm telling you, I don't like that guy. He's an asshole."

"He says you might want to go talk to your witness again, long and short of it," Benton said. "And maybe Jaime will want to, since it seems related to her big animal-cruelty case. But maybe first all of us should meet him at Oscar's apartment while we've got the chance."

"The lady lives across the street," Marino said. "She was drinking when I saw her this afternoon. She started talking about getting another dog. I don't know why she wouldn't have said something about Loudin earlier. We were talking about dogs and Jaime's anti-cruelty task force. We could go see her first, since we're right here, then go to Oscar's. He's on the other side of the park, not far from where your apartment is. Not far from John Jay."

"I think we should split up." Berger's voice. "You two go to Oscar's. Marino and I will stay here."

"I'd like to get back to John Jay," Scarpetta said. "How does it work if the IP traces to John Jay? Wouldn't the person who sent the e-mails have to be located there?"

Silence.

Scarpetta repeated her question and said, "Lucy? You still with us?"

"I'm sorry," Lucy said. "I forgot I was here."

"I didn't know she was on the phone," Benton said. "Maybe you could set your cell phone on the desk. I'm sorry, Lucy. Hello, Lucy."

The cell phone clunked as Scarpetta set it down.

Lucy said, "Whoever Scarpetta six-twelve is would have had to be physically within range of John Jay's wireless network to join it. For example, the person would have to be there using one of the college's computers—which isn't likely at almost midnight, when the buildings were locked, and that's when the last e-mail was sent, right before midnight on December twenty-eighth. Or the person could have brought his or her own laptop or something smaller such as a BlackBerry, an iPhone, a PDA, some device that's capable of logging on to the Internet. And that's what I'm thinking—that this individual had something like a PDA and just stood on the sidewalk in front of one of the buildings and hijacked the wireless network. I'm assuming the cops found Terri's cell phone? Or a BlackBerry or PDA if she had one? The photograph Scarpetta six-twelve sent? It could have been sent by a BlackBerry, a PDA, something like that, as I've mentioned."

"Her cell phone's being gone through." It was Marino. "No other phones, BlackBerries, or devices you could use for the Internet. Assuming the inventory we got here is correct. Just the one phone. Plain vanilla flip phone. Was on the kitchen counter, plugged in, recharging. That and the earpiece. Also recharging."

All of them continued to discuss and speculate, and then there was a brief lapse as Marino and Berger contacted the e-mail provider for Scarpetta six-twelve.

They got the information Lucy needed.

"The password's *stiffone,* all one word." Berger spelled it for Lucy over the phone. "Marino, maybe you could get with John Jay's security to find out if they noticed anyone in front of the classroom building late on the night of December twenty-eighth, and again yesterday, mid-afternoon?"

"In both instances, the twenty-eighth and last night," Benton said, "the building would have been closed due to the hour and the holiday."

"Are there security cameras?" Berger asked.

Lucy said, "You know what I'm thinking. I'm thinking the IP's deliberate to make it look like the e-mails are really from Aunt Kay. She's connected with John Jay, so why wouldn't she be sending e-mails from their wireless network? Point is, whoever's stolen Aunt Kay's identity by sending these e-mails doesn't care if the IP was traced, and likely hoped or even assumed it would be. Otherwise, this person would have used an anonymous proxy—a program on a remote server that grabs files for you and disguises your real address. Or some other type of anonymizer that gives you a temporary address every time you send an e-mail, so people can't find your real IP."

"That's my big battle." Berger made her favorite complaint about the Internet.

It was one Lucy liked to hear. The devil Berger fought was one Lucy knew.

"White-collar crime, stalking, identity theft," Berger added. "I can't tell you my aggravation."

"What about the account information for Scarpetta six-twelve?" Marino was asking Lucy, as if nothing dysfunctional had ever gone on between them.

He was just more guarded, which made him somewhat polite, for once.

"Anything more than the generic they gave me?" he asked.

"Name's listed as Dr. Kay Scarpetta. Address and phone number are her office in Watertown. All public information," Lucy said. "No profile, no options that would have required the person who set up the account to use a credit card."

"Same thing as Terri's accounts." Berger's voice.

"Same thing with a million accounts," Lucy said. "I'm

in Scarpetta six-twelve right now, and the only e-mails sent or received were to and from Terri Bridges."

"Don't you think that might hint it was Terri who opened that account to make it look as if Kay were writing to her?" Berger suggested.

"What about the MAC, the machine access code?" Benton asked.

Lucy said, as she scrolled through e-mails, "Doesn't match either of these laptops, but all that means is Terri or someone didn't carry one of these laptops to John Jay and send the e-mails from that network. But you're right. The sole purpose of Scarpetta six-twelve seems to be for an imposter to correspond with Terri Bridges, which would have added credence to the theory that the imposter and Terri were the same person, were it not for one thing."

The one thing she was talking about was on her screen.

"I'm talking as I'm going through the Scarpetta six-twelve account," she said. "And this is something that's really important. Really, really important."

So important, Lucy almost couldn't believe it.

She said, "At eight-eighteen last night, Scarpetta six-twelve wrote an e-mail that was saved as a draft and never sent. I'm forwarding it to all of you, and I'm going to read it out loud to you in a sec. This rules out Terri or Oscar writing it. Do you hear what I'm saying? This e-mail I'm talking about rules out either one of them being Scarpetta six-twelve."

"Shit." Marino's voice. "Someone wrote an e-mail

while this place was crawling with cops? Fact is, her body was probably already at the morgue by then."

"Her body arrived at the morgue at around eight, as I recall," Scarpetta said.

"So someone writes an e-mail to Terri and decides not to send it for some reason." Lucy tried to work it out. "As in maybe the person somehow found out Terri was dead right while in the middle of writing to her? And then just saved the e-mail as a draft?"

"Or wanted us to find it and make that assumption, draw some sort of conclusion from it," Scarpetta said. "Remember, we don't know how much of this is intended to deliberately lead us or, better put, mislead us."

"That's my hunch." Berger's voice. "This is deliberate. Whoever's behind it is smart enough to know we'd see these e-mails eventually. The person wants us to see what we're seeing."

"To jerk us around," Marino said. "And it's working. I'm feeling jerked around as hell."

"Two things are indisputable," Benton said. "Terri had been dead for hours by the time that e-mail was written and saved as a draft. And Oscar was already at Bellevue, so he definitely wasn't sending e-mails to anyone. So he couldn't have written the one you're talking about. Lucy? Can you read it, please?"

She read out loud what was on her screen:

```
Date: Mon, 31 December 2007 20:18:31
From: "Scarpetta"
To: "Terri"
```

Terri,

After three glasses of champagne and some
of that whiskey that costs more than your
books, I can be candid. In fact, I'm going
to go ahead and be brutally candid with you.
It's my New Year's resolution—to be brutal.

While I think you're bright enough to have
an excellent grasp of forensic psychology, I
don't think you could ever do anything but
teach, if you insist on staying in the field.
The sad fact? Suspects, inmates, victims
would never accept a dwarf, and I don't know
how jurors would respond, either.

Would you ever consider being a morgue
assistant where your appearance is immate-
rial? Who knows? Maybe one day you could
work for me! —Scarpetta

Lucy said, "The IP's not John Jay. Not an address
we've seen so far."

"I'm glad she never got that." Scarpetta sounded
solemn. "That's terrible. If she wasn't sending them to
herself, after all, she probably really did think they were
from me. And Oscar probably thought so, too. I'm glad
neither she nor Oscar ever read that, glad it was never
sent. How incredibly cruel."

"That's what I'm getting at," Marino said. "The person's a piece of shit. Is playing games, having fun with
us. This is for our benefit, to fuck with us, rub our noses
in it. Who else was going to see this unsent e-mail except

those of us investigating Terri's murder? Mainly it's for the Doc's benefit. You ask me, somebody's really got it in for the Doc."

"Any idea where that IP traces? What the address is, if not John Jay?" Benton asked Lucy.

She said, "All I've got is a range of numbers from the Internet service provider. They aren't going to tell me anything unless I hack into the mainframe."

"I didn't hear that," Berger said to her. "You didn't just say that."

25

For the first time since Marino had attacked her last spring, Scarpetta found herself alone with him.

She set down her crime scene case outside the bathroom doorway in the master bedroom, and she and Marino both looked at the stripped mattress beneath a window that had draperies drawn across it. They examined photographs of what the bed had looked like when the police had arrived last night, and the soft, sexy clothing that had been laid out on top of it. There was an uneasiness between the two of them now that they were inches from each other, with no one else around and no one to overhear them.

His big index finger began tapping an eight-by-ten of the clothing on the perfectly made bed.

He said, "You think it's possible the killer did this, like

maybe he was going through some fantasy shit after the fact? Like maybe he was playing out a fantasy of her dressing up for him in red or something?"

"I doubt it," Scarpetta said. "If that was his intention, why didn't he do it? He could have forced her to dress any way he'd wanted."

She pointed at the clothing on the bed in the photograph, and her index finger was smaller than his pinkie.

"The clothes are laid out the way they would be if someone extremely organized was planning what to wear last night," she explained. "Just as she had set up everything else for the evening, with methodical deliberation. I think that's how she went about her normal routines. She'd timed her dinner preparation, perhaps had taken the wine out a few hours earlier so it would be the temperature she wanted. She'd set the table and had arranged flowers that she'd bought at a market earlier in the day. She was in her robe, perhaps had just showered."

"Did it look to you like she'd just shaved her legs?" he asked.

"There wasn't anything to shave," Scarpetta said. "That's not how she removed her hair. She went to the dermatologist for that."

Photographs made sliding sounds as he shuffled them around, looking for ones that showed the interior of Terri's closets and drawers, which the police had not left in their original ordered state. He and Scarpetta started looking through socks and hose, undergarments and gym clothes, everything jumbled up and in disarray from multiple pairs of gloved hands digging through them and sliding hangers around. The police had rooted through quite a variety of high-heel platform pumps and sandals with stiletto heels, rhinestones, chains, and ankle straps, in different sizes, ranging from three to five.

"Finding ones that fit is one of the biggest challenges," Scarpetta commented, looking at the pile of shoes. "An ordeal, and I'm going to venture a guess she did a lot of her shopping over the Internet. Possibly all of it."

She returned a pair of studded flip-flops to the carpet beneath a hanging rod, which, unlike everything else she'd noticed in the apartment, had been installed lower than usual, so Terri could reach it without a tool or a step stool.

She said, "I'll also stick with my theory that she was influenced by consumer reviews. Possibly even for her provocative tastes."

"I'd give this maybe three stars," Marino said, holding up a thong he'd just pulled out of a drawer. "But you ask me, the thing about rating underwear? It all depends on who's wearing it."

"Victoria's Secret. Frederick's of Hollywood," Scarpetta observed. "Open mesh and fishnet. Lace teddies, crotchless panties. A corset. She was wearing a red lace shelf bra under her robe, and it's very difficult for me to imagine she wasn't wearing panties to match."

"I don't think I know what a shelf bra is."

"It rather much does what the name implies," she said. "The object of the game, to enhance and accentuate."

"Oh. The one he cut off her. Doesn't look like it would cover anything important."

"It wouldn't, and wasn't supposed to," she said. "That's why she would have been wearing it to begin with, assuming it wasn't the killer's idea."

Scarpetta returned the lingerie to its drawer and for a moment couldn't look at Marino as she remembered the sounds and smells of him, and his shocking strength. It wasn't until later that she'd felt him, when pain mapped out where he'd been in damaged flesh that burned and throbbed all the way to the bone.

"That and all the condoms," Marino said.

He had his back to her, opening drawers in a night-stand. The condoms had been collected by the police.

"You see from the pictures, she must have had a hundred condoms in this top drawer," he said. "Maybe this is a Benton question, but if she was a neat freak—"

"Not if."

"In other words, she was uptight. Everything had to be exactly right. So does it make sense for someone like that to have this wild side?"

"You mean for someone obsessive-compulsive to like sex?"

"Yeah."

Marino was sweating, and his face was red.

"Makes perfect sense," Scarpetta said. "Sex was a way to relieve her anxiety. Perhaps the only acceptable way for her to be uninhibited, to give up control. Or better put, to delude herself into thinking she was giving up control."

"Yeah. She gave it up as long as it was according to her plan."

"Meaning she never really gave it up. She couldn't possibly. That's not how she was programmed. Even when she appeared to be giving up control—during sex, for example—she wasn't. Because it wasn't Oscar or someone else who decided what she would buy. I doubt it was he or any of her partners who decided what she would wear or whether she would have body hair. Or even whether Oscar would have body hair. My guess is she decided what they would and wouldn't do. And where and when and how."

She remembered what Oscar had said about Terri's liking his body perfectly sculpted and perfectly clean and smooth. She liked sex in the shower. She liked to be dominated, to be tied up.

"She called the shots," Scarpetta said. "Until the end. That was the fun part for the person who killed her—controlling her absolutely."

"It makes you wonder if Oscar finally couldn't take it anymore," Marino said, stopping short of whatever else he was about to say.

Scarpetta stood in the bathroom doorway and looked in at the white marble and French gold fixtures, and the corner soaking tub with its showerhead and curtain pulled back. She looked at the polished, veined grayish stone floor and imagined the contusions Terri would have had if her assailant had sexually assaulted her on it, and was fairly certain that didn't happen. The weight of the assailant, even if the person were a hundred and nine pounds, like Oscar, would have caused contusions in areas that contacted the floor, especially if her wrists were tightly bound behind her.

Scarpetta outlined her thoughts to Marino as she studied the gilt-framed oval mirror above the vanity, and the chair with the gold metal back shaped like a heart. Her reflection looked back at her. Then Marino's chest was in the mirror as he looked at everything she was looking at.

"If he wanted to watch her die," Marino said, "maybe he also wanted to watch her being raped. But as I'm standing here looking at the mirror, I don't see how that could have happened if he was a normal-size person. If he'd been standing behind her, I'm saying. Well, I don't see how he could have."

"I'm also not so sure she could have been raped without exhibiting at least some injury," Scarpetta said. "If her wrists had been strapped together behind her back and he had gotten on top of her, even if it was on the bed, she likely would have had abrasions or contusions or both, posteriorly. Not to mention the bed didn't look touched, based on the photographs. And the clothing on them didn't look disturbed."

"She had no injuries to her back."

"None."

"You're pretty sure her wrists was already bound."

"I can't prove it. But his cutting her robe and bra off suggests she was bound at the time."

"What makes you so sure she was bound behind her back instead of in front? I know that's what Oscar told the police. Is that what you're basing it on?"

Scarpetta held out her wrists, the left one on top of the right, as if they were bound by a single strap.

"I'm basing it on the pattern of the furrow on her

wrists, where the groove was the deepest, where there was sparing, et cetera," she said. "If she'd been bound in front, it's likely the strap would have been inserted under this wrist"—she indicated her right one—"with the locking block a little to the right of her right wrist bone. If they'd been bound behind her back, the position would have been reversed."

"The killer right-handed or left-handed, in your opinion?"

"Based on the direction he pulled the strap during tightening? Consistent with someone left-handed, assuming he was facing her when he bound her. For what it's worth, Oscar's dominant hand is his right one. And I probably shouldn't tell you that."

She and Marino put on fresh gloves, and she stepped inside the bathroom and lifted the vanity chair and set it in the middle of the floor. She measured the height of it from its turned-up metal foot to the black fabric seat, which had darker areas, stained areas, that added to her theory.

"Possibly residues of the lubricant," she said. "Nobody noticed because it was never considered that she might have been sitting in this chair when she was garroted, in front of the mirror. Maybe some tissue and blood on the legs from her thrashing. Let me see."

She looked with a magnification lens.

"I can't tell. But maybe not. Not really surprised. Since her injuries are to the tops of her legs, not the backs of them. You still carry those little tactical lights that can blind people?"

Marino dug into his pocket and pulled out his flash-light and gave it to her. She got down on her knees and shone the light under the vanity, illuminating smears of dark dried blood under the counter's edge, not visible unless one was on the floor, looking. She found more blood on the underside of the vanity drawer, which was unpainted plywood. Marino squatted, and she showed him.

She took photographs.

"I'm going to swab all this, but not the chair," she said. "What we're going to do is wrap it up, and it goes to La Guardia. Can you step out for a minute and tell Jaime we need an officer who can escort this chair to Lucy's jet and be on that jet and receipt it to Dr. Kiselstein at the airport in Knoxville? Lucy can set it up. In fact, knowing her, she already has."

She studied the chair.

She decided, "The lubricant is moist, so we don't want anything plastic like poly tubing or basically shrinkwrap. I think paper so it continues to air-dry, maybe a Mammoth Bag, and then place the entire thing in a large evidence storage box. Be as creative as you can. I don't want any chance of bacteria, and I don't want anything rubbing against any surface of it."

Marino left, and Scarpetta retrieved a roll of string, a roll of blue evidence tape, and a pair of small scissors from her crime scene case. She set the chair against the tile wall and began measuring and cutting string to correlate with Oscar's and Terri's heights, and the lengths of their legs and also their torsos. She taped the strings to the wall directly above the chair as Marino reappeared in the doorway. Berger was with him.

"If you can give Jaime my notepad and pen so she can take notes and you can free up your hands. What I'm about to show you," Scarpetta said, "is why I don't believe Oscar could have committed this murder. I'm not saying it's impossible, but I'm going to show you why it's unlikely. A little simple math."

She directed their attention to the different lengths of string taped to the tile wall above the chair.

"This is all based on the theory that Terri was seated in this chair. What's relevant is the length of her torso, which is eighty-four and a quarter centimeters. . . ."

"The metric system ain't my thing," Marino said.

"About thirty-four and an eighth inches," she said. "I measured her in the morgue, and as you know, people with achondroplasia have abnormally short limbs, but their torsos and heads are relatively the same size as a normal adult's, which is why they seem disproportionately larger. That's why little people can drive cars without sitting on cushions but need extended pedals so their feet can reach the accelerator, the brake, the clutch. In Terri's case, her torso is about the same length as Jaime's and mine. So I've taped a segment of string to the wall"—Scarpetta showed them—"that's exactly the length of Terri's torso, and positioned it so it begins at the seat of the chair and ends here."

She pointed to the piece of blue tape fastening the top end of the string to the wall.

"The distance between the chair cushion and the floor

is twenty-one inches," she continued to explain. "So if you add thirty-four and an eighth and twenty-one, you get fifty-five and one-eighth inches. Oscar Bane is four feet tall. In other words, forty-eight inches tall."

She pointed to the string that represented his height.

Berger commented as she wrote, "Not even as tall as Terri was when she was sitting."

"That's right," Scarpetta said.

She lifted the "Oscar string," as she called it, from the wall and held it out parallel to the floor, and did the same with the "seated Terri string." She asked Marino to hold both, level and parallel to the floor.

She took more photographs.

Then Benton was behind Berger, and a uniformed officer was with him.

The officer said, "Someone need a chair escorted to a private jet headed to the bomb factory in Oak Ridge? The chair's not going to explode or nothing, right?"

"You bring the evidence packaging I asked for?" Marino asked him.

"Just like UPS," the officer said.

Scarpetta asked Marino to continue holding the Oscar and Terri strings while she explained to Benton what they were doing.

"And his arms are very short, about sixteen inches from his shoulder joint to the tips of his fingers, which would have given him less leverage," she added, looking at Benton. "Your reach is a good eight inches more than that, and if you'd been standing behind Terri while she was seated, you would have towered over her by almost twenty inches, giving you tremendous leverage. As opposed to Oscar. Imagine someone his size trying to pull up and back with force while the victim is thrashing about in the chair."

"And he's not even level with her when he's doing it? I don't really see how he could," Marino agreed. "Especially if he kept doing it to her over and over again, allowing her to regain consciousness, then strangling her into unconsciousness again, like you said. I don't care how much he can bench-press."

"Actually, I don't think there's any way he could have done it," Berger said.

"I'm worried about him," Scarpetta said. "Has anybody tried to call him?"

"When I talked to Morales," Benton said, "I asked him if anybody knew where Oscar was or had heard from him. He says the police have Oscar's cell phone."

"He voluntarily gave that up?" Scarpetta asked.

"Along with a lot of other things, yes," Benton said. "Which is too bad, at least about the phone. I wish he had it, because he's not answering his apartment phone, which doesn't surprise me. I don't know how we're going to reach him."

"I think what we ought to do is split up, as I suggested earlier," Berger said. "Benton? You and Kay meet Morales at Oscar's apartment and take a look. Marino and I will make sure this chair gets packaged properly. We'll make sure the swabs you just took and any other evidence goes directly to the labs. Then we'll head across the street and see what the neighbor has to say about Jake Loudin."

Scarpetta carried the chair out of the bathroom and set it down for the officer who was to package and escort it.

Berger said to her, "If you're still at Oscar's apartment when we're done, we'll meet you there. Lucy said she'll call me if she finds out anything else important on her end."

26

Oscar Bane lived on Amsterdam Avenue in a ten-story building of insipid yellow brick that reminded Scarpetta of Mussolini's fascist constructions in Rome. Inside the lobby, the doorman wouldn't let them near the elevator until Morales showed his badge. He looked Irish, was portly and elderly, wearing a uniform the same green as the awning outside.

"I haven't seen him since New Year's Eve," the doorman said, his attention fixed to Scarpetta's big crime scene case. "I guess I know why you're here."

Morales said, "That so? Tell me why we're here."

"I read about it. I never saw her."

"You mean Terri Bridges?" Benton said.

"Everybody's talking about it, as you might imagine. I hear they let him out of Bellevue. It's not nice the names they're calling him. You gotta feel sorry for anyone made fun of like that."

No one had heard from Oscar, as far as Scarpetta knew. No one seemed to have a clue where he was, and she was extremely worried someone might harm him.

"There's five of us who work the door, and we all say the same thing. She'd never been to this building or one of us, at least, would know. And he'd gotten strange," the doorman said.

He directed his attention to Scarpetta and Benton because he obviously didn't like Morales and wasn't trying very hard to hide it.

"Now, that wasn't always the case," the doorman continued, "and I know that for a fact because I've worked here for eleven years, and he's been in the building about half that time. He used to be friendly, a real nice guy. Then all of a sudden he changed. Cut his hair and dyed it the color of a marigold, got quieter and quieter, stayed in his apartment a lot. When he'd come out to walk or whatever, it was at odd times and he was as nervous as a cat."

"Where does he keep his car?" Morales asked.

"An underground parking garage around the block. A lot of the tenants park there."

"When was this?" Benton asked. "When you noticed something different about him."

"I'd say it was the fall. October or so when it started becoming obvious that something was going on. Knowing what I do now, I have to wonder what he got tangled up with, you know, with the girl. Put it this way, when two people get together and one of them changes for the worse? You figure it out."

"Is someone on the door around the clock?" Benton asked him.

"Twenty-four-seven. Come on. I'll take you up. You got a key, right?"

"I assume you have one?" Benton said.

"Funny you would mention that." His green-gloved finger pressed the elevator button. "Mr. Bane took it upon himself to change his lock some months back, around the time he started acting odd."

They boarded, and he tapped the button for the tenth floor.

"He's supposed to give us a key. We got to have a key in case of an emergency, and we've kept asking him, and we still don't have one."

"Sounds to me like ol' Oscar doesn't want anybody in his place," Morales said. "I'm surprised you didn't kick him out."

"It was getting to where there was going to be a confrontation with the building manager. Nobody wanted that. We kept hoping he'd get around to it. Sorry it's so slow—slowest elevator in the city. You'd think we got someone on the roof pulling us up with a rope. Anyway, Mr. Bane keeps to himself. Never has visitors. Has never caused any problems around here, but like I said, he started acting a little unusual, and about the same time he changed his locks. I guess you just never know about people."

"Is this the only elevator?" Scarpetta asked.

"There's a freight elevator. We ask the residents to use it when they take out their dogs. Not everybody wants to be on an elevator with a dog. Poodles are the worst. The big standard ones? They scare me. I'm not getting on an elevator with one of those. Rather ride with a pit bull."

"If someone took the freight elevator, would you be aware of it?" Morales asked. "Like if somebody tried to slip by you?"

"Don't see how they could. They'd still have to come in and out of the front of the building."

"No other access at all? I mean, we're sure Oscar hasn't come in tonight, and nobody saw him?" Morales asked.

"Not unless he climbed up the fire escape and came through the roof," the doorman said, as if Oscar would have to be Spider-Man.

Scarpetta recalled noticing a zigzag of horizontal platforms connected by stairs on the west side of the building.

The elevator stopped, and the doorman stepped out into a hallway of old green carpet and pale yellow walls. Scarpetta looked up at a steel-framed plastic dome in the ceiling that wasn't an ordinary skylight.

"That's the roof access you mean?" she said to the doorman.

"Yes, ma'am. You'd have to have the ladder. Either that or use the fire escape and come through somebody's window."

"And the ladder's kept where?"

"In the basement somewhere. That's not my department."

"Maybe you could check and make sure it's still there," Benton said.

"Sure, sure. But obviously he didn't come in or out that way, or the ladder would be under the roof hatch, right? You're starting to make me nervous now. Like maybe we should have some cops on the roof. Since they let him out of Bellevue, now you're giving me the willies a little."

He led them down to the end of the hall, to Oscar's dark wooden door, the number on it 10B.

"How many apartments on this floor?" Scarpetta asked. "Four?"

"That's right. His neighbors work, aren't around during the day. Out a lot at night because they're single, got no kids. For two of them, this isn't their only residence."

"I'll need their information," Morales said. "Not just them but a list of everybody who lives in the building."

"Sure, sure. There's forty units, four per floor. Obviously, this is the top floor. I won't call it a penthouse, because the apartments aren't any nicer up here than on the other floors. But the view's better. From the ones in the back you can see the Hudson pretty good. I gotta tell you how shocked I am. Mr. Bane sure doesn't seem like the type to do something like that. But you know what they say. They never do, right? And then he did start getting weird. I'll check on the ladder."

"A little reminder, pal," Morales said to him. "Mr.

Oscar Bane's not been charged with a crime. Nobody's saying he killed his girlfriend. So be careful what you spread around, got it?"

They had reached Oscar's door, and Morales had a key that Scarpetta recognized as belonging to a high-security Medeco lock. She noticed something else that she didn't want to draw attention to while the doorman was standing there—a strand of black thread, maybe eight inches long, on the carpet directly below the bottom door hinge.

"I'll be downstairs," the doorman said. "You need me? There's a house phone in the kitchen. A white wall phone. Just dial zero. Who do I call about the ladder?"

Morales gave him his card.

The doorman looked like he didn't want it, but he had no choice. He walked back toward the elevator, and Scarpetta set down her crime scene case, opened it, and handed out gloves. She picked up the piece of thread and examined it under a magnifying lens, noticing a thick knot on one end that had been coated with what appeared to be a flattened bit of colorless soft wax.

She suspected she knew the purpose of the knotted thread, but the door was almost twice as tall as Oscar, and he couldn't possibly have reached the top of it without assistance.

"What you got?" Morales said.

He took the thread from her, looked at it under the lens.

"If I had to guess," she said, "it's something he draped over the top of the door so he could tell if it had been opened in his absence."

"What a clever little guy. Guess we better find out about that ladder, huh? How did he reach the top of the door?"

"We know he's paranoid," Benton said.

Scarpetta placed the thread in an evidence bag she labeled with a Sharpie as Morales unlocked the door and opened it. The alarm started beeping, and he stepped inside and entered a code he had written on a napkin. He turned on the lights.

"Well, look here, we got another ghostbusting gizmo," he said flippantly, bending down to pick up a straightened coat hanger on the floor just inside the door. "Either that or Oscar was roasting marshmallows. I'm looking for a line of flour across the floor like the crazies do to make sure aliens haven't entered their houses."

Scarpetta examined both ends of the straightened coat hanger, then looked at the small flattened piece of wax inside the plastic bag.

"It's possible this is how he'd get the thread on the top of the door," she said. "He'd stick the waxy knot on the tip of the coat hanger. There's an indentation consistent with the diameter of the wire. Let's see if I might be right."

She shut herself out of the apartment, and there was just enough space between the door and the floor for the coat hanger to fit. She slid it back inside the apartment, and Morales opened the door.

"Looney Tuney," he said. "I don't mean you, of course."

The living room was immaculate and masculine, with

walls painted a deep shade of blue and hung with a fine collection of original Victorian maps and prints. Oscar had a fondness for dark antiques and English leather, and an obsession with anti-mind-control devices. They were strategically placed everywhere, inexpensive spectrometers, radio frequency field strength and TriField meters, for the supposed detection of various surveillance frequencies such as infrared, magnetic, and radio waves.

As they walked around the apartment, they discovered antennas and strips of vinyl-coated lead, and buckets of water, and odd contraptions like aluminum foil–lined metal plates wired to batteries and homemade copper pyramids, and hard hats lined with soundproofing foam and topped by small sections of pipe.

An aluminum foil tent completely enclosed Oscar's bed.

"Wave-jamming devices," Benton said. "Pyramids and hats to block out sound waves, beamed energies, including psychic energies. He was trying to create a bubble force field around himself."

Marino and a uniformed officer were carrying a box the size of a washing machine as Lucy got out of a cab in front of Terri Bridges's brownstone.

Lucy slung a nylon satchel over her shoulder, paid the fare, and watched them load the box into the back of a police van. She hadn't seen Marino since she'd threatened to blow his head off last spring in his fishing shack, and decided the best approach was to walk right up to him.

"This the officer who's going to be on my jet?" she said.

"Yeah," Marino said.

"You got the tail number and the pilots' names, right?" she said to the officer. "It's Signature at La Guardia, and when you go inside, Brent should be waiting for you. He's the PIC, will be in a black suit, white shirt, blue striped tie, and has on pants."

"What's a PIC?" The officer slammed the back of the van shut. "What do you mean he has on pants?"

"Pilot in command, sits in the left seat, your trivia for the night. Make sure he knows you've got a gun, just in case he forgot his glasses. He's blind as a bat without his glasses. Which is why he wears pants."

"That's supposed to be a joke, right?"

"There are two pilots. FAA regs—only one needs to see, but both must have on pants."

The officer looked at her.

He looked at Marino and said, "Tell me she's kidding."

"Don't ask me," Marino said. "I don't like to fly. Not anymore."

Berger emerged from the building and came down the steps, in the cold, blustery wind, with no coat on. She pushed her hair out of her face and pulled her suit jacket together, folding her arms against the cold.

"We'd better get our coats," Berger said to Marino.

She didn't say anything to Lucy but touched her hand

as the two of them walked with Marino to his dark blue Impala.

Lucy said to Marino, "I'm going to check out the wireless network Terri was using. If you'd make sure whoever's securing her apartment doesn't have a problem with my being in there so I don't end up cuffed and on the floor—or maybe he doesn't. I may not need to go inside her apartment if the entire building's on the same network, but I've got a couple of interesting things to pass along."

"Why don't we get out of the cold and sit in the car," Berger said.

She and Lucy got into the back, and Marino climbed into the front. He started the engine and turned on the heat as the van with Terri Bridges's vanity chair pulled away from the curb. Lucy unzipped her satchel and pulled out her MacBook. She opened it.

"Two important things," she said. "First is how Terri hooked up with whoever Scarpetta six-twelve is. The John Jay website. This past October ninth, about a month after Benton and Kay became visiting lecturers, Terri—or whoever was signed on as Lunasee—posted a notice on a John Jay website bulletin board asking if anybody knew how she might get in touch with Aunt Kay."

Berger was putting on her coat, and Lucy caught the subtle scent of spices and bamboo, and the oil of bitter orange blossoms—Berger's fragrance, from a perfume house in London. Lucy had asked about it earlier, hoping it wasn't one more lovely thing about Berger that was left over from Greg.

"The posting is archived, obviously," Lucy said.

"How'd you find it?" Marino turned around, his face almost indistinguishable in the dark.

"Looks like you've lost a lot of weight," Lucy said to him.

"I quit eating," he said. "Don't know why other people haven't thought of it. I could write a book, make a lot of money."

"You should. A book with blank pages in it."

"That's what I'm thinking. No food and nothing in the book. It works."

Lucy could feel his scrutiny of her, of Berger, of the two of them sitting close. Marino had sensors that told him where people were in relation to each other, and where they were in relation to him. It was all connected, in his way of thinking.

Lucy watched Berger read what was on the MacBook's screen:

```
Hi Everyone,
    My name's Terri Bridges, and I'm a foren-
sic psych grad student trying to get hold of
Dr. Kay Scarpetta. If anybody has any con-
nection with her, could you please pass on
my e-mail address? I've been trying to track
her down since last spring to interview her
for my thesis. Thanks. —TB
```

Lucy read it out loud to Marino.

She opened another file, and the photograph of

Scarpetta from this morning's column in *Gotham Gotcha* filled the display.

"This was on the same bulletin board?" Berger asked.

Lucy held up the laptop so Marino could see the off-putting photograph of Scarpetta in a morgue, pointing a scalpel at someone.

"The original image," Lucy said. "So the background's not been Photoshopped out. As you recall, in the photo on *Gotham Gotcha*, it's just my aunt and you got no idea about the context, except you assume she's in a morgue. But when we get the background back, we see a countertop with a monitor for security cameras, and beyond is a cinder-block wall with cabinets. But when I did some image enhancement of my own"—she touched the trackpad and opened another file—"I got this."

She showed them an enlargement of the transparent plastic shield covering Scarpetta's face. Reflected in it was the vague image of another person.

Lucy moved her finger over the trackpad and opened another file, and the image reflected in the face shield was more refined.

"Dr. Lester," Berger said.

"That figures," Marino said. "Someone like her would hate the Doc."

Lucy said, "We can establish a few things that may or may not be related. The photograph on the Internet this morning was taken in the New York ME's office during a case or cases when Dr. Lester was present, and that's who my aunt was talking to. Obviously, Dr. Lester didn't take the photograph, but my guess is she knows who did, unless she just didn't notice when it was being done. . . ."

"She would know," Berger said decisively. "She watches her fiefdom like a vulture."

"And no," Lucy said. "I didn't find the image on the John Jay website, although it's possible this photograph is floating around out there on the Internet and a fan sent it in to *Gotham Gotcha*."

"How do you know Dr. Lester didn't send it to *Gotham Gotcha*?" Marino asked.

"I'd have to get into her e-mail to figure that out," Lucy said.

"And you won't," Berger said. "But it's not Lenora's style. Her MO at this stage in her unhappy life is to dismiss people, treat them as if they don't matter. Not draw attention to them. The only person she's desperate to draw attention to is herself."

"I saw the two of them being real cozy with each other earlier tonight," Marino said. "Her and Morales in the park at Bellevue, next to the DNA building. They met on a bench for a few minutes after Benton and the Doc left the morgue. I happened to see it because I was waiting to pick them up. My read on it is Dr. Lester wanted to update Morales on what the Doc did in the morgue, what she found out. But for what it's worth, Dr. Lester was text-messaging somebody when she walked off in the dark."

"I'm not sure that means anything," Berger said. "Everybody text-messages these days."

"That's bizarre," Lucy said. "She meets with him in a dark park? Are they . . . ?"

"I tried to imagine it," Marino said. "I couldn't."

"He has a way of sidling up close to people," Berger said. "They might be friendly. But not the other. No. I'd say she's not his type."

"Not unless he's a necrophile," Marino said, as if there were such a word.

"I'm not going to make fun of anyone," Berger said, and she meant it.

"Point being," Marino said, "I guess it sort of surprised me because I don't think of her as having anything personal enough with anybody to merit her text-messaging them."

"It's more likely she was text-messaging the chief medical examiner," Berger said. "Just speculation. But that would be like her to pass on information to him, especially if she could take credit for what somebody else did."

"Covering her ass because she probably missed stuff," Lucy said. "So she wanted to call the chief right away. I'd have to get into his e-mail to figure it out."

"And you're not going to do that," Berger said.

Her shoulder was solidly against Lucy's as she said it.

Lucy was so aware of Berger's every motion, sound, and scent, she could be on LSD, based on what she'd read about it: an increased heart rate and higher body temperature, and crossover sensations such as "hearing" colors and "seeing" sounds.

"It might be something like that," Marino was saying.

"She's a pilot fish. Has to swim after the sharks to get the leftovers they drop. I'm not making fun of her. It's the truth."

"What's the Terri connection in all this?" Berger asked.

Lucy replied, "The photograph was sent to her, specifically, to the user account called Lunasee."

"Sent by?" Berger asked.

"Scarpetta six-twelve sent it to her the first Monday of December, the third, and what's not making much sense is for some reason Terri, I'm going to say it was Terri, deleted it, and whoever sent it also deleted it, which is why it wasn't in the trash. I had to restore it with the neural networking programming."

Marino said, "You're telling us the photo was sent December third, and both parties immediately deleted it that same day?"

"Yes."

"Was there a message with it?" Berger asked.

"Showing you that right now."

Lucy moved her finger on the trackpad.

"This," she said.

```
Date: Mon, 3 December 2007 12:16:11
From: "Scarpetta"
To: "Terri"
Terri,
    I know you like primary source material,
so consider this an early Christmas present—
for your book. But I do not want to be cred-
ited with having given this to you, and will
```

deny it if asked. Nor will I tell you who
took it—wasn't with my permission (the idiot
gave me a copy, assumed I'd be pleased). I'm
asking that you move the photo to a Word file
and delete it from your e-mail as I've just
now deleted it from mine. —Scarpetta

"Terri Bridges was writing a book?" Marino asked.

"I don't know," Lucy said. "But based on what Jaime and I have seen of this master's thesis? Could very well be that's where it was headed."

Berger said, "Especially if she really believed all this material was coming from Kay, and I do think she believed that. I think Lunasee was Terri. For the record. Although I know it's speculative."

"I do, too," Lucy said. "Obviously, the critical question is whether whoever's been posing as my aunt in these e-mails to Terri has anything to do with her murder."

"What about the IP?" Marino asked.

"When can you guys get the info from the ISP—the Internet service provider—to identify the customer? Because the address I get is a twenty-something block of the Upper East Side that includes the Guggenheim, the Met, and the Jewish Museum. That's not real helpful."

Lucy knew the exact location but wasn't going to be forthcoming about it. Berger didn't like her to break the rules, and Lucy had her friends in the world of ISPs, some of them going back to her federal law-enforcement years, and others further back than that, who knew people who knew people. What she'd done was no different from cops getting a warrant after they'd already opened the trunk of a car and discovered a hundred kilos of cocaine inside.

She said, "Also right around in that area, which is basically Museum Mile, is Dr. Elizabeth Stuart's dermatology practice."

Berger's face was close to hers in the dark backseat, her fragrance a spell.

Berger said, "Right around in that area? How *right around* are we talking about?"

"The dermatologist to the stars has an apartment that's the entire thirtieth floor in the building where her office is," Lucy said. "She's away for the holidays. Her office doesn't reopen until Monday the seventh."

27

Scarpetta waited to go inside the library until she could find an excuse to be alone, and Lucy's call provided it.

Leaving Morales and Benton in the bedroom, she walked back toward the living room and entered the library as Lucy told her over the phone about a posting on the John Jay website and asked if she was aware of it. Scanning shelves of old psychiatric volumes, Scarpetta told her that she wasn't.

"I'm sorry to hear it," Scarpetta added. "Everything I'm hearing makes me feel sorry, really sorry. I wish I'd known she was trying to get hold of me."

She didn't see the book Oscar had told her about, *The Experiences of an Asylum Doctor*, where he claimed to have hidden the CD. Her doubts about him proliferated. What kind of game was he playing with her?

"And the photograph on the Internet this morning," Lucy said. "Taken in the morgue here in New York. You were talking to Dr. Lester. Does that sound familiar?"

"I have no recollection of anybody taking my picture when I've been there or I would have thought of it when I first saw the photo today."

"When you look at the photo again, fill in the background with a countertop and a security camera video display. Maybe you can figure out where the person might have been standing. Maybe that will tell you something."

"It would have been from the direction of an autopsy table. There are three of them in the autopsy suite, so maybe it was somebody there for another case. I promise I'll think about it carefully, but not right now."

All she could think about right now was talking to Oscar again and telling him the book wasn't here. She could imagine his reply. *They* must have gotten hold of the CD. That would explain the thread on the floor outside his door. *They* had gotten in. That's what he would say. She hadn't mentioned the book or the hidden CD to Morales or Benton. She couldn't tell them the book and CD were there, and she couldn't tell them that they weren't. She was Oscar Bane's physician. What had gone on between the two of them, within reason, remained confidential.

"You got something to write with?" Lucy asked. "I'm giving you Dr. Elizabeth Stuart's phone numbers. The dermatologist."

"I know who she is."

Lucy explained that the photograph was e-mailed to Terri Bridges on December 3, at around noon, from an Internet coffee shop across the street from Dr. Stuart's office. She gave Scarpetta a cell phone number, and also a number for a time-share presidential suite at the St. Regis in Aspen, Colorado, and said Dr. Stuart always stayed there under her husband's name, which was Oxford.

"Ask for Dr. Oxford," Lucy said. "Amazing what people will tell you, but I didn't pass along all this to anyone else. Jaime has this thing about going through legal channels, imagine? Anyway, can you ask Morales something for me and then tell Benton to call me?"

"I'm walking that way now."

"I'm in the foyer of Terri's brownstone, logged on to the wireless network, which is accessible to all the apartments," Lucy said. "And it's broadcasting, meaning it's visible to anybody on it. There's a device on it."

Oscar's home gym was in the master bedroom, his foil-tented bed in the midst of it, and Benton and Morales were talking.

"What is it you want me to ask him, exactly?" Scarpetta said.

She could see why Morales was popular with women and begrudgingly respected but resented by just about everybody else, including judges. He reminded her of a couple of the star athletes on scholarship at Cornell when she was there as an undergraduate, these scrappy, supremely self-assured young men who compensated for their relatively small stature by being wiry and fast, brazen and outrageous. They listened to no one, had little regard for their team or coaches, and were intellectually lazy but scored points and were crowd pleasers. They weren't nice people.

"Just ask him if he's aware that there's a camera," Lucy was saying.

"I can answer that," Scarpetta said. "He installed a surveillance camera on the roof. Marino knows about it. Is Jaime with you?"

Scarpetta didn't realize why she'd asked until the words were out. It was something she sensed, maybe had sensed it the first time she'd seen them together when Lucy was scarcely more than a child, at least in Scarpetta's mind, practically a child. Berger was a good fifteen years older than Lucy.

Why did it matter?

Lucy certainly wasn't a child.

She was explaining to Scarpetta that Berger and Marino had gone across the street to talk to a witness. She hadn't been with them for a good half-hour.

Maybe it was the simple logic that a prosecutor as busy and important as Jaime Berger was unlikely to spend her evening inside a Greenwich Village loft watching a computer run a program. Anything Lucy discovered could have been relayed over the phone or electronically. While it was true that Berger was known for being hands-on and extremely energetic and fierce when it came to absorbing crime scenes in person and directing the evidence to be analyzed and quickly, and on occasion showing up at the morgue if there was an autopsy she wanted to see and Dr. Lester wasn't the ME doing it, she didn't watch computers. She didn't pull up a chair in the labs and watch gas chromatography, microscopy, trace evidence examination, or low copy number DNA amplification in the works.

Berger gave marching orders and had meetings to go over the results. It bothered Scarpetta to think of Lucy and Berger alone in that loft for hours. Scarpetta's uneasiness about it likely went back to the last time she'd seen them together, five years ago, when she'd appeared unannounced at Berger's penthouse.

She hadn't expected to discover Lucy there, confiding in Berger about what had happened in that hotel room in Szczecin, Poland, offering details that to this day Scarpetta didn't know.

She'd felt she was no longer the center of her niece's life. Or perhaps she had seen it coming, that one day she wouldn't be. That was the truth, her selfish truth.

Scarpetta told Benton that Lucy needed to talk to him. He hesitated, waiting for a signal from her that she was all right.

"I'm going to check his cabinets," she said, and that was her signal.

Benton should leave the bedroom so he could have a private conversation.

"I'll be down the hall," Benton said, entering a number on his cell phone.

Scarpetta could feel Morales watching her as she walked into Oscar's bathroom. The more she saw of the way he lived, the more depressed she was by his obvious deteriorated mental state. Bottles in the medicine cabinet made it clear he believed his own nightmares, and the date on several prescription bottles validated the timeline, too.

She found l-lysine, pantothenic and folic and amino acids, bone calcium, iodine, kelp, the sort of supplements taken by people who had suffered radiation damage or feared they had. Beneath the sink were large bottles of white vinegar that she suspected he was adding to his baths, and early last October he had filled a prescription for eszopiclone, which was used to treat insomnia. Since then, he had refilled the prescription twice, most recently at a Duane Reade pharmacy, on December twenty-seventh. The name of the prescribing doctor was Elizabeth Stuart. Scarpetta would call her, but not now and not here.

She began going through a small closet where Oscar kept the expected over-the-counter medications and first-aid necessities such as Band-Aids, rubbing alcohol, gauze—and a lubricant called Aqualine. She was looking at it when Morales walked in. The price sticker was missing from the unopened jar, so she had no idea where it had been purchased.

"Isn't that sort of like Vaseline?" he asked.

"Sort of," she replied.

"You think the labs can tell if this is the same stuff that was recovered from her vagina?"

"It's more commonly used as a healing ointment," Scarpetta said. "To treat burns, irritated or cracked skin, atopic dermatitis, eczema, that sort of thing. None of which Oscar has, by the way. Popular with runners, bikers, race walkers. Rather ubiquitous. You can get it at any pharmacy and most grocery stores."

It almost sounded as if she was defending Oscar Bane.

"Yeah. We know little Oscar's quite the little walker, flat-footed fella that he is. The doorman says he goes out in his little warm-ups almost every day, no matter the weather. The ladder's on the roof, how about that for strange? The building's got no idea why. I'm thinking the little guy climbed up the fire escape and came in one of his windows, then went out through the roof access and pulled the ladder up behind him. That explains why it's on the roof."

"Why might he do that?"

"To get in." Morales stared intensely at her.

"And opening his window wouldn't set off the alarm?" she asked.

"It was set off. I called the alarm company to inves-ti-gate. Not long after Oscar checked out of Belle-vue, yup, the alarm went off. The service called his apart-ment, and a man answered and said it was an accident and gave the password. It's not that loud. The building wouldn't have heard it, especially if it was deactivated quickly. So what do you think?"

"I don't have a thought about it."

"Shit, you have thoughts about everything, Dr. CNN. That's what you're known for. You're known for all these amazing thoughts you have."

He walked to the closet she was searching. He bumped against her as he picked up the jar of Aqualine.

"Chemically," he said, "we could tell if this is the same stuff recovered from her body, correct?"

"Certainly," she said, "you could determine what it's not, such as K-Y jelly, which has certain antiseptic and preservative additives like sodium hydroxide and methylparaben. Aqualine is preservative-free, mainly mineral oil and petrolatum. I'm pretty sure nothing like this was found in Terri's apartment. At least it's not on the evidence inventory, and I checked the medicine cabinet, looked around when I was just there. You would know better than anybody."

"Doesn't mean he didn't bring it in his murder kit, and leave with it. I'm not saying Oscar did, I'm saying the killer did. But I'm also not saying they aren't the same person, either."

Morales's brown eyes were intense on hers. He seemed to be enjoying himself, and at the same time angry.

"But you're on the money about nothing being in her apartment," he said. "Last night I didn't know we were looking for a lubricant because the autopsy hadn't been done yet. But I did look when I went back."

This was the first she'd heard that he'd gone back, and she thought about Terri's guest room office and Marino's comment that it appeared someone had groomed the carpet in there.

"After your buddy Marino found her laptops, I went back and checked out the place to make sure there wasn't anything else missed," Morales said. "By then I knew the autopsy results, had talked to Pester Lester. So I poked around for a lubricant. Nope, not there."

"We noticed the carpet in her office," she said.

"I bet you did," he said. "My mama taught me to clean up after myself, straighten the fringe on the rug, be dutiful and responsible. Speaking of, guess I'd better bag up a few of these things. Did I tell you I got a search warrant just in case we found something good?"

He flashed her a bright, toothy smile and winked.

They returned to the bedroom with its gym equipment and foil tent. She opened a closet and scanned a shelf that had more foam-lined helmets and several antennas. She rifled through clothing, most of it casual, and noted plastic panels in the pockets of several blazers, yet another type of shield, and she remembered Oscar's anxious comment in the infirmary about not having any protection with him.

On the floor were pairs of small snow boots, dress shoes, Nikes, and a wicker basket filled with hand grips, jump ropes, ankle weights, and a deflated fitness ball.

She picked up the Nikes. They looked old and not suitable for a serious athlete with potential joint and foot problems.

"These are the only running shoes?" she asked Morales. "Seems like he would have a better pair than this. In fact, multiple pairs."

"I keep forgetting what they call you," he said.

He moved next to her.

"Eagle eye," he said. "Among other things."

He was close enough for her to see faint reddish freckles scattered over his light brown skin, and she smelled his loud cologne.

"Wears a Brooks Ariel made especially for people who overpronate and need a lot of stability," he said. "Kind of an irony."

He waved his hand around the bedroom.

"I'd say your fan Oscar could use all the stability he can get," Morales added. "Good for flat-footed people. Wide-bodied, unique tread pattern. I got the pair he was wearing last night and dropped it off at the labs. With his clothes."

"Meaning he wore what, exactly, when he checked himself out of Bellevue a little while ago?" she asked.

"Another eagle-eye question."

She kept inching away from him, and he continued to crowd her. She was almost in the closet, and she placed the Nikes back on the floor and stepped around and away from him.

"Last night when I agreed to take him to the crazy hotel," Morales said, "I made a little deal. I said if he'd let me have his clothes, we'd stop by his apartment first so he could get a jump-out bag. Then he'd be all set when he was ready to leave."

"Sounds like you were expecting he wouldn't stay long."

"I was expecting exactly that. He wasn't going to stay long because his reason for being there was to see Benton and, most of all, you. He got his dream come true and he boogied."

"He came in here by himself last night to get his so-called jump-out bag of clothes?"

"Wasn't under arrest. Could do what he wanted. I

waited in the car, and he went in, took him maybe ten minutes. Max. Maybe that's why his little booby trap thread was on the floor. He forgot to drape it over the top of the door when he was leaving. He was a little upset."

"Do we know what was in his jump-out bag?"

"One pair of jeans, a navy blue T-shirt, another pair of his Brooks running shoes, socks, underwear, and a zip-up wool coat. The ward's got an inventory. Jeb went through it. You met Jeb."

She didn't say anything as they stood near the aluminum-foil tent, eye to eye.

"The corrections officer outside your door this afternoon. Making sure you were safe," he said.

She was startled by Rod Stewart singing "Do Ya Think I'm Sexy?"

The music ringtone on Morales's personal digital assistant, a hefty and expensive one.

He pressed his Bluetooth earpiece and answered, "Yeah."

She walked out and found Benton inside the library, his gloved hands holding a copy of a book, *The Air Loom Gang.*

Benton said, "About a machine controlling someone's mind back in the late seventeen hundreds. You okay? I didn't want to interfere. Figured you'd yell if you needed me to crush him into a cube."

"He's an asshole."

"Read that loud and clear."

He returned the book to its empty slot on a shelf.

"I was telling you about *The Air Loom Gang*," he said. "This apartment's like a scene out of it. Bedlam."

"I know."

Their eyes met, as if he was waiting for her to tell him something.

"Did you know Oscar had a bag packed with clothing on the ward, in case he got the urge to leave?" she said. "And that Morales brought him over here last night?"

"I knew Oscar could leave whenever he chose," he replied. "We've all known that."

"I just think it's uncanny. Almost as if Morales was encouraging him to leave, wanted him out of the hospital."

"Why would you think that?" Benton asked.

"Some things he said."

She glanced around at the open doorway, worrying Morales might suddenly walk in.

"A feeling there was a fair amount of negotiating going on last night when he drove Oscar away from the scene, for example," she said.

"That wouldn't be unusual."

"You understand the predicament I'm in," she said, scanning old books again, and disappointed again.

Oscar said the book with the CD would be in the second bookcase, left of the door, fourth shelf. The book wasn't there. The fourth shelf was stacked with archival boxes, each of them labeled *Circulars*.

"What should he have in his collection that he doesn't, in your opinion? To make it more complete." Benton said it for a reason.

"Why do you ask?"

"There's a certain corrections officer named Jeb who tells me things. Unfortunately, Jeb tells a lot of people things, but he sure didn't want you getting hurt today when you were in the infirmary, and he wasn't happy at all with your making him step outside. When I called and found out Oscar was gone, Jeb and I had a chat. Anyway, what's Oscar missing in here?"

"I'm surprised he doesn't have *The Experiences of an Asylum Doctor*. By Littleton Winslow."

"That's interesting," Benton said. "Interesting you would come up with that."

She tugged his sleeve and they got on the floor in front of the second bookcase.

She started pulling archival boxes off the bottom shelf, and was beginning to feel unhinged, as if she'd lost her GPS, anything that might tell her which direction was the right one. She didn't know who was crazy and who wasn't, who was lying or telling the truth, who was talking and to whom, or who might turn up next that she wasn't supposed to see.

She opened an archival box and found an assortment of nineteenth-century pamphlets about mechanical restraints and water cures.

"I would have thought he'd have it," she said.

"The reason he doesn't is because there's no such book," Benton said, his arm against hers as they looked at pamphlets.

His physical presence was reassuring, and she needed to feel it.

"Not by that author," Benton added. "*The Experiences of an Asylum Doctor* was written by Montagu Lomax about fifty years after Littleton Winslow, son of Forbes Winslow, wrote his famous *Plea of Insanity*, his *Manual of Lunacy*."

"Why would Oscar lie?"

"Doesn't trust anyone. Truly believes he's being spied on. Maybe the bad guys will hear where he's hidden his only proof, and so he's cryptic with you. Or maybe he's confused. Or maybe he's testing you. If you care about him enough, you'll come into this library just as you have, and figure it out. Could be a number of reasons."

Scarpetta opened another archival box, this one filled with circulars about Bellevue.

Oscar had said that she and Benton would be interested in what he'd collected about Bellevue.

She lifted out a manual on nursing, and an in-house published directory of the medical and surgical staff between 1736 and 1894. She picked up a stack of circulars and lectures going back to 1858.

At the bottom of the box was a thumb drive attached to a lanyard.

She pulled off her gloves, wrapped the thumb drive in them, and handed them to Benton.

She got up and felt Morales before she saw him, in the doorway. She hoped he hadn't seen what she'd just done.

"We got to leave right now," Morales said.

He was holding a paper bag of evidence, the top of it sealed with red tape.

Benton returned the archival box to its bottom shelf and got up, too.

She saw no sign of the glove-wrapped thumb drive. He must have slipped it into his pocket.

"Jaime and Marino are across the street—not here, across the street from Terri's apartment in Murray Hill," Morales said, keyed up and impatient. "The witness who called in the animal-cruelty report? She's not answering her phone or the intercom. The light's out at the building's entrance, and the outer door's locked. Marino said when he was there earlier, the outer door wasn't locked."

They were walking out of Oscar's apartment. Morales didn't bother resetting the alarm.

"Apparently, there's a fire escape ladder and a roof hatch," he said, tense and impatient. "The roof hatch is propped open."

He didn't bother with the deadbolt, either.

28

One tenant had returned home since Marino was here earlier, the man in 2C, the second floor. When Marino had walked around to the side of the building a few minutes ago, he could see lights on and the flickering of a TV behind opaque shades.

He knew the tenant's name because he knew the names of everyone. So far, the tenant, Dr. Wilson, a twenty-eight-year-old resident physician at Bellevue, wasn't answering the intercom.

Marino tried again, while Berger and Lucy stood by in the cold wind, watching and waiting.

"Dr. Wilson," Marino said, holding in the intercom button. "This is the police again. We don't want to force our way into the building."

"You haven't said what the problem is." A man's voice,

presumably Dr. Wilson's, answered through the speaker by the door.

"This is Investigator Marino, NYPD," Marino repeated himself, tossing Lucy his car keys. "We need to get into Two-D. Eva Peebles's apartment. If you look out your window, you'll see my unmarked dark blue Impala, okay? A female officer is going to turn on the grille lights so you can see for a fact it's a police car. I understand your being reluctant to unlock the door, but we don't want to forcibly enter the building. When you came in, did you see your neighbor?"

"I can't see anything. It's too dark out," the voice replied.

"No shit, Sherlock," Marino said to nobody in particular, the button released so Dr. Wilson couldn't hear him. "He's been smoking pot, what you want to bet? So he doesn't want to let us in."

"Is this Dr. Wilson?" Marino asked over the intercom.

"I don't have to answer your questions and I'm not going to unlock the front door. Not after what happened across the street. I almost didn't come back."

One of his windows slid up, and the shade moved.

Marino was sure the guy was stoned, and he remembered what Mrs. Peebles said about her neighbor who smoked pot. Son of a bitch. More worried about getting charged with possession than about whether the elderly widow in the apartment across from his might be in trouble.

"Sir, I need you to unlock the front door right now.

If you look out the window, you're going to see the entrance light is out. Did you turn the light out when you came in earlier?"

"I didn't touch any lights," the man's voice said, and now he sounded nervous. "How do I know you're police?"

"Let me try," Berger said, and she pushed the intercom button on the panel to the right of the door while Marino shone his flashlight on it, because they were completely in the dark.

"Dr. Wilson? This is Jaime Berger with the district attorney's office. We need to check on your neighbor, but we can't do that if you don't let us into the building."

"No," the voice came back. "You get some other real police cars here, maybe I'll think about it."

"That probably made things worse," Marino said to her. "He's been in there smoking weed, I guarantee it. That's why he opened his damn window."

Lucy was inside Marino's car, and the high-intensity red and blue flashing lights started bouncing off glass.

"I'm unmoved," the voice came back again, even more resolute. "Anybody can buy those."

"Let me talk to him," Berger said, shielding her eyes from the rapid bursts of blinding blue and red.

"Tell you what, Dr. Wilson," Marino said into the intercom. "I'm going to give you a number I want you to call, and when the dispatcher answers, you tell him there's a guy outside your building who says he's Investigator P. R. Marino, okay? Ask him to verify it, because they know I'm right here right now with Assistant District Attorney Jaime Berger."

Silence.

"He's not going to call," Berger said.

Lucy trotted back up the steps.

Marino said to her, "How 'bout doing me another favor while I stand here and babysit."

He asked her to return to his car and radio the dispatcher. She asked him what happened to his portable radio, or were police not bothering with portable radios anymore. He said he'd left his in the car and maybe she could grab it for him while she was requesting an unmarked backup unit and an entry tool kit, including a battering ram. She said it was an old door and they probably could pry it open with a Gorilla Bar, and he said he wanted more than just a Gorilla Bar, and that he wanted the prick doctor who was stoned on the second floor to get an eyeful of a Twin Turbo Ram like they used to bust in doors at crack houses, and maybe then they wouldn't need to use it because the asshole would buzz them in. Marino told her to request an ambulance, just in case Eva Peebles needed one.

She wasn't answering her phone or the intercom. Marino couldn't tell if any lights were on inside her apartment. The window that her computer was in front of was dark.

He didn't need to give Lucy radio codes or any further instructions. Nobody needed to teach Lucy a damn thing about being a cop, and as he watched her duck inside his car, he felt a tug from the past. He missed the old days when the two of them rode motorcycles together, went shooting, worked investigations, or chilled out with a six-pack, and he wondered what she was carrying.

He knew she was carrying something. For one thing, there was no way in hell Lucy would run around unarmed, even in New York. And he knew a Pistol Pete jacket when he saw one, and he'd noticed hers the instant she'd gotten out of the cab while he and the other officer were loading the packaged chair into the back of the van. What looked like a black leather motorcycle jacket had an outside breakaway pocket big enough to hold just about any pistol imaginable.

Maybe she was carrying the forty-caliber Glock with a laser sight that he'd given to her a year ago this past Christmas, when they were both in Charleston. Well, wouldn't that be typical of his lousy luck. He'd never gotten around to transferring the title over to her before he'd vanished from her life, so if she did anything that was whacked out, the damn gun would be traced straight back to him. All the same, the idea that she might care enough about the gun to risk breaking New York law and maybe going to jail made him feel good. Lucy could have any gun she wanted. She could buy an entire gun factory, probably several of them.

She climbed back out of his unmarked car as if it belonged to her, and jogged back to them, and he was thinking he should come right out and ask her if she was carrying, and if so, what, but he didn't. She stood next to Berger. There was something between them and it hadn't escaped his notice any more than the Pistol Pete jacket did. Berger didn't stand or sit close to people. She never let anybody break through the invisible barrier that she had to have around her, or believed she had to have around her. She touched Lucy, leaned against her, and watched her a lot.

Lucy handed Marino his portable radio.

"You must be a little rusty. Been out of real policing too long?" Lucy said to him with a serious tone and straight face, what little he could see of her face in the dark. "Bad idea leaving your radio in the car. Little oversights like that? Next thing, somebody gets hurt."

"If I want to take one of your classes, I'll sign up for it," he said.

"I'll see if I have room."

He got on his portable radio and called the unit en route to find out where he was.

"Coming around the corner now," came the reply.

"Hit your lights and siren," Marino said.

He pressed the intercom button.

"Hello?" the voice answered.

"Dr. Wilson. Unlock the door right now or we're going to break it down!"

A siren screamed, and he heard a buzz and he shoved open the door. He flipped a switch, turning on a light inside the small foyer, and directly ahead were the polished old oak stairs leading up, and he slid out his pistol as he got back on the air and told his backup to cut the lights and siren and stay put and watch the front of the building. He ran up the steps, Lucy and Berger right behind him.

He could feel the cold air coming in from the open roof hatch when they reached the second floor, and the lights were out there, too. Marino searched the wall to flip them on. He could see the night sky through the opening in the ceiling, and he didn't see a ladder, and his sense of urgency and his premonition grew. Most likely, the ladder was on the roof. He stopped at 2D and noticed the door wasn't completely shut. He guided Berger to one side and briefly met Lucy's eyes. His system was on high alert as he pushed the door open with his foot and it softly thudded against the inside wall.

"Police!" he yelled, and he had his gun out, gripped in both hands, the barrel pointed up. "Anybody here? Police!"

He didn't have to tell Lucy to shine her light into the room. She was already doing it, and then her arm snaked past his shoulder and she flipped a switch, and an old, ornate chandelier cast the room in a soft glow. Marino and Lucy stepped inside and motioned for Berger to stay behind them. Then nobody moved for a moment. They looked around, and sweat was cool as it rolled down Marino's back and sides, and he wiped his forehead with his sleeve as his eyes darted to the tan corduroy recliner he'd been sitting in earlier, and the couch where Mrs. Peebles had been drinking her bourbon. The wall-mounted flat-screen TV was on, the volume off, and the Dog Whisperer was silently talking to a snarling beagle.

Old wooden Venetian blinds were drawn in all the windows. Lucy was close to the computer on the desk, and she tapped a key. The computer screen filled with what looked like the *Gotham Gotcha* website gone berserk.

Gotham Gotcha! was rearranging into OH C THA MAGGOT! And the New York skyline was black against flashing red, and the Christmas tree from Rockefeller Center was upside down in Central Park, and a snowstorm struck and lightning flashed and thunder clapped inside FAO Schwarz right before the Statue of Liberty seemed to blow up.

Berger quietly stared at it. She stared at Lucy.

"Go on," Lucy told Marino, indicating she'd cover Berger and him while he began clearing the apartment.

He checked the kitchen, a guest bath, the dining room, and then he faced the closed door leading into what he assumed was the master area. He turned the cut-glass knob and pushed the door open with his toe as he swept the bedroom with his gun. It was empty, the king-size bed neatly made and covered with a plaid quilt with dogs embroidered on it. On the nightstand was an empty glass, and in a corner was a small pet carrier but no sign of a dog or cat.

Lamps had been removed from the two nightstands and placed on either side of an open doorway, illuminating the edge of black-and-white tile. He positioned himself to one side of the bathroom as he quietly approached, and swung his gun around and pointed it as he noticed a slight movement before he could see what it was.

Eva Peebles's frail nude body was suspended by satiny gold rope that was looped once around her neck and tied to a chain in the ceiling. Her wrists and ankles were tightly lashed with translucent plastic straps, her toes barely touching the floor. Cold air blowing through an open window had created an eerie oscillation, the body slowly twirling in one direction, then the other, as the rope twisted and untwisted, again and again.

Scarpetta feared that the person who murdered seventy-two-year-old Eva Peebles had also killed Terri Bridges. She feared that person might be Oscar Bane.

The thought had entered her mind the minute she'd entered the bedroom and seen the lamps on the floor and the body suspended by a gold rope that had been removed from a drapery in the dining room and attached to a short length of iron chain. The alabaster half-globe light fixture that had been attached to the chain's S-link was inside the tub, on top of folded clothing that she could tell from where she was taking photographs in the doorway had been cut open at the seams and removed from the victim after her ankles and wrists were bound, most likely while she was still alive.

On the shut white toilet lid were several unmistakable shoe prints no bigger than a boy's, with a distinctive tread pattern. It appeared the assailant had stood there to access the overhead fixture, and from that height, someone four feet tall could have managed quite well, especially if the person was strong.

If Oscar Bane was the killer after all, Scarpetta had misinterpreted and misjudged, in part based on what a tape measure had told her, and she'd been steered by her integrity as a physician, and there was no room for mistakes or confidentiality when people were dying.

Maybe she should have kept her opinions to herself and encouraged the police to find Oscar immediately or aggressively prevented his release from Bellevue to begin with. She could have given Berger cause to arrest him. Scarpetta could have said a number of things, not the least of which was that Oscar had faked his injuries, had lied to the police about them, lied about an intruder, lied about why his coat was in the car, lied about a book and a CD in his library. The ends would have justified the means, because he'd be off the street, and possibly Eva Peebles wouldn't be dangling from her ceiling.

Scarpetta had been acting too much like Oscar's goddamn doctor. She'd made the mistake of caring about him, of feeling compassion. She should stay away from suspects, restrict herself to people who can't suffer anymore and therefore are easier to listen to, to question, to examine.

Berger returned to the bedroom and stood at a sensible distance, because she was experienced with crime scenes and wasn't wearing the disposable protective clothing that covered Scarpetta from head to toe. Berger wasn't the sort to allow her curiosity to override her coolheaded judgment. She knew exactly what to do and what not to do.

"Marino and Morales are with the only person currently at home," Berger said. "A guy you'd never want for your family doctor, whose apartment, as I understand it, is about fifty degrees because the windows are open. You can still smell the pot in there. We've got officers outside to make sure nobody else enters the building, and Lucy's dealing with the computer in the living room."

"The neighbor," Scarpetta asked. "He didn't notice the damn roof hatch was open and all the lights were out? When the hell did he get home?"

She was still surveying before touching anything, the body slowly twirling in the uneven light of the lamps.

"What I know so far is this," Berger said. "He says he returned home around nine, at which time the lights weren't out and the roof hatch wasn't open. He fell asleep in front of the TV and didn't hear a thing, assuming someone entered the building."

"I'd say it's a safe assumption that someone entered the building."

"The ladder to the roof hatch is kept in a utility closet up here—same scenario as across the street. Benton says the ladder is definitely on the roof. It appears the assailant was either familiar with this building or with buildings set up like this one, like Terri's, and found the ladder. He went out through the roof and pulled the ladder up after him."

"And the theory about how he got in?"

"Theory of the moment is she must have let him in. Then he turned out the lights on his way up to her apartment. She must have known him or had reason to trust him. And the other thing. The neighbor says he didn't hear any screams. Which is interesting. Possible she didn't scream?"

"Let me tell you what I'm seeing," Scarpetta said. "And then you can answer your own question. First, even without moving any closer, I can tell by her suffused face, her tongue protruding from her mouth, the sharp angle of the noose high under her chin and tightly knotted behind her right ear, and the absence of any other apparent ligature marks, that the cause of death is probably going to be asphyxiation by hanging. In other words, I don't think we're going to find that she was garroted or strangled by a ligature first, and then her dead body was suspended by a drapery cord from a light-fixture chain."

"I still can't answer my question," Berger said. "I don't know why she wouldn't have screamed bloody murder. Someone straps your wrists behind your back, your ankles—tight as hell with some sort of flex-cuff. And you're nude. . . ."

"Not flex-cuffs. Looks like the same type of strap used on Terri Bridges's wrists. And also like Terri's case? The clothes were cut off." Scarpetta pointed to what was in the tub. "I think he wants us to know the chronology of what he does. Seems to go out of his way to make it pretty clear. Even left the lamps where he'd set them so we could see, since the only light in here, in the bathroom, is the one he removed and placed in the tub."

"You're conjecturing he set up the lamps like that for our benefit?"

"For himself first. He needed to see what he was doing. Then he left them. Made it more of a rush for whoever found her. The shock effect."

"Sort of like Gainesville. The severed head on a bookshelf," Berger said, looking past her, at the body slowly twirling in its infernal, mocking pirouette.

"Sort of," Scarpetta said. "That and the body winding and unwinding, which may very well be the reason the window's open. I'm guessing it was his final brushstroke on his way out."

"To artificially speed up the cooling of the body."

"I don't think he gave a damn about that," Scarpetta said. "I think he opened the window so the air blowing in would do exactly what it's doing. To make her dance."

Berger silently watched the body slowly dance.

Scarpetta retrieved her camera and two LCD chemical thermometers from her crime scene case.

"But since there are buildings everywhere around us," Scarpetta said in a hard voice, "he would have, at the very least, had the blinds shut while he was doing his handiwork in here. Otherwise, someone might have seen the entire ordeal. Maybe filmed it with a cell phone. Posted it on YouTube. So he was callous enough to draw up the blinds before he left, to make sure the wind blew in and created his special effects."

"I'm sorry you had to encounter Marino like this," Berger said, aware of Scarpetta's anger but not the reason for it.

Scarpetta's mood had nothing to do with Marino. She'd dealt with that drama earlier and felt quite done with it for the time being. It wasn't important right now. Berger was unfamiliar with Scarpetta's demeanor at crime scenes because she had never worked one with her, and had no clue what she was like when confronted with such blatant cruelty, especially if she was worried that a death might have been prevented, that maybe she could have helped prevent it.

This had been an awful way to die. Eva Peebles had suffered physical pain and abject terror while the killer had his sadistic fun with her. It was a wonder and a pity she didn't die of a heart attack before he'd finished her off.

Based on the sharp upward angle of the rope around her neck, she wasn't rendered unconscious quickly, but likely suffered the agony of not being able to breathe as the pressure of the rope under her chin occluded her airway. Unconsciousness due to a lack of oxygen can take minutes that seem forever. She would have kicked like mad had he not bound her ankles together, which might be why he'd done so. Maybe he'd refined his technique after Terri Bridges, realizing it was better not to let his victims kick.

Scarpetta saw no sign of a struggle, just an abraded bruise on the left shin. It was very recent, but that was as much as she could say about it.

Berger said, "Do you think she was already dead when he hung her from the chain?"

"No, I don't. I think he bound her, cut her clothes off, placed her in the tub, then slipped the noose around her neck and hoisted her up just far enough for the weight of her body to tighten the slipknot and compress her trachea," Scarpetta said. "She couldn't thrash about so much because of her bindings. And she was frail. At most she's five-foot-three and weighs a hundred and five pounds. This was an easy one for him."

"She wasn't in a chair. So she didn't watch herself."

"This time, I don't think so. That's a good question for Benton as to why. If we're talking about the same killer."

Scarpetta was still taking photographs. It was important she capture what she was seeing before she did anything else.

Berger asked, "Do you have a doubt?"

"What I feel or think doesn't matter," Scarpetta said. "I'm staying away from that. I'll tell you what her body's telling me, which is there are profound similarities between this case and Terri's."

The shutter clicked and the flash went off.

Berger had moved to one side of the doorway, her hands clasped behind her back as she looked in and said, "Marino's in the living room with Lucy. She thinks the victim might have something to do with *Gotham Gotcha*."

Scarpetta said without turning around, "Crashing the site wasn't a good way to deal with it. I hope you'll impress that upon her. She doesn't always listen to me."

"She said something about a morgue photograph of Marilyn Monroe."

"That wasn't the way to handle it," Scarpetta said to the flash of the camera. "I wish she hadn't."

The body slowly turned, the rope winding and unwinding. Eva Peebles's blue eyes were dull and open wide in her thin, wrinkled face. Strands of her snowy hair were caught in the noose. The only jewelry she had on was a thin gold chain around her left ankle—just like Terri Bridges.

"She admitted to it?" Scarpetta asked. "Or is it the process of elimination?"

"She's admitted nothing to me. I'd prefer it stay that way."

"All these things you'd rather she not tell you," Scarpetta said.

"I have plenty to say to her without doing so in a way that might be disadvantageous," Berger said. "But I get your point completely."

Scarpetta studied the black-and-white tile floor before stepping her paper-booted feet inside. She set one thermometer on the edge of the sink, and tucked the other under Eva Peebles's left arm.

"From what I gather," Berger said, "whatever virus brought down the website also enabled her to hack into it. Which then allowed her to hack into Eva Peebles's e-mail—don't ask me to explain it. Lucy's found an electronic folder containing virtually every *Gotham Gotcha* column ever written, including the one posted this morning and a second one posted later in the day. And she's found the Marilyn Monroe photograph, which Eva Peebles apparently opened. In other words, it seems this woman"—she meant the dead one—"didn't write them. They were e-mailed to her from IP addresses that Lucy says have been anonymized, but since this is yet another violent death that is possibly related to e-mails, we won't have any trouble getting the service provider to tell us who the account belongs to."

Scarpetta handed her a notepad and pen and said, "You want to scribe? Ambient temp is fifty-eight degrees.

Body temp is eighty-nine-point-two. Doesn't tell us a whole lot, since she's thin, unclothed, the room's been steadily cooling. Rigor's not apparent yet. Not surprising, either. Cooling delays its onset, and we know she called nine-one-one at what time, exactly?"

"Eight-forty-nine, exactly." Berger made notes. "What we don't know is exactly when she was in the pet shop. Only that it was approximately an hour before she called the police."

"I'd like to hear the tape," Scarpetta said.

She placed her hands on the body's hips to stop its slow, agitated turns. She examined it more closely, exploring it with the flashlight, noting a shiny residue in the vaginal area.

Berger said, "We know she said she believed the man she encountered was Jake Loudin. So if he's the last person to see her alive . . . ?"

"Question is whether he literally was the last person. Do we know if there might be any personal connection between Jake Loudin and Terri Bridges?"

"Just a possible connection that might be nothing more than a coincidence."

And Berger began telling her about Marino's earlier interview, about a puppy that Terri didn't want, a Boston terrier named Ivy. She continued to explain that it was unclear who had given the sick puppy to Terri, perhaps Oscar had. Perhaps someone else. Perhaps it originally had come from one of Jake Loudin's shops, hard to know, maybe impossible to know.

"I don't need to tell you that he's very upset," Berger

said, and she meant Marino. "Always the biggest thing any cop fears. You talk to a witness, and then the person is murdered. He's going to worry he could have done something to prevent it."

Scarpetta continued to hold the body still as she got a closer look at the gelatinous material clumped in gray pubic hair and in the folds of the labia. She didn't want to close the window—not before the police processed it with whatever forensic methods they deemed best.

"Some sort of lubricant," she said. "Can you ask Lucy if her plane has already left La Guardia?"

They were three rooms away from each other, and Berger called her.

"Bad luck is good luck in this case. Tell them to hold off," Berger said to Lucy. "We've got something else that needs to go down there . . . Great. Thanks."

She ended the call and said to Scarpetta, "A wind shear warning in effect. They're still on the ground."

29

The shoe impressions recovered from the toilet seat in Eva Peebles's bathroom were an exact match to the tread pattern of the shoes that Oscar Bane had been wearing last night when he'd allegedly discovered Terri's body.

More incriminating were fingerprints lifted from the glass light fixture that the killer had removed from the ceiling and placed in the tub. The prints were Oscar's. At shortly past midnight, a warrant was issued for his arrest, and an all points bulletin went out over the air and over the Internet.

The "Midget Murderer" was now being called the "Midget Monster," and police nationwide were looking for him. Morales had also alerted Interpol, in the event Oscar somehow managed to evade airport and border security and escaped the country. There had been plenty of reported sightings. In fact, the latest news break as of the three a.m. broadcast was that some little people, especially young men, were staying home for fear of harassment or worse.

It was now almost five o'clock Wednesday morning, and Scarpetta, Benton, Morales, Lucy, Marino, and a Baltimore investigator who insisted on being called her surname, Bacardi, were in Berger's penthouse apartment living room, and had been, for about four hours. The coffee table was covered with photographs and case files, and cluttered with coffee cups and bags from a nearby all-night deli. Power supply cords ran from wall outlets to the laptops they were plugged into, everybody tapping keys and looking at files as they talked.

Lucy was sitting cross-legged in a corner of the wrap-around couch, her MacBook in her lap, and every now and then she glanced up at Morales, wondering how she could be right about what she was thinking. Berger had a bottle of Knappogue Castle single-malt Irish whiskey and a bottle of Brora single-malt Scotch. They were clearly visible behind glass in the bar directly across from her. She'd noticed the bottles immediately when everyone had first gotten here, and when Morales had noticed her noticing, he'd walked over to look.

"A girl with my taste," he'd said.

The way he'd said it had given Lucy a sick feeling she couldn't shake, and she'd had a hard time concentrating on anything since. Berger had been sitting next to her in the loft when they'd read the alleged interview in which

Scarpetta supposedly told Terri Bridges that she drank liquor that cost far more than Terri's schoolbooks. Why hadn't Berger said anything? How could she have the same extremely rare and expensive whiskeys in her own bar and not mention that detail to Lucy?

It was Berger who drank the stuff. Not Scarpetta. And more unsettling than that was Lucy's fear about who Berger might drink it with. That was what had entered her mind when Morales had noticed her noticing the bottles in the bar. He was almost smirking, and whenever he looked at her now, there was a glint in his eyes as if he'd won a contest Lucy knew nothing about.

Bacardi and Scarpetta were arguing, and had been at it for a while.

"No, no, no, Oscar couldn't have done my two." Bacardi was shaking her head. "I hope I'm not offending anybody when I say dwarf, but I can't get used to saying little people or little person. Because I've always called myself a little person because I'm not the longest drink of water, like we say down south. I'm an old dog. No new tricks, can barely hang on to the ones I got."

She might be relatively short, but she wasn't little. Lucy had seen countless Bacardis in her life, almost all of them on Harleys, women on the downhill side of five feet who insisted on having the biggest touring bike, about eight hundred pounds of metal, their boots barely touching the pavement. In one of her earlier manifestations with the Baltimore PD, Bacardi had been a motorcycle cop, and she had a face that went with it, one that had enjoyed too much intimacy with the sun and wind. She squinted a lot, and did a fair amount of scowling, too.

She had short dyed red hair and bright blue eyes, was sturdy but not fat, and probably thought she'd gotten dressed up when she'd decided on her brown leather pants, cowboy boots, and snug scoop-neck sweater that exposed the tiny butterfly tattooed on her left breast and plenty of cleavage whenever she'd bend over to dig into her briefcase on the floor. She was sexy in her own way. She was funny. She had an Alabama accent as thick as fudge. She wasn't afraid of anything or anyone, and Marino hadn't stopped looking at her since she'd walked through the door carrying three boxes of files from the homicides that had been committed five years ago in Baltimore and Greenwich.

"I'm not attempting to make the point that a little person could or couldn't have done anything," Scarpetta replied.

Unlike most people, she was always polite enough to stop typing, to unglue her eyes from her computer screen when she talked to someone.

"But he couldn't have," Bacardi said. "And I don't mean to keep interrupting like Old Faithful going off, but I just had to get this out and make sure all of you are hearing me. Okay?"

She looked around the room.

"Okay," she answered herself. "My lady, Bethany, was almost six feet tall. Now, unless she was lying down, there's no way someone four feet tall could have garroted her."

"I'm simply pointing out she was garroted. Basing that on the photographs you've shown me and the autopsy findings I've reviewed," Scarpetta patiently said. "The angle of the marks on her neck, and the fact there are more than one of them, et cetera. I'm not saying who did or didn't do it—"

"But that's what I'm saying. I'm saying who did or didn't. Bethany didn't kick or struggle, or if she did, by some miracle she didn't scrape or bruise herself. I'm telling you, someone normal size was behind her, and both of them were standing up. I think he raped her from behind while he was doing it, because that's what got him off. And same thing with Rodrick. The kid was standing up, and this guy was behind him. The advantage the perp had in my cases is he was big enough to control them. He intimidated them into letting him bind their hands behind their backs. It doesn't appear they struggled with him at all."

"I'm trying to remember how tall Rodrick was," Benton said, and his hair was very messy, his face covered with stubble that reminded Lucy of salt.

Two all-nighters, back-to-back, and he looked like it.

"Five-foot-ten," Bacardi said. "One hundred and thirty-six pounds. Skinny and not strong. And not much of a fighter."

"We can say all of the victims have one thing in common," Benton then said. "I should say all of the victims we know about. They were vulnerable. They were impaired or at a disadvantage."

"Unless the killer's Oscar," Berger reminded everybody.

"Then the odds change. I don't care if you're a skinny kid on oxys. You're not at a disadvantage, necessarily, if your assailant is only four feet tall. And I hate to keep saying it, but unless there's another logical explanation for how his fingerprints turned up at Eva Peebles's crime scene? And prints made by a size-five women's shoe, a Brooks Ariel? And Oscar just happens to wear that exact same shoe, and he buys it in a size-five women's?"

"Can't overlook the fact he's disappeared, either," Marino said. "He's got to know we're looking for him, and he's choosing to be a fugitive. He could turn himself in. It would be in his best self-interest. He'd be safer."

"You're talking about someone profoundly paranoid," Benton said. "There is nothing on earth that would convince him it's safe to turn himself in."

"That's not necessarily true," Berger said, looking at Scarpetta.

She was going through autopsy photographs and didn't notice Berger's thoughtful stare.

"I don't think so," Benton said, as if he knew what was on Berger's mind. "He wouldn't do it, not even for her."

Lucy decided that Berger must be hatching a plan for Scarpetta to make an appeal to Oscar.

Morales said, "Don't know how we'd get the message to him, anyway. Unless she calls his home phone. Maybe he can't resist, is checking his messages."

"Never happen," Benton said. "Be Oscar for a minute, get inside his mind. Who's going to call him that he wants to hear from? The only person who mattered to him, the only person he seemed to trust, is dead. And I'm not sure how much he trusts Kay anymore. No matter. I don't believe he's checking his voicemail remotely. He already thinks he's being monitored, spied on, which is the main reason he's hiding, in my opinion. The last thing he's going to do is take the chance he might end up on the enemy's radar again."

"What about e-mail?" Morales asked. "Maybe if she sent him an e-mail? Sent it from Scarpetta six-twelve. I mean, he believes that really is you."

He looked at Scarpetta, who was looking up at everyone now, listening to them strategize about what she might do that could convince Oscar to turn himself in to the police. Lucy could tell by the look on her face that she wasn't interested in playing bait and switch with Oscar Bane. Except now she could. Confidentiality didn't matter anymore. Oscar was a fugitive from justice. There were warrants out for his arrest and, barring some miracle, when he was apprehended, he would go to trial and he would be convicted. Lucy didn't want to think about what might happen to him in prison.

Lucy said, "I think he would assume we've been in his e-mail. He's not going to log on to his account. Not unless he's stupid or desperate or losing control. I agree with Benton. You want my suggestion? Try television. Unless he believes people can find him when he turns on a TV in a Holiday Inn, that's probably the only thing he's monitoring. He's watching the news."

"You could make an appeal to him on CNN," Berger said.

"I think that's genius," Morales agreed. "Go on CNN

and tell Oscar to please turn himself in. That it's the best plan for his useless life, under the circumstances."

"He can call his local FBI field office," Benton suggested. "Then he doesn't have to worry about falling into the hands of some rural sheriff's department that doesn't know what the hell is going on. Depending on where he is."

"He calls the FBI, they'll take the credit for his arrest," Morales said.

"Who gives a flying fuck who takes the credit," Marino said. "I agree with Benton."

"So do I," Bacardi said. "He should call the FBI."

"I appreciate everybody deciding on that for me," Berger said. "But actually, I tend to agree with you. It's much riskier if he ends up in the wrong hands. And if by some chance he's no longer in the U.S., he can still call the FBI. As long as he ends up back here, I don't care who gets him."

Her eyes found Morales.

She added, "Credit isn't an issue."

He stared back at her. He looked at Lucy and winked. The mother-fucking prick.

Scarpetta said, "I'm not going on CNN and asking him to turn himself in. That's not who I am. It's not what I do. I don't take sides."

"You're not serious," Morales said. "You telling me you don't go after the bad guys? Dr. CNN always gets the bad guy. Come on. You don't want to ruin your reputation over a dwarf."

"What she's telling you is she's the advocate of the victim," Benton said.

"Legally, that's correct," Berger said. "She doesn't work for me or the defense."

"If everybody's finished speaking on my behalf and has no further questions, I'd like to go home," Scarpetta said, getting up and getting angrier.

Lucy tried to remember the last time she'd seen her aunt as angry as she was right now, especially before an audience. It wasn't like her.

"What time do you expect Dr. Lester to start Eva Peebles's case? I mean really start it. I'm not asking what time she said she'd start it. I don't intend to show up down there and sit around for hours. And unfortunately, I can't start the case without her. It's unfortunate she's doing it at all."

Scarpetta looked directly at Morales, who had called Dr. Lester from the scene.

"I don't have control over that," Berger said. "I can call the chief medical examiner, but that's not a good idea. I think you understand. They already think I'm a meddler down there."

"That's because you are," Morales said. "Jaime the Meddler. Everybody calls you that."

Berger ignored him and got up from her chair. She looked at her very expensive watch.

She said to Morales, "Seven o'clock is what she said, is that right?"

"That's what Pester Lester said."

"Since you seem to be so chummy with her, maybe you could check and make sure she really is going to start the case at seven, so Kay doesn't take a taxi down there after being up all night, and then sit."

"You know what?" Morales said to Scarpetta. "I'll go pick her up. How 'bout that? And I'll call you when we're en route. I'll even swing by and get you."

"That's the best idea you've had in a while," Berger said to him.

Scarpetta said to both of them, "Thanks, but I'll get myself there. But yes, please call me."

When Berger returned from seeing Scarpetta and Benton to the door, Marino wanted more coffee. Lucy followed Berger into her spacious kitchen of stainless steel, wormy chestnut, and granite, deciding she had to say something now. How Berger responded would determine if there was a later.

"You heading out?" Berger's tone turned familiar as she met Lucy's eyes and opened a bag of coffee.

"The whiskeys in your bar," Lucy said, rinsing the coffeepot and refilling it.

"What whiskeys?"

"You know what whiskeys," Lucy said.

Berger took the pot from her and filled the coffeemaker.

"I don't," she said. "Are you telling me you want an eye opener? I wouldn't have thought you're the type."

"There's nothing funny about this, Jaime."

Berger flipped up the on switch and leaned against the counter. She really didn't seem to know what Lucy was talking about, and Lucy didn't believe her.

Lucy mentioned the Irish whiskey and the Scotch that were in her bar.

"They're on the top shelf behind glass, in your own damn bar," Lucy said. "You can't miss them."

"Greg," Berger said. "He collects. And I did miss them."

"He collects? I didn't know he was still around," Lucy said, feeling worse, maybe the worst she'd ever felt.

"What I mean is those are his," Berger said with her usual calm. "If you start opening cabinets in there, you'll see a fortune in small-batch this and single-malt that. I did miss them. They never entered my mind, because I don't drink his precious whiskeys. Never did."

"Really?" Lucy said. "Then why does Morales seem to know you have them?"

"This is ridiculous, and it's neither the time nor the place," Berger said very quietly. "Please don't."

"He looked right at them as if he knew something. Has he ever been here before this morning?" Lucy said. "Maybe the Tavern on the Green gossip is more than that."

"I not only don't have to answer that, I won't. And I can't." Berger said it without an edge, almost gently. "Maybe you could be so kind as to ask who wants coffee and what they might want in it?"

Lucy walked out of the kitchen and didn't ask anyone anything. She unplugged her power supply. She calmly looped the cord around her hand and tucked it into a pocket of her nylon case. Then the MacBook went inside.

"Got to head back to my office," she said to everyone as Berger returned.

Berger asked about coffee, as if everything was fine.

"We haven't listened to the nine-one-one tape," Bacardi suddenly remembered. "I want to hear it, anyway. Don't know about everyone else."

"I should hear it," Marino said.

"I don't need to hear it," Lucy said. "Someone can e-mail the audio file to me if they want me to hear it. I'll be in touch if I have any new information. I'll see myself out," she said to Jaime Berger without looking at her.

30

"Poor doormen," Scarpetta said. "I think I spooked them more than usual."

When they arrived at their luxury apartment building, one glimpse of her crime scene case and the doormen always stayed clear. But this early morning, the reaction was stronger than usual because of the news. A serial killer was terrorizing New York's East Side, and may have killed before, years earlier, in Maryland and Connecticut, and Benton and Scarpetta looked pretty scary themselves.

They stepped onto the elevator and rode up to the thirty-second floor. The minute they were inside the door, they started undressing.

"I wish you wouldn't go down there," Benton said.

He yanked off his tie as he took off his jacket, his coat already draped over a chair.

"You've gotten swabs, you know what killed her. Why?" he said.

Scarpetta replied, "Maybe just once today people will treat me as if I have a mind of my own or even half the one I used to have."

She dropped her suit jacket and blouse into the bio-hazard hamper near the door, a practice so normal for them, it only rarely occurred to her what an odd sight they would be if anybody was watching, perhaps with a telescope. Then she thought of the new helicopter the NYPD had gotten, something Lucy had mentioned. It had a camera that could recognize faces up to two miles away, or something like that.

Scarpetta unzipped her pants and tugged them off, and she grabbed a remote from the Stickley mission oak coffee table in a living room full of Stickleys and Poteet Victory oils on canvas. She closed the electronic blinds. She felt rather much like Oscar, hiding from everyone.

"I'm not sure you agreed with me," she said to Benton, both of them in their underwear and holding their shoes. "And by the way, this is us. Are you happy? This is what you married. Someone who has to change when she comes through the door because of the antiso-cial places she visits."

He took her in his arms and buried his nose in her hair.

"You're not as bad as you think," he said.

"I'm not sure how you mean that."

"No, I did agree with you. Or yes, I did. If it weren't—" He held out his left arm behind her head, still holding her close, and looked at his watch. "Quarter past six. Shit. You might have to leave in a minute. That part I don't agree with you about. No. Babysitting Dr. Lester. I'm going to pray for a big storm that prevents you from going anywhere. See your favorite painting in here? *Mister Victory's Balancing Elements*? I'm going to pray to the Great Spirit that the elements will be balanced, and you'll stay home and take a shower with me. We can wash our shoes together in the shower like we used to do after crime scenes. And then you know what we did after that."

"What's gotten into you?"

"Nothing."

"So you agree about my not going on television," she said. "And please do pray. I don't want to babysit her. Everything you said is true. I know what happened to Eva Peebles. She and I discussed it in her bathroom. I don't need to discuss it with Dr. Lester, who doesn't listen and isn't as open-minded as Eva Peebles was. I'm tired and stressed out and sound like it. I'm angry. I'm sorry."

"Not at me," he said.

"Not at you," she said.

He stroked her face, her hair, and looked deep into her eyes, the way he did when he was trying to find something he'd lost, or perhaps thought he'd lost.

"It's not about protocols or whose side you're on," he said. "It's about Oscar. It's about everybody who's been brutalized. When you're not sure who's doing what or how or why, it's better to stay behind the scenes. This is a good time to stay away from Dr. Lester. To carry on quietly. Jesus," he suddenly said.

He returned to the hamper and fished out his pants. He reached into a pocket and pulled out the thumb drive still wrapped in the pair of purple gloves.

"This," he said. "This is important. Maybe the Great Spirit just heard my prayer."

Scarpetta's cell phone rang. It was Dr. Kiselstein at Y-12.

She said to him before he could say anything, "Lucy said it got there safely. I apologize a thousand times. I hope you weren't waiting. I'm not sure where."

Dr. Kiselstein's German-accented voice in her earpiece: "Since I usually don't receive samples from private jets, I treated myself and listened to music on the iPod my wife gave me for Christmas. So small, I could wear it as a tie clip. It was no problem. I know McGhee-Tyson, the Air National Guard base, except, as I said, usually not the jet of a millionaire. Usually a C-one-thirty or some other cargo plane bringing us something from Langley that NASA won't admit to. Like faulty heat shields. Or prototypes, which I like much better because nothing bad has happened. Of course, when they are strange deliveries from you, it's always bad. But I do have some results, as this is timely, I realize. No official report of the analysis. That will be a while."

Benton gave up hovering. He touched her cheek and headed to the shower.

"What we have, basically, is an ointment that is mixed with blood, possibly sweat, and silver salts, and along with this are fibers of wood and cotton," Dr. Kiselstein said.

Scarpetta moved toward the sofa. She got a pen and notepad from an end-table drawer and sat down.

"Specifically, silver nitrate and potassium nitrate. And carbon and oxygen, as you would expect. I'm e-mailing images to you, taken at different magnifications up to one thousand-X. Even at fifty-X you can see the blood, and the silver-rich regions are quite bright due to their higher atomic number. You can also see silver nitrate in the wood—small, whitish silver-rich specks evenly dispersed over the surface."

"Interesting it's evenly dispersed," she said. "Same with the cotton fibers?"

"Yes. Visible at higher magnifications."

To her an even dispersement implied something that might have been manufactured as opposed to a random transference due to contamination. If what she suspected was correct, however, they were likely dealing with both.

She asked, "What about skin cells?"

"Yes, definitely. We are still at the lab, and this will be going on for a day or two. No rest for the wicked. And this is very difficult because you sent many samples. What I'm calling you about is just two of them. One from each case. The chair and a swab. You might think the cotton and wood fibers are from the swabs you used on the body, and yes, maybe no. I can't tell you. But not so with the chair, because you didn't swab the chair seat?"

"No. That wasn't touched."

"Then we can conclude the cotton and wood fibers in the material on the chair cushion are there for another reason, perhaps transferred by the ointment, which presents a challenge as it's nonconductive. That requires us to use variable pressure, which maintains the high vacuum in the gun needed to create the electron beam as the rest of the chamber is backfilled with dry filtered air. And we have reduced the scattering of the electron beam by minimizing the working distance. I suppose I am making excuses. The ointment is difficult to image because the electron beam actually melts it, I'm afraid. It will be better when it dries."

"Silver nitrate applicators for cauterizing skin, possibly? That's what comes to my mind right away," she said. "Which might explain the presence of blood, sweat, skin cells. And a mixture of different DNA profiles if we're talking about a communal jar of a healing ointment. If we're talking about a source being, perhaps, a medical office? For example, a dermatologist?"

"I won't ask about your suspects," Dr. Kiselstein said.

"Anything else interesting about the chair?"

"The frame is iron with trace elements of gold in the paint. There was no one sitting in it when we placed it in the chamber. Suspects and punishment aren't my department." They hung up.

Scarpetta tried Dr. Elizabeth Stuart's numbers and got voicemail. She didn't leave a message and stayed on the sofa, thinking.

She believed she was dealing with Marino just fine until she decided to call him and realized she didn't have his cell phone number. So she called Berger, and the way the prosecutor answered, it was as if she knew who it was and that the call was personal.

"It's Kay."

"Oh," Berger's voice. "It said restricted. I wasn't sure."

When Lucy called, it came up as restricted. Scarpetta had a feeling something was going on with them that wasn't good. Lucy had been very subdued during the meeting. Scarpetta hadn't tried to call her, was assuming she was still with Berger. Maybe not.

Berger said, "Morales called a few minutes ago, said he's getting your voicemail."

"I've been on my phone, with Y-Twelve. I'm not going to be able to head to the morgue right this minute."

She gave Berger a quick summary.

"Then that's a common denominator," Berger decided. "The dermatologist. Terri went to her. And you said Oscar does. Or did."

Scarpetta had revealed that detail during the meeting just a little while ago, because she no longer was bound by patient-physician confidentiality. It wasn't right not to divulge the information, but she'd felt uncomfortable doing it. Just because the situation had changed legally didn't mean it felt that way to her. When Oscar had talked to her and wept so bitterly, he really hadn't anticipated the day when she'd betray him, no matter how many times she'd warned him and encouraged him to get a good lawyer.

She was so conflicted. She resented him, was incensed by him, because she felt she should be someone he could trust. And she resented him, was incensed by him, because she didn't want his goddamn trust.

"I need to tell Marino what Y-Twelve has discovered," Scarpetta said to Berger. "I don't know how to reach him."

Berger gave her two numbers and said, "Have you heard anything from Lucy?"

"I thought she might be with you," Scarpetta said.

"Everybody left about a half-hour ago. She left right after you and Benton did, minutes after you did. I thought she might have caught up with you. She and Morales weren't getting along."

"He's not somebody she would like."

After a pause, Berger said, "That's because she doesn't understand a number of things."

Scarpetta didn't respond.

"We get older and there really aren't absolutes," Berger said. "There never were."

Scarpetta wasn't going to help her.

"You're not going to talk about it, and that's fine." Berger's voice, still calm, but something else was in it.

Scarpetta shut her eyes and pushed her fingers through her hair, realizing how helpless she felt. She couldn't change what was happening, and it was foolish and wrong to try.

"Maybe you could save me a little time," Scarpetta said. "Perhaps you could call Lucy and let her know about the Y-Twelve results. You do it instead of me, and I'll try to find Marino. And while you have her on the phone, perhaps you might try a different tactic. Be very, very hon- est with her, even if you think she'll get incredibly upset or might use it against you. Just give her the facts even if you think it might ruin your case, cause you to lose something. That's hard for people like us, and that's all I'm going to say. I'm wondering if Bacardi—God help me, I can't get used to calling any real person that—would know if either Bethany or Rodrick was seeing a dermatologist in Baltimore or Greenwich in 2003. I noticed in the police report that he was taking Accutane for acne."

"Implying a dermatologist," Berger said.

"I would hope so. That's not an insignificant medication."

"I'll pass all this on to Lucy. Thank you."

"I know you will," Scarpetta said. "I know you'll tell her whatever she needs to hear."

Benton was out of the shower and wrapped in a thick robe, stretched out on the bed. He was scrolling through something on his laptop, and Scarpetta moved it out of the way and sat next to him. She noticed the red thumb drive plugged into a port.

"I'm not clean yet," she said. "I probably smell like death. Would you still respect me if I told a lie?"

"Depends on who it's to."

"To another doctor."

"Well, then, that's fine. For future reference, lawyers are preferable if you're going to lie to someone."

"I went to law school and don't appreciate lawyer jokes," she said, smiling.

She combed her fingers through his hair. It was still damp.

She added, "I'll tell my lie in front of you, and it won't seem as much a sin. I can't wait to get in the shower and brush my teeth. And these . . ."

Realizing she still had her dirty shoes in one hand while she touched his hair with the other.

"I thought you were going to wait and take a shower with me," she said. "And we'd wash our shoes."

"I planned to take a second one," he said. "I haven't washed my shoes yet."

Scarpetta got up from the bed and used the landline.

This time she didn't call Dr. Stuart's presidential suite directly or her cell phone, she tried the St. Regis front desk. She said she was from CNN and trying to reach Dr. Stuart, who she realized stayed there under the name of Dr. Oxford.

"Hold on, please."

And then Dr. Stuart was on the line.

Scarpetta told her who she was, and Dr. Stuart said brusquely, "I don't discuss my patients."

"And I generally don't discuss other doctors on television," Scarpetta said. "But I might make an exception."

"What is that supposed to mean?"

"It means what it means, Dr. Stuart. At least one of your patients has been murdered in the past twenty-four hours, and another one is being accused of that murder and another murder, and more charges could follow, and he's vanished. As for Eva Peebles, who also was murdered last night? I don't know if she's one of your patients. But what I do know is that forensic evidence indicates you'd be wise to be helpful. For example? I'm wondering if a certain woman from Palm Beach who has a home in New York might also be your patient."

Scarpetta gave her the name of the paraplegic whose DNA was found in Terri Bridges's vagina.

"You absolutely know I can't release information about my patients."

Dr. Stuart said it in a way that confirmed the woman was her patient.

"I absolutely know how it works," Scarpetta said, and to be sure, she added, "Just tell me no if she's not your patient."

"I'm not going to say no to anything."

Scarpetta went through the same routine with Bethany and Rodrick, without telling Dr. Stuart why she wanted to know. If the dermatologist had been acquainted with them, she wouldn't need Scarpetta to tell her the two had been murdered five years ago. She would know that.

"As you might imagine, I have plenty of patients from the Greenwich area, because I have an office in White Plains," Dr. Stuart said as Scarpetta leaned against Benton and looked at what he was scrolling through.

It looked like sections of maps someone had been e-mailing to Oscar—allegedly.

"I'm not saying whether those two people have ever been seen by anyone in my practice," Dr. Stuart said. "I will tell you that I remember the young man's death. Everyone was shocked. Just as we are by what's just happened in New York. I saw it on the news last night. But the reason I remember Greenwich is because the Aston Martin dealership—"

"Bugatti," Scarpetta said.

"I use the Aston Martin dealership. It's very close to Bugatti," Dr. Stuart said. "That's why the boy's murder hit home. I've probably driven within a block of the spot where he was found or killed. When I've taken my Aston Martin in for service. That's the reason I remember, if you understand what I'm saying. Actually, I don't have that car anymore."

She was hinting that neither Rodrick nor Bethany had been her patient and that she would have been aware of a sadistic sexual homicide because it had reminded her of a car that cost more than some people's homes.

"Do you have anybody working for you or somehow connected with your practice who the police should be aware of?" Scarpetta asked. "Or let me ask it in a way easier to answer. What might you be thinking if you were me?"

"I'd be thinking about the staff," she said. "In particular, part-timers."

"Which part-timers?"

"Part-time techs, residents, particularly those who do menial things in the offices and come and go. For example, work at one of my offices during their summer breaks or after hours. It could be anything from cleaning up to answering the phones and paging the physician on call. I have one who's also a vet tech. But has never been a problem. It's just he's more of an unknown, and I don't work with him personally. He's rather much a cleaner-upper and assists other doctors. I have a huge practice. More than sixty employees at four different locations."

"Vet tech?" Scarpetta said.

"I believe that's what he does for his full-time job. I know he has something to do with pet stores, because he's gotten a few of my staff puppies. A vet tech who helps with the pets in these places. Probably not in a way I want to know about, truth be told," Dr. Stuart said. "He's an odd duck, tried to give me a puppy once, on my birthday last summer. One of those Chinese crested dogs that has no fur except on its head, tail, and feet. This was maybe an eight-week-old puppy that looked deformed, as if it had alopecia, and all it did was shiver and cough. He wrote in a card that I could tell everyone I was doing hair removal on dogs now, that I was adding pet dermatology to my practice, or something like that. It was peculiar and I wasn't amused and made him take the puppy back. Frankly, it was an extremely upsetting experience."

"Did you ever ask him what happened to the puppy?"

"I have a good idea."

She said it ominously.

"He likes to give injections, put it like that," Dr. Stuart said. "He's very good with needles, has some phlebotomy training. Look, this is making me very upset. His name is Juan Amate."

"That's his full name? Often Hispanic names include the mother's maiden name, not just the surname."

"That I don't know. He's worked out of my Upper East Side office for the last several years. Maybe three or four years, not sure. I don't know him personally, and he's not allowed in the room when I'm with a patient."

"Why?"

"Frankly? Most of the patients I see personally are VIPs, and I don't allow part-time techs to assist me. I have my regular assistants, who are accustomed to dealing appropriately with very well-known people. You don't have a part-time tech drawing blood from an A-list movie star."

"Did you personally see Terri Bridges or Oscar Bane, or would that have been one of your other doctors?"

"I wouldn't have reason to know them personally. But I do have a few other little people who are patients, since obesity is one of the most common problems, and an unfortunate side effect of dieting can be skin problems. Acne, premature lines and creases on the face and neck, and if one doesn't have the proper fat intake, the skin doesn't hold moisture as well, so now we add dry flakiness to the list."

She didn't see Terri or Oscar personally. They weren't important enough.

"Is there anything else you can tell me about Juan Amate?" Scarpetta said. "I'm not saying he's done anything wrong. But I don't want anyone else hurt or dead, Dr. Stuart. Do you know where he lives, anything like that?"

"Have no idea. I doubt he has much money. Olive complexion, dark hair. Hispanic. Speaks Spanish, which is helpful. Speaks English fluently, which is a requirement in my practice."

"Is he a U.S. citizen?"

"He should be. But that's not for me to check on. I suppose the answer is I don't know."

"Anything else you can tell me? For example, do you have any idea where the police might find him right now, to ask questions?"

"No idea whatsoever. I know nothing else. I just didn't like it when he gave me that Chinese puppy," she said. "I felt there was something mean about the gesture. As if he were jerking me around somehow—of all people? To give *me* an extremely ugly dog with hair and skin problems? I just remember it being very upsetting, and then I looked bad to my staff because I made him take the pathetic little thing out of there immediately, and he said he didn't know what he'd do with it, as if I was sentencing the pitiful creature to . . . Well, it's as if he wanted to make me look heartless, and I think I actually started almost thinking about firing him after that. Obviously, I should have."

Benton had placed his hand on Scarpetta's bare thigh, and when she ended the call, he put his arm around her and directed her attention to what he had been looking at while she was on the phone.

He scrolled through maps, scores of them.

"Track logs," Benton said. "These thick colored lines, the dark pink ones?" He traced one that ran from Amsterdam to an Upper East Side location on Third Avenue. "An actual track mapped by a GPS."

"Simulated or real?" Scarpetta asked.

"I think these are real tracks. It appears they're recordings of routes Oscar took, hundreds of them. Some kind of recording process was on while he was going to various locations. As you can see."

He scrolled through about a dozen maps.

"Most of them either begin or terminate at the address of his apartment building on Amsterdam. Based on what I'm seeing, these track logs began this past October tenth and ended December third."

"December third," Scarpetta said. "The same day the morgue photograph of me appears to have been simultaneously deleted in Scarpetta six-twelve's and also Terri's e-mail."

"And the same day Oscar called Berger's office and ended up on the phone with Marino," Benton said.

"What the hell is going on here?" Scarpetta said. "Was he walking around with some kind of bracelet or something that has a GPS chip, and maybe using a PDA that has a GPS, and downloading all of his movements and perhaps e-mailing it to himself? To make it appear he's being followed, spied on, all those things he's said?"

"You saw his apartment, Kay. Oscar believes this stuff. But if someone else has been sending these track logs to him, can you imagine?"

"No."

Benton scrolled through more of them. Locations for grocery stores, several gyms, office-supply stores, or as Benton put it, just locations where he might have walked but didn't actually go inside the restaurant, bar, or other business.

"And as you can see," Benton said, rubbing her back, "as time goes on, his destinations become more erratic and variable. He's changing his locations daily. None of the tracks are the same. You can actually see his fear, the way he's zigzagging, literally all over the map. Or his simulated fear. If, once again, he's staged all this. But his fear seems real. His paranoia isn't faked, I really don't think so."

"You can imagine how this will look to a jury," Scarpetta said, getting up. "It will look like the mad cyber professor manufactured this elaborate plan to make it appear he's the target of some clandestine organization or hate group or God knows what. It will look as if he followed himself, so to speak, with a GPS, and planted all sorts of bizarre devices all over his apartment, and carried them on his person and in his car."

She finished undressing, because she had to get into the shower. There was so much to do. And Benton's eyes were intense on her as he got off the bed.

"No one on earth will believe him," she said as Benton put his hands on her and kissed her.

"I'll help you take your shower," he said, guiding her in that direction.

31

The wind buffeted Lucy as she sat on concrete as cold as ice on the brownstone's roof and took photographs of the camera attached to the footing of the satellite dish.

It was an inexpensive Internet camera that included audio, and was connected to the building's wireless network and served any tenant who wished to join it.

It also served somebody else. It served Mike Morales, and not in the way everybody thought, which was why it hadn't occurred to Lucy to check. And she was furious with herself.

Since it was known that another device was connected to the network—the camera that Morales said he had installed himself—it hadn't entered Lucy's mind to access the log to the wireless router. It hadn't occurred to her she ought to check the router's admin page.

Had she done that last night, she would have discovered what she now knew, and she tried Marino again. For the past half-hour, she'd tried him and Berger, and had gotten voicemail.

She didn't leave a message. She wasn't about to leave a message the likes of the one she had.

This time Marino answered, thank God.

"It's me," she said.

"You in a wind tunnel, or what?" he said.

"The camera you saw Morales install up here on this roof, where I'm right now sitting? He wasn't installing it when you surprised him up here. He was probably removing it."

"What are you talking about? I saw him . . . Well. Yeah, you're right. I didn't actually see him do anything. I just got off the phone with your aunt, let me tell you real quick, because she's trying to get hold of you. Something about our person of interest being tracked by a GPS or something? And he might work as a vet tech at Dr. Stuart's office? Long and short of it, Terri might have known the killer through the dermatologist's office, some Hispanic guy . . ."

"Listen to me, Marino! This fucking camera's been up here for fucking three weeks! And it's motion-sensitive, so every time it records something it's e-mailing it to someone who's about to get hacked into. I've got Morales's damn IP. I've got his fucking machine access code, and it's the same fucking one as Scarpetta six-twelve. Do you understand what that means?"

"I'm not fucking retarded."

Just like the old days. How many times had he said that to her over the years?

"It means whoever set up this camera and is getting images e-mailed from it is the same person sending e-mails to Terri, pretending to be my aunt. Probably some type of PDA, and the asshole stands out in front of John Jay, hijacks their wireless network, so that's what the IP comes back to. The machine access code is also the same one for the device used to e-mail the photograph to Terri—the photograph e-mailed from the Internet café near Dr. Elizabeth Stuart's office. Morales is the one who instructed Terri to delete that photograph on December third. . . ."

"Why?"

"He plays fucking games, that's why. He was probably in the morgue when the damn photo was taken, probably is behind it. Just like the photo of Jaime at Tavern on the Green. He probably orchestrated that and sent it to *Gotham Gotcha*."

"Then he's probably connected to *Gotham Gotcha*."

"Got no idea, but I do know Eva Peebles worked for whoever *Gotham Gotcha* is. And I doubt she could tell you who *Gotham Gotcha* is, if she were still alive to tell us anything, poor lady. Nothing in her computer identifies who it is. I'm setting up sniff packets even as we speak, looking at info at junction points. Fuckhead Morales. He's probably your fucking Hispanic vet tech, too. Fucking piece of shit. I'm about to pay him a home visit."

She was typing on her MacBook as she talked, doing a port scan. Marino had gotten deadly quiet.

"You still there?"

"Yeah, I'm here."

"You want to tell me why the fuck a cop would put up a surveillance camera three weeks before a murder?" she said.

"Jesus Christ. Why would he be sending shit pretending to be her?"

Lucy heard a woman's voice in the background. Bacardi.

"Why don't you ask him," Lucy said. "He's probably the one who gave Terri the brilliant idea to post something on the John Jay site about her needing to get in contact with my aunt. And Terri does, and then, miracle of miracles, guess who writes her? He obviously knew Terri or he wouldn't have been e-mailing her. He's probably the fucking vet tech, like I said, and she knew him because of the dermatologist."

"He probably gave her the sick puppy. Thought it was funny." Marino's voice, muttering. "Then Eva Peebles gets it. The puppy dies. She dies. What'd she do to deserve any of this? Wonder if he's the one who fixed things in Terri's apartment. What the landlord was talking about. That would be like him to be a pal, a confidant, to someone who could use a big strong pissant like him. Be like him to get someone like Terri, a forensic psych grad student, to post something on a website, to fuck with everyone. But why the Doc?"

"Because he's a failed doctor, and my aunt isn't. I don't know why. Why does anybody do anything?"

"You're not going to remove the camera, right? We don't want him knowing it's down."

"Of course not," Lucy said as the wind ripped at her, as if trying to rip her off the roof. "He'd probably come up here to remove the damn thing, and last thing he expected was you climbing up the fire-escape ladder. Now he has to cover his ass. So he puts on the big act that he's installing a surveillance camera in case the perp returns to the scene of the crime. Well, bullshit. I've got the log open right here on my laptop. This camera's e-mailed over ten thousand images in the past three weeks and is still grinding away even as we speak. According to the tab status, the asshole's accessing the network right now. You'll be happy to know I've disabled the audio function. Not that you'd hear a damn thing up here but wind."

"You absolutely sure about this?" Marino said.

"And I'm in. This is completely illegal," Lucy said.

"Oh, God," she said, shocked, as she scrolled through video files.

Video files in Mike Morales's personal e-mail account. His username was Forenxxx.

She landed on a video file that had been recorded by an entirely different device than the rooftop camera. She opened it and clicked play.

"Oh, Christ," she said. "A recording made New Year's Eve. Only this one isn't from the roof, it's from inside Terri's apartment. Oh, shit. Oh, shit."

Berger's penthouse was two levels, the master area on the upper one, where she and Lucy watched the murder of

Terri Bridges on a huge plasma flat screen in a sitting area off the bedroom.

It was almost more than either one of them could stomach, and there was virtually nothing either of them hadn't seen. They sat rigidly on a sofa, watching Terri's face in her vanity mirror as a pair of latex-gloved hands garroted her from behind with a rubbery blue tourniquet, the type used in doctor's offices when blood is being drawn. Victim and assailant were nude, her hands bound behind her back as she kicked savagely from the chair with the heart-shaped back, while he almost lifted her off it as he strangled her into unconsciousness.

Then he would release the pressure and, when she was revived, start again.

She said nothing the entire time, just made the expected awful guttural gagging sounds as her eyes bulged and her tongue protruded from her mouth and spittle ran down her chin. It took exactly twenty-four and a half minutes for her to finally die, because that's how long it took for him to ejaculate and finish her off, because he had no further interest.

He flushed the condom down the toilet, and he turned off the camera.

"Let's start it again," Berger said. "I want to listen a little more carefully to what's said when he takes her into the bathroom. I'm getting the impression they'd had sex before. And the other things said suggest maybe why he did this. The premeditation factor. He may have had motive that went beyond his sexually sadistic compulsions. Did she call him Juan? Or was that just a sound she made?"

"I suspect she'd been having sex with him long before she had it with Oscar," Lucy said. "Based on the familiarity, the comments he's making. She would have known him from Dr. Stuart's office—for a couple of years. I don't care if we don't yet know for a fact that he's Juan Amate. I'm telling you they're the same person. They have to be. I think she might have said Juan. I agree, hard to tell."

She pressed the play button on the remote. The film began mid-sentence with a shot of the vanity and Terri's terrified face in the oval mirror. Behind her was a man's naked body. He moved, adjusting himself and the camera angle, exposing his erect condom-sheathed penis, poking it between her shoulder blades as if it were the barrel of a gun. He was visible only from the waist down.

"Just our usual, baby, with a little extra hot sauce thrown in," the killer's voice said.

"I don't know," she said, her voice quavering as his gloved hand held up a scalpel in the mirror and twirled it, and its steel blade caught the light.

The sound of fabric slitting as he cut open her robe, her lacy red bra. It was a shelf bra, and her breasts protruded from it, her nipples exposed. He slit off her matching red lacy panties. He turned the camera on the pink robe and pink slippers and the bra as he dropped them into the tub. His gloved hands waved the cut lacy red panties in front of the camera lens.

"Capturing the flag." His Hispanic voice. "In my pocket so I can enjoy later, right, little girl?"

"Let's don't," she said. "I don't think I can."

"Should have thought about that when you told the little man all our secrets."

"I didn't tell him. You sent the e-mails. That's how."

"Now, that was a really big mess you made. How's that going to work? He complained to the fucking DA. How's that going to work, baby? I trusted you. I did you a favor. And you told him."

"I never told him. He told me. You were sending him the e-mails, and finally he told me. He got freaked out. Why? Why are you doing this?" And it sounded as if she said Juan.

"You gonna ask me why anything?" The scalpel stroking the air, almost touching her cheek, then withdrawing and vanishing.

"No."

"So, who's your man? The little one. Or me?"

"You are," her terrified face said to the mirror, his gloved hands pinching her nipples.

"Now you know that's not right, or you wouldn't have told him." The killer's voice chiding her.

"I promise I didn't. He found out because of the e-mails, those maps you sent him. He told me. You scared him."

"Now, baby." Pinching her nipples harder. "I don't want to hear no more of your lies. And now I gotta figure out how to get that fucking thing out of his ass before somebody else does."

Lucy hit pause, and the recording froze on a blurry image of Terri's wide-eyed face talking while his hands squeezed her breasts in the mirror.

"Right there," Lucy said. "The way he says it. Possible

he's hinting he's going to murder Oscar? He's going to be the one to retrieve the thing out of his ass?"

"I'm wondering the same thing," Berger said.

She triple-underlined a key phrase in notes on her legal pad: *Terri's idea—GPS?*

She said to Lucy, "I don't think there's any doubt about how this started—that Terri asked Morales to follow Oscar, because she was a jealous, controlling person. It wasn't her nature to trust anyone, and before she'd even considered making any sort of a commitment to him or perhaps telling her family about him, she wanted proof he was honorable."

"If one can make psychopathology logical."

"We have to. Jurors expect reasons for things. You can't just say someone's evil or felt like it."

"She may have said something about wanting to know what Oscar was up to, but I doubt an implanted GPS was her idea," Lucy said. "I don't think she ever imagined Morales would do her the favor, and then take it a little further by anonymously e-mailing GPS track logs to Oscar to drive him crazy, to torment the living hell out of him. The e-mailing of the tracking logs stopped when Oscar finally said something about it to Terri, and she obviously must have flown all over Morales about it."

"Right. That's what Morales is referring to." Berger indicated the frozen image on the TV screen. "She did the wrong thing and complained to Morales, berated him, perhaps. A guy like this? You insult his narcissism? And then he's the typical psychopath and blames it on her because she's the one who wanted Oscar spied on.

Suddenly, it's her fault that Oscar called my office and reported everything."

"To Marino, on December third," Lucy said. "And at that point, Oscar destroyed his computer's hard drive and hid the thumb drive in his library, where my aunt and Benton found it. And Morales stopped e-mailing the logs to him, because Terri knew, and the gig was up."

"Kay mentioned the thread on the carpet outside Oscar's apartment door. The roof access and fire escape. I'm wondering if Morales went in there trying to find this log, and while he was at it, planted a jar of Aqualine. I'm wondering if he came in through the window, set off the alarm, then left through the roof access so the doorman didn't see him. He had a key and the alarm code, the password. After killing Terri, he got some unexpected surprises. Oscar demanded to go to Bellevue. He demanded to see Benton and Kay. Now the stakes have been raised considerably. Morales has some worthy adversaries to deal with. Including you. He wants that damn tracking log so it's not traced back to him by someone like you. And he wanted Oscar to take the fall for at least four homicides."

"A classic case of someone who's decompensating," Lucy said. "Morales didn't need to kill Eva Peebles, not really. For that matter, he didn't need to kill Terri. He used to be smart and stick with strangers. What I still can't figure out is why would Oscar let anybody do that?"

"You mean the implant."

"We just listened to him say it. He stuck something

in Oscar's ass and has to get it back. What else could that mean? I'm thinking there's only one thing. But you don't just walk up to someone and say, hey, can I implant a GPS microchip under your skin?"

Berger placed her hand on Lucy's bare knee and leaned against her to pick up the cordless phone. She called Scarpetta for the second time in the past hour.

"Us again," Berger said. "Maybe you and Benton should just come over here."

"I can. He can't," Scarpetta said.

Berger put her on speakerphone and set the handset upright on the coffee table inside her handsome sitting area of leather and glass, and Agam polymorphic paintings and serigraphs that seemed to change and shimmer as Berger moved.

Greg's room.

Where he used to plant himself in front of the TV while Berger was alone in bed, in the adjoining room, sleeping or working. It took her a while to figure out that one of the reasons he started keeping such strange hours, as if he were on UK time, was because he was on UK time. He'd sit in this room, and at some point after midnight New York time, he'd call his friend the barrister, who would just be waking up in London.

"Benton's with Marino and Bacardi," Scarpetta said. "They went out. He was rather cryptic about it. I've not heard anything from Dr. Lester. Still. I'm assuming you haven't."

Morales had dropped off Dr. Lester at the ME's office earlier, because he didn't know then what Lucy was about to find out. Now he was aware people were looking for him, because Berger had contacted him. All she'd had to say was, "I think you need to explain some things."

She'd gotten as far as mentioning silver nitrate and Dr. Stuart, when he hung up on her.

"I suppose someone will tell me if I need to go down there," Scarpetta said. "Although I seriously doubt it's an issue, she really should x-ray Eva Peebles carefully. I'm repeating myself, because you don't want her body leaving the morgue until every inch of it has been x-rayed. Same thing with Terri's body. X-rayed again, every inch of it."

"That's what I'm getting around to," Berger said. "This idea of the microchip implant. When you talked to Oscar, did you get any idea that might lead you to believe he'd ever, for any reason, allow something like that? Lucy and I are watching this God-awful video again, and that's what the killer is implying. Morales, I mean. We know it's him."

"Oscar would never allow that," Scarpetta said. "What's far more likely is he complained about painful treatments, specifically, laser hair removal. And he has had hair removed from his back, possibly from his buttocks. He has no hair at all except on his face, his head. And he has pubic hair. He mentioned Demerol to me. If someone came in with scrubs and a mask on, and Oscar was on his belly, he would never have seen the tech or necessarily recognize him later. At Terri's apartment, for example, when Morales encountered Oscar at the crime scene? Oscar wouldn't necessarily connect him with some backroom tech at Dr. Stuart's office."

"In the video, we think Terri calls him Juan. We're not sure. You need to listen," Berger said.

Scarpetta said, "They're doing R-and-D with wireless GPS glass-encapsulated chips that have miniature antennas and a power supply that can last up to three months. About the size of a grain of rice, maybe smaller. One of them could have been implanted into his buttocks and he'd never know, especially if it's migrated, buried itself in deeper, which happens. We could find it with an X-ray, if we can find him. And by the way, he's not the only one paranoid about this sort of thing. The U.S. government has a number of pilot programs, and a lot of people fear that mandatory chipping is on the horizon."

"Not me," Berger said. "I'll move."

"You'll have plenty of company. That's why some call it Mark of the Beast Six-Six-Six technology."

"But you didn't see anything like that in Terri's X-rays?"

"I've been looking," Scarpetta said. "I have the electronic files of that and everything else, and I've been doing nothing but work on all of this since we last spoke. The answer's no. It's very important that Dr. Lester get more films, and I want to see them. Especially focusing on the back, the buttocks, the arms. People who have been implanted with microchips usually get them in their arms. Morales would know a lot about microchip technology for the simple reason it's used to tag animals. He would have seen microchips implanted in pets at the vet's office. He may have done the implanting himself, a simple procedure that requires nothing more than the chip and an implant gun fitted with a fifteen-gauge needle. I can be there in maybe half an hour."

"That would be fine."

Berger reached across Lucy again and ended the call. She returned the handset to its charger. She scribbled more notes and underlined words and phrases. She looked at Lucy for a long moment, and Lucy looked back, and Berger wanted to kiss her again, to resume what had begun when Lucy first appeared at her door and Berger had pulled her by the hand straight up here. Lucy didn't even have time to take off her coat. Berger didn't know how she could think about something like that right now, with that hideous image frozen on the big flat screen. Or maybe that was why she was thinking about it. Berger didn't want to be alone.

"That's what makes the most sense," Lucy finally said. "Morales implanting the GPS chip in Oscar while he's in the dermatologist's office. Probably thought he was getting a shot of Demerol in his butt. Terri probably had said something to Morales about Oscar, about not knowing if she could trust him, probably when she and Oscar first started dating. And Morales did his thing and acted like her best friend, her confidant."

"Big question. Who did Terri think Morales was? Juan Amate or Mike Morales?"

"I'm betting Juan Amate. Way too risky if she knew he was an NYPD cop. I think she did call him Juan. I do think that's what I heard."

"I think you're right."

"If she was screwing around with him, does that compute?" Lucy said. "Morales wouldn't care if she was seeing someone else?"

"No. As I just said, he acts like your best friend. Women confide in him. Even I have, to an extent."

"To what extent?"

They had never returned to the subject of the whiskeys in her bar.

"I shouldn't have to say it," Berger said. "But Morales and I didn't have that, and I don't think you believed we did or you wouldn't be sitting here. You wouldn't have come back. The Tavern on the Green rumors. That's all they are—rumors. And yes, no doubt he started them. He and Greg liked each other."

"No way."

"No, no. Not that way," Berger said. "One thing Greg doesn't have any ambivalence about is what he likes to fuck, and it definitely isn't men."

32

Scarpetta refilled coffees and carried them out on a tray with a few things to eat. She believed that sleep deprivation was healed by good food.

She set down a platter of fresh buffalo mozzarella, sliced plum tomatoes, and basil dribbled with cold-pressed unfiltered olive oil. In a sweetgrass basket lined with a linen napkin was crusty homemade Italian bread that she urged everyone to pass around, to break it with their hands, to tear off pieces. She told Marino he could start, and he took the basket, and she placed small plates and blue-checked napkins in front of him, then one in front of Bacardi.

Scarpetta set her own place on the coffee table next to Benton's, and she sat next to him on the couch, leaning forward, because she could stay only a minute.

"Just remember," Benton said to her, "when she hears about it, and you know she will, you don't talk about what I'm about to do. Either before or after I've done it."

"Damn right," Marino cut in. "Her damn phone will start ringing off the hook. I gotta tell you I don't feel so hot about this. I wish I could think about it some more."

"Well, we can't," Benton said. "We don't have the luxury of time to think about much of anything. Oscar's out there somewhere, and if Morales hasn't gotten to him already, he will. All he has to do is track him down like a hunted animal."

"Like he's been doing," Bacardi said. "Now a guy like that makes you believe in the death penalty."

"Much better if we get a chance to study them," Benton said matter-of-factly. "Killing them serves no useful purpose."

He was impeccably dressed in one of his hand-tailored suits that he never wore on the ward, a deep blue with a lighter blue pinstripe, a light blue shirt, and silvery blue silk tie. The makeup artist at CNN wouldn't need more than fifteen minutes with him. There was little Benton needed to improve his appearance, maybe a little powder and a breath of spray on his platinum hair, which needed a trim. To Scarpetta, he looked the same way he always had, and she hoped he was doing the right thing. That both of them were.

"I won't say anything to Jaime. I'll stay out of it," she said, and she realized she had started calling her Jaime about the same time Jaime had started spending so much time with Lucy.

All these years, and she usually referred to her as Berger, which was rather distant and perhaps not particularly respectful.

Scarpetta said to Benton, "I'll tell her she can take that up with you. It's not my network and, contrary to popular opinion, I don't run your life."

Marino's cell phone rang. He lifted his PDA and squinted at the display.

"IRS. Must be about all my charitable trusts," he said, pressing his flashing blue earpiece to answer. "Marino . . . Yup . . . Just hanging out. You? . . . Hold on. I'm going to start writing."

Everyone got quiet so he could talk. He set down the PDA on the coffee table and placed his notepad on his wide knee. He started scribbling. Upside down or right side up, Marino's writing looked about the same. Scarpetta had never been able to read it, at least not without tremendous annoyance, because he had his own version of shorthand. No matter the cracks he made, in truth, his writing was far worse than hers.

"I don't mean to be a smart-ass about it," Marino said. "But first off, when you said Isle of Man, where the hell is that? I assume it's one of these Caribbean tax havens or maybe one of those islands near Fiji. . . . Now, that's something. Never heard of it, and I've been there before. I mean to England. . . . I realize it isn't exactly in England. I know Isle of Man's a fucking island, but in case you flunked geography, England's a fucking island."

Scarpetta leaned close to Benton's ear and wished him good luck. She felt like telling him she loved him, which was unusual with people around. But for some reason she wanted to say it, but she didn't. She got up and hesitated, because Marino seemed about to get off the phone.

"No offense, but we knew that. We got that address," Marino said.

He looked at Bacardi and shook his head as if the IRS agent he was talking to was dumber than a bag of hammers—one of Marino's favorite expressions.

He said, "That's right . . . Nope, you must mean One-A. So it's Terri Bridges. I know it's an LLC and you don't got a name yet, but that's her apartment . . . No. Not Two-D. She's in One-A." He frowned. "You sure, I mean damn sure? . . . Wait a minute. That guy's a Brit, right? Well, he's Italian but lives in the UK, is a UK citizen . . . Okay. So it fits with the Isle of Man shit, I guess. But you'd better be right, because in maybe half an hour, that fucking door's getting kicked in."

Marino touched his earpiece and disconnected the IRS without a thanks or a good-bye.

He said, "*Gotham Gotcha*? We don't have the name of whoever it is, but we know where the person has an apartment. Upstairs from Terri Bridges. Two-D. Unless something's changed and nobody told us, still nobody home in that building. Tenant's an Italian financial guy named Cesare Ingicco, domicile is Isle of Man, where

his company is actually located, and Isle of Man's not the
Caribbean, just so you know. The LLC renting his apartment is this offshore one that Lucy dug up info about.
Guarantee the guy doesn't actually live there, that it's
someone else working out of that apartment or maybe
no one working out of it. So sounds like we need a warrant
and should go in there. Or maybe we go in and then
get a warrant. Whatever. We don't waste time, since Eva
Peebles indirectly worked for this Cesare Ingicco guy
across the street but probably not the one who actually
lives across the street, probably on his island and we're
going to find—you watch—that he dealt with Eva over
the phone, long distance. Eva didn't know shit, whatever
the case. How fucked up is that?"

"Why don't I hook up with some of your guys over
there," Bacardi said. "I think you should hang around
this area. When Benton goes live on the air, all hell
might break loose."

"I agree," Benton said. "Morales is going to know,
if he had any doubt at all, that we think he might be
after Oscar, and the rest of the world is after him, after
Morales."

"You think there's any chance at all Oscar and
Morales are partners in all this?" Bacardi asked. "Maybe
I'm crazy, but how do we know they don't work as a
team, sort of like Henry Lee Lucas and Ottis Toole. And
to this day there are plenty of people who think the Son
of Sam didn't act alone, either. You just never know."

"Extremely unlikely," Benton said as Scarpetta put on
her coat by the door. "Morales is far too narcissistic to

work with anyone. He can't work with anyone else no matter what he's doing."

"You got that right," Marino said.

"But what about Oscar's shoe prints and fingerprints we found in Eva Peebles's apartment?" Bacardi made a good point. "I don't know if we should just ignore them and assume they were doctored or there's a mistake."

"Guess who collected the shoe prints and finger-prints?" Marino said. "Fucking Morales. Plus, he has a pair of Oscar's sneakers, from when he took his clothes the other night."

"Anybody witness him lifting the prints off the light fixture?" Bacardi went on. "It's not easy to cheat. I mean, it's one thing if it's a pair of sneakers you took from the suspect. But it's another to take his fingers and leave prints, so to speak. My point is you got to have a pretty clever conspiracy to process prints at a crime scene and have them get a hit in the computer system. In IAFIS."

"Yeah, well, Morales is a clever guy," Marino said.

Bacardi got up and said, "I'm going to go on over to Murray Hill. Who's meeting me?"

"Sit back down." Marino tugged softly on the back of her belt. "You ain't taking a damn cab. You're a homicide detective. I'll drop you off and head right back here. I got a battering ram in the trunk you can have. I pinched it last night when they brought me one at the Peebles scene, special order. Oops. I forgot to give it back."

"I'm going," Scarpetta said. "Everybody be careful, please. Mike Morales is an evil man."

———

"Actually?" Berger said to Lucy. "And I've never told anybody this before."

"You don't have to tell me anything," Lucy said.

"I think Morales may have broken in the barrister for Greg, and in typical fashion, Morales goes from being the philanderer to the confidant you can tell your troubles to. The more I think about it, he's very bizarre that way, among other ways. To say the least."

"You think Greg knew?"

"No, I sure don't. Should I get us more coffee?"

"How do you know Morales was screwing around with the barrister?"

"It's not hard to tell these things when you're in an office with other people. I don't pay much attention, or maybe it appears I don't, but it registers. In retrospect, it becomes clear. Morales has probably done this sort of thing countless times, practically under my nose, or I've heard stories. He seduces someone into cheating on the boyfriend, the husband, and next thing, Morales has a bedside manner if not caretaking relationship with his victim. Helps her patch things up. Or he gets to know the man he fucked over, who doesn't know he's been fucked over, because Morales loves being pals with someone who has no idea he's the devil. Sadistic games and more sadistic games. He and Greg used to sit downstairs and drink his expensive liquor and talk. Probably about me, at least some of the time. Not in a good way."

"How long ago?"

"Morales got transferred into investigations about a year ago. It was right about that time. Toward the end. Not long before Greg moved to London. I'm sure Morales encouraged it. Might even have been his idea— for Greg to just end it with me."

"Maybe so Morales could start something with you?"

"Finish me and start me. He'd get off on that," Berger said.

"Then Greg is how Morales would have gotten the idea for the Irish whiskey and Scotch he wrote about in that phony interview he sent to Terri, when he was pretending to be my aunt," Lucy said. "And Greg shouldn't have let himself be talked into anything. Fuck that. He made his choice. And Morales won't be finishing or starting anything, except he's going to finish himself. You watch."

"If you check the bottles downstairs," Berger said, "my guess, he and Greg put a hefty dent in both of them. Morales would want the most expensive thing in the bar. That's him, all right. And it was a nasty dig to imply Kay routinely drinks whiskey that costs five, six, seven hundred dollars a bottle and say it was more than Terri's schoolbooks. He was painting quite the portrait of her, and if she'd finished her thesis, her so-called book? That would have been extremely unfortunate. I'm sure it's occurred to you he might be *Gotham Gotcha*. Seems that sort of thing would be right up his alley."

"The IP of whoever writes those columns is ano-nymized, and the Internet service provider has an account that traces to an LLC with an address in the

Isle of Man," Lucy said. "Which has one of the strongest offshore trust jurisdictions in the world. The machine access code doesn't match anything I've seen so far, so those columns aren't written on any laptop or any other device we're familiar with, nor is it one used to send any e-mails we've been looking at. Problem is, jurisdictions like the Isle of Man, Nevis, Belize offer such stringent privacy protection, it's very difficult to penetrate the shield and find out who's behind an LLC. I've got a contact at the IRS pulling some strings for me. Interesting it's the UK. I would have expected the Caymans. As in about seventy-five percent of all hedge funds registered. But I don't think Morales is *Gotham Gotcha*."

"The implication, of course, is whoever it is, this person has a lot of money parked offshore," Berger said.

"Of course she would," Lucy said. "Her endorsements alone, her product promotions. She's probably getting staggering kickbacks wired into accounts that are sheltered. My hope is she's a little too clever about bypassing certain tax laws, and that's what will lead us to a physical address. I mean, she rents, she owns, she's paying bills, or someone is on her behalf, and she's likely got a place in this city and was paying an employee in this city, and we know that for a fact. Someone was wiring Eva Peebles money from the UK on behalf of *Gotham Gotcha*. This agent who used to be ATF and now is IRS, I gave him Marino's name, too, and he's tying down more info from Eva Peebles's bank. I want to know who *Gotham Gotcha* is and where the hell she is. And if she's screwing the IRS? Oh, well. Have fun in prison."

"She? Her?"

"After that first column came out, I ran language analysis on maybe fifty archived ones. No, I really don't think it's Morales who writes those columns and has a site like that. Would require too much maintenance, too much work. He's a hit-and-run guy, just like everybody says. He's got a careless streak in him, and that's going to be what nails him in the end."

"You ran this analysis on the website about the same time you crashed it?" Berger said.

"I didn't crash it. Marilyn Monroe crashed it."

"A subject for another day. For the record, I don't approve of infecting sites with worms," Berger said.

"Same words and phrases constantly pop up, and allusions, metaphors, similes." Lucy was talking about the language analysis she ran.

"How can a computer possibly recognize a simile?" Berger asked.

"An example. Search for the words *like* and *as*, then the computer searches for those followed by adjectives, nouns. *Like the long hard leg of a chair—as if he had three of them.* And here are a few more good ones from *Gotham Gotcha*'s purple prose. *Gently curved like a firm banana inside Calvin Kleins that seemed melted on him.* Then let me see if I remember. *Her tiny tits as flat as cookies, her nipples as small as raisins.*

Berger said, "And your computer recognizes a metaphor how, exactly?"

"Discrete bodies of information with nouns and verbs that are inconsistent with each other. *My skull hibernated in the wet nest of my hair. Skull* and *hibernate* in the same sentence would be flagged as an inconsistency. As would *nest* and *hair,* if you look at them literally. But what you have metaphorically is a line from the Nobel Prize–winning poet Seamus Heaney. I'm sure you knew that wasn't purple prose."

"So your neural networking software reads poetry when it's not busy tracking assholes on the Internet."

"What it's telling me is the author of *Gotham Gotcha* is likely female," Lucy said. "One who's snide, petty, resentful, and angry. A woman competitive with other women. A woman who so intensely loathes other women, she'll mock one who was sexually assaulted. She'll humiliate and degrade the victim all over again. Or try."

Berger picked up the remote and pressed play.

Terri's panicky face in the mirror talking as latex-gloved hands kneaded her breasts. Her eyes were watering. She was in pain.

Her voice shook badly as she said, "No. I can't. I'm sorry. Don't be angry with me. I don't want us to do this."

Her lips and tongue made sticky sounds, her mouth was so dry.

The killer's voice. "Sure you do, baby. You love being tied up and fucked, don't you? So this time we're going for the jackpot, you know?"

Gloved hands set a jar of Aqualine on the counter, screwing off the lid, and his fingers dug into it. He smeared it into her vagina while she stood with her back to him, and he took his time, his condom-sheathed erect penis pushing hard into her upper back. He sexually assaulted her with the lubricant and his fingers. He raped her with fear. Unless he'd penetrated her with his penis off camera, that wasn't what he did. It wasn't what he wanted.

The chair scraped across tile as he made her sit.

"Look how pretty you are in the mirror," he said. "Sitting all pretty. Almost the same height as when you're standing. Who else can I say that about, right, little girl?"

"Don't," she said. "Please don't. Oscar's going to be here any minute. Please stop. My hands are numb. Please take it off. Please."

She was crying but trying to act as if this was just that—an act. She was trying to act as if he really wasn't doing anything harmful. It was a sex game, and based on references and demeanor, it seemed a certainty they'd had sex before, and domination might have been part of the drama. But nothing like this. Nothing even close. A part of her knew she was about to die, and die horribly, but she was doing her best to will it not to be so.

"He gets here at five, poor little punctual Oscar. It's your fault, you know," Morales's voice said to her face in the mirror. "From now on, baby, it's what you created. . . ."

Berger turned it off again. She wrote down a few more of her thoughts.

It all added up. But they couldn't prove one damn

bit of it. They had not yet seen Mike Morales's face, not once. Not in this video recording or the one he'd made when he'd murdered Bethany in his crappy Baltimore apartment the summer he'd finished medical school at Johns Hopkins in 2003, and not in the recording he made months later when he murdered Rodrick and dumped his graceful young boy's body near the Bugatti dealership in Greenwich, where Rodrick probably found his way onto Morales's radar because of the vet's office where Morales had worked part-time. It was probably where he'd met Bethany, only a different vet's office, that one in Baltimore.

In both those cases he'd done the same thing he'd done to Terri. He bound the victims' wrists. He was wearing surgical gloves when he penetrated them digitally, using the same type of lubricant. Back then, five years ago, he was about to start the NYPD police academy, and his part-time work was with veterinarians, not dermatologists. But veterinarians use cauterizing applicators and lubricants like Aqualine. Morales's pilfering a partially used jar of lubricant from his workplace was part of his MO, perhaps going back to his first murder.

Berger had no idea how many people he'd killed, but she wondered if the reason he used the lubricant was to confound police with a mixture of different DNA profiles.

"He would think that was funny," she said to Lucy. "He must have been thrilled when one of the profiles actually got a hit in CODIS and turned out to be the paraplegic from Palm Beach. What a big ha-ha that must have been."

"He won't get away with it," Lucy said.

"I don't know."

The police not only hadn't found Morales yet, but at the moment there was no warrant for his arrest. The overwhelming problem, which would continue to be a problem, was proof. The scientific evidence did not prove Morales had killed anyone, and recovering his DNA at Terri's crime scene and even from her body meant nothing, since he was inside the apartment and had actually touched her when he'd checked her vitals. He was the lead investigator in her case and had touched everything and everyone connected to it.

And his face wasn't on the video recordings. And he wasn't on video coming into or leaving Terri's apartment building because he probably had used the roof access night before last, pulling the ladder up after him. Then returning it to its closet later. Prior to that, when he'd been with her, probably it was somewhere else. Not Terri's apartment. That was too risky. Someone might have remembered seeing him in the area. Morales was too smart to take a chance like that.

It was possible, Berger considered, he used the roof then, too. She wouldn't rule it out, and she might never know.

Morales was smart as hell. He'd finished Dartmouth, Johns Hopkins. He was a sadistic sexual psychopath, perhaps the most outrageous and dangerous one Berger had ever come across. She thought of the times she'd been alone with him. In his car. In Tavern on the Green. And in the Ramble, when she'd paid a retrospective visit to that crime scene where the marathon runner had been raped and manually strangled, and now Berger had to wonder about her. Did Morales kill that woman, too?

She suspected it. Couldn't prove it. A jury wasn't likely to trust any identification based on the sound of his voice, which, like O.J. and the bloody glove, could be altered on demand so he didn't sound exactly like the murderer in the recordings. That man spoke with a heavy Spanish accent. Morales, when speaking normally, had no discernible accent. A case wasn't going to be won solely based on forensic voice analysis, either. Didn't matter how sophisticated the software.

It wasn't likely anyone—certainly not a prosecutor as seasoned as Berger—was going to suggest anything as ridiculous as making a comparison of Morales's penis with the penis in the video recordings, a normal penis, uncircumcised, nothing unusual about it, nothing remarkable one way or another, and wearing a condom over it was reminiscent of someone having a stocking over his face. Were there any identifying features, so much as a freckle, they were masked.

The most the cops could do—or Lucy could do—was prove these violent, seemingly damning videos were in his e-mail account, but where did he get them? Having them didn't prove he'd killed anyone or even done the filming with a camcorder he must have set up on a tripod. Lucy was the first to say that getting jurors to

understand IP addresses, machine access codes, ano-
nymizers, cookies, packet sniffing, and about a hundred
other terms that were part of her easygoing vernacular
was like a throwback to the early days, the late eight-
ies and early nineties, when people like Berger were first
trying to explain DNA to judges and jurors.

Eyes glazed over. Nobody trusted it. She'd spent an
inordinate amount of time and energy on satisfying the
Frye standard whenever she tried to admit DNA evidence
into court. In fact, DNA hadn't helped her marriage,
not that much could have. But with the proliferation of
new scientific techniques had come new pressures and
demands, the likes of which no one had ever anticipated
or seen. Maybe if forensic science had stayed where it
was when she was still at Columbia, living with a woman
who eventually broke her heart and scared her straight
into Greg's arms, she would have had something left
over for her private life. Gone on more vacations, or even
gone on one when she didn't bring a briefcase. Gotten
to know Greg's children, really gotten to know them.
Gotten to know people she worked with, like Scarpetta,
who'd never received so much as a card from Berger after
Rose died, and Berger had known about that.

Marino had told her.

Maybe Berger would have gotten to know herself.

"Kay will be here in a second. I've got to get dressed,"
she said to Lucy. "Actually, maybe you should get
dressed."

Lucy was in a Jockey undershirt and briefs. Both of
them had been watching what were called snuff films in

some markets, and neither of them had on much in the way of clothing. It was still early, not even ten a.m., but seemed more like late afternoon. Berger felt as if she had jet lag. She was still in the silk pajamas and robe she'd put on after getting out of the shower minutes before Lucy had shown up at her building.

In the space of less than five hours since Scarpetta, Benton, Marino, Bacardi, and Morales had been in her living room, Berger had learned the grotesque truth and had watched it as if it was happening before her eyes. She'd witnessed the tortured deaths of three people who had fallen prey to a man who was supposed to protect them: a doctor who never was, who shouldn't have become a cop, who shouldn't have ever been allowed within a mile of any living creature.

So far, only Jake Loudin had been located. He wasn't about to admit he might know Mike Morales, might actually use him to euthanize pets that didn't sell or God knows what he used him for. Maybe Morales went by the name of Juan Amate when he entered the basements of pet shops and added yet one more layer of misery to the world, for a fee. Maybe Berger would get lucky and find a way to coax Loudin into admitting, in exchange for a reduced sentence, that he'd called Morales last night after Eva Peebles was in the wrong place at the wrong time, a pet store basement. Berger really didn't think that Loudin had asked Morales to murder anyone. But Eva Peebles's existence was becoming an inconvenience that gave Morales the excuse to have a little more fun.

The intercom buzzed as she finished getting dressed,

and Lucy was sitting on the bed, because they had been talking nonstop.

Berger picked up the house phone as she buttoned her Oxford cloth shirt.

"Jaime? It's Kay," Scarpetta's voice said. "I'm at your door."

Berger pressed the zero on the keypad and remotely unlocked it, and said, "Come in, I'll be down in a minute."

Lucy said, "All right with you if I take a quick shower?"

33

Marino watched Headline News on his PDA as he walked swiftly along Central Park South, leading with his shoulder, weaving through other pedestrians like a football player with the goal in sight.

Benton, in his blue pinstriped suit, was sitting at a table across from a correspondent, Jim somebody. Marino couldn't remember, because it wasn't one of the more famous ones at this hour in the day. Below Benton's name in bold block letters was:

Dr. Benton Wesley, Forensic Psychologist,
McLean Hospital

"Thanks for joining us. And with us is Dr. Benton Wesley, former chief of the FBI's behavioral science unit at Quantico, and you're now, actually, at Harvard, and here at John Jay?"

"Jim, I want to get straight to the point because this is extremely urgent. We're appealing to Dr. Oscar Bane to please contact the FBI. . . ."

"Let me just back up and tell our viewers this is in reference to cases that you can't miss, no matter where you look—the two absolutely appalling homicides committed in New York over the past couple of nights. What can you tell us about those?"

Just ahead was Columbus Circle and the Time Warner skyscrapers, where Benton was in the studio this very second. This was a bad idea. Marino understood why Benton didn't think there was a choice, and why he didn't want to ask Berger first. He didn't want her held accountable, and Benton didn't answer to her. He didn't answer to anyone. Marino understood, but now that Benton was making his appearance on international TV, something didn't sit well about it.

"What we're asking is if he's listening, to please call the FBI." Benton's voice on live TV, through Marino's earpiece. "We have reasons to be very concerned about Dr. Bane's safety, and he is not—and I repeat—is not to contact local police or deal with any other authorities. He's to call the FBI, and he will be escorted to safety."

One of the things Scarpetta always said is never push somebody until that person has nothing to lose or nowhere to go. Benton always said it, too. So did Marino. Then why were they doing this? First, Berger had called Morales, and Marino had thought that was a terrible idea. She'd basically given him a heads-up, maybe gloating a little as she stuck it to him. The brilliant Morales busted, caught. Berger was one hell of a prosecutor. She was tough, all right. But she shouldn't have done that, and Marino still wasn't sure why she had.

He had a funny feeling it was personal, at least in part. Scarpetta didn't do anything like that, and she'd had her chance. When they were in Berger's living room from midnight on, Scarpetta could have said a lot of things to taunt Morales, whom she didn't like or trust any more than Marino did, even though they didn't yet know his hobby was starring in his own damn snuff films. But Scarpetta had been completely professional, her usual self, with Morales sitting right there. If she'd thought he was a murderer but didn't have a shred of proof, she would have kept her thoughts to herself. That's who she was.

"I have to say, Dr. Wesley, this is probably the most unusual plea I've ever heard. I mean, maybe *plea* isn't the right word, but why . . ."

Marino glanced down at the tiny figures bantering on his PDA. Berger's building was maybe two more blocks away. She wasn't safe. You push someone like Morales too far and rub his face in it, then what? Then he's going to do something. Who's he going to do it to first? The same lady he's been trying to conquer ever since he became an investigator. The same lady he lies about, giving everybody the bullshit impression he has sex with the sex crimes DA. Not true. Not even close.

Morales wasn't her type.

Marino had had a feeling he'd figured out who Berger's type was, some rich guy like Greg. But as he'd watched Berger and Lucy together while everyone was in Berger's living room, then watched Lucy follow her into the kitchen and suddenly leave the apartment, he'd changed his mind and had no doubt whatsoever.

Berger's weakness, her passion, wasn't men. Emotionally, physically, she was hardwired a different way.

"Oscar has every reason in the world not to trust anybody right now," Benton was saying. "We have reason to believe certain fears he's voiced to authorities about his own safety have merit. We're taking them very, very seriously."

"But hold on. There are warrants out for his arrest, for murder. Excuse me, but it sounds like you're protecting the bad guy here."

"Oscar, if you're listening to me"—Benton faced the camera—"you need to call the FBI, whatever field office is local, wherever you might be. You'll be escorted to safety."

"Seems like everybody else ought to be worried about their safety, don't you think, Dr. Wesley? He's the one police suspect killed those—"

"I'm not going to discuss the case with you, Jim. Thank you for your time."

Benton unclipped his mike and got up from the table.

"Well, this has been an unusual moment in the New York crime investigation. Two murders have rocked this New Year, and the legendary—I guess I can use the

word *legendary*—profiler Benton Wesley is appealing to
the man everybody thinks did it . . ."

"Shit," Marino said.

No way Oscar was going to call the FBI, God, or anyone else after hearing that.

Marino logged out and closed his browser as he
walked fast. He was sweating under his old leather Harley jacket, and the cold air was making his eyes water.
The sun was trying to escape heavy, dark clouds. His cell
phone rang.

"Yeah," he answered, dodging people as if they had
leprosy, not looking at any of them.

"I'm going to talk to a couple agents in the field office
here. About what we're doing," Benton said.

"I guess it went okay," Marino said.

Benton hadn't asked for a critique, and he didn't
respond to it.

"I'll make a few calls here at the studio, then head
over to Berger's," Benton said, and he sounded down in
the dumps.

"It went good, I think," Marino said. "Oscar will hear
it. No doubt about it. He's got to be in a motel or something, and that's all he's got is TV. They'll keep playing
the segment all day and night, that's for sure."

Marino looked up at the fifty-two-story glass-and-
metal building, fixing on the penthouse facing the park.
The grand entrance had *TRUMP* in huge gold letters.
But then, so did everything expensive around here.

"If Oscar doesn't ever see it on TV"—Marino seemed

to be talking to himself now, Benton had gotten so quiet—"then I don't want to think about why that might be. Unless he's done surgery on himself, his every move is tracked by GPS—you know whose GPS, right? So you did a good thing. The only thing you could do."

He continued until he realized the call had been lost. Marino had no idea he'd been talking to no one.

The gun barrel jammed against the base of Scarpetta's skull didn't evoke the fear she would have imagined. She really couldn't comprehend it.

There seemed to be no synapse between her actions and consequence, cause and effect, if and then, now and later. All she was vividly aware of was a dismay of biblical proportions that it was her fault Morales was inside Jaime Berger's penthouse, and that at the end of Scarpetta's life she had managed to commit the only sin that was unforgivable. She was to blame for tragedy and pain. Her weakness and naïveté had done unto others what she had always warred against.

Everything was her fault, after all. Her family's poverty and the loss of her father. Her mother's unhappiness, her sister Dorothy's borderline personality and extreme dysfunction, and every harm that had ever befallen Lucy.

"He wasn't there when I rang the bell." She said it again, and Morales laughed at her. "I wouldn't have let him in."

Berger's eyes were unblinking and fastened to Morales as she stood motionless at the foot of her spiral staircase, her cell phone in hand. Above her was a gallery displaying magnificent works of art in her magnificent penthouse, the New York skyline all around them beyond a curved wall of spotless glass. Ahead was the sunken living room with furniture in fine woods and earth-tone upholsteries where all of them had sat not that long ago, allies, friends, together in a campaign against the enemy, who now was revealed and was here again.

Mike Morales.

Scarpetta felt the barrel of the revolver leave her skull. She didn't turn around. She kept her eyes on Berger, hoping she understood that when she'd gotten off the elevator and rung the bell and announced herself, she was alone. Then suddenly, a force out of hell grabbed her arm and escorted her through Berger's door. The only reason she might have been the slightest bit forewarned was a comment one of the concierges had made when Scarpetta had entered the building a few minutes ago.

The lovely young woman in her lovely suit had smiled at her and said, "The others are waiting for you, Dr. Scarpetta."

What others?

Scarpetta should have asked. Dear God, why hadn't she? All Morales had to do was show his badge, but even that hadn't been necessary, most likely. He'd been here hours earlier. He was charming, persuasive, didn't like to be told no.

Morales's eyes looked around, his pupils dilated, and his latex-gloved hands dropped a small gym bag to the floor. He unzipped it. Inside were the retracted legs of a tripod and colorless nylon ties, and other items Scarpetta couldn't discern, but it was the ties that caused her heart to pump harder. She knew what those ties could do, and she was afraid of them.

"Just let Jaime go and do what you want to me," she said.

"Oh, shut up."

As if he found her tedious.

In one snap, he lashed Berger's wrists behind her first, and led her to the couch and pushed her down hard, making her sit.

"Behave," he said to Scarpetta, and he lashed her wrists next, very tightly.

Instantly, her fingers contracted and the pain was terrific, as if something metal was clamped around her wrists, compressing blood vessels and biting into bone. He pushed her down on the couch, next to Berger, as a cell phone started ringing upstairs.

His eyes slowly moved from the cell phone he had removed from Berger's grip to the gallery upstairs and the rooms beyond it.

The cell phone rang, then stopped, and water was running somewhere. And it stopped. And Scarpetta thought about Lucy the same time Morales did.

"You can stop this now, Mike. You don't need to do this . . ." Berger started to say.

Scarpetta was on her feet and Morales shoved her hard, and she fell back onto the couch.

He bounded up the spiral stairs, his feet scarcely seeming to touch them.

Lucy toweled off her very short hair and breathed in a lungful of steam inside one of the nicest showers she'd been in for a while.

Greg's. Glass-enclosed, with rain-forest showerheads, body jets, steam bath, surround-sound music, a heated seat if you wanted to just sit and listen to music. Berger had Annie Lennox in the CD player. Maybe it was a coincidence, since Lucy had played it last night in the loft. Greg and his whiskeys, and his fine things, and his barrister, and Lucy was baffled by a man who truly knew how to live but had chosen someone he could never do it with, all because of a slight genetic murmur.

Sort of like being one digit off in math. By the time you finished the long, complicated equation, you were light years from the answer, and you failed. Berger was the right person but the wrong answer. Lucy felt a little sorry for him but not for herself. For herself she felt a happiness that was indescribable, unlike anything she'd ever known before, and it seemed all she did was relive and relive.

It was like listening to the same intoxicating piece of music again and again, as she'd just done in the rain shower, every touch, every look, every accidental intention that resulted in a grazing of bodies that was so erotic and at the same time so moving because it really meant something. It wasn't cheap. It wasn't guilt-ridden or headed into shame. It felt perfectly right, and she simply didn't believe it could be happening to her.

This was a dream she'd never known enough to have,

because no part of her had ever feared or wanted it any more than she had nightmares about extraterrestrials or fantastic dreams about flying machines and race cars. Those didn't exist or were real and within reach. Jaime Berger wasn't an impossibility or a possibility that had ever crossed Lucy's mind, although certainly during early encounters she'd felt a giddiness, a nervousness, on the rare occasions she'd been around her, as if she were being offered an opportunity to toy with a very large, undomesticated cat, like a cheetah or a tiger, that she would never be in the same room with, much less pet.

Lucy stood up inside the steam-filled shower, unable to see through the clouded glass, contemplating how best to have an open conversation with her aunt, to explain, to just talk.

She pushed open the door at the same time a shape moved in front of it, and steam dissolved around Mike Morales's face. He smiled at her, a pistol pointed inches from her head.

"Die, bitch," he said.

The door yielded to one blow of the battering ram and slammed against the wall.

Bacardi and a uniformed officer whose name she thought was Ben walked into the soft music of Coldplay as they entered apartment 2D and were confronted by Dr. Kay Scarpetta.

"What the hell?" Bacardi said.

Scarpetta was all over the walls. Posters, some of them

from ceiling to floor, not poses but newsy photos of her on the set of CNN or walking through Ground Zero or in the morgue, preoccupied and unaware that someone was taking what Bacardi called a "thinking action shot." Didn't mean the person was doing something powerful, but he or she was doing it mentally.

"It's like a freakin' shrine," said Ben, or whatever his name was.

The apartment at the back of the building, one floor above Terri Bridges's, was unfurnished except for a simple maple desk facing a wall and, tucked under it, a small office chair. On the desk was a laptop, one of those new PowerBooks or AirBooks or whatever they were called, expensive and weighing almost nothing. Bacardi had heard stories about people accidentally throwing them away with a stack of newspapers, and could see how that might happen. The laptop was plugged into a charger, and "Clocks" was playing on iTunes—the volume turned low, playing over and over again, God knows for how long, because someone had selected repeat on the menu.

Also on the desk were four bud vases, cheap cut glass, and in each one a withered rose. She went to the desk and pulled down one of the rose petals.

"Yellow," she said.

Officer Ben, as she now thought of him, was too busy looking around at the shrine to Scarpetta to care about a few dead roses, or to understand that from the female perspective, yellow mattered. Bacardi's need of reassurance wanted red when it came to roses, but her instinct knew better. A man who gave you yellow roses was one you'd never have, and that's the one you wanted and should move heaven and earth to get. She glanced at Officer Ben, for an instant fearing she just might have said that out loud.

"Well, guess what?" she said, her voice bouncing off old plaster walls as she walked on bare hardwood floors, going from room to room. "I don't know what we're supposed to do, because it looks like the only thing in here's a computer and toilet paper."

When she walked back in, Officer Ben was still looking around at photographs of Scarpetta that were as big as Times Square in proportion to their location. He shone his flashlight on them as if that might tell him something.

"While you gawk," Bacardi said, "I'm going to call Pete—Investigator Marino to you—and find out just what the hell we're supposed to do with *Gotham Gotcha*. You got any idea how to arrest a website, Ben?"

"Ban," he corrected her. "For Bannerman," he said.

His light trailed over the huge posters like a comet on its last legs.

"If I were Dr. Scarpetta," he said, "I might hire a couple bodyguards."

34

The house phone rang, and Berger told Morales it was the intercom.

"It's probably security," she said from the couch, and she was pale and in pain.

Her hands were cherry-red behind her back. Scarpetta couldn't feel her own hands at all now. They could be rocks.

"They probably heard the gunshot." If a voice could be gray, Berger's was gray.

When Morales had bounded up the stairs after the cell phone sounded up there, the ring tone a familiar one, Scarpetta had asked the question that would change eternity for her.

She'd said to Berger, *"Is Lucy up there?"*

Berger's answer was her wide eyes, and then they heard the gunshot.

It had sounded like a metal door slamming shut, almost like the steel barrier doors at Bellevue.

And silence.

And now Morales was back, and at this point, Scarpetta no longer cared about anything in this world except Lucy.

"Please get an ambulance," she said to him.

"Let me tell you what's up, Doc." He waved the pistol and was becoming more bizarre. "What's up is your little superhero niece has a fucking bullet in her fucking head. You imagine the IQ I'm killing off this morning, whew."

He picked up the unzipped gym bag and walked around the couch, to the front of it. Displayed on the PDA clipped to his low-riding jeans was a GPS track log, a heavy pink line snaking through a map of someplace.

He dropped the gym bag on the coffee table and squatted next to it. His latex-gloved hands reached inside the bag, and he pulled out a small pair of Brooks running shoes and a plastic Baggie containing the polyvinyl impressions Scarpetta had made of Oscar's fingertips. The Baggie was greasy, as if Morales had oiled or lubricated the polyvinyl impressions. He balanced the revolver on his thigh.

He removed the impressions from the Baggie and slipped them over the fingers of his left hand, and that was the first time Scarpetta realized he was left-handed.

He held the gun with his other hand, and stood up and splayed his left hand with its freakish irregular white rubbery fingertips, and he grinned, his pupils so dilated it was as if he had black holes for eyes.

"I won't be around to reverse the reverse of them," he said. "These are reversed."

Slowly moving his rubbery fingertips and enjoying himself.

"Right, Dr. Sherlock? You know what I'm talking about. How many people would think of it?"

He meant that since the prints were from an impression, they would be reversed when they were transferred to a surface. Morales must have remedied that when he'd photographed the prints he'd planted on the light fixture in the tub at Eva Peebles's apartment. Whoever photographed and lifted the prints in Berger's apartment would discover a reverse-sequence arrangement, a mirror image of what was expected, and wonder how that could have happened. A fingerprints examiner would have to make adjustments, display different perspectives to make an accurate geometric analysis for a comparison of these planted prints with Oscar's prints in IAFIS.

"You answer when I talk to you, bitch." Morales got up and loomed so close Scarpetta smelled his sweat.

He sat down next to Berger and stuck his tongue between her lips and slowly rubbed the gun between her legs.

"Nobody would think of it," he said to Scarpetta as he fondled Berger with the barrel of the revolver and she didn't move.

"Nobody-would," Scarpetta said.

He got up and started pressing various silicone fingertips on the glass coffee table. He went to the bar, flicked open a glass door, and plucked out the Irish whiskey. He picked out a colorful tumbler that looked like hand-blown Venetian glass, and he poured whiskey into it. He left Oscar's prints all over the bottle and the tumbler as he drank in gulps.

The apartment phone rang again.

Again, Morales ignored it.

"They have a key," Berger said. "They hear something in this building and you don't answer, they'll finally come in. Let me answer it and tell them we're fine. Nobody else needs to be hurt."

Morales drank some more. He swished whiskey in his mouth and waved his gun at Berger.

"Tell 'em to go away," he said. "You try anything, everybody's dead right now."

"I can't pick it up."

Morales exhaled an exasperated breath as he came close and picked up the cordless phone and held it against her mouth and ear.

Scarpetta noticed tiny specks of red on his light-skinned face, like his freckles but not his freckles, and something moved inside her like plates of the earth sliding before a huge quake.

The pink line on the map on the PDA snaked, moving. Someone or something moving fast. Oscar.

"Please call an ambulance," she said.

Morales mouthed *Sorry*, and shrugged.

"Hello?" Berger said into the phone he held. "Really? You know what? Probably the TV. A Rambo movie or something he's got on. Thanks for your concern."

Morales removed the phone from her drained face.

"Hit zero," she said with no inflection. "To disconnect the intercom."

He hit zero and dropped the cordless phone into its charger.

Marino touched the door with his index finger and pushed it open an inch as he slid his Glock out of a pocket in his leather jacket and the alarm-system chime sounded its warning tone that a door or window had been breached.

Marino swung himself around inside Berger's penthouse, the pistol in both hands. He crept forward, and through an archway he saw the sunken living room that reminded him of a spaceship.

Berger and Scarpetta were on the couch, their arms behind their backs, and he knew by the looks on their faces that it was too late. An arm snaked up from behind the wraparound couch and poked a gun in the back of Scarpetta's head.

"Drop it, asshole," Morales said as he stood up.

Marino was pointing his Glock at Morales, who had a gun buried in the back of Scarpetta's blond hair, his finger on the trigger.

"You hear me, Gorilla Man? Drop the fucking gun or you're going to see genius brains all over this penthouse apartment."

"Don't do it, Morales. Everybody knows it's you. You can quit," Marino's mouth said while his thoughts streaked through possibilities that kept pinning him against the same wall, a wall he couldn't get away from no matter what.

He was trapped.

He could pull the trigger, and Morales would pull the trigger. Maybe Morales would be dead, leaving Berger and Marino. But Scarpetta would be dead.

"You got a little problem with proof, Gorilla Man. Anybody ever call you that?" Morales said. "I like that. Gorilla Man."

Marino couldn't tell if he was drunk or high. But he was on something.

"Because . . . because"—he sniggered—"you're the proverbial knuckle dragger, now, aren't you. Va-nil-la Go-ril-la. How you like that?"

"Marino, don't drop your gun," Scarpetta said with amazing steadiness, but her face looked dead. "He can't shoot everyone at once. Don't drop your gun."

"You know, she's such a hero, ain't she?" Morales jammed the barrel hard against her skull, and she winced silently. "One brave lady, having all these stiffs for patients who can't thank her or complain."

He bent over and touched her ear with his tongue.

"Poor thing. Couldn't work with living people? That's what they say about doctors like you. That and you gotta have the air-conditioning on fifty or you can't sleep. Put the fucking gun down!" he yelled at Marino.

Their eyes locked.

"Okay." Morales shrugged. He said to Scarpetta, "Sleepy time, and you get to see your precious little Lucy again. Did you tell Marino I blew her brains out upstairs? Say hello to everyone in heaven for me."

Marino knew he meant it. He knew people meant it when they really didn't care, and Morales didn't care. Scarpetta was nothing to him. Nobody was anything to him. He was going to do it.

Marino said, "Don't shoot. I'm going to put my gun down. Don't shoot."

"No!" Scarpetta raised her voice. "No!"

Berger said nothing, because there was nothing she could say that would make a difference. It was better for her to say nothing, and she knew it.

Marino didn't want to put his gun down. Morales had killed Lucy. He would kill every one of them. Lucy was dead. She must be upstairs. If Marino kept his gun, Morales couldn't kill all of them. But he'd kill Scarpetta. Marino couldn't let him do that. Lucy was dead. All of them would be dead.

A tiny red laser dot landed on Morales's right temple. The little dot flickered and was shaking badly, then slowed and moved just a little, like a ruby-red firefly.

"I'm putting my gun down on the floor," Marino said, squatting.

He didn't look up or back. He didn't let on he saw anything as he set his Glock on the Oriental rug, his eyes never leaving Morales's.

"Now stand up real slow," Morales said.

He raised the pistol away from Scarpetta's head and

pointed it at Marino as the red firefly crawled around his ear.

"And say *Mommy,*" Morales said as the laser dot went perfectly still on his right temple.

The gunshot was a loud spit from the gallery, and Morales dropped. Marino had never actually seen that for real, someone dropping like a puppet with its strings cut, and he bolted around the couch and grabbed the gun off the floor as blood poured out of the side of Morales's head, spreading across the black marble floor. Marino grabbed the phone and called 911 as he ran into the kitchen for a knife, and changed his mind and grabbed a pair of poultry shears out of the cutlery block, and snapped through the ties around Scarpetta's and Berger's wrists.

Scarpetta ran upstairs and couldn't feel her own hand on the railing.

Lucy was just inside a doorway that led from the gallery into the master bedroom, blood everywhere, great smears of it from where she'd crawled across the bathroom floor, then across hardwood, to where she'd shot Morales with the Glock forty-caliber pistol next to her. She was sitting up, leaning against the wall, and shivering, a towel in her lap. She was so bloody, Scarpetta couldn't tell exactly where she'd been hit, but it was her head, possibly the back of her head. Her hair was soaked with blood, and blood was running down her neck and her naked back, pooling behind and around her.

Scarpetta struggled out of her winter coat, then her blazer, and got on the floor next to her, and her hands felt dead as she touched the back of Lucy's head. She pressed her blazer against Lucy's scalp and Lucy complained loudly.

"It's going to be all right, Lucy," Scarpetta said. "What happened? Can you show me where you've been shot?"

"Right there. Ow! Jesus Christ! Right there. Fuck! I'm okay. I'm so cold."

Scarpetta ran her hand down Lucy's slippery neck and back, couldn't feel anything, and her hands were beginning to burn and tingle, but her fingers didn't seem to belong to her.

Berger appeared at the top of the stairs.

"Get towels," Scarpetta said to her. "Lots of them."

Berger could see Lucy was alert, she was all right. Berger hurried toward the bathroom.

Scarpetta said to Lucy, "Is any spot tender back here? Tell me where you feel pain."

"Nothing back there."

"You sure?" Scarpetta did the best she could, gently palpating with a hand that wasn't working right. "Making sure you've got nothing going on with your spine."

"It's not back there. It feels as if my left ear's gone. I can hardly hear anything."

She scooted behind Lucy so that she was sitting behind her, her legs stretched out on either side of her, her back against the wall, and she carefully felt the back of Lucy's heavily bleeding scalp.

"My hand's pretty numb," Scarpetta said. "Guide my fingers, Lucy. Show me where it hurts."

Lucy reached back and took her hand and guided it to a spot.

"Right there. Goddamn that hurts. I think it might be under the skin. Shit that hurts. God, don't press on it, that hurts!"

Scarpetta didn't have her reading glasses on and couldn't see anything but a blur of bloody hair. She pressed her bare hand against the back of Lucy's head and Lucy yelled.

"We have to stop the bleeding," Scarpetta said very calmly, kindly, almost as if she was talking to a child. "The bullet must be right under the scalp, and that's why it's hurting when we apply pressure. You're going to be all right. You're going to be just fine. The ambulance will be here any minute."

There were furrows around Berger's wrists, and her hands were bright red and were very stiff and awkward as she opened several large white bath sheets and tucked them around Lucy's neck and under her legs. Lucy was naked and wet and must have just stepped out of the shower when Morales shot her. Berger got down on the floor next to them, and blood got all over her hands and her blouse as she touched Lucy and told her repeatedly that she would be fine. Everything was going to be fine.

"He's dead," Berger told Lucy. "He was about to shoot Marino, to shoot all of us."

The nerves in Scarpetta's hands were waking up and angry, a million pins sticking, and she vaguely perceived a small, hard lump at the back of Lucy's skull, several inches to the left of the midline of it.

"Right here," she said to Lucy. "Help me, if you can."

Lucy lifted her hand and helped her find the perforation, and Scarpetta worked the bullet out, and Lucy complained loudly. It was medium- to large-caliber, semi-jacketed, and deformed, and she handed it to Berger and pressed a towel firmly against the wound to stop the bleeding.

Scarpetta's sweater was soaked with blood, the floor around her slippery with it. She didn't think the bullet had penetrated the skull. She suspected it had struck at an angle and expended most of its kinetic energy within a relatively small space within milliseconds. There are so many blood vessels close to the surface of the scalp, it bleeds alarmingly, always looks worse than it is. Scarpetta pressed the towel very firmly against the wound, her right hand on Lucy's forehead, holding her.

Lucy leaned heavily against her and shut her eyes. Scarpetta felt the side of her neck and checked her pulse, and it was rapid but not alarmingly so, and she was breathing fine. She wasn't restless and didn't seem confused. There were no signs she was going into shock. Scarpetta held her forehead again, pressing hard against the wound to stop the bleeding.

"Lucy, I need you to open your eyes and stay awake. You listening? Can you tell us what happened?" Scarpetta said. "He ran upstairs and we heard a gunshot. Do you remember what happened?"

"You saved everybody's life," Berger said. "You're going to be fine. All of us are fine."

She was stroking Lucy's arm.

"I don't know," Lucy said. "I remember being in the shower. Then I was on the floor and my head felt as if someone hit me with an anvil. Like I got hit with a car in the back of my head. For a minute I was blind. I thought I was permanently blind, and suddenly I saw light, and images. I heard him downstairs, and I couldn't walk. I was dizzy, so I crawled over to the chair, kind of slid myself over the wood to where my coat was and got the gun out of it. And I started to see again."

The bloody Glock was on the bloody floor near the railing of the gallery, and Scarpetta remembered it was one Marino had given to Lucy for Christmas. It was Lucy's favorite gun. She'd said it was the nicest thing he'd ever given to her, a pocket-size forty-caliber pistol with a laser sight and boxes of high-velocity hollowpoints to go with it. He knew what she liked. He was the one who'd taught her to shoot when she was a child, when the two of them would disappear in his pickup truck, and later Lucy's mother—Scarpetta's sister, Dorothy—would call and curse, usually after several drinks, and scream at Scarpetta for ruining Lucy, threatening to never let Lucy see her again.

Dorothy probably never would have allowed Lucy to visit were it not for the minor problem that she didn't want a child, because Dorothy was a child who would always want a daddy to take care of her, to dote on her, to adore her the way their father had doted and depended on Scarpetta.

She pushed Lucy's forehead with one hand and held the cloth against the back of her head with the other, and her hands felt hot and swollen now, her pulse pounding in them. The bleeding had slowed considerably, but she resisted looking. She continued the pressure.

"Looks like a thirty-eight," Lucy said, shutting her eyes again.

She must have noticed the bullet when Scarpetta had handed it to Berger.

"I want you to keep your eyes open and stay awake," Scarpetta said. "You're fine, but let's just stay awake. I think I hear something. I think the rescue squad's here. We're going to the ER and we'll do all those fun tests you like so much. X-rays. MRI. Tell me how you're feeling."

"I hurt like shit. I'm okay. Did you see his gun? I'm wondering what it was. I don't remember seeing it. I don't remember him."

Scarpetta heard the door open downstairs, and the clatter and confusion of tense voices as the squad came in, and Marino hurried them up the stairs, all of them talking loudly. He stepped out of the way, looking at Lucy in her bloody bath sheets, then at the Glock on the floor, and he leaned over and picked it up. He did the one thing you never do at a crime scene. He held it in his bare hands and walked off with it, disappeared into the bathroom with it.

Two paramedics were talking to Lucy and asking her questions, and she was answering as they buckled her into the stretcher, and Scarpetta was so busy with that, she didn't notice Marino had somehow ended up back downstairs, and was there with three uniformed officers. Other EMTs were lifting Morales's body onto yet another stretcher, nobody bothering with CPR because he had been dead for a while.

Marino was dropping the magazine out of the Glock—Lucy's Glock—it seemed, and clearing the chamber while an officer held a paper bag open. Marino was telling them about Berger remotely unlocking the apartment door and letting him in without Morales knowing. Marino was making up a story about him creeping as close as he could, then deliberately making a sound so Morales would look up.

"Giving me just enough chance to get off a round before he shot someone," Marino lied to the cops. "He was behind the Doc with his revolver pointed at her."

Berger was with them, and she said, "We were right here on the couch."

"A hammerless thirty-eight," Marino said.

He was pointing all this out, taking the blame, not the credit, for killing someone, and Berger was going along with it flawlessly. It seemed her new role in life was keeping Lucy out of trouble.

Legally, Lucy absolutely couldn't have a handgun in New York City, not even inside a residence, not even for self-defense. Legally, the handgun still belonged to Marino because he'd never gotten around to the paperwork, to transferring his gift over to Lucy's ownership, because so much had gone on after that Christmas a year ago in Charleston. Nobody had been happy with one another, and then Rose wasn't herself and no one knew why for a while, and Scarpetta wasn't capable of fixing their world as it seemed to fly apart, like an old golf ball that's lost its skin. It had been the beginning of what she'd decided, not all that long ago, was the end of them.

Her bloody hand held Lucy's bloody hand as the paramedics clattered the stretcher toward the elevator, one of them talking on the radio to the ambulance in front of the building. The doors opened and Benton was stepping out in his pinstripe suit, looking just like he did on CNN when she'd watched him on her BlackBerry as she'd walked to Berger's apartment.

He took Lucy's other hand and looked into Scarpetta's eyes, and the sadness and relief on his face was as deep as anything could possibly be.

35

Scarpetta's well-known name was not what got her a table at Elaine's, where it wasn't possible for anyone to be important enough to earn indulgences or sovereign immunity if the legendary restaurateur didn't like the person.

When Elaine took up residence every night at one of her tables, an expectation drifted up like cigarette smoke from an earlier day when art was adored, criticized, redefined—anything but ignored—and anybody in any condition might walk through the door. Contained within these walls were echoes of a past that Scarpetta mourned but didn't miss, having first set foot in here decades earlier, on a weekend getaway with a man she'd fallen in love with at Georgetown Law.

He was gone, and she had Benton, and the décor at Elaine's hadn't changed: black except for the red-tile floor, and there were hooks for hanging coats, and pay phones that as far as Scarpetta knew weren't used anymore. Shelves displayed autographed books that patrons knew not to touch, and photographs of the literati and film stars filled every spare inch of wall all the way to the ceiling.

Scarpetta and Benton paused at Elaine's table to say hello—a kiss on each cheek, and *I haven't seen you in a while, where have you been?* Scarpetta learned she had just missed a former Secretary of State, and last week it was a former Giants quarterback she didn't like, and tonight, a talk show host she liked even less. Elaine said she had other guests coming, but that wasn't news, because the grande dame knew everybody expected in her salon on any given night.

Scarpetta's favorite waiter, Louie, found just the right table.

He said to her as he pulled out her chair, "I shouldn't bring it up, but I've heard everything that's gone on." Shaking his head. "I shouldn't say it—to you of all people. Gambino, Bonanno? It was better back then. You know? They did what they did, but they had their reasons, know what I mean? They didn't go around whacking people for the hell of it. Especially doing some poor lady like that. A dwarf. And that elderly widow. Then the other woman and the kid. What chance did they have?"

"They didn't," Benton said.

"Me? I believe in cement shoes. There's special situations. You don't mind me asking, how's the little . . . you know, the other dwarf doing? I feel like I shouldn't use that word because a lot of people say it in the pejorative."

Oscar had contacted the FBI and was fine. A GPS microchip had been removed from his left buttock, and he was taking a rest, as Benton put it, at the private and posh psychiatric unit at McLean called the Pavilion. He was getting therapy and, most of all, was being given the gift of feeling safe until he could sort himself out. Scarpetta and Benton would head back to Belmont in the morning.

"He's doing okay," Benton said. "I'll tell him you asked."

Louie said, "What can I bring you? Drinks? Calamari?"

"Kay?" Benton said.

"Scotch. Your best single-malt."

"Make that two."

Louie said with a wink, "For you? My special stash. A couple new ones for you to try. Anybody driving?"

"Strong," Scarpetta said, and Louie headed to the bar.

Behind her, at a table by a window overlooking Second Avenue, a big man wearing a white Stetson sat alone, working on what looked like straight vodka or gin with a twist. Now and then he craned his neck to check the score of a basketball game playing silently on the TV above his head, and Scarpetta got a glimpse of his big jaw and thick lips, and long white sideburns. Then he stared at nothing, slowly turning his glass in small circles on the white tablecloth. Something about him was familiar, and she envisioned footage she'd seen on TV and was seized by the shock that she was looking at Jake Loudin.

But it wasn't possible. He was in custody. This man

was small, rather thin. She realized he was an actor, one who wasn't busy anymore.

Benton studied the menu, his face obscured by a plastic laminated menu with Elaine on the cover.

Scarpetta said to him, "You look like the Pink Panther on a stakeout."

He closed the menu and placed it on the table, and said, "Anything in particular you want to say to everyone? Since you've orchestrated this little gathering for reasons beyond being sociable. I just thought I'd mention it before they show up."

"Nothing in particular," Scarpetta said. "Just wanted to air out. I feel everyone should air out before we go home. I wish we weren't going. It doesn't seem like we should be there and everyone else is here."

"Lucy will be absolutely fine."

Tears touched Scarpetta's eyes. She couldn't get over it. A sense of dread held her heart like unwelcome hands, and she was conscious of her near loss, even in her sleep.

"She's not meant to go anywhere." Benton pulled his chair closer and took her hand. "If she were, she would have checked out a hell of a long time ago."

Scarpetta held her napkin to her eyes, then stared up at the silent TV, as if she cared about whoever was playing basketball.

She cleared her throat and said, "But it's almost impossible."

"It's not. Those revolvers? The ones I'm always telling you are such a terrible idea because they're so light-weight? Well, you see why, only in this case the luck was in our favor. The recoil is unbelievable. Like having your hand kicked by a horse. I think he jerked when he pulled the trigger, and probably Lucy moved, and small-caliber, low-velocity. Plus, she's meant to be with us. She's not meant to go anywhere. All of us are fine. We're more than fine," Benton said, pressing his lips against her hand, then kissing her on the mouth tenderly.

He didn't used to be so openly affectionate in public. He didn't seem to care anymore. If *Gotham Gotcha* still existed, they would probably be an item in it tomorrow—Scarpetta's entire dinner party would be.

She had never visited the apartment where the anonymous author wrote her cruel and vindictive columns, and now that she was sure who it was, she felt pity for her. She completely understood why Terri Bridges turned on her. Terri was receiving heartless and belittling e-mails from her hero, or thought she was, and when she'd had enough, she gave her alter ego the assignment to eviscerate Scarpetta publicly. Terri had pulled her own trigger, firing several rounds at a woman whose perceived mistreatments were the last straw in a lifetime of mistreatment.

Lucy had determined that Terri had written the two New Year's Day columns on December 30, and they had been in a queue and had been automatically sent to Eva Peebles after Terri was already dead. Lucy also discovered that on the afternoon of December 31, just hours before Terri was murdered, she deleted all her e-mails from Scarpetta612, not because she sensed she was about to die, for sure, in Benton's opinion, but because she had just committed her own crime, anonymously, against a medical examiner whom she would finally meet, in the morgue.

Benton believed Terri had a conscience, a sizable one, and that's why she'd deleted the hundred-some e-mails she'd thought were between Scarpetta and her. Terri's anxiety had dictated she should eradicate any evidence that there might be a connection between *Gotham Gotcha* and Terri Bridges. By deleting the correspondence, she'd also expunged her fallen hero from her life.

That was Benton's theory. Scarpetta didn't have a theory except that there would always be theories.

"I wrote Oscar a letter," she said as she opened her handbag and pulled out an envelope. "I'm thinking everyone should read it, that I'll show it to them. But I want to read it to you first. Not an e-mail but a real letter on real paper, my personal stationery, which I haven't used since God knows when. I didn't write it in longhand, though. My penmanship gets only worse with time. Since there will never be a court case, Jaime said it's perfectly fine to tell Oscar whatever I want, and I have. I've done my best to explain to him that Terri was dealt hardships by her family, and it was this early programming that compelled her to control everything within her reach. She was angry because she'd been hurt, and hurt people often hurt back, but beneath it all she was a good person. I'm giving you a bit of a summary, because it's long."

She slipped four folded pages of heavy, creamy paper out of the envelope and carefully smoothed them open. She skimmed until she found the part she wanted Benton to hear.

She quietly read to him:

. . . In the secret room upstairs where she wrote her columns were the yellow roses you gave her. She saved every one of them, and I'm betting she never told you. No one would do something like that if the feelings weren't profoundly important, Oscar. I want you to remember that, and if you forget, re-read this letter. That's why I wrote it. Something for you to keep.

I also took the liberty to write her family and express my condolences and tell them what I could, because they have many, many questions. Dr. Lester, I fear, hasn't been as helpful as they'd like, so I've filled in the blanks, most of those conversations over the phone, with a few exchanges by e-mail.

I've talked about you, and maybe by now you've heard from them. If you haven't, I feel sure you will. They said they wanted me to tell you what Terri did in her will, and they intend to write you about it. Maybe they have.

I won't divulge the fine points of her wishes, because it isn't my place to do that. But in keeping with her family's request to me, I'll pass along this much. She left a considerable sum to the Little People of America, to start a foundation that offers assistance in medical care for those who want and need procedures (such as corrective surgeries) that medical insurance won't cover. As you know,

much of what can and should be done is unfairly
deemed elective: orthodontic care, for example,
and in some instances, bone lengthening.

Suffice it to say, Terri had a very kind heart. . . .

Scarpetta had read as much as she could, because the
wave of sadness was rolling over her again. She folded
the pages and tucked them back into their envelope.

Louie appeared with their drinks and just as unob-
trusively was gone, and she took a sip and it warmed her
on its way down and its vapors lifted her brain as if it had
retreated into a cloistered place and needed courage.

"If you think it won't interfere with your patient's
treatment"—she handed Benton the envelope—"would
you see that he gets this?"

"It will mean more to him than you imagine," Benton said, sliding it into the inside pocket of his jacket, a
buttery black leather jacket.

It was new, as was the belt with its Winston eagle-head
buckle, and the handmade boots he had on. Lucy's way
of celebrating when she, quote, dodged another bullet, was to buy people gifts. Not inexpensive ones.
She'd gotten Scarpetta another watch she really didn't
need—a titanium Breguet with a carbon-fiber face—to
go with the black Ferrari F430 Spider that she said
she'd also gotten Scarpetta. It was a joke, thank God.
Scarpetta would rather ride a bicycle than drive one of
those things. Marino had a new motorcycle, a racing red
Ducati 1098 that Lucy was keeping for him in her han-
gar in White Plains, because she said he wasn't allowed

to ride anything with fewer than four wheels in the city. She'd rather rudely added that he had to maintain his weight or he wouldn't fit on a Superbike no matter how super it was.

Scarpetta had no idea what Lucy might have given Berger. She didn't ask questions unless Lucy wanted her to ask them. Scarpetta was being patient as Lucy continued to wait for judgment that Scarpetta had no intention of rendering because it wasn't what she felt. Not remotely. After getting over the initial shock of it, although there was no justification for shock, not really, Scarpetta couldn't be more pleased.

She and Berger had actually gone out to lunch last week, the two of them alone at Forlini's near One Hogan Place, and had sat in a booth that Berger said was almost named after Scarpetta. She'd said it was a lucky booth because it was the break-up booth. Scarpetta had said she didn't see how that could be construed as lucky, and Berger, who, it turned out, was a Yankees fan and used to go to games and thought she might do so again, had replied that it depended on who was up to bat in the bottom of the ninth.

Scarpetta didn't need to watch baseball to get the gist of things. She'd simply been glad that a booth named after New York's fire commissioner wasn't the hot seat it might have been in the not-so-distant past. Few people knew as much about Scarpetta as Jaime Berger did.

"I didn't answer your question," Benton said, watching the door. "I'm sorry."

"I forgot the question."

"Your letter. Thank you for reading it to me, but don't read it to them."

"I didn't think so."

"They don't need proof that you're a decent human being." Benton's eyes on hers.

"It's that obvious."

"Everyone knows that shit on the Internet, the e-mails Morales sent pretending to be you, and all the rest of it? We know who you are and who you aren't. Nothing that's happened is your fault, and you and I will continue to talk about this, say the same thing again and again. It takes a long time for your emotions to catch up with your intellect. Besides. I should feel guilty. Morales got all that shit from Nancy what's-her-name, and Marino never would have had that flake for a therapist had I not sent him to that damn treatment center and even wasted my time conferring with her."

"She should never have talked to Morales, I agree. But I can see why she would."

"Nope," Benton said. "Never should have happened. He probably seduced her over the phone. I don't know what he said, but she should never have told him one word of what Marino had confided in her. It's such a HIPAA violation, she's history. I'm seeing to that."

"Let's don't punish anybody. There's been enough punishment, enough of people not getting along and fighting each other's battles and making each other's decisions and paying people back. Indirectly, that's why Terri's dead. That's why Eva's dead. If Terri hadn't been paying everybody back . . . Well, if Marino wants to go after his former lamebrain therapist, let him do it himself."

"You're probably right," Benton said. "And they're here."

He got up so Marino would see him in the crowded dark, and the party of four, which included Marino's new girlfriend, Bacardi, who did have a first name—it was Georgia—and also Berger and Lucy, squeezed their way through the crowded dining room and paid their respects to Elaine and bantered about things Scarpetta couldn't hear. Then everyone was pulling out chairs and sitting down, and seemed in fine spirits. Lucy had on a Red Sox baseball cap, probably to tease Berger, who naturally hated the Red Sox, but mainly to cover a small shaved spot.

That was it. An insult to Lucy's vanity, the bullet wound on the back of her head healed, the minor contusion to her brain gone. Marino had rather much summarized as only he could that Lucy was a-okay because there was nothing up there to hit but bone.

Louie was back with plates of Elaine's famous calamari, and he took orders without writing anything down, and Berger and Lucy wanted to try his special stash of Scotch, and Bacardi didn't live up to her name and asked for an apple martini, and Marino hesitated, then shook his head and looked uncomfortable. Nobody paid any attention, and Scarpetta knew what had happened. She reached behind Lucy and touched Marino's arm.

He leaned back and his wooden chair creaked, and he said, "How ya doin'?"

"Have you ever been here?" she asked him.

"Not me. Not my kind of joint. I don't like having private conversations with Barbara Walters two tables away."

"That's not Barbara Walters. They have Red Stripe, Buckler, Sharp's. I don't know what you're drinking these days," Scarpetta said.

She wasn't encouraging him to drink or not drink. She was saying she didn't care what he was drinking, and that only he should care about it, and what she cared about was him.

Marino said to Louie, "You still got Red Stripe?"

"You bet."

"Maybe a little later," Marino said.

"Maybe a little later," Louie repeated along with the rest of the orders, and was gone.

Berger was looking at Scarpetta, and she cut her eyes toward the man in the white Stetson sitting by the window.

"You know what I'm thinking," Berger said to her.

"It's not him," Scarpetta said.

"I almost had a heart attack when I walked in the door," Berger said. "You have no idea. I thought, How can that be possible?"

"He still where he ought to be?"

"You mean hell?" Lucy cut in, seeming to know exactly what they were talking about. "That's where he ought to be."

"Don't go getting any ideas, Rocky," Marino said to her.

That used to be his nickname for Lucy, because

she never knew when to quit swinging and was always challenging him to boxing and wrestling matches, until she turned twelve and got her period. His middle name was Rocco, so his calling her Rocky had always struck Scarpetta as a bit of projection going on. What he loved in Lucy was what he loved in himself and just didn't know it.

"I don't care what anybody says, I'm crazy about those damn movies," Bacardi said as Louie was with them again already. "Even the last one, *Rocky Balboa*. I always cry at the end. I don't know why. Real blood and guts? Not a tear. But the movies? I'm a mess."

"Anybody driving?" Louie said again, and then answered himself, his usual routine, "Of course not. Nobody's driving. I don't know what happened. Gravity," he added, letting them know their drinks were strong. "I start pouring, and gravity takes over. I can't lift up the bottle, and I keep pouring."

"My parents used to bring me here when I was a kid," Berger said to Lucy. "This is old New York. You should absorb every detail, because one day there won't be anything left of an era when everything was better, even if it didn't seem so at the time. People would come in here and actually talk about art and ideas. Hunter Thompson. Joe DiMaggio."

"I've never really thought of Joe DiMaggio talking about art and ideas. Mainly baseball—but not Marilyn Monroe. We all know he didn't talk about her," Lucy said.

"You better hope there's no such things as ghosts," Benton said to his almost niece. "After what you did."

"I've been wanting to ask you about that," Bacardi said to Lucy. "Wow. Now, this has got a hell of a lot of apples in it."

She tucked her arm under Marino's and leaned against him, and a butterfly tattoo lifted out of her tight knit top on a swell of bosom.

Bacardi said, "Since the damn thing crashed, and what a mystery that is, I never got to see the damn photograph. It's fake, right?"

"What do you mean?" Lucy asked innocently.

"Don't play your dumb-as-a-fox role with me." Bacardi smiled and sipped her apple martini, not daintily.

Scarpetta said to Berger, "You must have seen some interesting people here when you were a kid."

"Many of the people in the pictures on the walls," Berger said. "Half of them Lucy has never heard of."

"Here we go again. It's a damn wonder anybody serves me a drink," Lucy said. "I'm still ten. I'll be ten my entire life."

"You weren't around when JFK was shot, not when Bobby was, not when Martin Luther King was. Not even for Watergate," Berger said.

"Was there anything I missed that might have been good?"

"When Neil Armstrong walked on the moon. That was good," Berger said.

"I was around for that, and when Marilyn Monroe died." Bacardi worked her way back into the discussion. "So let's hear it. Tell me about the photograph. The worm, or whatever the media's calling it."

"There are dead pictures of her on the Internet," Marino said. "A couple of 'em. That's what happens. Some asshole who works in a morgue sells a picture. We could stop letting people bring in their phones," he said to Scarpetta. "Make them leave them in the morgue office like I have to leave my gun when I go into lockup. Have a safe or something."

"It's not a real photograph," Lucy said. "Not exactly. Just from the neck up. The rest of it I cut and pasted and enhanced."

"You think it's true she was murdered?" Bacardi asked very seriously.

Scarpetta had seen the altered photograph and what Eva had written about it, and was quite familiar with all of the records pertaining to the case. If she hadn't been more than halfway through her single-malt Scotch, straight and neat, she might not have been so candid.

"Probably," she said.

"Probably not smart to say that on CNN," Benton said to Scarpetta.

She took another sip. The Scotch was smooth with a peaty finish that drifted up her nose and evaporated somewhere in her brain, deeper than before.

"People would be surprised if they knew what I don't say," she said. "Eva Peebles had it mostly right."

Lucy curled her fingers around her glass, raising it to her aunt, then to her lips, exploring it with her nose and tongue the way a Tastevin treats a fine wine. She looked at Scarpetta from the shadow of her baseball cap and smiled.

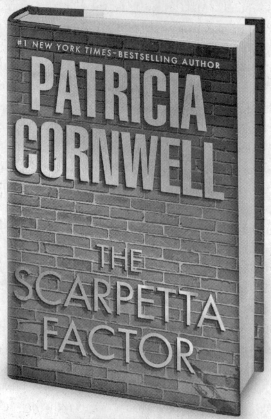